Never Come Down

Michelle Black

Hard Shell Word Factory

For Doug

Copyright © 1996 Michelle Black
Trade paperback
ISBN: 0-7599-0443-X
Published December 2001
eBook ISBN: 1-58200-075-1
Published February 1999

Hard Shell Word Factory
PO Box 161
Amherst Jct. WI 54407
books@hardshell.com
http://www.hardshell.com

All characters in this book have no existence outside the imagination of the author, and have no relation whatsoever to anyone bearing the same name or names. These characters are not even distantly inspired by any individual known or unknown to the author, and all incidents are pure invention.

Originally published by Wolf Moon Press

Cover art design by Ann T. Weaver from the original watercolor, *"Leap Year."*

Chapter One

"THERE ARE NO RULES ABOVE 10,000 FEET." I read this cryptic message on no fewer than four car bumpers during my brief lunch at the Tenmile Cafe. I knew immediately I would like it here—who could not love a place that so revered anarchy?

After a morning filled to the brim with activity, I was almost too tired to ponder any deeper meanings for this curious slogan. Leaving my home in Philadelphia before dawn, I had flown into Denver, rented a Jeep Wrangler—the most macho, stud vehicle I had ever seen in my life, one that made me feel like the reigning Miss Kick-Butt Colorado—and arrived at the mouth of the Tenmile Canyon, all by 11:00 a.m.

My growling stomach, still on Eastern time like my watch, forced me to pull into the first restaurant I could find upon reaching the tiny mountain town of Columbine, where the city limits sign optimistically proclaimed: "Welcome to Columbine—All the Civilization You'll Ever Need." We'll see about that, I thought with a doubtful smirk.

As I finished my scrambled eggs and toast, I casually studied the other diners in the Tenmile Cafe. They seemed to fall into two distinct fashion categories. They wore either jeans with hiking boots or neon spandex. The latter group presumably belonged to the expensive mountain bikes parked near the door. I belonged to neither camp, with my khaki slacks, my tailored blouse, and my sensible sandals which now proved a little too bare for this chilly mountain climate.

My waitress was a pretty young woman with long, straight brown hair and jeans-with-hiking-boots. She wasn't wearing make-up and she wasn't wearing a bra. Her ample breasts bounced noticeably when she walked, a fact not lost on the male mountain bikers who openly ogled her every time she passed their booth. If she minded this attention, she didn't show it. I asked her for directions to Leap Year, Colorado.

"You got four-wheel drive?" she queried first.

I nodded confidently, but her question made me nervous. I had been warned that Leap Year was off the beaten path, but I hoped there would at least *be* a path. She proceeded to give me directions so elaborate, I ended up writing them out on a napkin.

"What sends you up to Leap Year?" she asked, sitting down in my booth with a friendly intimacy that caught me off guard. I instinctively stiffened, but reminded myself that this was the West and everyone was friendly out here or so I'd been told.

"I've inherited some property there," I responded. 'Some property' was actually a modest understatement. I had inherited the entire town of Leap Year. Not that this was saying much—Leap Year was a ghost town. When Grady died—Grady was my great, great-aunt who lived to be over one hundred years old—she left me everything she owned and that included the entire incorporated space of Leap Year, Colorado.

"Good luck, honey," the waitress called as I left. I don't know which bothered me more: the fact that my drive required "good luck"— not exactly a confidence builder—or that the waitress called me "honey." Why would a woman of about my own age—twenty-six—be calling me honey? Oh well, maybe that was just more of this Western friendliness thing.

I pulled out of the cafe parking lot feeling mild irritation at the lecherous mountain bikers and their adolescent breast worship. Being recently divorced, I was admittedly not objective on the subject of the male gender. Suffering more from an angry, bitter spirit than a broken heart, I had resolved to spend a summer traveling and inheriting Grady's "town" had given me a perfect opportunity. Leap Year was to be but the first stop on a wide-open itinerary. I would stay here only long enough to get a look at the place and list it for sale with a real estate agent.

I was convinced this experience would cleanse me somehow, improve my bruised outlook on life. My older sister Jane feared my self-esteem was at ground zero after my divorce and encouraged me— no, browbeat, me into coming on this trip.

"Jump right back into the saddle," she advised. "You need to get your confidence back. Seduce the first handsome cowboy you meet out there, preferably one with trail dust still in his hair. Have a lightweight summer romance. Nothing serious. He wouldn't even have to be a cowboy. A carpenter would do—they're good with their hands, right? Don't pick anybody too deep. No late night debates on the origin of the universe. Just into bed by ten, lights out by eleven."

I sighed after getting these marching orders. Another relationship was the last thing I wanted or needed just now, but I assured Janey I would do my best.

When the gravel road turned to rocky dirt path, I knew I must be getting close, just as the waitress had instructed. The drive proved more challenging than I was used to and at times I crept along, gently easing the jeep over boulders, large and small, that made the road an endless series of speed bumps. Too new at mountain driving to concentrate on anything but avoiding death, I largely missed the spectacular scenery included with the drive at no expense. The last fourteen miles of the trip took over an hour. The route switch-backed tortuously up the mountain. With one final, heart-stopping twist, a town appeared. A weathered sign announced for anyone interested: "Leap Year, Colo., Elevation 10,214." I smiled to myself, thinking at least I wouldn't have to worry about any "rules."

Leap Year, I was told, started as a mining town, boomed during the 1870's and '80's, then slowly died over the next few decades. Grady was its last living resident.

Now just one street remained with a collection of buildings on either side in varying states of decay. About a dozen were still standing, with the rest collapsed or nearly so. Some were just roofs on the ground, others were unrecognizable piles of rubble. The lawyer settling Grady's estate had warned me the land was virtually worthless when I told him I wanted to sell it. Now I feared he might be right.

I had no trouble locating Grady's house from the lawyer's description: a two-story Victorian with two bay windows, a large veranda stretching from the front to the south side of the house, and a mansard roof with a lot of shingles missing. Once-yellow paint had blistered off long ago in the harsh mountain sunshine. It was easily the nicest house in the town, standing tall over the tiny buildings and cabins that surrounded it.

I parked the Jeep in front of the house and waded knee-deep through weeds and wildflowers to reach the porch. I held my breath as I climbed each badly decayed step. They creaked and felt spongy, but held. The lawyer had promised to arrange for the electricity to be turned on. I flipped the switch next to the door and breathed a sigh of relief as the porch light snapped on.

I stepped inside the house and felt as though I were entering a time warp. The clock had stopped somewhere around 1930, judging from the style of the living room furniture. Without pausing to decide if I liked the place or not, I smiled with the realization this was my house. My house. I actually owned something, however briefly. I was thrilled.

I then headed straight to the study and located Grady's desk. In a note she enclosed in her will, she instructed me to find a very important letter addressed to me in the top drawer. I reached for the drawer handle, but sneezed first. The house was dusty.

The drawer was so tightly stuffed that opening it was a struggle and took several jerks. I yanked out a conglomeration of paper several inches thick and walked over to the bay window where I brushed off the seat of the wooden rocker and sat down to sort through them. I found old bills, junk mail, newspaper clippings, warranty information, receipts—a little bit of everything.

I paused in my search long enough to walk out to the Jeep to collect some snacks I bought at a gas station. The wind picked up and turned sharply cooler. Thunder rumbled in the distance. The afternoon thunderstorm promised on the car radio would roll in soon. I looked up and down the deserted street uneasily, suddenly feeling too alone. The waitress back at the cafe had mentioned that sometimes drug dealers hid out up here. She said she thought they were harmless, though they sometimes looked pretty creepy— "like they took more drugs than they sold."

I hurried back into Grady's house and resolved to drown my nerves with a healthy dose of diet soda and taco chips. The air in the old house was musty, so I opened one of the windows of the bay. The breeze smelled of the approaching storm. Munching away, I settled back into the rocker and I sifted my way through yet another heap of paper.

After about ten minutes of sorting, I finally caught sight of my name handwritten on one of the papers. It was obviously a letter— maybe it was *the* letter. Grady's handwriting was difficult to read, all large and shaky, like she wrote it after drinking twelve cups of coffee.

> *Dear Darcy,*
>   *When you read this, I shall have passed on. Do not grieve for me. I have already lived far more years than any person has a right to. I have decided to break a promise I made nearly seventy-five years ago, but I think the truth must come out in all things—that is the natural way of the world. My mother made a confession on her death bed that I feel I must now share with someone—*

I chuckled. Family secrets? Deathbed confessions? Pretty heady stuff. I rubbed my eyes with a yawn. My four-thirty wake up call was telling on me.

>   *She could have taken the story to her grave, but she chose to tell it. I don't think she told the truth to "save her*

soul"—my mother was never a religious woman and did not request a priest to attend her even though I know she was baptized and confirmed a Catholic. No, she unburdened herself because she knew I had a right to know the truth, even if lies are easier to live with. When I get through with this story (if I ever get started, you must excuse my rambling—I guess I am getting old) you will know that the lies I grew up with were far preferable to the truth.

Please remember, before you judge my mother, that she always did what was best for her children. You may not agree with what she did—who could? We are speaking of crimes, after all—crimes of a shocking magnitude. But she did them for her children.

So, I will tell you of my mother's sins and I will also share with you her great secret. It was never of any use to me, but perhaps you will have better luck. I hope I am doing the right thing. This knowledge was a curse to my mother and everyone else who knew of it.

A LOUD banging noise interrupted my reading with a jolt. I dropped the letter and everything else slipped off my lap. Someone was knocking on the front door. Completely startled, I jumped up from the rocker and stared at the door, unable to decide what to do.

The loud knocking continued. A man's voice shouted "Hello? Hello?" I approached the door warily. I wasn't planning on company in a ghost town. The knocking grew more insistent and obviously was not going to go away. Adrenaline caused my heart to pound as I placed my hand on the door knob. Reasoning that intruders don't knock and yell "hello," I took a deep breath and opened the front door a crack.

"Yes?"

"Who are you?" demanded the man. So much for Western friendliness.

"Who are *you*?" I shot back, annoyed by his rudeness.

He glanced down both sides of the porch and then back at me, frowning. "Look, this is private property."

"I know. I'm the new owner." I frowned back defiantly.

He cocked his head, still skeptical.

"I inherited this place from my great-aunt." I was doubly annoyed at being required to identify myself to this stranger.

"Oh." He visibly relaxed now and looked like this explanation changed everything. "Are you Darcy? Darcy Close?"

I nodded dumbly, incredulous that he knew my name. Now this hostile, would-be intruder was all smiles and offering me his hand. I reluctantly shook it. He had rough workman's hands.

"I'm Evan Allender. Sorry I came on so strong," he explained. "They asked me to keep an eye on this place since your aunt died. You know—keep the vandals away. The house was broken into a couple of times since she died. I threw one bunch out myself, called the sheriff on the others."

He looked big enough to throw squatters off the property. At least six-two, lanky, but strong-looking, he was maybe thirty. He had long, strawberry blond hair, pulled into a pony tail that stuck out the back of his ball cap. His freckled face was sunburned and he wore a drooping red-gold handlebar mustache. He was handsome in a funky sort of way.

Both his cap and his faded tee shirt bespoke an allegiance to the Chicago Cubs. He wore a plaid flannel overshirt with one elbow split out. As for the rest of his attire, he definitely fell in the jeans-with-hiking-boots contingent, although his shoes were more workman's boots.

"How did you know my name?" I asked.

"I knew old Miss McAllister real well. I did a lot of work for her. Did you see the bathroom?"

"Umm...no. I really just got here." Bathroom? Why would he be asking about that? He looked crestfallen that I had not seen it. "Is there something wrong with the bathroom?"

He seemed slightly embarrassed now. "Oh, I just did it, that's all. I remodel—carpentry, plumbing, that sort of thing. Well, I'm not actually licensed to do plumbing, but your aunt didn't mind. She was kind of anti-government, anyway. I do good work, though. Here, I'll show you." He brushed past as if I had invited him in.

Did he say carpenter? *Carpenter*? A mere coincidence? Who's to judge? A carpenter had been sister Jane's second choice after cowboy. I smiled to myself at the thought of her invisibly shoving me in his direction. *Once more unto the breach....*

I obediently followed him upstairs, knowing all the while that back home I would never have allowed a strange man in my house for any reason on earth. He ushered me into the bathroom with a look of accomplishment on his face.

I was properly impressed. "This...this is beautiful," I gasped. It looked like something out of a decorating magazine. Marble countertops, ornate fixtures—and a whirlpool bathtub.

"This house is a genuine historical landmark, but your aunt wasn't too much on history. She liked her creature comforts. She sank seven grand into this room. I tried to talk her into going with something kind of Victorian—you know, in keeping with the style the house. Maybe a cast iron tub on feet, something like that. But she wanted the Jacuzzi for her arthritis. Hell, she was a hundred years old. Who was I to argue?"

I had been afraid Grady's house might not have indoor plumbing. What a shock. "You did a wonderful job."

"Well, I guess I better leave you alone now that I know you're not a vandal. Call me if you need anything." He turned to leave, then snapped his fingers and spun back. "That reminds me. I was supposed to give you a message when you got here—you don't have any phone service. The lines went down last winter and the phone company didn't bother to fix them because nobody was living up here. The old lady's lawyer told them you wanted service so they said they'd be working on it sometime soon. If you want, I'll call them and tell them you're here."

"That would be really great if you could."

I followed him back downstairs, asking on the way, "Have you lived here long?"

"Nearly fifteen years in the county. I moved up near Leap Year about three, four years ago. We're your closest neighbors. We live in that crappy-looking trailer you probably saw on your way up—the one with the half-built log cabin next to it. It's going to be a great house, if I ever get the damn thing finished."

"Does your wife help you in your business?" I assumed the "we" meant he was married. So much for Jane's idea.

Evan smiled at this. "Oh, no, she wouldn't know a Hilty gun from a rip saw. She teaches acupuncture at the community college. That's down valley about seventy miles."

"Quite a commute."

He nodded in agreement. "About three hours up and two hours down in the winter. Less in the summer."

It amused me how everyone in the mountains gave directions with the words "up" and "down" rather than the more conventional east, west, etc.

We said our goodbyes and I went back upstairs to marvel at Grady's luxurious bathroom. I started playing with the whirlpool tub. I turned on the jets too soon, causing water to shoot me straight in the face, the rest hit the ceiling. I almost didn't hear Evan banging on the door again a few minutes later. He must have forgotten something.

I hurried back down to the door, arriving breathless.

"Hi," I struggled to say as I gulped in air.

"You okay?"

"It's...just...I'm...not used to the altitude." I tried to smile to cover my embarrassment.

"We wondered if you wanted to go down into Columbine with us and grab some mocha latte at the Tenmile."

I glanced out to his truck and saw a young man sitting in the cab. He looked a lot like Evan so I assumed this was perhaps a younger brother. Maybe they were in business together.

"Well, um...I—"

"Ah, come on. You'll love it." Evan raised his eyebrows expectantly as I hesitated.

"It's the least I can do," he persisted. "I don't want you to think your new neighbor is a jerk."

"I don't think you're a jerk," I assured him with an awkward smile. An oddball, maybe. Perhaps a serial rapist. Who knows? Going with them was crazy. Yet Evan seemed so nice, so genuine, so...neighborly. My new Western philosophy said: Take a chance! Go for it.

I accepted his invitation and we walked out to his truck, a rusty white Toyota with "Allender Construction" printed on the side.

"Don't tell me, let me guess," said Evan slyly as we walked. "You couldn't wait to turn on the Jacuzzi, right?"

I laughed and blushed as I pushed my wet bangs off my forehead.

As I climbed into the cab, Evan introduced me to the young man—boy really—he appeared to be in his late teens. "Darcy Close, this is Reilly."

Reilly and I exchanged awkward smiles and nods. The forced intimacy of the small cab was shy-making.

"Down to the Tenmile," Evan intoned as he swung the little truck onto the rocky road, "For the cinnamon rolls and the mocha latte and...Marlena."

Reilly groaned. I assumed this was some kind of inside joke between the brothers and Reilly was the butt of it. Reilly's hair was darker blond and much straighter than Evan's. He wore it cut off sharply at chin level and kept raking it back from his forehead with his fingers.

"*Marlena...Marlena,*" sang Evan, in a jovial mood.

"Marlena?" I asked tentatively, feeling left out.

"Marlena owns the Tenmile. She's the love of Reilly's young life," explained Evan.

"Stop it, Dad."

Dad? I guess the surprise registered on my face, for Reilly turned to me and snidely announced, "He's older than he looks."

"Sad but true," said Evan with a mock sigh. I was certain I was not the first to mistake them for brothers. "Thirty-six, I confess. Hey...I just realized something—I've been your father half my life."

"Wow, I'm impressed," droned Reilly.

"Cut the sarcasm, Sidewinder, we have company."

Reilly turned and gave me a vague half-smile, as an apology of sorts.

"I understand your mother teaches acupuncture," I said to him to make conversation.

"My mother designs jewelry," he informed me as though I had made a rather stupid mistake.

"Reilly's mom split when he was three," Evan explained.

"And I've been raising him ever since," dead panned Reilly.

"You heard from your mom lately?" Evan asked his son.

"She called me last week to wish me a happy birthday."

"Your birthday was last *month*."

"I know."

Evan let out a sigh that said he was annoyed with his ex-wife. "She still in Tucson with that rodeo guy?"

"He's in the hospital. He got gored by a bull."

This was certainly the first conversation I had ever been a part of that included a bull goring. As fascinating as that was, I could sense the mood of the Allenders was taking a header, so I jumped in to change the subject.

"I didn't know the Tenmile Cafe even had espresso."

"They just got the machine last week. It's not on the menu yet—they haven't totally figured out how it works. We're Marlena's guinea pigs. Reilly has to see Marlena at least three times a week and me...I just go to sightsee."

Probably to get even with his father for the teasing about his crush on Marlena, Reilly added, for my benefit, "There's a waitress on the day shift who never wears a bra."

"Am I going to be a party to sexual harassment?" I asked, feigning lofty disdain.

"I plead guilty to *looking*, that's all," said Evan. "We would rather die than offend Celeste."

"We probably *would* die if we offended Celeste," said Reilly, quite seriously.

"Celeste has a big boyfriend," Evan explained.

"A *very* big boyfriend. He used to be a lineman for the Broncos until he blew out his knee."

Then Reilly turned to his father. "Do you suppose Mike is the only black person in the county?"

"Probably the only one who lives here year-round."

"Oh, come on," I said, incredulous at this demographic. "Are you trying to say that there is only one black person in the entire county?"

"That's about the size of it. There are a few Indians, a few Hispanics, but mostly just your standard issue lily-white European rejects. That Mike—he's got it made. He's got money, he's got fame. And he's got Celeste."

"Dad's a breast man," Reilly said to me, probably to further annoy his father.

Evan elbowed his son playfully said out of the corner of his mouth: "Jeez, Reil, Darcy's gonna think we're a couple of perverts."

"Then she'd be a very perceptive woman," said Reilly.

"Watch out, Darcy. Reilly likes older women. Marlena's a good ten years older than I am."

Son shot father another warning look, so father changed the subject this time. "Hey, I've got a rock 'n' roll lyrics trivia question for you both: What place lies about 'a mile down on the dark side of Route 88'?"

"Greasy Lake," I answered without hesitation. Both men stared at me in surprise.

"That was too easy," said Evan. He thought for a moment. "Okay, what did the fireman in 'Penny Lane' keep in his pocket?"

"A portrait of the Queen."

"Who's Sting's favorite whore?"

"'Roxanne.'" I felt like a contestant on a game show. Success was making me cocky. "Come on, give me a tough one."

Evan sighed with a mock frown. "Okay...what did R.E.M. say we got instead of St. Peter's?"

I paused for dramatic effect, then—truly showing off—I lightly answered, "A truck stop."

"Wow, she's good," said Reilly. "Nobody beats Dad at Lyric Trivia."

As the truck slammed and jerked its way down the switchbacks, I longingly wished I had the nerve to drive like Evan, who appeared to be paying so little attention to what he was doing. He careened around the hairpin turns I had so cautiously curbed. We arrived at the Tenmile

Cafe in less than half the time it had taken me to make the same trip and just a step ahead of the thunderstorm.

We sat in a booth by the window with me on one side and Evan and his son on the other. As the braless waitress named Celeste approached, both men watched with reverent attention. She was wearing a thin stretchy top and her breasts moved like twin slinkys beneath it.

"She's wearing the leotard," Reilly whispered as though in pain. He sucked in his breath. "That's my favorite."

Evan motioned him to be quiet as she arrived at our table. He smiled across the table at me as though to say how-can-you-put-up-with-us? I smiled back, ever the good sport. He gave Celeste our order and after she jotted it down she looked up from her pad and recognized me from this morning.

"Well, hi. Did you get up to Leap Year all right?"

I told her I had and thanked her for her directions.

"I don't get to give directions that often. In a town this small, everything is usually measured by its distance from the stoplight."

The stoplight. That must mean there was only one. This really was a small town. I tried not to smile at this as Celeste retreated to the kitchen with my two companions wistfully watching her go. Conversation was about to resume when an elderly man wearing a cowboy hat and a neck brace attached with velcro came over to our table.

"How did a nice young lady like you get hooked up with a couple of coyotes like these?"

I giggled self-consciously, not knowing how to answer the old codger.

"You're addressing the new mayor of Leap Year, Jim," said Evan. "This is Miss Darcy Close. Darcy, this is Jim Knobe."

Ignoring Evan, old Jim leaned close to me and continued the tease. "Watch out for this one." He gestured toward Evan. "A notorious womanizer."

"Now, Jim," protested Evan. "You know I'm retired. Reilly's the womanizer now."

"Reilly's a womanizer-in-training," continued Jim, still pretending to speak only to me. "He's studying at the feet of the master."

"I'll be on my guard every minute," I assured him, playing along.

"How's the neck, Jim?" asked Evan, who then explained to me, "Jim cracked up his snow mobile last winter."

Jim stood up and frowned, shaking his head as much as someone could in a neck brace. "Not good, not good at all. I been thinking of driving over to the college and seeing if your dear lady could maybe help me."

"Well, she sure cured my back," said Evan to Jim. To me, he said, "That's how I met her. I fell off a roof, broke my foot and my wrist, did something godawful to my back. Doctors couldn't do a thing, but keep me on pain killers."

"That was our Year of Worker's Comp." Reilly sounded nostalgic.

"I finally gave up on modern medicine and started searching out alternatives. Greta was the first person to really help."

"So she moved in to provide round-the-clock therapy," added Reilly with undisguised contempt. Father shot son a warning look this time.

"My only problem," said Jim, "is that I have a little trouble understanding her. My hearing is so bad anyway and with her accent."

"She's Swedish," Reilly said to me and then added nastily, "We all have trouble understanding Greta." He obviously meant more than her accent.

Jim sensed a family quarrel coming on and turned to leave, rapping on the table with his knuckles in a kind of "goodbye" gesture and saying, "Take care now. Hope I see more of you, young lady."

Jim had no more than left when Marlena sauntered over, bringing out our order herself. Marlena was a handsome woman, tall, thin, late forties, looking like she was born to wear those tight jeans and that soft pink sweater. Her graying hair was short and curly, parted on the side in a girlish way. Her tanned face carried deep laugh lines of someone who smiled often, but she smiled more with her mouth than her eyes, as though she found the world a place of endless bemusement rather than a real hoot.

"Celeste told me you boys were back. And who's your friend?"

"Marlena, I'd like you to meet Darcy Close. The proud new owner of Leap Year."

"Our heiress. At last we meet you. We were all wondering what you'd be like." Marlena smiled at me in a rather chilly way. Almost as though she were sizing me up as a potential rival, but for who? Evan, who was married, or Reilly, who was barely out of high school?

"How are we doing on our Mocha Latte today, boys?" Marlena leaned against the side of our booth, resting the round tray against her skinny hip.

"Let's ask Darcy's opinion," said Evan. "She's from back East. She's probably an expert on this stuff."

I was not a fan of espresso, but I wanted my new friends to like me so I said, "Excellent," with great enthusiasm.

"Well, boys, do you think Darcy might locate the Hidden Vein?"

"What's the Hidden Vein?" I asked innocently.

"It's Leap Year's answer to the Lost Dutchman Mine," explained Evan. "People have been looking for a legendary lost vein of gold for over a hundred years. Hard to say how the rumors got started."

"Is that why Grady bought up all of Leap Year?" The lawyer told me Grady started buying up the vacant houses and lots from the 1930's onward and finally ended up with the whole town—one hundred and forty-six acres and an abandoned railroad water tower. She even owned the mineral rights to the dozens of played-out mines in the area.

Evan and Marlena both chuckled at this.

"That's the theory at least," said Marlena. "People used to tease her about buying the whole town. She would just say she was looking for something her parents lost a long time ago."

These comments caused me to think about Grady's letter—her cryptic mention of a "secret." Could it involve the Hidden Vein? "Maybe I shouldn't sell the place after all."

"Oh, don't sell it," said Evan.

"I don't really have a choice. There are a bunch of unpaid taxes on the land. If I don't sell it, the county will."

Marlena then turned her attention to Reilly, probably not wanting me to remain in the spotlight any longer than necessary. "How's life been treating you, Sidewinder?"

Reilly gave her a hangdog expression and coyly moaned, "My love life's in the Dumpster, Marlena."

"You always say that, but I don't believe it. A cute boy like you. What woman could resist you?" With a tough smile, she turned and headed back to the kitchen area.

"See there," teased Evan. "She thinks you're cute."

Reilly looked abjectly miserable. "Cute like a puppy dog."

When Reilly got up to use the men's room, I leaned forward over the table and asked Evan in a slightly coquettish way, "What's the story on you and Marlena?"

Evan pursed his lips and whispered, "How did you know about that? Are you psychic or something?"

I shrugged mysteriously. It was actually a lucky guess.

"When I first came up here, Marlena sort of adopted me. I moved here from Chicago right after Sandy and I split. Sandy's Reilly's mom. Reilly was staying with my parents while I tried to get something going with my carpentry. It was the late Seventies, they were throwing up condos like crazy out here. Marlena let me stay with her, she put my name around to get me jobs—she knows everybody. She and her husband had just split up. I was her lap dog for about a year."

"Lap dog?"

"I got fed and watered and came when I was called." He didn't sound like he was entirely comfortable with his year as a "kept man." Before Reilly returned to the table, Evan leaned forward and whispered: "Don't tell Reilly. He'd have a fit."

When the brief rainstorm ended, we left the cafe. Reilly stayed in town and Evan drove me back up to Leap Year. On the way home, he questioned whether I thought it wise to hang out in Leap Year all by myself. I think his implication being I was too pampered to tough it out in such an extreme and remote location. I informed him that if a one hundred-year-old lady could survive alone there, surely I could manage a week or so. I climbed out of the truck, feeling huffy. Little did he know he was dealing with the reigning Miss Kick-Butt Colorado.

"Look," said Evan to change the subject. He pointed down the canyon. "It's still raining down there. That's about seven or eight miles from here."

I marveled at the fact we could see so far away, but Evan said that was nothing. "Go up on that ridge up there over the old Northern Star mine sometime. You'll be able to see over a *hundred* miles. It's a great place for a picnic. 'Course there's probably still some snow up there now. Parts of it hold snow year-round."

"The Tenmile Range is beautiful," I mused.

"Uh...you're standing in the Tenmile Range. You're looking at the Gore Range." He smiled at my ignorance in an indulgent way, making me feel less stupid. I immediately liked this about him. I tried to get over my disappointment that he had a wife.

He leaned his head out the window and called to me. "How about coming over to dinner at my house tomorrow night? I'd like for you to meet my girls."

Girls? Plural? Did he have a harem? He pulled off his sunglasses and suddenly looked very handsome to me. I said I would be happy to come and was told to arrive around seven.

"Black tie optional," he called, laughing as he shifted the truck back into gear. When he drove off, I saw what I already half-expected to on the back bumper: THERE ARE NO RULES ABOVE 10,000

FEET.

I shook my head and returned to my seat in the bay window to read what was left of the first page of Grady's letter.

> *The story played out before I was ever born. It began in the fall of 1879, when my father first came West to the gold fields of Colorado—*

Chapter Two

The story played out before I was ever born. It began in the fall of 1879, when my father first came west to the gold fields of Colorado.

CONOR MCALLISTER had not segregated himself from the company of women for so long a time that he did not notice that the young widow, Mrs. Kelly, was flirting with him. The question was not whether she was flirting, but why? She was great with child, hugely with child, probably due any day, probably overdue. Why would a woman in that condition be flirting at all and why on earth with him?

Not that he was a stranger to women's wiles. Before his marriage, he had been considered one of Philadelphia's most eligible bachelors. He was good looking, with regular features and light brown hair that curled at the back of his neck. His eyes were blue and his mother had always told him he had the prettiest eyes she had ever seen on a boy. He knew better than to trust his mother's opinions since she doted on him, her only child, but he would learn from experience early on that his looks won him rewards he did little to earn.

He also noticed that young Widow Kelly was pretty. At least she had a pretty face as she tilted her chin with its tiny dimple, toward him. Her speech indicated she had been born in Ireland, but Conor guessed she must have come here as a young child, for only a faint lilt remained, not the thick brogue he had heard among the recently emigrated servants in his parents' house.

Conor caught himself wondering what her figure would look like when it was not so swollen with child. Then he glanced away, embarrassed at having such an inappropriate thought. There was a lot of gossip going about the town of Leap Year concerning this woman and this baby she was expecting, a baby that seemed to be arriving too many months after the death of her husband. Conor had heard the gossip and he had only just arrived in town three weeks before. Of course renting a room above the saloon and having made the acquaintance of the saloon owner meant that he was privy to a great deal of gossip.

The paternity of Mrs. Kelly's baby was a matter of great

speculation. Her late husband, a miner lost in a mine collapse the previous year, was not a candidate. Since her husband's death she had begun to take in laundry for the miners—a lucrative business which adequately if not lavishly supported her four children plus the one on the way. She did not live with any man and was never seen in the company of anyone other than her boarder, the elderly Mrs. Atwater whom everyone called "Granny" though she was no one's relation, but was, like Mrs. Kelly, a miner's widow.

A popular theory, especially at the saloon, was that Mrs. Kelly was providing the miners with services beyond just laundry. With a male population of nearly 2,000 and a female population of less than 300, she would not have been the first matron to augment the family income in this manner. The miners had a lot of money to spend and virtually nowhere to spend it. A willing woman could name her price.

Rape was another possibility—an unfortunate consequence of the unusual ratio of men to women, or so everyone said. Still, Mrs. Kelly was the only one who knew and she wasn't talking.

Conor had happened upon Mrs. Kelly as he walked back to town from a visit to the Northern Star Mine. Snow clouds were gathering and a few flakes had begun to fall. Snow in October. This amazed Conor, but everything about the Rocky Mountains had been amazing so far. Just before arriving in the town of Leap Year, as he made his way south down the Tenmile Canyon, he had looked up the eastern face of the canyon wall to see three enormous breaks in the forestry that seemed to form the letters S-K-Y. He never asked anyone about this apparition later because he was afraid he had imagined it. Of course, Leap Year carried its own set of surprises. Upon first setting foot on its boarded sidewalks, Conor was presented with a man, thrown out of the saloon, who landed at Conor's feet. The man smiled up at Conor rather drunkenly and said with great cordiality, "Good day, friend." Conor responded with similar courtesy, carefully stepping over the man and continuing on his way.

Perhaps he was just easy to impress or perhaps there really was something indefinably spectacular about this place. Unlike all the other residents of Leap Year, he had come not to seek his fortune in the gold rush, but to report on it.

Thaddeus Applebee, Conor's best friend from boarding school and college, owned a small weekly newspaper and had hired Conor to go out West and report back on the recent series of gold and silver strikes in the mountains. A new gold rush was in the offing and stories about it were of interest to everyone.

He had spent the day getting a tour of the Northern Star Mine from its owner, Gideon Reynolds. Reynolds told him that gold had been mined here as early as the 1860's, but the area had been too remote to develop properly. Then, new strikes were made in 1878, first with 'free gold'—gold exposed in blowouts, veins eroded into view for the naked eye to see. But those strikes were only the beginning. An almost unbelievably rich silver belt had been uncovered and lode mining had begun in earnest with miners boring tunnels into the canyon walls and down through its floor twenty-four hours a day.

The Northern Star was the largest of the mines in the Tenmile Mining District and currently the richest, but facts like these changed on a daily basis as new strikes were made. Conor had found Reynolds to be a quiet, serious man, not prone to boasting, and this made his fantastic descriptions all the more compelling. Conor had left with his head buzzing from the tales of treasure and overnight millionaires.

On the walk back to town from the Northern Star Mine, he had caught sight of Mrs. Kelly struggling to split wood in the yard beside her house. She had a large kettle boiling over a small fire in the yard. It was filled with laundry. She was groaning and cursing with the effort of swinging the heavy ax and missed her target about three out of every four tries.

Conor's first impulse was to hurry on by, but some remnant of chivalry wouldn't let him. He couldn't stand to see a woman in her condition having to undertake such heavy labor. And then there was the weather. Snow was falling. A cold night ahead. She would need this wood for more than her laundry kettles.

He strode into her yard. "May I help you?" He pulled off his hat in a polite gesture.

She glanced up from her work, somewhat startled. "Oh, thank you, but I'm doing fine." She swung and missed again.

Conor covered his mouth with his hand to hide a smile. She looked up at him again, this time with a sheepish grin. He set his notebook on the ground, put his hands on his hips and waited. When she missed again, she leaned the ax handle against the ground, sighed and wiped beads of perspiration from her brow. Conor was reminded of what Thoreau had observed: Wood warms you twice.

"If you really wouldn't mind..." she said, smiling prettily, giving up. Conor removed his coat and set to work. He hated splitting wood; it had been one of his punishments as a child. His family hadn't even needed the wood, they heated with coal. But his father liked the look and smell of a wood fire in the parlor after dinner on winter evenings and if young Conor had committed any infractions during the day or gotten low marks, he was sent out to split the wood and kindling while a servant, whose usual job it was, sat by smirking.

At least no one was smirking now. In fact, he had the satisfaction of doing someone a good turn. For the first time in a long time, he felt rather like a good Christian. His mother would be pleased by something like this. Then again, his mother would probably not have approved of his associating in any fashion with a woman with a reputation like Mrs. Kelly's.

He almost chuckled out loud at the thought of his mother's reaction, had she known he was living in a room over a saloon. A saloon with a brothel in the back, no less. Four women worked in little tent-like shelters behind the main building. The saloon was called the Lucky Chance, because its proprietor's name was Brandon Chance, but it was also called the Last Chance and the Lost Chance, depending on the mood of its patrons.

Brandon Chance had been Conor's first acquaintance in Leap Year. He was called Brandy by everyone who knew him—a good name for a saloon keeper. Conor was disappointed to find out Brandy didn't stock any of his namesake, however. Conor liked Brandy straight off, but didn't care for living over the saloon. The noise and music went on until all hours making it almost impossible to sleep. And Brandon was charging him the exorbitant rate of five dollars per week. "Because the room is heated," Brandy explained. "You don't know just how cold it gets up here, friend." The "heat" came from the stove in the main floor below. The stove pipe extended up through Conor's room on its way to the roof and it did put out plenty of heat for the small space.

The room had no windows, but Brandy proudly pointed out the "window" in the ceiling. Conor had never seen this arrangement before, but Brandon assured him it was superior to a normal window in that it provided "light, air, and privacy." Conor leased the room, not because he liked it but because there were no other rooms in town. The Northern Star Hotel had burned down in September and would not be rebuilt until spring thaw, six months from now.

As Conor moved in and paid for his first week in advance, Brandy leaned close and in confidential tones advised him that if he ever desired feminine companionship of an evening, such could be arranged for a very reasonable fee. "I could send someone up here," Brandon said with a wink. "You don't really want to visit the cribs." By cribs, he referred to the little tents out back. "They're out there for the miners and other rough types. I can see you're a gentleman and used to much better."

Conor had thanked him for the offer and politely said he would think about it. Brandon had laughed and said over his shoulder as he left, "You'll think about it a lot come winter. Winter nights up here are long and cold."

Some evenings he cracked open the skylight to let in some fresh air. As he lay on the lumpy little mattress, he could hear the women in the cribs below with their customers. It was odd to eavesdrop on such activities, at once embarrassing and fascinating. But he wasn't seriously tempted. The women were not very attractive and not particularly clean. Then there was the once-a-week "airing" of their bedding. The mattresses and sheets were hauled out and laid across ant hills. When asked about this strange practice, Brandon advised him the ants ate the lice. Conor wasn't tempted at all after that.

Still, on the warmer nights, with the skylight open, he had to listen to what seemed like the whole world coupling except him.

"MY SON, JOE, usually chops and splits for me," explained Mrs. Kelly as Conor worked his way through her short pile of logs. "He's twelve and he's in school right now."

"Does Leap Year have a school?" Conor asked between whacks. He was trying to carry his share of the conversation. She didn't look old enough to have a twelve-year-old. Or maybe she did, he was no judge of age. She could perhaps have been his age, thirty, and had married young.

"No, not yet. They have to go down to Columbine, you know, the town below. The Methodist preacher gathers up all the children of school age and hauls them down there in his wagon. Isn't that sweet of him? Of course, with winter coming on—I don't know how long that's going to last. There's talk of finding homes down there for the children to stay at through the week so they would only come home on the weekends."

"My parents sent me away to boarding school when I was twelve. I hated it."

"They couldn't afford to keep you?" Mrs. Kelly's pretty face was downcast with concern.

Conor tried not to laugh. "They just thought the experience would be good for me, that's all."

"And was it?"

Conor paused and wiped his brow. "Cold rooms, bad food, Latin verbs, chapel every day...and the teachers would beat us unmercifully."

He resumed his task.

"That sounds a perfect nightmare," she said. He could not see her face now, she was busy stirring the clothes in the big kettle and tending the fire beneath it. She walked back. "Strangers—people outside your own family—actually beat you?"

"'Spare the rod and spoil the child' was the school motto." Conor was making this up, but the beatings had been real. A birch rod had been the disciplinary instrument of choice. And good-looking boys like Conor had more to worry about than the beatings, but he was certainly not going to tell Mrs. Kelly about that. In fact, he had never told another living soul what had happened to him one rainy April afternoon when he was fourteen. His classics tutor had caught him cheating on an exam. If the school's officials were informed of this, Conor would be immediately expelled—sent home in disgrace to face the wrath of his father. He wished to avoid this at all costs—and the tutor knew it. He could still, sixteen years later, hear the voice of the tutor whispering in his ear: "I'm not going to hurt you, Conor. I would rather die than hurt you. You're my favorite, you know. Now there's a good boy, and look at you. Nature has blessed more than your handsome face, my dear." Conor escaped with no worse than a prolonged fondling from the lecherous old man, but sickening memories of that afternoon tormented him for years, intruding upon his thoughts at unexpected moments like a cloud crossing the face of the sun.

He finished the last log and leaned on the ax handle to catch his breath. He still was not used to the altitude. The slightest exertion left him breathless and sometimes dizzy. Brandon had even warned him to go easy on alcohol consumption in the early weeks. "Liquor really packs a whollop up here until you're used to it. Makes cheap drunks of most of these fellas. Bad for business," he joked.

Seeing he was finished, Mrs. Kelly rushed in the house and fetched a cup of water. As he gulped it down, she said, "I don't know how ever to thank you, Mr...?"

"McAllister. Conor McAllister. Forgive me for not introducing myself." He had forgotten introductions because he already knew her name. But he couldn't admit to know or he would be admitting he had listened to all the idle talk and he thought himself above that sort of thing. In truth, though, his new friend Brandy was a world class gossip and he enjoyed listening to him rattle on at length. Then again, in his new career as a journalist, was this not part of the trade?

"And I am Elodie Kelly, Mrs. Kyle Kelly, but my husband is recently deceased."

Not recently enough, Conor snickered to himself, but said, "Sorry to hear that, Ma'am." He picked up his coat, which had a light dusting of snow on it.

When he handed her back the empty glass, she drew an apple from the pocket of her apron and offered it to him. Before he could take it, she warned, with an impudent smile, "It might be from the Tree of Knowledge."

"If this is Paradise," he returned, taking the apple, "we're overdressed." It wasn't like him to speak so freshly to a woman he barely knew, but she seemed to invite it.

A delightful, trilling laugh was her response, making him feel rather clever. Then she sobered and said, "Sunday supper, that's it. You must come to Sunday supper."

"No, really, that's all right. I didn't do this for a reward. You owe me nothing, really." He began to back his way out of her yard.

"Five o'clock," she continued, smiling mischievously. "We'll be having chicken."

"I really can't, I'm sorry. It's a generous offer and I'm much obliged by it, but I'm afraid—"

"Five o'clock, Mr. McAllister, I'll see you at my table on Sunday." She continued to smile and jutted out her dimpled chin, then turned and went in her house, leaving him still lamely protesting in the yard.

Conor sighed. What had he gotten himself into? Sunday was just day after tomorrow. Sitting down to a table full of strangers filled him with dread.

HE TRUDGED the mile and a half back to the saloon and went to bed with a meager supper of bread and cold coffee. A home-cooked meal would be a welcome change, he reasoned. Then again, she had four children. They would be there. He really didn't care much for children. He lay down upon his narrow bed, but could not sleep.

Two years. Two years since Allison's death. He knew the anniversary only too well because he had just celebrated his daughter's second birthday before leaving Philadelphia. His in-laws had given a nice dinner party and his little girl had been dressed in a darling party dress which she efficiently destroyed with cake and ice cream. It had all been very amusing, but Conor couldn't get the hang of being cheerful. He had tried all evening, even drinking far too much in an effort to shake off his depression.

He had gone to the kitchen to fetch another bottle of wine and had caught a bit of the cook's conversation with the kitchen maid. "Not much of a father is he?" the maid was saying. "Nor likely ever to be," said the cook. "Some men don't ever catch on to it."

Upon hearing this, Conor took the bottle of wine and left the house without a word to anyone. The overheard discussion of his parenting skills had cut rather close to the bone. What the women said was true—he wasn't much of a father and he knew it. He hadn't even been able to come up with a name for his daughter. After two nameless weeks, the baby was christened "Beatrice" by his mother-in-law. Beatrice had been Allison's favorite name, the name she had given to all her dolls in childhood. The doll collection had remained in her bedroom even after he had taken up residence there. How he had hated all those stupid dolls. Conor finished off the wine in his room at home. The second anniversary of one's wife's death was as good an excuse to get drunk as any.

He was so ill the next day he couldn't go to work, not that he ever had too much trouble finding reasons not to show up there. He hated working for his father at McAllister Bootworks, but returning to work there had been a condition of his moving home again after Allison's death. This hangover was even worse than usual. He swore never to touch alcohol again, but this proved to be a piecrust promise: Made to be broken.

Downstairs that morning, through his headachy haze, he overheard sounds of his mother-in-law paying a call on his mother. She came to complain of his uncouth behavior at his daughter's birthday party. She said her husband was so insulted by Conor's leaving the house without saying goodbye, that he felt like never inviting him back.

Lilly McAllister tried to make excuses for her son, but it was not easy to explain Conor's antics. The inconsolable grief excuse was getting old. "But you've got to invite him back sometime," reasoned Lilly. "You've got his daughter."

"Some father he is," sniffed Allison's mother, echoing the sentiments of her kitchen staff without realizing it.

CONOR STOOD up on his bed and opened the sky light to see if it was still snowing. It was, but only lightly. He heard laughter coming from the saloon and feminine giggling coming from the cribs. He closed the glass and lay back down again. He fell into a fitful sleep, stirred by dreams of the Garden of Eden, in which the naked Eve strangely resembled the odd young widow, Mrs. Kelly.

Chapter Three

THE BRIGHT morning sun against my eyelids woke me up with a start. I glanced around, disoriented, blinking, to realize I had fallen asleep in Grady's rocker. Had I really slept the entire night through? It didn't seem possible, yet the last thing I remember from the evening before was sorting amongst Grady's endless papers, pausing to read whatever caught my fancy, and getting more and more sleepy in the process.

I had planned to return to Columbine before dark and stay at the little motel on the edge of town. I stretched and rubbed my stiff neck, still unable to comprehend I had actually dozed off in such an uncomfortable position. Had the house cast a spell on me?

Surviving a night all alone in a ghost town gave me new found confidence. I could stay here and save the price of a motel room. That would spare my careful travel budget a lot.

I spent the day in Columbine, buying necessities for the house and returned to Leap Year in time to get ready for dinner with my new neighbors.

I arrived at Casa Allender promptly at seven, bringing a bottle of wine purchased in Columbine's only liquor store. It bore a label I had never heard of and I renamed it in my mind "Chateau Leap Year," in honor of my new real estate.

I drove down to Evan's house and parked in front of the trailer. The log cabin was larger than the trailer but its walls were only three feet high at this point. Two of the largest dogs I had ever seen bounded out to greet me. They looked like a gray version of Irish Setters but were the size of small horses. As soon as I got out of the car, both jumped on me at once, knocking me straight to the ground. Fortunately, they were licking rather than biting, but still I cowered on the ground until two young girls pulled them off of me.

"Rhett! Scarlett! No, no. Sit!" the girls yelled. "They won't hurt you. They're just saying hello, that's all."

Evan ran out into the yard. "Oh, for Christsakes, girls, get them in the house. Darcy, are you okay?"

"Fine." I was a bit dazed. I looked around for my present of wine.

It had smashed against a rock in the course of my fall. Evan pulled me to my feet and I brushed myself off. I felt a little overdressed in my slacks and sweater. Evan was barefoot in shorts and a tank top. He was, however, wearing an earring so maybe he was dressed up a little. The two little girls, whom I now realized were twins, wore faded, mismatched shorts and shirts that looked like they had been purchased in a garage sale. They wore earrings, too, fancy beaded affairs.

"Oh, damn, look at your wine. I'm sorry, Darcy. What a welcome—bet you can't wait to come back now. You'll have to forgive Rhett and Scarlett, they're obedience school dropouts."

"What are they?" I tried to recover my breath as we walked up the steps to the door of the trailer.

"Irish Wolfhounds. Largest canine breed on the planet. Each weighs around one-eighty. Cost more to feed than the kids. They're great, though. They'll love you to death."

Evan ushered me in the door and announced: "Come meet Team Allender, otherwise known as The Brady Bunch on Acid."

Rhett and Scarlett escaped from their little mistresses and galloped over to me once again. I dodged the inevitable crotch sniff and made my way to the couch with Evan as an escort. The girls sat on the floor in front of me momentarily on either side of the dogs.

"Darcy, this is Summer and this is Winter."

I struggled to keep a straight face upon hearing the names of Evan's daughters. He not only looked like an aging flower child, he named his kids like one, too. "Summer and Winter," I repeated, unable to think of anything else to say. After all, hadn't my mother admonished me at least a thousand times: If you can't think of something nice to say, say nothing?

"Daddy's two favorite seasons," Winter informed me proudly. Her face was identical to her sister's, but fortunately for the uninitiated, she wore her dark hair in a short, straight bob, not unlike her older brother's, while her sister had long hair reaching nearly to her elbows. The girls had inherited their father's height, unlike Reilly who was barely taller than me.

"Most people say spring and fall are their favorite seasons," I said to Evan, though he was on his way back to the kitchen.

"Up here, spring is mud season," he called from the kitchen. "Nothing good ever happens during mud season. I wouldn't name anybody after that. Now fall—fall is okay, but basically you just spend fall waiting for that first snow."

Left alone with the girls, I tried to make conversation. "So...I understand your mother teaches acupuncture."

"Our mother is a flight attendant," said Summer.

"She gets to stand up when all the passengers have to wear their seat belts," Winter added, with pride.

"Greta is the pin pusher," said Reilly, striding into the room and sitting down next to me on the couch. "Their mother's name is Beth."

I wondered when I was going to be introduced to the elusive Greta. I had first assumed she was in the kitchen, but now realized Evan was in there alone, preparing dinner. And how many wives did Evan have, anyway? Every time the subject came up, he seemed to have gained another. It was interesting how much both Reilly and his half-sisters resembled their father without resembling each other in the slightest.

The girls began playing with the dogs, who had finally adjusted to my presence. Reilly leaned in a little closer to me than felt comfortable and, with eyes full of mischief, whispered out of earshot of his sisters: "He likes you."

I frowned slightly at this oddball remark. Reilly moved back and added, this time in a conversational tone, "They're not really married, you know."

"Your father and Greta?"

"He and the Viking just live together. He's never been married."

"That's right," piped up Winter, jumping into the conversation. "Nobody's ever roped the Mustang." Then she shouted toward the kitchen: "Right, Daddy?"

"What, Honey?" Evan shouted back.

"Nobody's ever roped the Mustang."

"That's right."

Winter then pirouetted before the couch, struck a pose and sweetly announced: "We're all bastards in this house."

"Winter!" Her father's tone held the promise of a reprimand. Winter got an "uh-oh" look on her face and ran off into the kitchen.

"I thought I told you I didn't want to hear that word again," came Evan's lowered voice.

"It's true, isn't it?"

"Don't sass me, young lady."

Evan sounded funny coming on parental. Reilly leaned in too close again and said, "They aren't going to last the summer. She hasn't been home in three weeks and judging from his end of the phone conversations, there's big trouble in Little Stockholm."

Was Reilly pimping for his father or trying to line up his next step mother? I steered Reilly into safer conversational waters by getting him to talk about himself. He told me how he had a scholarship to attend the community college in the fall. He wanted to go to a university but couldn't afford it.

He participated in mountain bike races and then explained to me what they were. Then he proudly showed off the mountain bike he had in a state of semi-disassembly in front of the television set. He said the whole family liked to head into the mountains off road whenever they got the chance. He said his dad was a maniac on the downhills. "To brake is to admit defeat," was the family motto, borrowed from a tee shirt slogan.

He told me he wished he could leave home and get a job, but his father didn't like leaving the girls alone up here, so "Guess who got elected babysitter for the summer?"

An electric and an acoustic guitar each sat on stands in the corner of the small living room in what looked like a place of honor—a shrine almost. I asked who the musician was in the family and Reilly indicated his father. He said he used to play professionally, at least on weekends. Never made enough money at it to quit his day job, though.

Reilly worried that Evan was not working enough this summer. Summers were the only time of intensive building work in the county. "We go on welfare nearly every winter. A real ego-enhancing experience, let me tell you. If Greta really does catch the bus, I don't know what we'll do. It's not like we can get along on what *he* makes."

I was struck by how serious and mature Reilly was in comparison to his bohemian father. Maybe he had been correct in his comment that he had "raised" his dad.

Reilly went on to say that the only good thing about his father's unemployment was the fact that it gave him more time to work on the cabin. He had been working on it for years, but was hampered by the fact that the weather made it impossible to work in the winter, but outside employment usually came first in the summer. "It's going to be a great house when it's finished. Of course anything would beat this dump."

"Yeah," agreed Summer, who had quietly been observing me throughout Reilly's long talk. The twin girls may have looked alike, with their pretty heart-shaped faces and turned-up, freckled little noses, but their personalities were distinct. Winter was the outgoing, ebullient one; Summer more reserved, aloof, a watcher.

"It's on the table," called Evan and we went into the kitchen and sat down to eat.

"Dad and the Viking are vegetarians," Reilly explained as Evan served an Oriental stir fry of some sort.

"*Reilly...*" growled Evan.

"Dad and *Greta*," Reilly corrected himself. He added in a stage whisper: "We have to sneak down to the Tenmile to get our burger quotient."

Unperturbed, Evan poured us both a glass of wine, which he assured me was certainly not as nice as the wine I had brought. "We're not wine snobs in this house, I'm afraid. If it doesn't come with a screw top, you probably didn't drink it here," he joked.

The rest of the table conversation focused on me. I told them about myself, how I used to work in an art gallery, how I had an undergraduate degree in art history which was pretty worthless on the job market, how I was recently divorced. I tried to give the impression this divorce thing was of little consequence and didn't go into detail.

I told them what I knew of Grady, about how I was still trying to pin down just how we were related. I confessed I had no idea why she singled me out as her sole legatee. She never married or had children of her own, but she'd had dozens of great-great nieces and nephews to choose from, why had she picked me? We met only once when I was nine. The year was 1976 and my grandparents organized a family reunion of insane proportions to celebrate the Bicentennial. Since they lived in Philadelphia, they assumed everyone would want to come there to celebrate the Fourth. My grandmother researched the family tree and invited every relative she could locate, even ones she had never met. Grady, at ninety-three or thereabouts, was the oldest relative and one of the most obscure. She represented the Colorado branch of the clan and its connection to the eastern branch was a little hazy.

She surprised everyone by accepting the invitation and when she arrived, she proved to be a feisty, charming delight. My own memories of her were tainted by the fact that I was running a high fever on the day we spent together. I came down with a virus on the morning of July Fourth and by noon was so ill I could not take part in any of the festivities. For unknown reasons, Grady stepped forward to be my nurse and insisted that my parents and all the rest go off and enjoy the day's and night's big events.

I must have made quite an impression on the old girl, though I can't think why. I was a very ordinary nine-year-old, as far as I know. We spent the day and evening talking, talking, talking. She did most of the talking—my throat hurt—and the cadence of her speech delighted me. She sounded a lot like Mae West, but without all the spicy double-entendres. She had large, crinkly blue eyes and a jowly, sun-weathered face. She was probably glad to have a captive audience. Since her last brother died in the late Sixties, she had lived alone in Leap Year, seeing only the mailman once a week and coming into town once a month to buy groceries and see the nurse.

After the visit to Philadelphia, she told my mother I was "the cleverest little thing." We became pen pals, exchanging letters and Christmas cards over the years, but never saw each other again.

Evan spoke at length of Grady—he called her that too. He assumed that was actually her name, rather than a child's corruption of the title, "great-aunt." She apparently adopted the name in some past decade. He did a lot of repair work for her over the years. In exchange for one large job, she gave him the three acres on which his house—or houses—now sat.

"She was real sharp until the last year or so," he said. "Then once I went up to check on her and she stuck a shotgun in my face. She didn't know me from Adam. Her memory kind of came and went. Next time she saw me she was all smiles. I wouldn't let the kids go up there after the shotgun incident."

"She was guarding her treasure," said Winter seriously.

"Maybe so," laughed her father.

"Do you really think she might have had a treasure?" I was getting caught up in the gold fever at little bit myself. "She left me this letter talking about her parents and maybe the Hidden Vein, I think. Unfortunately I could only find the first page of it. Her drawers were in a total state of chaos."

Evan and his daughters glanced at each other. "I'm afraid we know why they're such a mess. Grady's house was burglarized the week she died. They totally trashed the place, dumped every drawer on the floor. The girls and I and Sam, the sheriff's deputy, tried to clean it up, but we just sort of stuffed everything back in the drawers."

"Still, it was nice of you to do that."

"It was my idea," said Winter. "We liked Grady. She was funny."

"And cool," added Summer. "Is it fun to live in a ghost town, Darcy?"

"A lot of things go bump in the night," I joked.

"You're awfully brave," said Winter, in awe of my accomplishment. Having my bravery praised like this made it impossible, vanity-wise, for me to admit that I had spent my first night in Leap Year by accident.

At the end of the meal, Reilly abruptly excused himself,

announcing he had a date. Evan looked annoyed, but handed him the keys to the truck anyway. Before leaving, Reilly leaned down and whispered something in Winter's ear. After he left, Winter announced: "I have a wonderful idea."

"What's that, Babe?" Evan was clearing the table. My offer to help wash had been turned down.

"Let's forget about the dishes and all go jump in the hot tub."

Evan must have read the less-than-enthused look on my face and said, "No, not tonight. I don't think Darcy's in the mood for that."

Both girls began begging me, but I told them I didn't bring a swim suit. They looked puzzled by this remark.

"It's not a swimming pool, Darcy," Summer informed me. "You don't need a swimming suit."

"I'm afraid modesty has never been a big priority around here, Darcy," Evan explained. "Girls, why don't you go get in the tub. Darcy and I will finish this wine on the deck." The girls were satisfied by this and scampered away to the hot tub, tossing their clothes off as they ran.

I followed Evan out back to the deck, which was easily the best part of the house. It was an elaborate redwood structure on two levels. I guessed he had built it himself and complimented him on it. At one end of the lower level, the girls bounced and splashed in the round, redwood tub. As soon as they saw Evan, they began whining for him to join them. They wouldn't let up and he finally gave in, asking me if I minded if he got in with them for a minute. "Trust me, we won't get any peace unless I do." He then proceeded to pull off his clothes, but before getting in the tub said, "Damn...we forgot towels," and unselfconsciously strode past me to retrieve some.

I replayed these last few seconds in my mind as a reality check: a man I had only just met was walking around naked before me as though this were the ordinary course of events. Had I entered a foreign country with strange new customs in driving up to Leap Year? Then again, had I entered the Twilight Zone? Or perhaps the Woodstock Zone? I took a deep breath of the cool evening air. Maybe the lack of oxygen up here removed one's inhibitions. I felt vaguely upset at my own comparative prudishness. I was thankful Reilly had left and yet...it now occurred to me that it was he who put the hot tub idea in Winter's head. What a corker.

Both girls came to my side of the hot tub and Winter asked, with a confidential tone, "Darcy, don't men look funny...you know, down there?"

I laughed in embarrassment and the girls laughed, too. Knowing whatever I answered might get repeated, I just made a vague gesture.

The girls did not want the matter to rest. "Daddy calls his penis 'Jack'," giggled Winter.

"Is that so?" I was giggling as bad as the girls now.

"Jack Sprat," sang Summer.

"One-eyed Jack" shrieked Winter. Both girls were beside themselves at their own wit.

"Did I hear someone taking Jack's name in vain?" said Evan as he returned with the towels—four towels, I noticed, not three. The girls jumped at the sound of their father's voice and dove under the water. Evan climbed in and when they resurfaced, he frowned in mock annoyance, saying, "Shame on you." Then he turned to me and added, "Shame on you, too, Darcy."

"I'm just an innocent bystander," I protested.

"You're a college graduate. I expected you to elevate tonight's proceedings, not sink to our level."

"I think Darcy is just shy, Daddy," said Winter. "I think she'd get in if you didn't look."

"Yes, Darcy, we'll hide his eyes," added Summer. She and Winter were positioned on either side of Evan and now covered his eyes with their hands. "Now don't let him peek," she commanded her sister.

"Don't let them pressure you, Darcy," said the now-blinded Evan. He sighed. "First our dogs attack you, then we force you to disrobe against your will. As you may have guessed, we don't get a lot of company up here—maybe this is why—who knows? Anyway, you can't imagine what a big deal this was—your coming over tonight...."

"Well, aw shucks, guys—I'm flattered." I was already pulling off my clothes, tingling with a what-will-happen-next? sensation. We were above 10,000 feet, after all. I slid into the hot water and knew that getting back out again was going to be murder, the night air had turned so cold. The girls dropped their blindfolding grip on their father's face and we all sat there quietly for a moment. To make an awkward situation even more so, Summer announced to the group: "Darcy's breasts are a lot bigger than Greta's."

Evan cringed at this remark and, if my face was not already red from the heat of the water, it was now. "This is why I had kids—so I could stay in a perpetual state of embarrassment. Summer, honey, we don't comment on people's appearance."

"But I meant it as a compliment."

"We don't comment on people's appearance," he repeated patiently.

The girls and their father laughed and joked and teased each other for another ten minutes or so. I watched them quietly, amazed and envious at how happy they seemed. I think Tolstoy was wrong when he said happy families were all alike. This was the oddest happy family I had ever met.

The girls got out and ran into the house to prepare the dessert. They had made homemade ice cream that afternoon in honor of my visit.

"They're cute," I told Evan after they left.

"They're a handful, but they're great. They're growing up though...I kind of hate that. I'll miss them."

"I bet they'll always be Daddy's girls."

Evan looked wistful. "Naw, puberty's gonna strike any day now. They'll belong to the rest of the world instead of just me...it happened with Reilly, it'll happen with them, too. It's never quite the same again. But I guess that comes with the territory."

As tactfully as I could, I asked if it weren't somewhat unusual for a father to have custody. I didn't say it, but I actually thought it was almost unheard of for a father—particularly one who had never bothered to marry the mothers—not only to have custody, but to want it.

"Life just keeps happening to me." He shook his head pensively. "I never get the chance to plan it out. Reilly's mom pulled a *'By the Time I Get to Phoenix'* number on me. I came home from work one day and found a note telling me Reilly was at my mother's. That's it—just Sayonara and good luck. So suddenly I'm this twenty-one-year-old single parent. With Beth—the girls' mom—she wanted to go back to work. She travels all the time, so it just made sense for me to keep them."

He explained that Beth was a flight attendant who flew out of Denver. He met her on a flight from Denver to Chicago when he was going home to attend his father's funeral. Fate placed them both on the return flight to Denver three days later. He related how she had recognized him as he boarded and had cheerfully asked him if he had enjoyed his visit to Chicago. He remembered laughing at her innocent question, since it was along the lines of: "Did you enjoy the play, Mrs. Lincoln?"

I asked him what the biggest difference was between living in Chicago and living up here—besides the scenery, of course. He looked beyond me, squinting into the distance, thinking this over.

"The biggest difference would have to be that back in Chicago—

and this is probably true for Philly as well—you're defined by what you do for a living. What you do is who you are. You're the doctor or the architect or the plumber or whatever. Here you're defined by what you do when you're *not* working. Here you're the rock climber or the skier or the mountain biker. You make a living any way you can—do whatever it takes to support your habit—namely, living up here. We're a bunch of junkies, really. Hooked on the altitude, I guess."

I thought about what he had said. It was true, where I came from, people were defined by their occupation. No wonder I never felt like I had an identity, I had never gotten around to deciding what I was going to be when I grew up. Maybe things would be different if I lived here. Maybe I would finally start being the 'me' I was always planning to be, if I ever had the time.

The girls announced that dessert was ready. Evan, in deference to my modesty, got out of the tub first. His red-gold hair was wet on the ends and stuck to his neck and shoulders. He had a good-looking body and he must have been proud of it, for he once again made no effort to cover himself. After he disappeared into the house, I slipped out, discreetly covered myself with a towel and struggled into my clothes underneath it, shivering in the cold, all the while.

As we finished the evening, the girls made all sorts of plans for outings that would include me: hiking to the old Northern Star mine, a picnic at the falls, an overnight camping expedition to watch the Perseids meteor display in August. Evan warned them not to "overwhelm" me on my first visit. Oddly, Greta's name was never mentioned.

I drove home alone to my ghost town and prepared for bed. Leap Year was so...*silent* after an evening with the Allenders. I missed all the activity and the human contact, however oddball. Drowsy, yet unable to sleep, the silence of Leap Year wore on my nerves. I went down to the kitchen to retrieve a small radio I had noticed sitting on the ledge of the window over the sink.

As I passed the desk on my way back to the stairs, the AA batteries fell out the back of the radio and one rolled under the desk. Cursing to myself, I got down on all fours to look for it and in doing so, noticed some more papers stuck underneath. I pulled them out and immediately recognized that two of the pages matched the letter from Grady. My drowsiness and my nerves vanished as I sat on the bare floor, held the pages up to the kitchen light coming over my shoulder, and excitedly began to read.

Chapter Four

My father's first dinner at my mother's house involved a little more drama than either of them anticipated, I think...

"IT'S TOO damned early in the year for a storm like this." Brandon Chance made this remark to no one in particular. He was staring out the front windows as he washed and dried glasses. The saloon was closed...it was Sunday. Brandy said the Lord rested on the seventh day and he could, too. But he usually ended up working most of the day anyway. So much catching up to do before the start of another week.

His economic prospects were looking bright for this winter. Old Reynolds had announced he was keeping three shifts going year round—the first time ever. Most years, Leap Year had become all but deserted in the winter. The altitude was too high, the snowfall too deep and the temperatures too extreme to keep any but the true diehards around. Even gold fever had its practical limits. But lode mining was different from placer mining. Down in the shafts, the temperature was a constant fifty-one degrees, summer or winter. The dark tunnels were a world unto themselves and the miners had to remind themselves whether it was day or night.

"How can you tell its going to be so bad?" Conor asked. He was seated at a table, putting the finishing touches on one of his mining sketches. It had been a productive week—two articles completed and a third nearly so. He got paid by the article, so he tried to work quickly.

"Look at them clouds, they're full of snow."

Conor got up and stood near Brandy and they looked together. Dark heavy clouds were coming up the canyon. Brandy shook his head. "It's only the first week of November. What's the winter going to be like? Gonna be a good night to turn in early and stay warm."

Conor gave a worried sigh. "I'm supposed to dine out tonight."

"You don't want to stray too far tonight. It's gonna be a blizzard for sure. I've seen clouds like that often enough to know what they can do. You don't want to venture anywhere you can't stay over."

"I'm not going far...a mile, a mile and a half. I'll be able to walk it no matter what the weather."

Brandy chuckled at his new friend's naivete. "And where might you be off to?"

Conor was evasive. He knew Brandy would make a field day of the fact he was dining with the young Widow Kelly. Brandy wouldn't let the matter drop, so finally Conor told him, with the expected result.

Brandy rolled his eyes and clucked his tongue. "My, my, my...our pretty, little widow. I was wonderin' why you got all fancied up."

Brandy was referring to the fact that Conor had shaved that morning. He had not shaved since arriving in Leap Year, having decided to grow a full beard like all the other men in town. This had left him with a scruffy three-weeks' worth of whiskers on his face. He did not know if it would be proper to show up at someone's home for Sunday supper looking so unkempt and had debated whether or not to shave ever since receiving Mrs. Kelly's dinner invitation.

Off the beard came, painfully, with several razor nicks, using lukewarm water from a tin cup heated by placing it next to the stovepipe that served as his heater. He had stared at his image in the little shaving mirror, wondering whether to take the mustache off as well. He had always been clean-shaven until his marriage to Allison. He had grown the mustache to please her. He frowned as he studied it; she had always liked the mustache better than he had. As he pinched his nostrils together and began to lather the shaving soap across his upper lip, he felt vaguely...*unfaithful*.

Conor didn't care to be teased about his dinner with the Widow Kelly and gestured to indicate the matter was of little consequence. "She wanted to pay me back for some work I had done for her. That's all."

"Too bad she's in the state she's in or I bet she'd pay you back real well. You know what they been saying, Mac, that she gives the miner's a lot more than clean laundry. Otherwise how'd she get that kid she's carryin'? Her old man's been gone more than a year—it sure as hell ain't him."

"What happened to him anyway?"

"Big disaster in the Northern Star Number Five. That was the newest shaft back then, real promising. Kyle Kelly was working deep in that one. We used to call him 'Crazy Kyle,' 'cause he'd do anything on a dare. I never liked him much. He was all right enough sober, but he was a mean, sorry son of a bitch when he was drunk, which was about every payday. He was the only one in there when a great thundering sound was heard and the whole of Number Five fell in. Never could even get to old Kyle's body."

"An accident with the dynamite?"

"Maybe...but it was more. Everything shook. I felt it here at the Lucky Chance. Knocked every glass I had off the wall. The engineer thinks there was something called an 'earthquake.' Said that part of the mine was too...unstable." Brandon shook his head with a smile. "Kyle must've pissed off the Tommyknockers but good to cause that."

Conor had been hearing about Tommyknockers ever since coming to the Tenmile. On his first day in town he had heard a little girl reciting a poem as she jumped rope. The catchy rhyme had told of how the Tommyknockers, supposedly the ghosts of dead miners, knocked on the walls of the mines to warn of an impending collapse. Miners who survived such disasters always swore they had heard the walls creaking and knocking just before a cave-in.

"Do you believe in Tommyknockers, Brandy?"

"I would if I had to work them shafts all day," laughed Brandon with a mock shiver. "Reynolds gave up on the Number Five after that. Those crazy Cornishmen were afraid of the shaft and they convinced all the rest to stay clear. Thought old Kyle's ghost would get 'em. By then the Seven and the Nine were into full production."

Brandy leaned closer to Conor and added in a confidential tone, "Some say old Kyle was on to something. Rumor had it he might have found a vein he wasn't telling Reynolds about. He always acted like he owned the Number Five. Used to insist on working alone."

"Was he highgrading?" Conor was learning to pick up the miner's lingo. 'Highgrading' meant stealing the ore.

"They searched him end of every shift. They search 'em all up there. Practically strip 'em naked to catch the thieves. Never even found so much as gold dust on Kyle, so they had to think his shaft was waste of time." Brandy sighed. "If he had a secret, it died with him."

Conor smiled at the mention of gold dust. Brandy paid two young boys every Sunday to sift through the sawdust swept up from the saloon floor to look for gold dust that had fallen from the miners' clothes. They usually came in to drink straight from a shift. Brandy garnered enough to make it worth his while to employ the two boys, who were at work in the back as they spoke.

As five o'clock approached, the snow grew heavier. A foot deep already, Conor was forced to borrow a pair of snowshoes from Brandon. He had to be taught how to walk in them and still didn't really have the hang of it by the time he left for the Kelly house.

"Watch out for yourself, Mac," Brandy had teased as he slowly made his way down the main road of town. "Widows can be mighty feisty."

Conor shook his head at this ludicrous remark, considering Mrs. Kelly's condition. The walk in snowshoes took him exactly twice the time he had allotted for the trip. He was embarrassed to arrive nearly half an hour late.

"We'd given up on you, Mr. McAllister," Mrs. Kelly greeted him brightly at the door. Her face was flushed and moist with the steam of the kitchen.

Conor apologized profusely as he struggled to unbuckle the snowshoes. Finally, Joe—the boy of twelve that Elodie had spoken of—came out on the porch and helped Conor rid himself of the unwieldy contraptions. They were set next to the door and Elodie led Conor by the arm into the Kelly cabin. She noticed immediately his clean-shaven face and was flattered he had made this effort on her behalf. She had thought him handsome even with his half-grown beard, but now...she very nearly could not take her eyes off him.

As cabins in Leap Year went, it was much larger than most, with three rooms on the main floor—a kitchen with room to eat in, a parlor, and a bedroom—and at least two bedrooms upstairs. The walls were dark and rough-hewn, as were the walls of all the dwellings he had seen in Leap Year, but the furnishings were of surprisingly good quality. Lace draperies decorated the small windows and the mantle of the stone fireplace held a statute of the Virgin Mary.

The family had truly believed the weather had kept Conor from attending the dinner and were already partaking of the meal. Mrs. Kelly sat Conor at the empty place left for him and introduced the rest of the family: Thirteen-year-old Mary Rose, five-year-old Donal, and two-year-old Mary Katherine, called Kitty. Then the elderly Mrs. Atwater was presented.

"Call me Granny—everyone does," she said loudly. She was nearly deaf and most things had to be repeated to her. Conor noticed the Kelly family, even little Kitty, who was just learning to talk, was used to this and did it without a second thought.

The food was delicious—chicken with gravy, mashed potatoes and yams, corn bread muffins. Conor appreciated the fact that this meal had been prepared at no small expense. Everything had to be purchased at the local market. Leap Year was so high, it had no growing season. The saying on food was: If you can't shoot it, you'll have to buy it.

The food was not the only expensive item on the table. Conor noticed the moment he began to eat that they were dining on fine china and silver. Conor dined on tin plates at the saloon and at the Belle of

Colorado Cafe—what passed for a restaurant in Leap Year—and had only been offered simple crockery by Mr. and Mrs. Reynolds when they had served him luncheon the first day he had toured the Northern Star and they were arguably the wealthiest couple in Leap Year, at least for the moment. He had not dined on china since leaving his parents' house. He was forced to reconsider his first impression of Mrs. Kelly as a poor miner's widow. Perhaps she had received a large financial settlement from Mr. Reynolds to compensate her for her loss. It took more than laundry to set so fine a table.

The dinner conversation began with a discussion of the weather. The Kellys, like Brandon at the saloon, were surprised to see a storm gathering of this intensity so early in the season.

"No school for me tomorrow," announced Joe, excited by the prospect.

"That's a foolish thing to rejoice over," snapped his mother.

"When winter sets in for good, there won't be any more school," Joe said to Conor.

"Don't be too sure of that, young man," said Elodie. "The preacher is going to find families for you to stay with down below and that's the end of it."

"But I don't want to go away," said Joe, into his plate. He dug in his fork, frowning.

Elodie made eye contact with Conor across the table and, giving him a broad wink, said, "Mr. McAllister, here, went away to school when he was about your age and he loved it. Didn't you, sir?"

Conor tried to keep a straight face. "Uhm...yes, it was most...edifying."

"What?" asked Rose.

Conor had just taken a mouthful of food, so Elodie answered for him. "He told me he loved every minute of it and he praised the day his wonderful parents made the decision to send him there."

"But, you need me around here, Ma," Joe protested.

"I need you more to get an education. I don't want you to end up in the mines like your father." Elodie's voice had a chilling finality to it.

"But miners make good money," said Joe, unable to concede defeat.

"The money is good, but the work is bad. Now, as I said before, that ends it. More chicken, Mr. McAllister?"

Conor knew Elodie was correct in saying the money was good. Miners made three dollars a day, five if they worked with the blasting powder. This at a time when the average man's daily wage was eighty cents. Only a lucky few lived to be older than Conor, though. Those that weren't the victims of accidents, like Kyle Kelly, succumbed to miners' lung from constantly inhaling the silica dust.

Little Kitty, as if on cue to change the subject, spilled her milk and Elodie and Granny Atwater simultaneously jumped up to attend to it.

Conor found the noisy chaos of the family more enjoyable than he had thought he would. The children were funny and lively. They spoke freely at the meal, something Conor had never been allowed to do at his parent's table, growing up. They asked numerous questions of him about Philadelphia. Joe had been studying the Declaration of Independence in school.

At one point, Elodie apologized for the constant stream of questions and asked the children to go easy on their visitor since he was "not used to children."

"Actually..." began Conor tentatively. "I have...a daughter." All eyes turned to him and he suddenly wished he had not mentioned this.

"How nice," said Elodie. "And would she be with your wife in Philadelphia?"

This was why he had wished he had not mentioned his daughter. He knew he would have to explain about Allison. "Umm...no. She is with my wife's parents."

The table now looked at him expectantly, waiting for the obvious explanation of his wife's whereabouts. Conor realized he must reveal the truth or else they might think she was in an asylum or something.

"My wife is..." Deceased? Passed on? Passed Away? Gone? Conor couldn't think of the appropriate words, all sounded wrong. "She...uh...didn't survive..." Conor wanted to bite his tongue at this moment. Why would anyone blurt out to a woman on the verge of giving birth that his own wife had died doing just that? Finally, he just said, "I don't have a wife."

"What?" asked Granny Atwater in a loud voice, not following Conor's mumbling.

"His wife is dead," shouted Elodie to Granny, enunciating the words carefully.

Conor stared at his empty plate, wishing he could go home. Elodie served a sweet raison bread with cream for dessert, which was wonderful, but Conor didn't talk much during the rest of the meal. By seven, dinner was completed and the children cleared the table. Conor was ushered into the little parlor and sat down on the sofa before the fire. Elodie brought him coffee and asked that he stay until the children were put to bed.

Joe came in and sat with him. They talked about the snow and about winter in the high country. They stepped outside to get more wood for the fire and for the stove in the kitchen and could hardly see the woodpile for the blowing snow. Another foot of snow had fallen during the course of the meal and drifts in some places reached as high as a man's head. When they returned to the house, Joe spoke to his mother about the blizzard that was threatening. Conor noticed the worried looks on their faces as he resumed his comfortable seat in the parlor.

Elodie took a momentary break from putting the children to bed to deliver to Conor a bottle of brandy. "Men like their brandy after a meal," she said as she poured him a glass. Conor smiled up at her, feeling "at home" in a sense for the first time since arriving in Colorado. He certainly hadn't tasted brandy since leaving his father's house. Mrs. Kelly's pale, heart-shaped face was so pretty in the firelight, with its dimpled chin. She had deep blue eyes with long dark lashes and soft, curly brown hair pulled back from her face with pins and combs. She left him to continue preparing all the children for bed.

Eventually, the noisy household became quiet, as all, even Granny, had disappeared upstairs. Elodie reentered the parlor and startled Conor. She stood before him with her hands folded.

"Joe informs me that you won't be able to return home tonight on account of the weather."

"No, no...I'll be all right," Conor assured her.

"Oh, no, you won't, Mr. McAllister. Have you looked outside? There is no more to see but white. I'm afraid you wouldn't find the road in front our house much less your way home."

Conor opened his mouth to protest again, but she raised her hand to silence him. "You're a newcomer to these mountains. Trust me, people have frozen to death in their own yards in weather like this. They've wandered and wandered, all the while just ten feet from their own door. Whether you like it or not, you'll be our guest tonight— imprisoned if you will." She smiled as she said this last and then knelt before him. "Let me help you with your boots."

Conor had just finished another glass of the brandy. He was drinking more than he knew he should, more than a good guest should, but every time his glass was empty Mrs. Kelly dutifully refilled it. He started to say that he did not need her help, and actually didn't want it, though he wouldn't have said this, but she had already started trying to work his left boot off.

"These are the finest boots I've ever seen," she remarked. She was having to struggle a great deal. The boots were still new and stiff. They had been a going away present from his father.

"My father makes boots," he informed her and tried to help with the ordeal.

"A cobbler, is he?" She succeeded in removing his left boot and went to work on his right.

Conor smiled at her calling his father a cobbler. His grandfather had been a cobbler, emigrating from Ireland before the turn of the century. His father was a businessman. He had never made a boot in his life, but had built the largest bootworks in the state. At the age of twenty-five, Ben McAllister had negotiated a contract with the United States Army to supply them with boots that had literally made the family fortune. The Civil War had brought almost more growth than the company could handle. Three presidents had worn McAllister boots and numerous generals, famous and otherwise. But for now, Conor was content to have Mrs. Kelly think his father was a cobbler.

Conor winced as Mrs. Kelly removed his right boot.

"Sore?" she asked.

"It's nothing. My boots are not broken in yet. They still torment me."

"I'll take care of that," she smiled and began massaging his stockinged feet.

"No, no...that's all right, please don't." He tried to pull his foot away from her, but she wouldn't relinquish it without a fight.

"Relax, Mr. McAllister...you need to relax. And don't you tell me this doesn't feel good. I know it does. Close your eyes and be glad you have a warm fire before you and someone to rub your feet. Come on now, that's it, close your eyes."

He sank back into the sofa and began to enjoy the slow steady motion of her hands on his feet. He didn't close his eyes, but watched her. She had a strange, serene expression on her face. The effect was almost hypnotic. Then she rested one of his feet against her bosom and began to massage his ankle. Kneeling on the floor as she was, he could no longer really see her huge belly, just her pretty face. He allowed himself the luxury of some highly impure thoughts.

Then he came to his senses. He realized he was sitting in the parlor of a woman he barely knew with his foot against her breasts. It was then that he came to terms with just how intoxicated he had become.

He was about to pull his foot out of her grasp, when she dropped it and slowly rose to her feet. She offered him her hand to pull him into a standing position.

"It's time for bed," she said.

The only sound was that of the howling wind sneaking around the door and window frames. Like one in a trance, he allowed himself to be led to her bedroom. He was confused at first. Was she offering him her bed to sleep in or did she mean for them to share it? He stood at the door of the room as she entered, setting the lamp on a chest by the bed.

When she closed the door behind him and began to undress, Conor finally found his voice. "Umm...uh...I will go sleep on the sofa."

"Stay here, Mr. McAllister. You'll find it much more to your liking. You're too tall for that sofa."

Was the woman mad? She blithely continued to undress. Shoes, stockings, dress. In no time she was sitting there before him in some sort of chemise. It was like a nightgown, but without sleeves.

"Mrs. Kelly—"

"*Elodie.* You're standing in my bedroom watching me take my clothes off so I think that puts us on a first-name basis, don't you...Conor?"

"Mrs. Kelly...I have no intention of—"

"Come sit down, Conor." She patted the bed beside her.

He almost laughed at the absurdity of it all. "This is quite simply insane."

She smiled and her face softened, suddenly she was less aggressive than before. "I'm sure it must seem so to you. You're from far away. From far down below. Things are different up here." She sighed, looking very tired, too tired to talk much longer. She pulled some pins and a large comb from her hair, causing it to suddenly cascade over her shoulders and down her back like a dark waterfall. "Maybe it's because we're closer to heaven. The angels can keep a near eye on us, you know. We don't need all those rules to live by that they take so seriously down below. Rather we do what we need to get by."

Conor had no idea what she was talking about. He had never been so unnerved by a woman before.

She suddenly ducked her head. "I know I am not attractive."

"No, no, it's not that. I mean, it is that, but it's not." He was stammering now. The alcohol was making it difficult to think coherently. Waves of lust and revulsion were washing over him so quickly he could not sort them out. "It's just that, well...you know." He gestured helplessly toward her waistline.

She smiled impishly. "Yes...I know."

Conor knew he was not getting through to her. He was growing exasperated. "If this is about my having split that wood for you—"

Elodie laughed softly. "No, no, dear Lord, no. I'm all alone in this world and so are you, Mr. I-don't-have-a-wife. And you're the handsomest man I've ever seen."

"I just...couldn't possibly." In the battle between lust and revulsion, lust was beginning to close in on victory.

The screaming of the winds grew louder. Drafts leaked around the single window. The room was cold. She looked squarely into his eyes and held his gaze for a long time. She leaned over and put out the lamp, plunging the room into total darkness. She said simply, "Come to bed."

For reasons he would spend months trying to understand, he did as he was told.

It was hurried from the start and over quickly. They both undressed him in a kind of frenzy. There were so many buttons—his jacket, his vest, his shirt, his trousers, his long underwear. He kept trying to kiss her amid all this frantic activity, but in the darkness he often missed her mouth and kissed instead her nose, her ear, her chin. His hand found her breast and she slipped the chemise off her shoulder so that he could touch her bare flesh. He was becoming so aroused he thought he would burst, but he also realized he had no idea how to approach her given the awkwardness of her shape. He had never touched his own wife when she was in this condition. He was too shy to confess his dilemma, but she seemed to know it without being told.

He heard her shifting her position. He groped for her blindly and soon understood she meant for him to take her from behind, like a hound takes a bitch in heat. It had never occurred to him that humans could assume this bizarre posture, but he was not inclined to debate the matter as he hurriedly drew up her gown and found his way in. After two years of complete abstinence, the feeling was overwhelming. Everything else ceased to exist for those few seconds. He held his breath to be silent, afraid someone would hear—and it was over.

Exhausted and gasping, he gently lowered the two of them down into the quilts and sheets sideways, still connected. They lay nested together like two spoons in a drawer. Conor buried his face in the ocean of her hair, hair that smelled like the wind just before a rainstorm. In the darkness, all was sensation. The sighing motion of her back against his chest, the soft flesh of her hips tucked into his lap, the warm wetness between her thighs, the curve of her calves on his shins. He couldn't have felt more content had he returned to the womb himself.

For the first time since leaving home, he fell effortlessly into a deep sleep.

SOMETIME LATER, there came a sound, a sharp sound, a crying out. Conor struggled to rouse himself. For a moment, he didn't know where he was. But a light was present in the room and the memories of a few hours before came flooding back. The sound, the voice was Elodie's and she was calling out for someone.

"Granny!" Her voice was tight with pain.

Conor instantly assumed he had hurt her in some way. He knew what he had done was wrong, terribly wrong. He sat up in bed in a panic.

Young Joe came to the bedroom door instead of Granny Atwater. Conor was horrified at the thought this woman's son had seen him in her bed.

Upon seeing Joe, Elodie snapped: "Get Granny—hurry!"

"Elodie?" Conor whispered tersely, using her given name for the first time ever. "What's wrong?"

"What do you think?" was her equally terse reply.

Conor stared dumbly, he didn't know.

"I'm birthing this baby, you fool!"

Granny Atwater bustled into the room wearing a tattered dressing gown. Conor was beside himself that yet another person had seen him in Elodie's bed. His clothes, where were his clothes? He was wearing his long underwear and still had on his shirt, though both were undone. Where were his trousers? He glanced around all over the floor. He struggled to button up his underwear and his shirt and thought he would go insane if he did not immediately locate his trousers.

Elodie let out a terrible cry.

A remarkably blasé Granny Atwater smiled and sat down on Elodie's side of the bed. "Well, dear girl, I see you took my advice."

She was looking at Conor when she said this. Just then his foot brushed against one of his suspenders and he realized his trousers were under the covers at his feet. He quickly pulled them on.

"Works every time. Old Granny knows a few tricks from thirty years of midwifing." The old woman laughed. "'Course I never knew just how you'd manage it with no husband in your house. You're the clever one. Clever Elodie always gets what she wants. Now let's see where we're at."

Conor was out of bed, finally. What was the old witch cackling about? She seemed to be referring to him for some reason. She was lifting Elodie's night dress.

Granny Atwater glanced over her shoulder to him. "Go on...you're not needed here." Then she laughed again, an old woman's laugh. "You've done your part."

Conor made a hasty exit and joined Joe on the sofa. Another terrible scream was heard. He felt a cold panic. He was certain Elodie was dying and it was surely his fault. Why had he done it? To satisfy his lust upon a pregnant woman was unthinkable. Had he gone temporarily insane? It was as though she had cast some strange erotic spell on him. He avoided looking at Joe, he was so ashamed of what he had done. Then it occurred to him that perhaps Joe was too young to know what went on between men and women in bed. He tried to remember how much he knew at Joe's age, but his thoughts were interrupted by yet another scream. Conor involuntarily cringed. He marveled at how calm the boy seemed in the face of such dire commotion.

"Does it bother you? Hearing that?" Conor asked him.

"It's not the first time," Joe smiled. "And anyway, I'm glad it's finally come. Ma said if she had to carry the animal for one day more she would lose her wits. She was near beside herself with the waiting."

Joe looked suddenly pensive. He furrowed his brow and asked quietly: "Are you going to be our new father, then?"

A sense of overwhelming shame returned to Conor. "Umm...uh...no. No, I'm not," he stammered. Apparently, finding a strange man his mother's bed was not a commonplace occurrence. Conor had idly wished that if Elodie had, in her widowhood, indeed become a prostitute as Brandon had implied, it would have somehow lessened his own dishonor.

The screaming stopped. Oh, no, she's dead, thought Conor. Joe rose expectantly, waiting for word from his mother's room. Finally, Granny stuck her head out and proclaimed: "Another girl."

Joe made a disappointed face.

"Is Mrs. Kelly all right?" Conor asked, afraid of the reply. Allison's death had left him with a permanent fear of women in childbed.

"Oh, she's fine, fine. No one drops 'em faster than our Elodie."

She was fine? He hadn't killed her? He was relieved to hear that Elodie had survived her lying in, but had no sooner thought this than a second humiliation presented itself. The old woman's words came back to him now. He recalled a dinner party at Allison's parents' house. They had been celebrating the news that Allison was with child. After dinner, her father had drawn him aside and warned him that no more marital relations should further occur until well after the baby's birth. He insisted it was a well-known medical fact that such activity could bring on premature labor or worse. Had Elodie enticed him into her bed, not for romantic or even lustful purposes, but rather to occasion the labor she had so long wished to arrive?

Conor busied himself rebuilding the fire in the small stone fireplace. The enormity of this woman's gall was beyond measure. It was not so much that she had seduced him. Women seduced men all the time. At nineteen, he himself had been seduced by one of his mother's friends and he certainly had not minded that. But Elodie hadn't just seduced him, she had used him for her own purposes, and that he could not forgive.

He knew, in his rational mind, that men used women time and again, especially in matters of the flesh. But never in his life had he heard of a woman doing likewise. This made the humiliation all the more unbearable.

He stepped out onto the porch of the cabin. Dawn chased the last of the snow clouds quietly over the mountain. In the grey light, Conor surveyed the magnificently transformed landscape. Every tree was a castle of snow. The mountains themselves, forbiddingly white. Conor saw his own breath hang like a cloud in the still and frozen air.

From the window of Elodie's bedroom, he heard the crying of the new infant. He thought of his daughter. Would she even remember him when he returned home next spring? He now wished he were not stuck here for the winter. The mountain passes could not be crossed after a certain point in the season and winter had come early this year. Perhaps he would winter in Columbine. A thousand feet below, the weather might be more equitable and the probability of crossing paths with the infamous Mrs. Kelly would be lessened.

On the other hand, he hated to give up the room at the saloon. As much as he disliked it, there were no other rooms to be had. With the mine running shifts this winter, every available space was being fought for. He was lucky to have the room to himself. Most miners shared a room with at least three or four roommates.

He stepped back into the cabin. Mary Rose was fixing breakfast for her younger siblings. Granny Atwater was still in Elodie's room, tending to her and the child. Joe offered him some oatmeal, but he declined politely. Bundling up, he went back out onto the porch to fasten on his snowshoes. It was awkward getting them on, with no place to sit. And he had never done it himself before. Brandon had fastened him in when he had left the saloon the day before. He finally got them attached, although one came immediately off in three steps. Securing it again, he began the long walk back to the center of town.

Chapter Five

I WOKE UP full of ambition. The mad tea party at the Allenders of the night before had put me in an exceptional mood. Plus I now had the discovery of the additional pages to her letter. I still didn't have it all, unfortunately, so I tackled the cleaning of Grady's house in earnest. Being alone in the town, she'd had no trash pick up and had apparently stowed away anything she didn't want any more in spare rooms. Some of the four bedrooms other than her own were packed from floor to ceiling. Fortunately nothing was deposited in them that rotted, the only smells being that of dust and old paper.

Hoping I could persuade Evan to haul the junk away in his truck, I spent the morning filling trash sacks. The refuse mostly consisted of old news papers. I sorted through them for interesting keepsakes. Maybe the Allender twins were right, maybe Grady did have some kind of treasure she was hiding. Who knows where she got the money to buy up the town over the years? And you don't spend several thousand dollars on a bathroom remodel from money you save from social security checks.

She didn't believe in banks. At least none were discovered by her lawyer. I found forty dollars in one of her kitchen drawers, but that was all so far. I suppose if she had a stash of money in the house, the burglars got it. I chuckled with the thought that perhaps Grady was one of the drug dealers Celeste, the waitress, had warned me about. Then a chilling thought hit me: What if Evan were one of them? He certainly looked the part. I didn't want to even consider the possibility. He seemed too nice, too connected to the community, too parental, too...poor.

The day was uneventful—except for jumping out of my skin twice over the discovery of a couple of mice. I made my daily trip into Columbine—this time for mousetraps. I managed to shave off a few minutes of the drive every time I made it. I was proud of my growing prowess at hairpin turns and switchbacks.

I stopped in at the Tenmile Cafe for a quick early supper and to use the public phone. I called my mother to check in as promised. I dreaded calling. I knew my mother would assault me with another diatribe on why I had no business being in this remote place by myself. I just about had the whole speech memorized, danger by danger. Today turned out to be my lucky day: I interrupted her bridge party, so she couldn't talk, but I could almost hear her scowling. Then I called the car rental agency and inquired about renting the Jeep by the month rather than the week. Getting Grady's house ready to put on the market was going to take longer than I had anticipated. Besides, I was having too much fun to leave now. Maybe I would spend my whole vacation right here in the Ten Mile Canyon.

Back at the counter at the Tenmile Cafe, I noticed a salient point: I did not look like a local. My clothes, my hair, everything bespoke *Tourist*. The county depended on tourism and the money it brought in, but I was soon to learn these affluent outsiders were the subject of mild derision whenever they were out of earshot. "More dollars than sense," was the saying. Why not be contemptuous of someone who owns a bicycle that cost more than your car and a car that cost more than your house?

I caught a glimpse of my image in the window: dark blond pageboy, nice, neat, conservative—boring. I was reasonably attractive, I knew this. My ego had not suffered such a battering in the divorce from Keith that I had no self-confidence, it just wasn't the right kind of attractive to go over in this strange new environment. I wanted to look more like Celeste—no make up, no bra, long unstyled hair worn casually pulled into a braid or something.

Marlena noticed me and came over to say hello. She seemed much more friendly this time. She asked me what I thought of the "Allender boys," as she called them. I told her I thought they were a couple of heartbreakers and confessed I had mistaken them for brothers when I first met them. She said everyone did, a fact that flattered Evan and annoyed his son.

"Reilly was in this morning," she added. Then she leaned over the counter and whispered in a teasing tone, "We talked about you behind your back."

"No wonder my ears were burning." We both laughed. "What could you have possibly discussed?"

She raised her eyebrows. "He said you were recently divorced."

"Not very recently. Almost a year now. It's nothing."

"Honey, I've been divorced. It's never 'nothing.'"

I shrugged. "It's such a boring story. My college sweetheart turned into the Husband from Hell during the three years I worked my backside off putting him through law school." Keith announced, between graduation and the bar exam that marriage was 'stifling' him and he wanted a divorce. Actually, it 'stifled' him right into an affair with a tall redhead who sat beside him in Creditor's Rights.

Marlena and I rolled our eyes and shook our heads at this in unison. Keith needed a meal ticket through law school and I got drafted. Oh, I'm not really sure he was ever that cold and calculating about it, but this interpretation tended to put everything into some kind of orderly perspective. I guess my basic problem was my failure to understand my role. When Keith came to me and told me he wanted out, he said he thought he had married too young, that he just hadn't been as ready to settle down as he thought. To his credit, that was probably the most honest thing he ever said to me. Maybe it was better to end it sooner rather than later, before we'd had the chance to screw up a couple of kids' lives as well as our own.

"You know, honey," Marlena drawled philosophically. "I believe that old saying about every ending being a new beginning."

"It's funny you should say that because I got the word about Grady and Leap Year right in the middle of all the nasty divorce stuff. It was the only good thing that happened to me. Right off, I thought I was going to get rich." I smiled self-consciously. "I guess that's not going to happen, though."

"Unless you find the Hidden Vein," Marlena kidded.

"Oh, yeah, right," I played along.

"Exactly. There you go. With me—and this was years ago—I'd just broken up with my husband and he'd no sooner left for California than I met someone who just turned my life around. Lord, he was a godsend. Something about him just made you want to smile when he walked in the room." She was looking into the distance, then she returned to the present with a casual shrug. "Didn't last, but it got me through a real low time."

I froze. I knew she was talking about Evan. She had to be. She was about to say something else when she broke off to look at someone in the parking lot.

"See that man out there?" she asked.

I saw a sort of derelict character staggering across the lot, bumping into a car as he tried to walk. He was filthy from head to toe, with long greasy hair and a stained, bushy beard. He wore a stocking cap on his head and a shaggy coat although it wasn't yet very cold. Had he been in the city, I would have called him a street person.

"I just hate it when they come down into town. They're always drunk or crazy or something. They talk to themselves or yell at people and they smell to high heaven. I'm going to call the sheriff if he doesn't get out of my parking lot. He'll scare the customers away."

"Where does he come from?"

"Who knows? Somewhere up the canyon. They live in tents and shacks. Squatters, really. They come down now and then. They say a bunch of them live up there somewhere. I guess you could call them mountain men."

"Mountain men," I repeated. "He sure doesn't look like Robert Redford did in 'Jeremiah Johnson.'"

"Honey, nobody looks like Robert Redford." I could tell Marlena found me quaintly amusing, probably in a 'dumb pilgrim' sort of way. "Don't go out into the parking lot until he leaves, Darcy. He might pull a semiautomatic on you."

The creepy guy eventually moved on. Marlena was about to return to the kitchen when she stopped and asked if I had any kind of weapon for protection up in Leap Year. I said no, that I really didn't know anything about guns.

"Do you really think I'm in any danger?" First Evan's comments, now Marlena's—my sense of security was on a roller coaster ride.

"Oh, no, not really, I guess. This county hasn't had a murder in fourteen or fifteen years. Most folks around here don't even bother to lock their cars or houses."

"Oh, come on." I found this tidbit as hard to swallow as Evan's assertions on the racial demographics. "I thought that attitude had gone out with the model-T."

"Well, you're wrong. Now I lock up the Cafe, of course, but I never lock my car unless I'm in Denver. I didn't mean to scare you, I guess I just don't like to think about you all alone up there." Then she made a sly face and with a voice that teased like a cat's purring, she added, "Maybe you ought to make better friends with that neighbor of yours. Word has it his bed is half empty this summer."

Jeez! Small towns. Give me a break. I was starting to get tired of people pushing me in Evan's direction. Had they held a town meeting on this? A referendum, maybe? All in favor of Evan getting it on with that new girl, say aye.

THE ALLENDER family was at my doorstep on Sunday morning. Evan and both daughters rambunctiously greeted me on the porch when I sleepily opened the door.

"We came to take you to church," announced Winter brightly.

They were obviously dressed for hiking, not Sunday service and I said something along the lines of, "Huh?"

Evan winked. "Get dressed. You'll see."

Anxious to appear ready for anything, I hurriedly pulled on some shorts, a tank top, and a sweater, dragged a brush through my hair and then covered it up with a canvas hat.

Following Evan out to the truck, I asked the girls what church they belonged to. They thought this was pretty funny and Winter said, "Daddy's an atheist, silly."

More confused than ever, I squeezed into the cab next to Winter, with Summer practically sitting on my lap.

"Daddy, did you remember your sunscreen?" asked Summer. "He has very sensitive skin," she informed me.

"Yes, ma'am." Evan gave her a small salute.

I had noticed as we got in that three backpacks lay in the back of the truck. I assumed they must have a picnic in mind. I asked where we were headed.

"About a mile down on the dark side of Route 88," Evan teased. "No, I'm gonna show you why you're so lucky to live here, Darcy."

We drove down to the main highway and headed south through the canyon.

"Look, Darcy," said Winter pointing to the heavily forested mountainside we were passing. "The SKY Chutes."

I stared dumbly at where she was pointing.

"We're too close to see them well," said Evan.

After several fleeting seconds of trying to focus, what they were talking about suddenly popped out. Across the face of the mountain, hundreds of feet in size, were the letters: S-K-Y, as clear as day.

"Who did that?" I asked, assuming the letters were man-made, that someone had chopped down the trees in that configuration.

The girls burst into giggles at my innocent and ignorant question.

"The mountain," answered Evan with a kinder smile. "Those are avalanche chutes."

I waited for more explanation and he continued. "Each mountain has some natural terrain that forms avalanche paths over and over again. All the trees are scraped away when that happens. That mountain just happened to know how to write. You can see it even better in the winter when the chutes are white."

"Reilly and his best friend, Jason, skied the *S* last winter," said Summer.

"Crazy fool," muttered Evan. "I think he has a death wish."

We drove over Follow The Sun pass which Evan explained was

used by the Ute Indians for ten thousand years. They summered every year in the Tenmile Canyon. Finally, we turned off onto a dirt road and began climbing through a pine forest. We reached a trail head of sorts and Evan parked the truck.

"Hope you like to hike," he said, as he and the girls donned their backpacks. "Don't worry, we brought plenty to eat and drink." He glanced down at my canvas sneakers. "I wish you had on sturdier shoes."

"I'll be all right," I assured him and we started on the trail. It turned steep almost immediately. The altitude and the general state of my fitness level had not prepared me for this. I dropped back and was trailing Evan and the girls soon, but pride kept me from complaining. After forty-five minutes of uphill walking, I was sweaty and breathless. "How much farther is it?" I asked meekly.

"Not more than another mile or two," Evan said, now pausing for me to catch up. "We picked a short one because we knew you weren't used to the altitude. How're you doing?"

"Fine, fine." I tried not to pant. Evan walked on ahead and Summer dropped back to walk with me.

"Where's Reilly?" I asked her, when I could find the breath.

"He's at home still asleep. He sleeps late a lot. And he and Daddy had another big fight last night. They're always fighting. Daddy says its Reilly's job to drive him crazy. He says that's what teenagers are supposed to do."

"It is, huh?"

"Daddy says he drove his father crazy when he was a teenager and now he's getting what he deserves from Reilly. He says that's the circle of life."

When I wasn't staring straight down at the rocky path in front of me, I occasionally glanced about and notice the profusion of wildflowers growing along the route. I asked Summer if she knew their names and she identified many of them effortlessly. I envied her knowledge and resolved to buy a book on the subject so I could do likewise. The only trouble was, every time I took my eyes off the trail to admire the flowers, I would trip on a rock and stumble. It was embarrassing.

I couldn't maintain Summer's pace for long and soon I was walking alone again. After another hour, I'd had enough. I liked this family and had to admit I was more attracted to Evan than I should have been, but I was very near my call-it-quits point. I was only going to let them torture so much and no more. My sweater was soaked in sweat and I pulled it off.

Evan stopped on the trail and let the girls pass by. "Not much farther," he assured me with a grin. The mood I was in, tempted me to punch him. He followed me as we continued higher and higher. The trees got shorter and shorter and finally there were no trees at all.

I struggled up the trail, breathless, tired, feet sore, leg muscles aching, when Evan tapped me on the shoulder. "Darcy, turn around," he said in a soft voice just above a whisper.

I stopped, turned around and...gasped. Before me lay a vast panorama of unparalleled beauty, a mountain range so grand in scope I found it difficult to immediately comprehend. This vista was beyond postcard pretty, beyond calendar art, beyond coffee table books...this was...this was...the most spectacular...the most dazzling...the most overwhelming visual extravaganza one could imagine.

"Oh, my God," I murmured.

Evan laughed. "She did it," he called to the girls. The girls rushed over and began laughing. Evan saw my look of confusion and explained. "Every time I bring someone up here, they always say, 'Oh, my God.' That's why we call it going to church."

I was still staring, open-mouthed, amazed, even reverent.

"I used to tell the girls the Rocky Mountains held up the sky—that we were looking at the roof of the world."

Winter rolled her eyes. "Oh, *Daddy*."

"There was a time when you believed me."

The girls shook their heads and ran on ahead. We found a flat spot to spread out a blanket. Evan and his daughters emptied their backpacks. There was champagne and orange juice, French bread, three cheeses, fresh strawberries, nectarines, and chocolate chip cookies which the girls had made themselves.

The girls complained that they did not get any champagne with their orange juice and Evan complained that he loved to eat nectarines but they were so messy and ruined his long mustaches. He told me he used to wear a full beard, but "got tired of winning Jesus look-alike contests." The girls thought that was very funny. I sensed some kind of family in-joke here, but didn't pursue it.

He gestured to the area just below us and said while we were on the 'Jesus subject,' the gnarled, twisted trees that grew in the harsh environment of tree line, called bristlecone pines, had probably been saplings at about the time of Christ. Evan insisted the pines were among the oldest living things on earth, that some were even four thousand years old, though the ones in Colorado were closer to two thousand.

After the girls finished eating, they ran off to play, with their father admonishing them to "stay out of the mines and off the tailings piles." They pouted a bit, then ran off again.

Evan said that once when Reilly was about nine, he was climbing on a tailings pile from an abandoned mine and inadvertently started a rock slide which rained down on hikers thirty feet below. Several ended up in the hospital, though all recovered fully.

"They threatened to sue me," Evan frowned at the memory. "I said 'Go fish,' like I had any money for their medical bills. They cooled off on the idea when they found out I didn't have any insurance."

Evan named off the various peaks we could see from our privileged vantage point and their elevations. He had climbed some of them. He said it was the current fad to "bag Fourteeners." In English, this meant climb a mountain of at least fourteen thousand feet in elevation. He had bagged seven so far and tried to do at least one new one each summer. He said he would take me with him next time if I was interested. He liked to get "an interesting group together" for these little one day expeditions.

In my supreme egotism, I instantly read as a compliment that I would be considered interesting enough to be included in such a party. I was grateful he was not holding my current poor hiking performance against me. It was my maiden voyage, after all.

By mid day, the sky began to cloud up and thunder was heard. Evan said we had to get below tree line because of the lightning danger. The picnic was quickly concluded and we were on the trail once again.

The Allenders returned me to Leap Year by late afternoon and politely refused my offer to stay for dinner. I was secretly relieved since I was not sure I had enough food for three more. I wanted to reciprocate for all their hospitality, though they didn't act as though they expected it. Also, I was fairly sure Evan's refusal was partly motivated by the girls' obvious exhaustion which was showing itself in increased whining and fighting between themselves.

I thanked Evan for the wonderful day and extended my hand to shake. Did he hold it longer than necessary or was this my hopeful imagination at work? My heart pounded like a twelve-year-old school girl. Evan shrugged off my thanks, saying the trip had given him an excuse not to work on his house. I waved goodbye to them and more reluctantly resumed my solitary ghost town life.

BY THE THIRD day of intensive work, I had Grady's house under control. Plus, I received an unexpected payoff: another page to the letter Grady had left for me. I had no way of determining if it were the next page to the letter or not. Her account tended to ramble within even a given paragraph, so it was hard to tell. This page seemed to be saying her father had artistic talent. I wondered if I would find any examples he might have left behind. I was beginning to find myself fascinated with Grady's parents and wanted to see what they looked like. She had indicated more than once already that her father was a real looker. Odd that she would make this remark about her father rather than her mother. I read the new page eagerly, like I had found a new piece to a jigsaw puzzle, half of whose pieces were missing.

After working so dutifully on the house, I decided to give myself some time off and go exploring. The day promised such fine weather, I fixed a sack lunch and went for a hike instead.

First I walked up to the old Northern Star mine, the major local landmark of Leap Year and it's only claim to fame. I decided to eat my lunch on the ridge above and behind the mine about a half mile, the spot where Evan told me I could see for a hundred miles. The walk up passed through some spectacular alpine flower fields. I had my new wildflower book with me and walked along, identifying numerous colorful specimens—blue larkspurs, Indian paintbrushes, elegant columbines in three different colors.

There were patchy snow banks sitting on the ridge. I was reading my book and crossing one such snow field when...the snow *collapsed* beneath me and down I fell through the earth itself!

Alice down the rabbit hole...falling, time stretched out, seconds like minutes...whacking my forehead as I fell farther...hitting my ear, hitting both elbows...landing squarely on my left ankle—the pain excruciating.

Then...silence...and darkness, except for a thin shaft of light fifteen, twenty feet above.

Where was I?

Chapter Six

My father was a gifted artist, though he never thought of himself as such. His talent was unschooled and came to him as naturally and effortlessly as breathing. He surprised his family when he was able to turn it into his career...

WINTER SPENT at altitude was worlds apart from anything Conor had yet experienced. It snowed so often, he wondered where the world got so much of the stuff. He purchased a pair of snowshoes of his own and quickly became proficient at trudging about in them. He often hired a horse from the livery and went out on little expeditions, learning new details about this strange and wonderful place. His articles and sketches were popular in Thaddeus Applebee's newspaper.

Conor was a good writer, having worked on the newspaper at college ten years before, and better still, was excellent at sketching. Applebee had published Conor's sketches before. They contained just the right amount of detail to transfer to the plates for printing. It had been Conor's artistic talent that had gotten him sent to the awful boarding school in the first place. Conor's father had disapproved of this hobby and was concerned that his youngest son was too much under the influence of his wife. He had only himself to blame. He had already raised four sons with his first wife and Conor, born two decades later by his second wife, often seemed almost like an afterthought. He was tired of child-rearing by the time Conor arrived and he had left the boy's upbringing almost entirely to Lilly, his wife. That may have been a mistake, he reasoned later, because although there was nothing particularly effeminate in his growing son's demeanor, he did like to draw and that was not an appropriately masculine pastime in Ben McAllister's view. He decided Conor needed toughening so at age twelve he had been packed off to a school with a reputation for strict discipline, good academics, and few fine arts. His mother reluctantly acquiesced in the boarding school decision solely due to the fact the Civil War had just broken out and the school's location in upstate New York would place her beloved son as far from harm's way as she could, at the time, imagine.

Conor met Applebee on the first day of school and when they realized they were both from Philadelphia, a bond was formed. They were an unlikely pair from the start. Applebee was as short and plump and funny-looking as Conor was tall and lean and handsome. Conor's mother once said that Conor and Applebee walking into a room together resembled the number "10." Conor immediately liked Applebee's wit. His verbal caricatures of their teachers and classmates were always razor sharp. If someone was being obnoxious or out of line, Applebee could be counted on to cut them dead with the perfect remark, whereas Conor was usually tongue-tied in such situations. Since Applebee was small and wore glasses, he was seldom invited to fistfight after one of these remarks. But whenever he was, he knew he could count on Conor, who was much more athletic, to aid in his defense. On one such occasion, when they were both sixteen, Conor had gotten his perfect nose broken in the scrape and Applebee had felt dreadful about it. He had made his physician father come all the way up from Philadelphia to treat Conor.

"Good god, son, you compelled me to leave bleeding soldiers to treat a broken nose?" Applebee's father had thundered after seeing his patient. "You led me to believe your friend was practically dying!"

Conor's nose healed only slightly crooked which, if anything, made his face even more handsome by throwing off the symmetry. As they grew older, Applebee began to additionally enjoy Conor's company for the female attention he attracted. Drawn initially to Conor, women and girls would often hang around long enough to discover Applebee's good traits, hidden though they were under a painfully plain exterior. He met more girls through Conor's castoffs than he could ever have managed on his own.

Conor's active social life benefitted his mother as well. Mothers of marriageable young ladies went out of their way to befriend Lilly McAllister, in hopes of helping their daughter's romantic chances with him. This circumstance provided her with a new start in Philadelphia society—an elite and tightly knit circle that for many years had quietly, politely shunned her. Conor's father had married her a little too soon after the death of his first wife *and* she was more than twenty-five years his junior *and* she had originally come into his house as the hired companion to his ailing wife, a stroke victim. But all these matters were quite forgotten, once Conor reached an age of eligible bachelorhood.

Conor's four older half-brothers teased him relentlessly about his popularity, but eventually the joke had gotten old, for it looked as if he would never settle down. It was their opinion he was being too hard to please and they told him so.

"You're not going to find the perfect woman, Conie-boy, she doesn't exist," his brother Ned had chided him at a family dinner one Christmas Eve after the women had left the table. Ned was married with three children and worked in the family business, McAllister Bootworks, with their father as did all of Conor's brothers.

"You've got to lower your sights and get realistic, little brother," said Bob, who was married with four children.

"Marriage isn't so bad, you know," added Will, the youngest of the "first set" of McAllisters, who was nevertheless sixteen years older than Conor. "Besides, you don't want to end up with some irate father sticking a shotgun in your back."

Will meant this as a joke, but Conor immediately looked down at his plate and the rest of the table shifted uncomfortably. It so happened that an episode not unsimilar to Will's suggestion had actually occurred just the summer before. Conor had improvidently involved himself with the daughter of one of their employees. He met the girl at the company picnic, during one of Conor's brief stints of employment at the bootworks. A generous financial arrangement was worked out and the matter was hushed up. Conor didn't know how many in the family knew about the misadventure, but obviously no one had told Will.

Only the oldest brother, Andrew, sat back and said nothing, all the while glancing at Conor with a knowing grin. Finally he leaned forward and said to his siblings, "Leave the boy alone. You all know you're just jealous." The whole table had shared a laugh at the truth of this. Conor smiled in thanks to Andrew who had two sons older than Conor.

A year and a half later, Conor proved Ned wrong. The perfect woman did exist. Her name was Allison and Conor proposed after a mere six-month courtship. Allison was charming, lovely, quiet, accomplished, came from a good family—in short, no one, not even Conor's mother who thought no woman alive was good enough for her baby, could find anything to complain about with Allison.

There was still the nagging problem of Conor's career, or lack of one. Conor had many talents, but was noticeably lacking in ambition. Applebee, on the other hand, was a born entrepreneur and straight out of college had transformed a failing daily newspaper into a successful weekly. In matters of career, Applebee was as industrious as Conor was lackadaisical. Applebee privately felt his best friend was more than a little lazy and certainly unmotivated—though he also thought Conor to be the victim of his father's extraordinary success. Not really having a steady income, Conor and Allison had to begin married life under his father's roof. This pleased his mother, but did not set well with his father at all. On more than one occasion, Ben McAllister was overheard to remark, "Are we ever getting rid of him?" Which was to say, Is Conor ever going to grow up?

The situation grew so tense, Conor and Allison eventually moved in with her parents. This pleased her mother, since Allison was soon to give birth to the couple's first child and she wanted to be close at hand. She knew something no one else besides Allison and their family doctor knew. Allison's health was more delicate than it appeared. Something wrong about the heart. The doctor had suggested that Allison should not ever have children, but this advice was ignored, hidden, for fear it would spoil her chances for marriage. Three weeks shy of their first wedding anniversary, Allison gave birth to a baby girl and tragically proved the doctor correct.

Allison's death left Conor morose and withdrawn and more at loose ends than ever. He seemed to take no interest in anything going on around him, including his newborn daughter. Allison's parents were only in their late forties and fortunately willing to raise their grandchild. They graciously extended Conor an indefinite invitation to continue his residence with them, but their attempts to involve him in the upbringing of his daughter were not very successful.

The child was colicky and difficult. The constant crying got on Conor's nerves. He would wander into the nursery from time to time in the early weeks and stare down at the squalling little red face and try to comprehend that he was somehow connected to this thing, whose birth he had looked forward to for so many months.

After awhile, he gave up trying and returned to his own parents' home. "Like the proverbial bad penny," his father had grumbled. His in-laws didn't say so, but they were actually glad to see him go. He wasn't contributing anything financially to his child's welfare—a fact which irritated Allison's father since Conor's family was considerably more well-to-do than Allison's—and Conor's aimless, melancholy presence at the dinner table every night added nothing to the demeanor of the household as it struggled to adjust to the loss of a beloved eldest daughter.

On his first night home after Allison's death, Ben took his son into his study for a talk. Conor followed him with foreboding. Being called into Dad's study after dinner always meant a whipping or a lecture, and with a wry smile, Conor had the impertinence to ask which it would be tonight. He thought this was a good joke, especially since he was now so much bigger than his father, indeed he was the tallest in the family, but his father was in no mood for jokes. Conor wondered if he had ever shared a good joke with his father. Ben McAllister seemed to save his humor for his business associates.

"Damn it, son, I brought you in here to discuss your future."

"I would never have guessed," Conor mumbled, taking another sip of the brandy he had carried in with him. He slouched down as low as possible in the uncomfortable chair before his father's desk.

"You're twenty-seven years old, for heaven's sake." Ben was exasperated, but tried to keep his irritation at bay. Lilly had made him promise to go easy on the boy.

"Twenty-eight, Thursday next," Conor corrected, staring at the detailed carving on the walnut desk front, trying to follow its pattern.

"That's an age when most men begin to prosper."

"Like you," Conor interjected sourly. He winced at the thought of getting the Army Contract story again, one of the staples of McAllister family history.

"Hell, yes, like me. I'm proud of my accomplishments. I thought marriage would mature you, give you some direction—"

"You want me to come back to work for you," Conor interrupted, feeling rude and out of sorts and more than a little drunk.

"What's wrong with that? You don't seem to have any other prospects at the moment."

Conor groaned. "We've tried this twice before, Dad. I'm just not cut out for the bootworks."

"It's not like I'm asking you to make the boots, for heaven's sake. You could be a salesman, or tend to the accounts, something with the figures—Ned's area. Ned could find something for you to do. Or maybe Bob—I'll talk to Bob. Bob could find something if Ned can't."

Something to keep me busy, thought Conor tiredly. He knew his father had mentioned Ned and Bob because they were the only brothers left he had not worked for in two previous times at the factory. The jobs with Will and Andrew had not worked out.

"Yes, all right, I'll give it another try." Conor rose to leave, then paused and waited to be dismissed. He was talking to his new boss, after all, instead of merely his father. Ben waved him on and he left, but not before an admonition that he was drinking too much. Conor held back on an angry retort that his drinking habits were his business, resolving instead to make the best of it with his father, to really try to fit in at the factory and find a place, any place, at least until something better came along.

But Conor was in hell for the next two years. He hated the

bootworks. It was noisy and the smell sickened him. He couldn't seem to locate a job that he was good at and his older siblings were forever treating him like the kid brother. He was so much younger than they were, it was as if he were permanently frozen in their minds as a ten-year-old, no matter what his true age.

Further, he was embarrassed by the deferential way the workers treated him because he was the owner's son. And then there was the unpleasant matter of periodically running into the man whose daughter he had gotten into trouble at the company picnic. That man wasn't at all deferential and glared at him whenever their paths crossed. Conor wished the man had been dismissed. He even hesitantly suggested this, only to have his father explode, "That man has worked for me for longer than you've been alive. He's the best tanner I've got. You'll go before he does!" Conor didn't bring up the subject again.

Then Applebee's offer came like a godsend. Now he was to be a journalist. *A journalist.* He liked the sound of it. And an artist, as well. Everyone was so impressed when he said he was going west. Going West. GOING WEST. Magical words. Full of promise. Going to gold country to report on the scene there.

Applebee exhorted him almost weekly by letter to send more, more. He claimed the articles were responsible for a 20 percent increase in his readership. Conor's mother had written to say that she was constantly being complimented by all her friends and even slight acquaintances on her adventurous son's moving accounts of life in the mountainous west.

Conor spent most of his mornings sitting at a table in the saloon writing his letters to Applebee. Applebee was publishing them under the title "Letters from the Gold Fields." The saloon was quiet in the mornings, until the first shift change at the mine. He had no desk or table in his room to write on so Brandy let him sit downstairs, even though he was drinking only coffee. Brandy bent the rules for him because he was a boarder and because he liked him.

One morning in mid-December he sat describing in detail an accident that had occurred at the Brown-Eyed Susan Mine the day before. A steam driven hoist was used in the mine to lower and raise ore carts by cable. The carts carried miners, two at a time, down into its seven underground levels. The carts then lifted ore out of the mine to be sorted. Useless ore was pitched down the growing tailings piles, while silver or gold ore was loaded onto waiting wagons for transport to the smelter. The day before at the Susan, the leather brakes on the hoist burnt out, dropping the cart containing two miners 180 feet to their deaths at the bottom of the shaft.

He was about to finish his letter when Angel, the youngest of the prostitutes, sat down and began looking at the pen and ink sketches he was going to send along.

"Pretty pictures," she said.

Conor looked up and acknowledged her compliment, but resumed writing without responding verbally. He had learned in his first month at the saloon that even the most innocuous pleasantry was interpreted by these women as an expression of commercial interest and if such wasn't forthcoming, they became surly.

"Bet you're writin' to your sweetheart," she persisted, scooting her chair closer.

Conor had the urge to shrink away, but didn't. "I'm trying to concentrate," he said softly, but bluntly.

"All right, all right." She got up in a huff and wandered away. She was hopelessly infatuated with Conor—this was apparent to everyone *except* Conor—but she was getting tired of his constant rebuffs. She had even been moved to ask Brandon if he thought there was something "wrong" with Conor. Brandy, who had himself been a bit offended by Conor's lack of interest in his "stable of fillies," as he called them, told her he could only conclude that Conor was still mourning his dead wife. This explanation had soothed Angel's wounded pride. She no longer felt she had to take his rejections quite so personally, but at some point her patience was going to run out.

Brandy came over with a fresh pot of coffee and refilled Conor's cup. "Angel botherin' you again?"

"No, no, it was nothing." Before Brandy left the table, Conor motioned him to sit down. There had been something he had wanted to discuss with his landlord since he had arrived. "I'm not morally offended by prostitution, Brandy, really I'm not. But isn't Angel too young to be, well, doing this sort of thing?" It had troubled him to see a child exploited.

Brandy grinned. "How old do you think she is?"

Conor shrugged. "Fourteen...fifteen?"

Brandy slapped his knee in delight. "That's what everybody thinks! And don't little Angel use it to her advantage." Brandy leaned in close to speak confidentially. "She's twenty-three. She's been in the business for years. She knows all the secrets of the trade."

"Secrets?" Conor's curiosity was piqued.

"Playin' the virgin's her best number. Real useful, too. I get a young fella in here, for example, and he's lookin' to have his first, but he's real nervous about it. Well, I draws him aside and tells him I know of this young thing wantin' to start in the business and would he like to be her first and all? Gets 'em every time. Then there's the ones scared to death of catchin' something. I give them the same story and they think they're safe." Brandy laughed and shook his head. "Little do they know Angel works more than the other three put together."

As Brandon rose, Conor looked back at Angel in a new light. She was less than five feet tall, with thin arms and no breasts. Her pinched and pointed face was fragile. Looks were certainly deceiving, if Brandon could be believed. Conor sighed audibly as he folded his papers together and addressed them to Applebee. All this talk of virgins had brought back unpleasant memories of his wedding night with Allison. What a disaster that had been. It still amazed him that things could go so wrong between two people who loved each other.

The wedding had been splendid. The reception had been elegant, if a bit overlong. Everyone had a good time. Endless toasts were made to the happy couple and the dancing had gone on long into the night. Conor's family and Allison's had pretended to be the best of friends. Even Conor's father had appeared to be in a good mood. But finally the festivities were over and the couple was alone. Problems began immediately. It seemed no one had informed Allison that losing her virginity was going to be painful. With each attempt, she grew increasingly upset and finally downright peevish.

"Are you certain you're doing it right?" she demanded. When he assured her he was, she queried, "How do you know you are?"

"I just do." Conor had tried to be patient, but he had not expected the woman of his dreams to question his sexual expertise on their wedding night. He had imaged she might be shy on their first time together, maybe even frightened, but *irritable*? Thinking he was being helpful, he added, "Don't worry, it won't always hurt."

"And how do you know that?" Her tone was sharpening like that of a prosecutor coming in for the kill.

Conor knew he had to answer very carefully. "I...I...just do."

"What you don't want to tell me is that there's been someone else. That's it, isn't it?" She narrowed her eyes. "How could you?"

"Allison...I'm twenty-seven years old." In his exasperation, he thought this explained everything, but Allison's belligerent frown told him otherwise. "You can't seriously have expected me to have waited."

"Didn't you expect *me* to?" she countered in a petulant voice he had never heard her use before.

Conor didn't have a ready answer to this one. He had previously considered her lack of sophistication one of her more endearing traits. Now it was coming back to haunt him in the worst way. He tried to reason with his twenty-year-old bride. "Allison, you just have to understand that men don't...save themselves for marriage like women do."

"Some men do, good men, Christian men," she snapped.

Conor groaned. He collapsed back into the pillows and stared at the dark ceiling. Except for a few chaste kisses during their engagement, holding Allison on the dance floor was the closest they had ever come to physical intimacy until this moment. His thoughts wandered back to the girl at that company picnic, how she had wrapped her legs around his hips while he was inside her and had whispered, with a wanton giggle, "You're trapped." He had often since imagined Allison doing likewise, but he knew now in an instant that was never going to happen. The stress of the wedding may have been wearing on them both, but even this knowledge did not stop him from snarling, "All right, I admit it, I've not led a perfectly moral life. In fact, I'm not perfect at all." The possibility that Allison was likewise not as perfect as he had imagined was beginning to dawn on him. "But we're married now, so I guess you're stuck with me!"

"Don't shout at me," Allison whined. She began to cry like a spoiled child.

He glumly took her into his arms, his anger subsiding, his disappointment still acute. "Listen to us. Arguing on our wedding night. What kind omen is that?"

Allison eventually calmed down and before the night was out they managed to consummate their marriage—Conor with an almost grim let's-get-it-over-with determination and Allison holding her breath, biting her lip and keeping her eyes shut tight. Conor went to sleep that night thinking how that company picnic had been a lot more fun than this.

CHRISTMAS spent with all the other single men at the saloon was a rousing, rather drunken affair, wholly unlike any Christmas Conor had ever spent with his large family in the East. He wrote a wryly amusing account of this for Applebee's paper and it drew the largest response of any of his writings. Applebee forwarded the many letters to the editor that poured in after its publication. Half the readers were entertained by this recounting of a bizarre holiday celebration, the other half were appalled by it, finding it sacrilegious and unwholesome to poke fun at such a sacred event. Many threatened to cancel their subscriptions, but

Applebee said he wasn't worried. Controversy only increased circulation as new readers were tempted to see what the fuss was all about.

There was one Christmas incident he didn't share with Applebee's readers. He was presented with a hand-knitted woolen sweater by the little prostitute, Angel. This placed him in an awkward position. He had no present for her and really didn't feel inclined to give her one. He tried to tactfully refuse the gift, but when he saw her crestfallen look, he knew he must accept it.

He also was fairly certain what she expected in return. This made him almost chuckle out loud, for it reminded him of the warnings all the proper young ladies in the East received from their mothers against accepting gifts from gentlemen lest the gentlemen think they're entitled to what Angel had in mind. Conor half-considered giving her what she wanted just to end the matter, but every time he thought of the grimy clientele she entertained each night, the notion of getting intimate with her made him shudder.

BETWEEN Christmas and New Year's, Conor received a sad message from home. Applebee had clipped out an obituary and attached a note drafted in his usual terse short hand:

"Kathleen Tompkins' husband killed in hunting accident. Attended funeral. Hate to admit it, but K. stunning in black. She asked about you."

The memory of Kathleen—that pint-sized terror—brought a wistful smile to his lips. Tiny, red-haired Kathleen was the brightest, bossiest, wickedly funniest, most outspoken woman he had ever known. Conor met her the day she came to work for his mother as a seamstress and they had become lovers so quickly it was impossible to sort out who had seduced whom.

She was his same age when they met, twenty-one, but decades older in spirit. Conor instantly loved how she always said exactly what was on her mind, well-received or not. Every thought that came into her quicksilver brain left her mouth unedited. This put most people off, but Conor thought she was terrific. In many ways, she reminded him of Applebee. They shared the trait of being able to sum up someone's character in a few bold strokes. Kathleen took special delight in verbally skewering the spoiled and often empty-headed debutantes he squired to parties. Conor would even supply her with the details of these soirees and his partners so she could then, late in the night, in his bed, make fun of the superficial crowd that populated his social life.

Sometimes he thought she was jealous of his world and the young ladies in it, though he knew she would never admit to this.

Conor used to call her "the little tyrant." "Demure" and "submissive" were not words in her vocabulary, thus making her very nearly the opposite of the feminine ideal of her day. Conor did not really appreciate the effect this had on the physical side of their relationship. Though she was a willing and frequent visitor to his tiny bedroom on the third floor of his parents' house, she laid down so many rules and regulations about what went on there he sometimes wondered why either of them bothered. She was obsessed with avoiding pregnancy—a goal he had no quarrel with—but her conception avoidance method of choice was withdrawal and he really didn't enjoy it. Spilling his seed all over her thighs or belly just wasn't as much fun as doing it the normal way—plus, he found it embarrassing. He was a spoiled little boy who had grown into a spoiled young man. He confided his dissatisfaction to an unsympathetic Applebee one day as they dressed after a game of tennis at the Men's Athletic Club.

With an irritated frown, Applebee had chided him, "You've no idea what a gem you've got with that girl and all you do is complain. Trust me when I tell you that *coitus interruptus* is better than no *coitus* at all. I'm an expert on the latter." Applebee was unabashedly fond of Kathleen. The three of them often dined together. Conor loved those evenings. Kathleen and Applebee delighted in trading insults. They tried to outdo each other. It could get quite outrageous. Conor would come home exhausted, with his sides aching from having laughed so much.

"What's that you say?" Michael Horrigan had asked. He was a somewhat arrogant young grain factor who occasionally played doubles with them. He had overheard the word *coitus* and decided to intrude upon their conversation.

"McAllister, here, is the most ungrateful man in the universe," answered Applebee.

"How so?"

"He has this sweet young something who visits his room nearly every night and he has the audacity to complain because she won't give him everything he wants."

"Won't let you in, huh?" Michael smirked.

"Oh, she'll let him in all right. She just won't let him stay very long," volunteered Applebee, with authority. "She's afraid of getting into trouble, and who could blame her?"

"*Applebee*," Conor whined, wishing now he'd kept his mouth shut.

"My wife's the same way," interjected Jeffrey Allen, their fourth in doubles tennis. Jeffrey was a couple of years older than the rest and was married with a young son. He, too, had been listening in on Conor's conversation with Applebee. "She laid down the law after Jeffrey Junior was born. She said no more babies for at least two years and if I didn't like it, I could find a new wife."

This revelation stunned the three young bachelors. They lived at a time when the sale of all artificial methods of contraception were banned by law and the practice itself was denounced from the pulpits as sinful and unnatural. It was privately considered the province of unmarried couples like Conor and Kathleen who sought to enjoy the benefits of marriage without taking on the responsibilities.

"You let a woman tell you what to do?" sneered Michael to Jeffrey, but implying Conor as well.

Jeffrey glanced about the assembled group and announced solemnly, almost sadly, "Yes." He then turned around and resumed dressing.

"If Conor's girl were mine," pontificated the obnoxious Michael, "I'd say, 'Listen, sweetheart, it's my way or the highway!'"

"Which probably explains why Conor has company at midnight and you don't," observed Applebee, as he cleaned his glasses on his undershirt. He didn't really like Michael. He tolerated his friendship because he and Conor could beat Michael at tennis.

"Can't we change the topic?" suggested Conor, who did not appreciate having his personal problems broadcast for the entertainment of the entire Men's Athletic Club changing room.

To which Applebee, with mock reverence, asked rhetorically, "*Is there another topic?*" Everyone laughed.

Then there had been the night Conor didn't quite withdraw in time. Kathleen, every bit as hot tempered as her mane of curly red hair would suggest—flew into a fury. She ranted and raved at him until he feared his parents, one floor down the mahogany-carved staircase, would hear. She was quite a sight, this tiny woman stomping around his room stark naked threatening to strangle him with her bare hands if she ended up with a baby after his mistake.

A week later, he caught sight of her in the garden. She loved doing her hand sewing in the garden and could always be found there whenever his parents were not at home. He took a deep breath and decided to approach her. He'd been avoiding her up until then for fear she'd throw another tantrum. He walked over to where she sat on the big stone garden bench and stood before her.

"Still mad at me, Kate?"

She glanced up at him, frowned, then returned her gaze to her sewing. "It's all right," she said in a flat voice. "I'm bleeding."

"You're what?" Conor sat down at her side, his eyes wide with alarm.

"The bleeding came. You're off the hook," she announced matter-of-factly.

"Should you see a doctor?"

"What for?" she asked, putting down her sewing for the moment. "I told you everything was all right."

"All right? You just said you were bleeding." Conor was thoroughly confused.

She frowned at him, incredulous. "Are you really that ignorant, Conor?"

Conor shrugged. He was. His knowledge, at the time, of the mechanics of the female reproductive system did not extend beyond what his own role was in producing an offspring.

Kathleen sighed and rolled her eyes. "Women bleed every month. Unless they're in a family way."

"All women?"

"All women between fifteen and fifty. It's from the womb." Then she leaned toward him and whispered in his ear, "It comes out where you go in."

"Oh." Conor reddened. The conversation had gotten entirely too female, making him squeamish.

Applebee later confirmed what Kathleen had told him. "Good God, you really are ignorant, Conor. I'll loan you one of my dad's medical books. That'll put you straight."

Kathleen eventually married a tailor. She met him in a fabric shop, not surprisingly. In the years that followed, Conor had replayed in his mind the night their affair ended countless times, wondering if he should have or could have made a different choice.

"We've got to talk," she had announced briskly as she shut his bedroom door. Talk was mostly what they ended up doing near the end. Although she spent nearly every week night in his room—not the weekends when he was usually out until all hours with his friends— they seldom made love more than once or twice a week. After three years together, they had settled into the habits of an old married couple.

Conor had been dozing even though he had been expecting her.

Apprehension gripped him as he struggled to awaken himself. She can't be pregnant, she can't, she can't, she can't.

"I've met someone."

Conor was so relieved her announcement didn't involve a blessed event it took him a few seconds to actually comprehend the implications of what she had said. He pulled back the covers and she slipped into bed next to him.

"He's asked me to marry him."

After an uncomfortable silence, Kathleen demanded, "Aren't you going to say *anything*?"

Conor shrugged, at a loss. "Do I know him?"

"No."

"Well, do you mind at least telling me?"

With a vaguely defensive tone in her voice, Kathleen launched into a description of the tailor, how they had met, how he wanted to open a tailor shop in a small town outside of Philadelphia, how he wanted her to work with him in this endeavor, how it had always been her ambition to own a shop.

"It sounds like you've already made up your mind," Conor remarked at the end of this recitation, which had sounded a bit rehearsed. He was jealous, of course. He was surprised and disappointed. He wanted to say something mean. "Do you share with him more than your sewing talents?"

"You don't have the right to ask me that," she snapped. "When did you ever earn the right to demand fidelity of me? You who go out with a different girl every night. The society pages would be quite at a loss for material if you left town, Conor."

He responded in a low and even voice. "I have never been intimate with another woman since the day we met and you know it, Kate."

She was still bristling. "You don't have the right to ask, but I'll tell you anyway—the answer is 'no.' He's never so much as kissed me. He's a proper and decent man."

"Oh, and I'm not. I forgot," Conor joked, unable to resist. She smiled faintly and he pulled her close.

"Conor, I don't want to leave you, but...I'm twenty-four—practically an old maid. I've got to think of the future. And these last three years—they haven't been especially easy for me, you know."

"They haven't?" This was news to Conor. He had always thought their relationship was simple and effortless.

"Conor, everyone in this house hates me except you. I mean,

some of the girls are in love with you and just jealous." Conor knew this, that several of the younger girls on his mother's household staff had crushes on him, though he had never given the matter too much thought. "They call me 'whore' and 'slut' to my face and those are the ones who will talk to me at all. I try to pretend I don't care, but—"

"Who said that?" Conor was angry. "Which ones? I'll tell my mother to dismiss them."

"And what would you give as the reason for their dismissal—that they called your whore by right name?"

"Oh, for God's sake, don't talk like that."

Kathleen shrugged unhappily and started to cry. She had never cried before in his presence. He held her head to his chest and combed his fingers through her long and tangled hair.

"Old Barrett warned me about you—years ago. The first time she caught me sneaking out of your room."

"What did Barrett say about me?" asked Conor. Mrs. Barrett was the formidable head of household. Under her stern and watchful eye, Lilly McAllister's house ran like a precision timepiece.

"I expected some big lecture on morality, but that wasn't the case at all. She gave very practical advice. She told me I was wasting my time with you, that you would never marry me, that you'd use up all my pretty years and then discard me, that you'd marry instead one of those ridiculous bits of fluff you partner at those fancy parties you attend."

"I thought Barrett liked me," complained Conor, not expecting such a brutal assessment from a woman who had practically raised him and always had doted on him.

"She does, Conor, but that doesn't make her blind to the truth."

"It's just...I can't get married now, Kate. I've got to finish school and...and—"

She placed her fingers over his lips to silence him. "She said something else about you. She said you were born with a face women said 'yes' to, but you never learned how to say 'no.' She said that would be your undoing. I don't know what she meant by that."

Conor didn't either, but Kathleen married her tailor within the month so whether he had made the right decision or the wrong one became a moot point. But now the tailor was dead. Conor pitied Kathleen her loss and thought bitterly on how God seemed to have nothing better to do than kill people's spouses. Kathleen...a widow. Suddenly, the word 'widow' caused the image of Elodie Kelly to appear in his mind. He shook his head and frowned.

Chapter Seven

"THERE—I heard it again."

"Help me!" I screamed, though my voice was raw and hoarse from shouting.

"There...didn't you hear it that time?"

"You're nuts."

"No, I'm not. It's a woman's voice."

"It's a cat yowling. Or the wind whistling through the mine or something. There's no woman around here." The second man's voice turned teasing, "Probably a ghost. It's near a ghost town, ain't it?"

"Down here!" I shouted.

"Look, Barry, there's a little book. Some kind of flower book."

"We've got to get back to work, Steve. Come on...this is stupid."

"What's this?" said the one named Steve.

The shaft of light above me darkened. I began yelling like crazy.

"Hey...where are you?"

"I'm down in this shaft of some kind—I fell. Help me."

"Are you hurt, Lady?"

"Just my foot. I think it's broken. I can maybe climb out if I had something to hang on to. I'm afraid I might fall further—I'm stuck on some kind of ledge."

"Well, hold on. I'm gonna go get some cable. We can just barely see the top of your head."

In a few minutes my rescue was at hand—as they say in melodramas. A cable was lowered and I tied it around me under my arms. Barry and Steve assured me they would not let me fall so I slowly began climbing, searching for hand and foot holds as I made my way back up. The crevice or shaft I had fallen into was only about one and a half to three feet wide at various points. I tried to sometimes place my weight on the injured foot, but whenever I did, I felt things moving around in there that weren't supposed to be moving. In fact, the whole of my left foot felt like a bag of broken glass. I also had a cut over my eyebrow that was swollen and kept bleeding annoyingly into my right eye.

At last I was back to the surface. My rescuers were two telephone repairmen. The moment I was out and saw them I burst into tears and blubbered something like: "You saved my life...thank you, thank you," then hugged them both.

When I told them my name they said it was my phone lines they had come up to work on. Barry, a stocky man in his middle thirties, said they had been eating a late lunch near the entrance to the old mine when they heard sounds coming from it. Steve, a tall, thin man of about fifty, thought Barry was crazy. He insisted that coming to a ghost town had put Barry in a "suggestible state." In the alternative, he thought Barry might be playing a joke on him. Either way, Barry demanded they go investigating. They both confessed the beauty of the day had encouraged them to search for a reason to "goof off."

They gave me water and what was left of their lunch—a bag of barbecue chips and a granola bar. Barry wrapped his jacket around me because he thought I might be in shock. He said he didn't know why you were supposed to do that to accident victims, but his brother was a volunteer fireman and he had said that's what you were always supposed to do.

Meanwhile, Steve was trying to remove my shoe from the injured foot. It was a flimsy, canvas shoe and he finally cut it off with his pocket knife. The top of my foot looked like it had swallowed a golf ball. I silently cursed myself for not buying some good, sturdy hiking boots. They might have protected my feet to have prevented or lessened the injury. I just wasn't a mountain woman yet.

With my arms slung around both their necks, the three of us slowly made it back down the ridge to their truck. We then began the long drive down into Columbine to take me to the clinic. Steve wanted to call in on his radio to get the rescue helicopter to fly in, but I adamantly refused. I insisted my injuries were not life threatening and the helicopter would not be needed if they wouldn't mind taking the time to drive me in.

They discussed this among themselves for a moment and, I think, concluded that this was as good a reason as any to avoid working the rest of the afternoon.

Once we reached the truck, I saw the clock on the dash board. It was now two-thirty. I had spent almost an hour and a half in my stone prison.

"What was it that you fell into?" Barry asked on the way to town.

"I have no idea. I was just walking along and then—boom—the ground wasn't there anymore."

"Maybe it was a big rabbit hole," joked Steve. "Sure your name ain't Alice?"

I laughed at this. Despite my aches and pains, I was so happy to be rescued, I was in a great mood. "You know that was exactly the thought that come to my mind as I fell."

Steve seemed pleased by this, then he said to his partner, "Do you think we'll get on TV for this?"

"Maybe the Denver stations, probably not national."

I mentally cringed at the idea this matter might be made public, but said nothing. How could I criticize the men who had saved my life?

"That hole must be connected to the mine," reasoned Barry. "Otherwise how could we have heard her calling for help through the mine entrance?"

"We knew you weren't in the mine because it's been sealed up for years, decades."

"Maybe it was an old well," I suggested, although the shaft seemed too haphazard in shape and too narrow to have been man made.

"Nobody's ever lived up there, I don't think," said Steve. "Who knows?" That ended the discussion as far as he was concerned and he turned on the radio as he drove. We listened to country and western music for the rest of the drive.

As we passed Evan's house, I noticed his truck in the yard. I was thankful he was home. I could call him to drive me home from the clinic, hopefully.

The clinic was a small, neat brick building in the center of Columbine. A nurse named Victoria Reno immediately took charge of my care. Nurse Reno was a slender woman of about fifty with close-clipped steel gray hair and large clear-framed glasses that kept slipping down her nose. Her brisk, no-nonsense manner was reassuringly professional, yet still approachable.

I was X-rayed and examined by her and a young student nurse who was an intern for the summer. There was no doctor on duty that day. The county shared a doctor with two other counties. Specialists came in on a once-a-week schedule.

My rescuers decided to say goodbye, so I wrote down their names and addresses and gave them each a farewell kiss. They blushed and grinned and exited with a bashful "twern't nothin'" humility.

Mrs. Reno whisked in the examining room with my X-rays. "I'm not a radiologist, but there's nothing too tricky to diagnose here. If your goal was to break your foot, you did a splendid job."

"Thanks," I responded with a weary smile.

"You're really so lucky, you know. You should never go out

hiking or anything else by yourself in these mountains. There are too many dangers."

"Yes, oh, yes. When I think what could have happened if those men hadn't come along when they did."

Mrs. Reno chuckled. "They're really quite proud of themselves. I suppose they have a right to be."

She then began to create a plaster splint to hold my foot in place. She said I would get a walking cast as soon as the swelling went down, probably in four or five days. A doctor would need to review my X-rays between now and then.

As she worked on my splint, I identified myself as Grady's great-niece. "The lawyer who settled my aunt's estate told me you took care of her a lot in the last couple of years. He said you handled all the arrangements after she died. I want to thank you for that."

"I liked your aunt. She was a remarkable woman. I hope I'm that feisty when I'm that age. Come to think of it—I just hope I get to see that age."

"I was just curious: What did she actually die of?"

Mrs. Reno straightened up and pushed her glasses up the bridge of her nose. "Well, old age, I guess. She was over a hundred, you know, so the coroner said no need to go to the expense of an autopsy. There was no question of foul play, of course. She was found on her kitchen floor by the mail carrier. She had passed away probably a few days before she was found."

"But how did they know there was no foul play if they didn't do an autopsy? I mean, her house was broken into just after she died and-"

I broke off, not wanting to sound so accusatory to a woman I had heard nothing but kind things about concerning Grady. She looked decidedly uncomfortable at my questions, like she knew the local authorities, in the interest of saving money, had not crossed all the 't's where Grady was concerned, just because she was old and had no family to make a fuss on her behalf.

"That's just the way we do things up here. Less formal than what you're used to in a large city, I'm sure." Her slightly curt tone told me to butt-out. Then she smiled, apparently not wanting to make an issue of this. I smiled back. She seemed like such a nice woman, it was hard to get mad at her, especially over something that was probably not her decision anyway.

She went on to tell me they didn't immediately know who to contact after Grady was found, so Grady's remains were cremated and I could retrieve them from a mortuary over in Brownleaf, a larger town down valley about sixty miles. Then she gave me some pain pills and asked if someone was coming to take me home.

I called Evan's number, but got the answering machine—the twins' voices recited in unison: "Little pig, little pig, we are very busy, you can leave a message, if you're not a sissy!" BEEP.

I left a brief message saying I had been in an accident and could he drive me home? The big 24-hour clock on the wall read 17:00. I counted on my fingers to realize that was now five o'clock. The student nurse washed the blood off my face and elbows. No stitches were needed.

I lay on the examining table, my foot elevated with an ice bag on it, in the half-lit room all alone amid its ugly stainless steel and crisp white linen and the smell of antiseptic. I felt horribly depressed. My wonderful summer had come to such an abrupt halt. I would probably have to go home right away. I was the proverbial fish out of water here, kidding myself that I could ever fit in. I hadn't even been rescued by my hero of choice—Evan. I couldn't even get him to give me a lift home.

Then at six-thirty, as though to springboard me from these morbid thoughts, Evan burst into the room wearing a sweaty tee shirt and black bicycling shorts. He had on bicycling shoes with no socks and his legs were splattered with mud.

"God, Darcy, what happened? I came as soon as I got your message, but I was out on my bike all afternoon. Did you roll your Jeep?"

I told him about my accident as the nurse's aide gathered my things. Without warning, he picked me up in his arms and carried me out of the clinic. This grand gesture embarrassed me, yet at the same time I enjoyed every minute of it.

"Evan, this is not necessary," I protested, half-heartedly.

"I only get chivalrous once a decade, so enjoy it while it lasts."

Everyone we passed stared at us, of course. I meekly waved goodbye to Mrs. Reno as we swept past her in the hall. She said, "Hello, Evan," with a bemused smile and waved back. Evan deposited me in his truck, then went back in and picked up the crutches I was to use.

"I'm gonna drive slow," he said. "I don't want you to have that foot bounced around any more than necessary. I know how you feel. I've been there. When I fell off that roof several years ago."

He spoke at length of his own accident on the way home. People always do that. Do they think it makes the injured person feel better?

Or is it a kind of one-up-man-ship?

I related the story of my ordeal and for some reason started crying in the middle of it. The pent up emotions of the day just spilled out. Evan reached over and patted my shoulder. He could barely reach it because I was sitting sideways with my back against the door so that I could keep my foot elevated on the seat. Then he patted my knee, which I thought was a bit forward. He turned on the radio. It was the public station and they were playing weird "space music." The effect was soothing, but eerie. Evan said he was anxious to explore the hole I fell into. He, like the repairmen, didn't think it could be a well. Maybe it was an old mine shaft. He said that he and Reilly liked to rock climb and would have to check it out.

We reached Leap Year just at twilight. Evan carried me in and set me down on the couch. He thought I should live downstairs until I pointed out Grady's only bathroom was upstairs, so up we went.

"Not that I'm volunteering to help, but can you get undressed okay?"

Not that I'd mind his help...but I assured him I could manage. He went downstairs to see if he could fix something for us to eat. The chips and candy bar the telephone men had given me had been the only thing I'd eaten since breakfast. I could hear him singing to himself downstairs as I hopped around the bathroom, getting out of my clothes, putting on my robe, and trying to clean myself up a little more. I was shocked at my first view in the mirror. The swelling over my eye was starting to go down, but the cut was rather nasty-looking. I left the bandage off, because I thought it made me look too pathetic. Alone in my house with Evan, my vanity shifted into overdrive.

I got into bed just as Evan entered the room. He was frowning. "Darcy, what do you eat? I couldn't find any food."

My eating habits were unconventional. I was known to eat breakfast cereal for dinner and ice cream sandwiches for lunch. I shrugged demurely to answer his question. He held a cereal box in the crook of his arm and munched on a handful of it. He offered me the box, insisted on propping my foot on several pillows, then went back downstairs for a bag of ice.

He returned and very gently balanced the plastic sack full of ice on my foot. He leaned over to inspect my splint, talking all the while about his own past breaks, and rested his hand absentmindedly on my knee again.

"Does it hurt much?"

"They gave me some painkillers at the clinic. I'm feeling very mellow at the moment." I showed him the prescription.

"Oh, that's a fun one. I used to take that for my back. You won't be awake much longer."

When he noticed where his hand was, he glanced at me for my reaction. I gazed up at him impassively, hoping I didn't look too hideous. Then he slowly, lightly began to run his hand down my thigh, all the while watching for my reaction.

"You're not stopping me," he observed quietly.

"No, I'm not..." I was hoping I sounded more sexy than sleepy, but at that moment, I wasn't sure.

We looked at each other for what seemed to be a long time. A silent negotiation of sorts taking place.

He shook his head with a doubtful smile. "Are you sure you want this?"

"Are you?"

He laughed. "Are you kidding? You've been giving me wet dreams since the day we met."

This goofy compliment thrilled me. He leaned down and kissed my thigh.

"That is certainly the first time a man has ever kissed my thigh before kissing my lips."

He pretended a look of confusion. "Is that how it goes—lips first, *then* thigh?"

"Typically."

"I'll have to remember that." He then recited to himself, "Lips first, then thigh, lips first, then thigh." He untied the sash of my robe and opened it. With a wry glance, he informed me, "Summer was right." He started kissing my breasts. He still had not made it northward to my face.

He abruptly stood up and pulled his sweat-stained tee shirt off over his head. He wadded it up and then sniffed it. "Oh, God...I really need a shower."

I had been wondering how to tactfully bring this up. "Don't run off now," he teased as he disappeared into the bathroom.

The five minutes he spent showering seemed an eternity to someone who had taken such a strong painkiller. Still, I had to ask myself, what the hell am I doing? Why am I getting involved with a man I barely know? He already has a steady girlfriend and he lives in a place I'll be leaving soon and...wait a minute—this is a classic one-night-stand. I've never had a one-night-stand before, never really wanted one...until now. Should I ask why or why not?

I was too groggy to figure out an answer. The exhaustion of the day's ordeal was beginning to set in as well. Stay awake, stay awake, I chanted to myself. I pinched myself, bit my lip, anything to keep alert. Falling asleep during sex would not make a good first impression.

I heard the shower shut off at last.

"Your soap makes me smell like a girl," he complained good-naturedly as he strode into the room, dropping his towel on the floor. His wet hair hung in curly ringlets, looking much redder now than blond.

"Darcy...Darcy...don't check out on me now. We're just getting to the good part."

I must have looked as sleepy as I felt.

He climbed into bed and I'm pretty sure we made love.

I WOKE UP in pain, but sublimely happy. I looked over adoringly at my prize. I couldn't see his face, just a tangled mass of golden red curls on the pillow and his freckled tan-pink shoulders. Whatever had happened last night must not have been too bad—at least he stayed. My sister Jane would be so proud of me.

I wiggled the toes of my injured foot. The swelling was still pretty bad and the skin was turning all the colors of the rainbow. Then I surveyed the rest of my naked body. It was a disaster area of bruises, a human war zone. I let out a moan of dismay, which woke up the sleeper at my side.

"What's wrong?" he murmured drowsily, shifting around to face me.

"I was just taking inventory of the damage." There was the bruise and cut above my eye, the swollen ear, two bruised elbows, one knee, a large bruise on my rib cage just below my left breast, and another large bruise on my right side near my hipbone.

Evan propped his head on one elbow and surveyed me as well. "What a mess," he agreed. "You didn't look that awful last night—if that's any consolation. Then again, maybe the light was just bad."

I leaned over and kissed him.

He chuckled. "Last night right after we did it the first time, I got this horrible fear. I thought—how well do I really know this woman? She might be crazy and say I raped her. The sheriff would've taken one look at your battered body, thrown me in the slammer and swallowed the key."

I playfully punched him. Then I got serious. "You know, I'm really better in bed when I'm fully conscious."

Evan grinned. "Prove it." He put his arms around me and I involuntarily winced. He released me and asked with an air of helplessness, "Is there anything I can touch that doesn't hurt?" When I didn't answer right away, he added, "At the risk of sounding like a self-serving jerk—would more drugs help?"

"I don't want to take anything. I want to be...*alert* this time. Aren't you tired of making love to someone who's nearly comatose?"

"But this was my first chance to take advantage of a cripple," he quipped. "And I finally got to live out my necrophiliac fantasies."

"Oh, stop it—I wasn't that bad...."

"Okay," he teased. "I'll give you one more chance."

Sometime after we made love, I remembered he had a family. Did they know where he was? Were they worried about him? I asked him.

"Everything's cool," he said, looking uncomfortable. "I, uh...I told Reilly I wasn't gonna be home til morning before I left to pick you up."

"That sure of yourself, huh?"

"It wasn't that...I mean, you needed someone to stay with you last night, right? It's not like I said, 'I'm gonna sleep with her.' That was just an added bonus." He was never serious for long.

"And what was Reilly's reaction?"

Evan grinned. "He was pretty certain I was going to sleep with you." He shrugged. "He's eighteen...all he thinks about is sex. You know, though, it was kinda strange. I expected him to pitch a fit about it and he didn't. He was pretty cool with the idea and that surprised me. Usually he hates all my girlfriends." Evan sighed. "We've had this intense sort of Oedipal thing going for several years."

Evan went on to say how Reilly never really got over Beth—the twins' mother—leaving. He was attached to Beth, which Evan said was odd since Beth "never really gave a damn about him." Evan couldn't understand how Reilly could take that breakup harder than the departure of his own mother. I asked about ages and he said Reilly had been about twelve the second time.

Evan decided we needed breakfast in bed and went downstairs to the kitchen. I lay back in Grady's bed watching the sun glow orange against the mountain range. Sunrises were different in the mountains than they were down below. There was no "rosy-fingered dawn" described by Homer. Instead, one just caught a reflection of the rising sun against the canyon walls. They momentarily turned a golden-y color that reminded me of the stuff they pour on your popcorn at the movie theater—the stuff they can't call butter because it isn't butter (God knows what it really is) so they call it "golden flavoring".

Instead of a rosy-fingered dawn, I watched a golden-flavored sunrise, which was okay with me. After all, I felt like I had discovered a new motherlode. Evan was quite simply the best lover I'd ever had or even imagined. I didn't mind, for once, that he had been with so many other women—at least he had learned a few things. Compared to him, my ex-husband, Keith, was a bumbling amateur in bed. Evan even used condoms without being asked, for Christsakes.

I deserve this, I told myself. I deserve this. This is my karmic reward for the divorce. The universe is in harmony once again. I tried not to listen to my inner, more ethical self who was busily pointing out that this dream lover already had a spouse, of sorts. Was cheating on a girlfriend—a live-in girlfriend, no less—as bad as cheating on a wife? Isn't this a telling comment on his true character? I remembered the old saying: if he'll cheat on her, he'll cheat on you. And me—once the victim of a philandering husband, now I was helping a guy victimize some other poor woman.

Then again...the things he could do with his hands, his fingers, his tongue—no more ethical debate, please—we're above ten thousand feet, after all.

He suddenly appeared at the bedroom door holding a gallon of milk. He had a look of disappointment on his face. "Darcy...*whole milk*?"

"But it tastes good, Evan."

He shrugged sadly and went back downstairs. I pondered the milk dilemma. Do I start buying low fat—which I can't stand—just to please him or do I maintain my individuality, my sense of self-worth, my independence and continue to drink whole milk? In good lap dog fashion, I resolved to buy both. Evan returned from the kitchen bearing French toast and coffee. No man had ever made me a hot breakfast in my life! I have died and gone to heaven, I have died and gone to heaven.

After breakfast, Evan spent a great deal of time arranging the pillows in such a way to allow us to lie face-to-face on our sides. My legs ended up wrapped around his waist with my injured foot on a pillow behind his back. Then we made love very, very slowly. Evan called this "playing Siamese Twins" because what we were doing at the moment was not "goal-oriented" enough to be considered "a real fuck."

"You're amazing," I giggled, realizing for the first time in my life that I had always been too serious about sex. "You've actually made me glad I broke my foot."

"Maybe I should have been a doctor."

"Doctors are supposed to cure people. You make them glad they're sick."

"But is there really a difference?" he challenged. We both laughed because I couldn't decide. Then suddenly, his sleepy, sexy smile changed to a look of panic. "Oh, shit! What time is it?" He reached over me to see his watch on the bedside table. "Oh, God, it's almost eleven! I'm supposed to see a guy about a job down valley at noon. Even if I leave right now, I'll be half an hour late." He jumped out of bed and headed for the shower. Before leaving the room, he turned with a helpless gesture and said with self-deprecating humor: "This is why I can't hold a job. I'm unreliable."

He returned from the shower, complaining once again: "You've got to get different soap. If I go to a job smelling like this, the guys'll think I'm queer."

As he pulled on his clothes, he explained he was to put in a bid to work on a new apartment complex. He had to stop by home first to change as he now realized all he had to wear was the dirty mountain biking clothes he had worn to the clinic. On his way out the door, he told me he was going to send the twins up to look after me in the afternoon.

JUST AFTER one o'clock, two Indians dressed in feathers and buckskins and covered with war paint burst into my bedroom.

"Don't move," warned Indian Number One, brandishing a rubber tomahawk.

"You're our captive," shouted Indian Number Two, aiming a bow with no arrows at me. "Should I tie her up?"

"No need to—she's not going anywhere."

"Oh, dear...whatever shall become of me?" I cried with great drama.

"We are going to trade you to the Cavalry for guns," Indian Number One informed me.

Indian Number Two, a.k.a. Summer Allender, had already lost interest in the attack and sat down on the bed to examine my splint and my multihued, swollen foot. "Does it hurt much?"

"Only when people—" Summer was jiggling up and down, "jump on my bed." The jiggling stopped.

"Don't talk to the prisoner," Indian Number One commanded.

"Oh, Winnie, come off it. We're here to nurse you, Darcy. What do you need us to do?"

"A cold drink would be nice," I suggested. Summer hurried off to the kitchen and brought back cans of pop for us three.

"So..." said Summer, in a grown up, conversational tone, "you and Daddy had a sleep over."

I was a little nonplused. I knew Evan was something of a free spirit and his family was not exactly a model of convention, but I was uncertain how to answer personal questions from one's lover's children. This was new territory for me.

"Is that what he told you?" I ventured cautiously. I was following the old maxim: when in doubt, dodge.

"Reilly told us at breakfast."

"Did you and Daddy have sexual intercourse?" Winter jumped in, getting right to the heart of the matter.

"Sexual intercourse?" I meekly repeated, completely nonplused now.

"We know all about it," Summer assured me. "We saw a movie about it in school last year. The boys saw one movie and the girls saw another. They told us to go home and talk to our parents about it and we told Daddy we thought it was gross."

"Yeah, gross," said Winter, making a sick face.

"But Daddy said we were too young to understand it all and that some day it would make sense. He said that lying between a woman's legs is the sweetest thing on earth—those were his exact words."

"And at the end it feels like sneezing."

"Sneezing?" I tried to keep a straight face, but couldn't.

"Yeah," Winter concurred. "You know—Ah-Ah-Ah-CHOOO!" She and her sister collapsed in giggles at this.

With some amusement, I tried to imagine my own father having such a conversation with me on the subject of sex. I did not recall him ever admitting that sex existed in the world, much less trying to verbalize what the experience felt like.

Summer solemnly concluded the sex education lecture with the admonition, "You're not supposed to do it until you get out of high school."

Winter grinned wickedly and confided, "Sandy and Daddy did it in high school. We checked the dates. Reilly was born right after they graduated from high school."

"June, 1975," added Summer, always the precise one. "They ran away from home and lived in a commune in Ontario."

"That's in Canada," Winter added for my benefit.

"When Reilly was born all the people in the commune sat around in a circle naked and chanted—"

"Naked and chanting?" I was completely agog.

"The chanting was supposed to make Sandy's pain go away," Summer continued.

"Childbirth is painful," Winter informed me gravely. "Did you know that?"

"So I've heard." My facial muscles were starting to ache from the pressure of trying not to laugh.

"Daddy said it didn't work because Sandy screamed her head off," Summer said. Both girls thought this was amusing.

"Then a really funny thing happened," said Winter, "Just when Reilly came out, Daddy fainted. Sandy never let him forget that. She said she did all the work and he got all the attention. And when people come to visit us that lived in that commune, they still tease Daddy about it."

"How long did they live in Canada?"

"Not long," said Summer. "When Grandma found out where they were, she made them come home."

"You haven't answered our question, Darcy," Winter reminded me.

"Some things are very private and I...don't feel comfortable discussing them." The girls exchanged looks, so I added, "Besides, I wouldn't want to do anything that would hurt Greta's feelings."

"We don't like Greta," Winter said in a confidential way.

"She doesn't like us," added Summer.

"She doesn't like kids."

"Or dogs," said Summer, passion rising in her pink cheeks. "She's always trying to talk Daddy into getting rid of Rhett and Scarlett. She says they're dirty and smelly and jump on people too much."

"Would you like to have an Irish Wolfhound puppy someday, Darcy?" asked Winter, as our conversation once again veered wildly off course, to my relief. "Scarlett is with puppy."

"With puppy...excuse me?"

"In the olden days, people used to say 'with child' instead of 'pregnant,' so I say that Scarlett is 'with puppy'."

"Rhett is the puppies' father, but Rhett and Scarlett are brother and sister, which is incest, you know, but Daddy says it's all right because they're just dogs."

I sunk down into my pillows, exhausted.

JUST BEFORE dark, Evan arrived with some dinner in a sack from home. "I hear you got a visit from my favorite Indian tribe this afternoon," he said, as he spread out the meal on a tablecloth on my bed. It was another vegetarian stir fry.

"I was their captive."

He looked instantly alarmed. "Did they tie you up?"

When I shook my head 'no', he was so relieved. "They once tied up Greta and left her. It was six hours until I got home." He rolled his eyes, "Whoever said Scandinavians don't have hot tempers? That was one angry Swede."

With a smirk, I couldn't resist bringing up one item of the twin's chatter. "It was a very educational afternoon. For example, I learned that sex was just like sneezing."

Evan groaned loudly and shook his head as if hating to be reminded of this. "I try to do a good job being a father, I really do." He sighed. "When they heard about sex for the first time, they reacted the way all kids do when they get the news—you know, 'oh, gross, that sounds awful,' and so forth—and like a fool, I try to talk some sense into them and go like, no, it's really beautiful and all that. So what do they do but repeat everything I said at school the next day. Out of context, it sounds pretty weird and I get this ferocious phone call from their teacher who does everything but come right out and call me a pervert. And so I go, Look, lady, I'm trying to raise three kids here on my own and I'm trying to do the best job I can and if you got any suggestions, well, you can...shove 'em!"

Evan then crossed his arms over his chest with a triumphant smile and added: "I didn't get called to drive on any more field trips after that."

BY THE FIFTH day of my convalescence, the swelling had reduced to the point I would soon be able to go back to the clinic for a real cast. I was excited to reach this point, it meant the dependence on the crutches would cease and I would be able to walk, drive the car and just generally rejoin the human race.

A part of me enjoyed being an invalid, though, thanks largely to Team Allender. Evan spent every night with me and the girls visited often, pedaling up the mountain to Leap Year on their little bikes. I worried I was reaching the end of the lease on my nine-day-wonder status, but their interest in me continued.

One afternoon, Reilly paid a call. He brought a sack of cinnamon rolls and a thermos of mocha latte from the Tenmile Cafe, compliments of Marlena who had heard all about my accident. She had given Reilly a job on the evening shift, washing dishes and bussing tables. That was the reason Evan had been coming up later to see me. He had to wait for Reilly to get home from work.

He said he liked his new job, but I wondered how anyone could like a job like that. I assumed the main attraction was proximity to Marlena. I decided, on the basis of one freshman course in Psychology, that Reilly was probably looking for a mother figure since his childhood had been so lacking in one. Then again, Marlena struck me as way too sexy to be anyone's idea of a mother figure.

"Dad can't stop talking about you," Reilly said with a coy smile and raised eyebrows. He was pacing around my room, he had refused to sit down. I don't think he was comfortable being in my bedroom. I had feared the conversation would head toward my new affair with his father and I had no concept of how to deal with it.

"That's nice." I tried to play it cool without coming off bitchy.

"So things are getting pretty serious, huh?" His voice and smile had almost a cat-and-mouse quality to them. His pacing was getting on my nerves. "I mean, the old man doesn't show up for too many breakfasts at our house anymore."

"I know what you mean, Reilly." My tone was cold now.

"The twins told me the Viking called last night before he left for your place. They said for once he didn't ask her when she was coming home. Sounds like she's history to me, what do you think?"

"I think I'd rather not talk about this."

"Suit yourself...just trying to help." He helped me eat the cinnamon rolls and finally left.

Reilly's matchmaking attempts took a more ominous turn the following day when the twins were on one of their visits. Winter was playing in one of the abandoned houses—Evan had already evaluated them and decided which ones were in strong enough condition to pose no danger of collapse. Summer was going out to join her, but paused at my door for a moment and turned to ask, "Darcy, does Leap Year have more than one street?"

"Just the one now. That's all that's left."

"And it's just called Main Street, right?" She looked confused, even troubled.

"As far as I know. Why do you ask?"

"Oh, nothing. It was just something Reilly said, it's nothing."

"You don't act like it's nothing..."

Summer smiled gravely. "He just said that if Daddy married you, we'd all live on Easy Street. I assumed that was somewhere in Leap Year, but I didn't know where."

What an odd, old-fashioned expression for an eighteen-year-old to use. Maybe he heard it on a movie or maybe he heard it from Marlena. He was certainly off base if he thought I had lots of money. Inheriting a town sounds a lot better than it really is. In truth, I didn't have much money at all. I was living on a small sum I had gleaned from the division of the meager assets I shared with Keith. I began the summer with exactly $3,412 in my account. I quit my job at the Randall Gallery, so I was proverbially working without a financial net, counting on making some money from the sale of Leap Year.

I had very carefully considered my finances before leaving home. I thought if I lived frugally, I could surely get through the summer without working. This extended vacation was my gift to myself after the divorce. Of course, my bank balance had dropped a lot since then, what with airline tickets, car rental, then all the miscellaneous expenses to bring Grady's house up to speed. I knew I was going to get hit with some medical bills for the accident—I had no insurance—but how much could a broken foot cost anyway? Two-fifty? Three hundred? I'd never had any real medical bills before.

"I think he was just making a joke, Summer. Besides, it's too soon to talk about things like marriage. I've only known your dad a few weeks, not even a whole month."

Summer came back into the room and sat down on the bed. "Greta's clothes are still in the closet in his room. I kind of don't think she's coming back now. Reilly says she's not." She looked up at me. "I don't think Greta's clothes would fit you. She's taller than you and really skinny."

Not to mention the fact that my breasts are bigger. I felt sad and awful having this odd conversation with this little girl about the women in her father's life.

She looked more pensive still. "I don't think my mom is ever going to live with us again. She and Dad don't get along at all. Whenever she comes to pick us up and Dad's around, she gets real tense and they say mean things to each other. She says she wants us to come and live with her sometime when she gets her life together, but I don't think that's going to happen anytime soon."

"I'm sorry."

Summer shrugged. "It's okay. What I wanted to tell you was that if you wanted to move in with us, it would be okay. It would be nice to have a girl in the house again. Girls are easy to live with—they don't leave the toilet seat up."

I nodded quietly in agreement. She then jumped up from the bed and said she'd see me later. Before she left the room, she remembered something and pulled a crumpled piece of paper out of her shorts pocket. I knew what it was instantly, without being told.

"Darcy, is this more of that letter from Grady? We found it yesterday when we were sorting that pile of stuff you asked us to." I had started paying the girls two bucks an hour to search through Grady's endless reams of papers for interesting stuff. They had previously lost interest in their jobs after about twenty minutes each, but at least they had managed to hit pay dirt.

"Oh, this is great!" I beamed with delight and thanked her over and over. She left with a proud smile on her face and I read more of Grady's parent's story.

Chapter Eight

Nearly six months passed before my parents' paths crossed again. My mother was a determined woman and not at all the sort to let a bad beginning stand in the way of what she wanted. My poor father probably had no inkling of what he was up against...

FOR THREE weeks in January Leap Year was snowed in. The storms would not let up long enough for even a single supply wagon or mail delivery—which came only once a week under the best of conditions—to make it up the tortuous switchbacks. Work at the mines was slowed by the numerous avalanches often swallowing up the mine entrances, or adits, as they were called.

Conor took a bad chest cold that kept him in bed for a week with a fever and a terrible, rattling cough. He had no idea the danger he was in. A congestion of the lungs, however trifling it may start out, could quickly turn fatal at such a high altitude. The ever-devoted Angel insisted on nursing him and he was too weak to resist her efforts. He soon became grateful for the broth she brought him three times a day and the foul-smelling, but effective, poultices she applied to his chest each morning. He recovered quickly under her care. With his fever gone and his cough less frequent, he advised her one morning that he no longer required a poultice.

"Don't be silly, Mr. McAllister, of course you do." She was already unbuttoning his long johns down his chest. He had gotten used to her seeing him in his underwear. Besides, of what use was modesty when dealing with a prostitute? One did not think twice about disrobing in the presence of one's doctor. A professional distance was simply assumed.

"I'm fine now. Much better, I assure you." His voice was still half an octave lower than normal.

"Well, I guess so," grinned Angel, noticing with her trained eye that Conor had an erection. She quickly continued to unbutton his underwear, not stopping at the waist this time.

"*Angel*," Conor half-heartedly protested, grinning and turning red with embarrassment. "You shouldn't...you mustn't—"

She had already taken him into her well-practiced hand. "Now, Mr. McAllister, your head may be sayin' 'no,' but the rest of you is sayin' somethin' else entirely."

He couldn't argue with this—he was as hard as a rock. Still, he knew if he let her do this, there would be no getting rid of her the rest of the winter. He thought quickly. "I...I wouldn't want to lose my very high regard for you."

In all of Angel's twenty-three years, no one had ever threatened her with respect. She was stunned. She didn't know what to say. She removed her hand from his underwear and stared at him. All the commotion triggered a convulsive coughing fit for Conor, which provided a needed diversion from the awkward situation. Angel left his room looking more moony and love struck than ever. Conor mentally congratulated himself on proving old Mrs. Barrett wrong: He did know how to say 'no.'

But what will I do about you? he said in his thoughts to the erection still poking out of his underwear. He decided to finish what Angel had started, thinking with a smirk, how often the school masters had warned the boys of the dangers of self-abuse. He, like all boys everywhere, had concluded, under the covers late at night, that blindness and insanity were a small price to pay.

Thoughts of school inevitably triggered memories of the classics tutor so he had to concentrate on something else quickly lest he spoil the mood. He decided to focus on the afternoon he had spent with the girl at the company picnic. His imagination drifted back to that breezy summer day, the tall, sweet-smelling grass, the plaid wool picnic blanket warmed by the late day sun. But instead of the girl's face he saw that of Elodie Kelly. It was Elodie smiling up at him from that blanket, reaching out for him, slowly parting her thighs for him, Elodie, with a mysterious smile on her face, whispering, *You're trapped.*

Why on earth did I think of *her*? he wondered afterwards, as he tried to figure out how to clean up the sticky semen now pooling around his navel without having to get out of bed. He settled on using a corner of his bed sheet. Then he started coughing again.

The short days and long nights of winter wore on. The cold made it easy to avoid contact with the young Widow Kelly. Conor was determined to keep a wide berth from the woman, even if she had rarely left his thoughts over the long, snowy months. He kept to his work and spent odd hours at the saloon. He knew he was probably drinking too much, but there was often little else to do most days. He sometimes played cards with the miners when he could get into a friendly game for matchsticks. He didn't have the money for any serious gambling. The only time he was in danger of running into to her was on visits to the mercantile. He always glanced about before entering the store to make sure the territory was clear.

He had been so successful at avoiding her that by the end of February, he was forced to conclude she was avoiding him as well and this thought was something of a relief. He caught glimpses of her now and then. That much was impossible to escape. Leap Year was too small to go for long without seeing nearly the entire population at one time or another, though the cold kept them inside more. She was usually in the company of one or more of her children. She had the new baby often strapped to her chest with a large woolen shawl. He still found himself wondering, at times like that, just who the baby's father might have been. She was never in the company of any man. Of course, he felt he knew a great deal more about her morals since their night together. An illegitimate child should come as no great surprise.

His disdain for this woman knew no limits. The shame and humiliation of what had transpired between them was at times almost too much for Conor to bear. Still, he could not purge himself of memories of that night. It was difficult to forget the strangest and most erotic event of his entire thirty years. Sometimes he even drew sketches of her when he was alone in his room. Sometimes he did portraits of her face, sometimes full figures, both clothed and unclothed. He had to invent the details, of course, for he had never actually seen any part of her body except her face and arms. He had touched her, touched nearly every part of her, but only in total darkness. He always destroyed the pictures the morning after creating them. Just looking at them in the cold light of day filled him with guilt and mortification.

In spite of his efforts, one sunny, frigid day when the snow was reflecting so brightly it hurt one's eyes to look at it, he stepped out onto the frozen sidewalk and directly into the path of Elodie Kelly, who firmly stood her ground.

"Good day to you, Mr. McAllister."

Conor tried to sidestep, without replying, but she anticipated his move and was once again in his path.

"*Good day to you*, Mr. McAllister."

Conor sighed in exasperation. At least she had not addressed him by his first name. "Good day, Mrs. Kelly. Would you mind letting me pass?"

"Perhaps I would mind, Mr. McAllister." Her tone was arch. For once, she was not accompanied by any of her many children. "I do not understand what wrong I have done to you that is so great you cannot even be civil to me."

Conor glanced around to see who might be observing him engaged in conversation with this woman. To his relief, no one was close by. He looked at the ground, then at the street, then somewhere above Elodie's head—anywhere at all to avoid looking her in the eye. In a terse voice that he struggled to keep low, he angrily responded to her boldness. "Mrs. Kelly, if you have even an ounce of decency or dignity left, I would assume you would wish to do as I do and pretend that the night we spent together never occurred."

"Excuse me, Mr. McAllister, but I do not recall holding a gun to your head and forcing you to do anything against your will."

She had him on this point, but he would not concede. "I was...I was intoxicated and...and..."

"Lonely."

The word stung him. He hated hearing it because it was true. How could this woman who was nearly a stranger to him know so much about him? Lust may have gotten him into her bed, but aching loneliness had kept him there. Falling asleep holding her warm body next to his had been the most satisfying thing that had happened to him in nearly three miserable years. He refused to be further humiliated by this irritating woman. He muttered "Good day," through clenched teeth, turned on his heel and walked in the opposite direction, leaving her standing there on the icy sidewalk in that frozen sunshine.

Chapter Nine

CAST DAY arrived at last. Evan drove me down into town to the clinic.

"What color do you want?" Nurse Reno asked. She presented me with a surprising array of color choices for my cast.

"You'd look good in pink," Evan offered.

"Pink would clash with a lot of my wardrobe." I was only half-serious.

"Fashion cannot be denied," Mrs. Reno asserted, with mock professionalism. "Choose carefully, you have to live with this thing for the next six weeks."

I was down to blue versus lavender. The lavender had too much purple in it, so I opted for the blue.

"Well, God forbid she should take my opinion on anything," Evan complained, pretending to pout.

Mrs. Reno smiled at Evan's carrying on and began the work of applying my walking cast. She forced my foot into the correct flex of ankle which unexpectedly caused me a lot of pain. I drew in my breath and Evan took my hand in his and let me squeeze it. I wondered if he had held Sandy's or Beth's hands when they were in labor. Then I remembered the twins' story about Sandy and the commune and the chanting and I almost laughed. I had asked Evan about this story and he had confirmed every word. He shrugged it off with: "It was the Seventies—what can I say?"

Evan surprised me in his willingness to act like we were a couple at the clinic. I had not been invited back to his house since the day we became lovers. Nor did he take me out to restaurants or other public places. I felt peevishly like the Other Woman, even though Greta was nowhere in sight.

When the cast was completed, Mrs. Reno told me I could put my weight on the foot as soon as I could do so without pain. "Let the pain be your guide, dear." Until then, I had to stay on crutches, though I was now down to one crutch.

Evan picked up a six-pack of beer and a frozen pizza to celebrate this new stage in my convalescence. We drove up to Leap Year and arrived by six. Evan said he could stay the evening as well as the night because it was Reilly's day off.

I popped the frozen pizza in the oven, happily noticing my growing freedom of movement, as I maneuvered about the kitchen with the aid of one crutch and occasionally placing weight lightly on my injured foot. I stood at the sink gazing out the window watching the sun sink behind the mountains. Evan came up behind me and began fondling my breasts and kissing my neck. I knew this meant he wanted to make love, immediately, as in, on the kitchen floor.

We were on knees-and-elbows doing just that when something extraordinary happened—my telephone rang.

"My phone is ringing!" I cried, stupidly stating the obvious. I had raised my head sharply, bumping Evan's chin in the process.

"Don't answer it," Evan whispered tersely, still on task, as they say.

"But I've got to—"

"No, no—I'm so close," he whined.

"Evan," I pleaded, "it's my first phone call." I tried to wriggle out from under him, but he grabbed my elbows and laid his full weight on me to block my escape.

"It's just the phone company calling to tell you that you've got...service," he panted. "We can't stop now—"

The phone kept ringing. Keep ringing...keep ringing...I prayed. Evan...damn you...hurry up! I got one arm free and began reaching for the phone cord. The telephone hung on the wall and the long coiled cord reached nearly to the floor. My fingers were only inches from it. Evan was moaning, finally coming, when I made one last swipe and grabbed the cord. The receiver fell to the floor and bounced. Evan jerked in surprise, then rolled off of me.

In as normal a voice as I could muster, I answered the phone.

A woman's low voice, in heavily accented English said: "I am seeking Evan Allender. Is he there, please?"

"It's for you."

Evan raised his head off the floor. "One of my kids?"

I covered the mouthpiece with the palm of my hand. "Someone with a Swedish accent."

Evan sat bolt upright, looking scared. "Oh, shit," he whispered, taking the receiver. With his free hand, he pulled off the condom and threw it on the floor. He struggled to yank his shorts back up.

I quietly left the kitchen and went upstairs to afford him some privacy. On the way up the stairs—which I now managed so much more easily—I heard him say, angrily: "What do you mean—'I sound like I just had sex'?"

I cleaned up and got dressed, then sat on my bed waiting for their conversation to end. I waited a long time and didn't hear much. Greta did most of the talking. Evan made a few "uh-huh's" and "Yeah, I guess so's" and finally some "okay's."

Just as darkness fell across the room, I heard the receiver click. Evan climbed up the stairs slowly and entered the bedroom looking like someone had died.

"Life just keeps happening to me," he announced mournfully. He lay down on the bed and stared at the ceiling.

"What is it?"

He sighed. "She's left me."

"She found out about us?"

"I suppose, but that's not it." He sat up, frowning, starting to look both miserable and angry. "She's found someone else."

"Oh," I said, trying to be sympathetic, but really fighting the urge to jump up and down at the prospect of graduating from Other Woman to Main Squeeze.

"Nineteen," he said, looking angrier. "*Nineteen*. She's left me for a god damned nineteen-year-old. One of her students. It turns out her roommate 'Chris' was short for Christopher, not Christine. No wonder *Chris* never answered the phone."

I awkwardly patted his shoulder.

"Nineteen. A year older than Reilly. I can't believe it." He shook his head, then added with great bitterness, "He's probably better than I am in bed. Hell, at nineteen, *I* was better than I am in bed." He flopped back down and stared at the ceiling once again.

I tried to imagine someone better in bed than Evan and couldn't. He let out another plaintive groan and I knew we were in for a regular whine-fest.

"How could she do this to me? Dumping me for a kid?"

I wanted to say—"you have me"—but I knew if I needed to point this out to him, it wasn't worth much.

Evan mournfully began a litany of everything that was wrong with his life. "My girlfriend leaves me for a kid a year older than my own son...my hairline is receding...I don't wake up with erections as often as I used to...I'm never going to finish my house...my truck needs a new transmission."

I put my arms around him and lay my head on his chest, trying to comfort him, but got no response. I sat up, thinking I smelled smoke.

An ear-piercing siren went off—the kitchen smoke alarm.

"Oh, my God—we forgot the pizza!"

Evan jumped out of bed and ran downstairs. I followed, more slowly, hobbling my best.

The kitchen was filled with smoke. Evan whacked on the smoke alarm to shut it off—possibly breaking it in the process. He tried to pull the blackened pizza from the oven, forgot a hot pad, burnt his hand, cursed, got a towel and threw the pizza into the sink and turned on the water. I opened the living room windows and Evan opened the window over the sink. He joined me in the living room.

"I told you not to answer the damned phone," he joked with a half-hearted smile. He walked over to me and we hugged. "Let's go out to eat."

He started to fetch my crutch, but I said no, I was going to force myself to walk on the cast. I still had to go gingerly, but was able to get out to his car on my own. I was elated to finally be "taken out." This seemed to confirm my new status as the former Other Woman.

Evan drove silently, still morose. As we neared his house he looked alarmed and said, "What the hell is this?" The house was completely dark, though it was only nine-thirty. He swung the truck into the yard to investigate.

We both got out of the car. Evan helped me walk by putting his arm around my waist. He opened the front door and flipped on the light.

There on the couch were Reilly and Marlena, making out like a couple of teenagers. They sat up in a hurry, blinking their eyes against the sudden brightness. They were still dressed, but this looked like a temporary circumstance.

"What the hell is going on?" Evan demanded like fathers have done from the beginning of time.

"Jeez, Dad...uh..."

"Hello, Evan," said Marlena, uncomfortably.

"I think I'll just wait in the car," I mumbled, taking the coward's way out. I slipped out from under Evan's arm and limped out to the truck.

I couldn't hear what was being said, but after a couple of minutes, Evan shouted, "Well, don't let me interrupt anything!" Then he slammed the front door and stormed out to rejoin me.

"What's up?" I asked tentatively.

"You mean besides Reilly's dick?"

"Evan...calm down."

"I thought we were gonna get something to eat," he practically yelled.

I wanted to tell him to back off, but thought silence was a safer choice.

"That horny cow," Evan fumed. "I thought she was cradle robbing when she was fucking *me*!"

It seemed to take forever to reach Columbine. By the time we pulled into the parking lot of the Tenmile Cafe—which seemed an ironic choice for the evening repast—Evan's anger had cooled to a low boil.

A young waiter came over to take our order. He greeted Evan by name. I still could not get used to the concept that everyone knew everyone. I was too used to the anonymity big cities automatically provide. I thought this intimacy was nice, yet had to be suffocating now and then.

I ordered scrambled eggs and pancakes. Evan studied the menu a long time, then announced he wanted a double cheeseburger with everything on it.

"A cheeseburger, really?" asked the young waiter in surprise. I assumed he was used to Evan's vegetarianism and was as astonished as I was at this sudden conversion.

"You got a problem with that, pal?" Evan glared at the boy and looked like he was ready to start a fist fight.

"Hey, no, man, anything you want." The boy scurried off.

I put my hands on the table and stretched them out to Evan, who took them in his hands. I asked where the twins were and he said Reilly had talked them into spending the night with one of their girlfriends in Columbine. Then he stared forlornly out the window and repeated, *"Life just keeps happening to me."*

The waiter brought our food. I began to eat, but Evan sat staring at his burger.

"I haven't eaten meat in three years," he said with an odd expression on his face. At that moment, I realized this cheeseburger was an act of defiance against the fickle Greta. Evan raised the burger to his mouth and reluctantly took a bite. He started to chew, then stopped, then started again. Suddenly, he looked at me with a mixture of nausea and panic on his face. He jumped up and bolted from the restaurant.

I looked out the window to the neon lit parking lot to see him bent over, vomiting. This had not been Evan's best day.

THE BEST thing about having an impotent lover is that you get to find out quickly if the attraction was only physical. Evan moped around for a week after Greta's kiss-off call. He would stop by each day to see how I was doing and then just sit around. Eventually, the talk would dry up and he would leave. I made a couple of attempts to entice him into bed, but he would morosely shrug and say, "I guess I'm out of order."

Greta found out what hours he was working and drove up and removed all her belongings from of the house when he wasn't there. He came home from work one day and found half the bedroom closet empty. According to the twins, he sat in the closet and cried for half an hour. The girls were upset by that and crawled into the closet with him and talked him into taking them out for pizza.

He suggested they invite me to eat pizza with them. They didn't object, so they picked me up on their way. The twins told me the closet story while Evan was ordering the pizza at the counter. They were worried about him and so was I. I was worried about *us*—that maybe there wasn't going to be an 'us' anymore. And I was tormented by jealousy that he was taking this breakup with the 'the Viking' so hard.

The girls chattered throughout the meal, but Evan listlessly ate his pizza and stared out the window into the parking lot, as though he were either looking for someone or worried that his truck was being stolen.

I told them about my new research project on Leap Year, how I was determined to find out about the Hidden Vein. I was spurred on by the continuing discovery of pages to Grady's letter, but fearful I was never going to find them all. I had convinced myself the Hidden Vein existed, that it was more than just an interesting local myth. I thought I could trust Grady's letter for that much, at least. The twins chimed in that they, too, were certain it was real and even Evan concurred.

I spent every afternoon of the previous week at the county library, usually arriving just ahead of the daily afternoon thunder storm. On the first day, I made the acquaintance of the librarian, a plump and pleasant woman in her early thirties, named Vonda. She brought her two-year-old son, Cody, to work with her every day. She said the county didn't pay her enough to afford a babysitter, so if they didn't like it, they could get a new librarian.

When she told me all this, I smiled and nodded sympathetically, as she tried to get Cody interested in something besides pulling books off the bottom shelf nearby. I thought about how Keith had once complained when a fellow classmate brought her young child to the law library one afternoon because she needed to study for finals and the child's grandmother, her usual sitter, was ill. Keith had thrown a fit and gotten the woman expelled to another part of the library because, even though the child was being quiet, its very presence was interfering with his precious concentration. Keith was such a jerk.

I told Vonda I was interested in local history, particularly Leap Year. She said it was too bad I had not come the summer before and could have talked to "old Miss McAllister." I chuckled and confessed I was her great-niece.

"Oh, you're our heiress," Vonda exclaimed, calling me the "heiress" just like Marlena had that first day. I felt like a local celebrity. She directed me to the shelf on Colorado history and I asked if there might be anything specifically on the Hidden Vein.

"Oh, you won't find anything about that in any of the traditional history books. That's just based on rumor and speculation."

"But how did the rumors get started?"

"Well, it had to do with Miss McAllister's mother. Her name—before she married Miss McAllister's father—was Elodie Kelly. Her first husband was a miner for the Northern Star. Well, he got killed in a mine collapse, but everybody thought he had found some gold before he died. I don't know why."

That sounded like pretty specious evidence to me, but who was I to judge? I asked Vonda if there were any books just on the Northern Star Mine. She said she knew of one and went to look for it. She returned empty-handed and puzzled. The book was absent from the shelf, yet the computer system did not show it had been checked out. She decided it had either been mis-shelved or somebody had walked out with it. She did find a short book on the owner of the Northern Star, Gideon Reynolds. The author's name caught my immediate attention: Conor McAllister.

After giving Cody a snack, Vonda showed me how to operate the microfilm machine which would allow me to read old Columbine newspapers from the era. Vonda insisted on bringing me a stool to prop up my cast. She was being such a dear, fussing over me as much as Cody. I then realized I was the only patron in the library all afternoon. She probably welcomed having another adult to talk to for a diversion.

"WHAT HAVE you learned so far?" Evan asked, finally taking an interest in my conversation with the twins as we finished our pizza.

"Not a lot, really. I read an old newspaper account of the big mine cave-in that killed Kyle Kelly. They think it was caused by an earthquake. I thought that was cool—I don't know why. I'm not sure I can trust everything I read in this paper. They devoted about as much space to the possibility of an earthquake as they did to a discussion of whether or not Tommyknockers were real."

Evan and the girls laughed at this, the first sign Evan's mood was improving. On the way home, though, he threw me a curve. "Hey, girls, what do you say we have Darcy sleep over at our house tonight?"

The girls said "sure" and "okay," while I made furious faces at Evan and pinched his elbow to indicate I thought this was a terrible idea.

"I don't have my toothbrush," I said, trying to make up an excuse for the girls' benefit.

"We won't tell your mother," said Evan. He seemed to be in a slightly better mood since dinner.

We reached their house and the girls got out of the truck. I held Evan back.

"I don't feel comfortable with this, Evan. You could have talked to me first."

"What's wrong? I mean, now we don't have to worry about you-know-who showing up. It'll be cool."

"That's not it. I just don't feel right about sleeping with you in front of your kids."

"That's why bedroom doors have locks on them, Darcy. And, I mean, it's not like I've never brought a date home, you know?" He kissed my forehead and flippantly added: "Just don't scream too loud when I make you come." He got out of the truck and waited for me to follow.

I sighed and got out, unable to deny him as usual, ever the good lap dog. At least he was talking like he wanted to make love again. I had feared he had lost interest in me.

We watched television for a while, then the twins went to bed. I saw them running to and from their bedroom to the bathroom to brush their teeth. Both were as naked as little wood sprites. I had the feeling I had entered the Woodstock Zone again.

I turned my attention to the guitars on their stands and asked Evan if he would play something. He said he wasn't in the mood and wasn't in practice, but after some coaxing, he picked up the acoustic guitar and began to play little snatches of this and that. He was good. I don't know why this surprised me.

He told me about the various bands he'd been in. The most successful had been a four-piece group called "Magical Thinking". I asked what sort of music they played.

"Covers, mostly," he said. "We could do R&B, rock, country, pop—anything they'd pay us to play. We were complete whores." He said he left the band several years ago, but didn't elaborate.

With a somewhat wistful smile, he put the guitar back on its stand and said, "It's time for bed."

His bedroom was small, too small for the big framed bed of chinked pine logs. It was just like beds I'd seen in decorating magazines only he had made it himself "for nothing" as opposed to the thousands of dollars these beds sold for in trendy stores.

We undressed and climbed in. I still felt ill-at-ease, knowing the girls were just on the other side of the wall. Evan was not similarly inhibited. He took me in his arms and began kissing me—the first real affection since the Fatal Phone Call. Then his eyes widened and he smiled. "I've got a surprise for you." An erection. His wayward virility had returned. We smiled at each other as he began to make love to me.

Then he stopped abruptly. "I forgot..."

"Forgot what?"

"You know...you know..."

I knew. He was talking about a condom. Although he used them religiously, he could not bring himself to ever actually say the word. "It's okay...don't stop now."

"You sure?"

I mentally calculated my cycle. My period was due in a couple of days. I felt certain there was no danger of pregnancy. "I'm sure."

"God, it feels so good," he whispered. "Darcy, I love you."

"I love you, too." At that moment, I didn't care if I got pregnant. I was ready to live in this awful trailer and have ten kids if Evan asked me to.

Afterward, I lay in his arms with my head on his chest. Pregnancy was on my brain. If I got pregnant, would I keep it or abort? "Evan, did having kids make you change your views on abortion?" I had always wondered this, but had never felt comfortable asking anyone before.

"I never had any views on abortion."

"None?"

"Well...I don't know...abortion, abortion—I caused two."

I sat up and looked down at him. The full moon lit the room with an eerie gray light. "Really?"

"So...what? I'm a criminal now?" His tone was almost defensive.

"I'm just curious, that's all. I just want to know everything about you. You've lived so much compared to me."

"Does that mean I'm worldly or just fucked up?"

"It means—I don't know—you're interesting." I wanted to flatter him.

Evan sighed. "Okay...here's the abortion story. It's not that interesting." He shrugged. "Beth got pregnant six months after the twins were born. We were among the small percentage of Really Stupid People who thought breast feeding was a form of natural birth control—big mistake. She said 'no way' was she gonna have another one so soon. We were still so overwhelmed with the twins and Reilly was dealing us fits—I think he didn't like all the attention the twins got. Anyway, the decision was easy—if decisions like that are ever easy. I don't think Beth ever looked back. I know I sure didn't."

"And the other one?"

Evan twisted his mouth with disgust. "That was somebody...somebody in between Beth and Greta." He sighed angrily. "I got hornswoggled on that deal."

Hornswoggled? Once again I felt the need for a Western-English dictionary.

"She told me she was on the Pill. Turns out she decided getting knocked up was a fast track to the altar." He shook his head with a bitter smile. "Not with this boy. I had to practically arm wrestle her into getting it—the abortion, I mean, but she eventually did it. Not one of my proudest moments."

He sighed angrily. "I was so mad I swore never to get myself in that situation again. I went down to a doctor in Brownleaf to get the Big V."

"Vasectomy?" I asked in awe.

"He talked me out of it. Said I was way too young—like it was any of his business. He said, 'Use condoms, stupid.' So I do. Have ever since. Can't say as I really like it, but it beats the alternative."

I smiled to myself, thinking how I assumed he used condoms to impress me with his caring concern, when all the while he had only his own self-interest at heart. Oh, well, I won either way.

We lay quietly for a while. Then he asked why I wasn't sharing any "awful stuff" from my past. I told him that aside from being briefly married to a jerk, I didn't have much to tell. "His name was Keith. He chopped up my heart and ate it for lunch."

"Well, I hope it gave him indigestion," offered Evan thoughtfully.

"I guess I could tell you the weird story about my father."

"Sounds juicy—let's hear it."

I sighed, both hating and wanting to tell this. "Until two years ago, my dad was this completely predictable guy. Very successful. He was the senior vice-president for one of the largest insurance companies in the nation. He and my mom had this nice ordinary life together and then one day—wham!—he just quits his job and announces he's going off to 'see the world'. The next thing we know, he's calling from New York to say good bye, that he's joined the merchant marine and he's going to be a cook on a freighter bound for Lisbon. Since then, he's been all over—Bangkok, Taiwan, Tokyo. The last time I heard from him he was in Marrakesh teaching some wealthy French family how to play tennis."

"Cool," said Evan appreciatively.

I had half expected this reaction from him. "It's not too cool when you're the one who gets deserted. This has nearly killed my mother. She still has no idea what motivated it. If he had left her for another woman, she wouldn't have liked it, but she could have understood it. But this...?" I raised my hand in a hopeless gesture. "Mid-life crisis? Searching for his inner child? Pick your psychobabble flavor of the month, I guess. Someday reality is going to reel him back in. I just hope my sister and mother and I can hang on until that happens."

I lay back down with my head on Evan's chest. I was tired. Telling family secrets was exhausting work. I had this awful, secret fear that someday reality was going to reel *me* back in. This fear came on me every time I got too happy.

"Did you tell your mother yet about your accident?"

"I called her before we left for the diner. She wasn't home so I left my new phone number on her machine. I'm just dreading that phone call. I know she'll make me come home."

Evan laughed in disbelief. "*Make* you come home? Are you kidding, Darcy? You're a grown woman—"

"I'm still twelve, according to her."

"She can't *make* you do anything. Tell her I said so."

"You don't know my mother," I teased. "My whole family thinks I'm completely inept. They even think the divorce was somehow all my fault—you know, like, "Poor, pitiful Darcy—she can't even manage to stay married.""

"Fuck them!"

"Yeah, you know, you're right. Fuck them!" Evan was making me feel good about myself. When was the last time someone had done that?

Evan spoke a little bit about his family, but just a thumbnail sketch. His father had been a cardiologist and Evan found gallows humor in the irony that he had died at fifty-six of a heart attack, never having taken any of his own professional advice. His two older brothers he described as "robo-yuppies." The oldest was the favorite son, the golden boy who had followed his dad into cardiology. The other was an investment banker for whom making money had become "a sacred, religious act."

Evan candidly admitted he had never been "college material"—a fact which bothered him less than it had his family. But he never regretted the choices he had made, especially in light of the fact that both his brothers were "drinking Maalox for breakfast by the time they were thirty."

His younger sister was a veterinarian. Although she, too, was a professional, she had managed to still be "cool" in spite of this defect in her character. His mother was "cool", too, even though she has "never missed out on an opportunity to tell me just how bad I've fucked up my life."

"Do you worry about Beth trying to take you to court, you know, like a custody battle?" I had heard a radio talk show discussing this very issue. They said it was in current vogue for vindictive ex-spouses to allege child molestation in order to wrest custody of the children back.

"Beth? Take me to court? Hell, no," Evan laughed. "Compared to her, I'm normal."

"What's wrong with Beth?"

Evan responded by pressing his finger against one of his nostrils and making a loud snorting noise. "She's got a real problem. How she passes the drug screenings her airline gives, I'll never know."

He smiled and pulled me close to him. "You're so damned sensible compared to all the other women I've been involved with. How did I ever get this lucky? I think Grady planned this, somehow."

I sighed. Good Old Ms. Normal and Boring. At least I had at last found someone to appreciate me.

THE NEXT morning I awoke just after dawn to find that my period had started. I had spent all night preoccupied with pregnancy and abortion for nothing! Of course, I had no tampons or anything to cope with it. There was already a bloodstain the size of a fist on the bed sheet—very embarrassing—so I was forced to wake up Evan and tell him my dilemma. We went off to the bathroom in search of anything Greta might have left behind. He tore through the medicine cabinet and the vanity under the sink to no avail.

He sat on the bathroom floor and looked up at me in exasperation. "She took everything. Even the aspirin! You know, she was really so cheap. I mean, we used to share all the expenses fifty-fifty and she used to keep track of what everybody ate!"

I didn't like talking about Greta, so I interrupted, telling him not to worry about my problem—that I would improvise with Kleenex or something until he took me home. He stood up with a feisty look on his face and suggested we return to bed.

I hesitated. "Are you sure you want to...I mean—"

He grabbed a couple of towels and told me making love to a bleeding woman turned him on in a "primal, voodoo, howling-at-the-moon sort of way." Mr. Uninhibited. I just rolled my eyes.

Much later, the twins made breakfast—French toast. This was the Allender breakfast of choice. Then Evan drove me home on his way to work. I was oddly depressed that I wasn't pregnant. But the mere fact that I was feeling this way scared me. Was I hearing my biological clock ticking for the first time?

To get my mind off babies and love affairs coming too soon after divorces, I drove down to the county library, as usual. I had become such a regular, I was starting to stay with Cody during his nap time so Vonda could sneak out for a quick errand. Today she was going to get her hair trimmed.

I settled in at my place before the microfilm machine, just as the brief thunderstorm began to rattle through. I hoped the sound of the storm would not awaken Cody. I lazily watched the rain blur the view from my window as it washed down the pane. I felt such a strange and pleasing contentment. My eyes wandered back to my screen and suddenly caught a byline—the name Conor McAllister popped into view. The article was an amusing story about some people who had gotten lost in a blizzard.

As I read the account with new interest, I thought for a moment about how most of the stories I had been reading by the other reporters had always been so melodramatic and serious. This newspaper story, which had as much potential for melodrama as any, instead focused on the humorous aspects of these hapless people and their plight. I decided immediately that I liked this Conor McAllister, and not just because we were related.

At the end of the article, I noticed an important tagline—it said the article was being reprinted with permission from another paper called the "Tuesday Gazette" in *Philadelphia, Pennsylvania.*

Chapter Ten

My parents might never have met again had it not been for the sudden appearance of Brandon Chance's wife in town...

NO ONE knew Brandon had a wife. He had never mentioned it. Some of his friends had known him nearly ten years and did not know this. In fact, he generally talked down the institution of marriage. But the truth was he not only had a wife, but a grown son as well.

On a snowy, bright day in late March, Mrs. Hannah Chance and her son arrived in Leap Year by freight wagon, with her exclaiming, "My heavens, the snow—and it's nearly April!" She was from Texas and not used to snow at all. She had assumed that by postponing her trip until Spring she would avoid the snow altogether. When she said this to the driver of the freight wagon, he laughed and shook his head at her ignorance of the seasons in the high country.

"Lady, I been snowed on every month of the year up here." He then helped her down out of the wagon seat where she had been squeezed between him and her son for the last three hours in the drive up from Columbine and unceremoniously dumped her two valises on the dirty snow of the main street of Leap Year.

"Joshua," she cried in impatience. "Stop your gawking and help me."

Josh snapped to attention and dutifully picked up the valises. He followed behind his mother as she purposefully made her way down the wooden sidewalk which was wet with melting snow and ice. The warm March sun was diminishing the snow banks, but its work would not be done until well into June.

The first woman Hannah encountered on the street was Elodie Kelly. Elodie was on a shopping mission and had her baby strapped to her chest and her two youngest children in tow.

"Excuse me, Ma'am," said Hannah, as polite as she could, though the arduous journey to Leap Year had made her distracted and irritable. Elodie stopped and nodded. "Might you direct me to the hotel in town?"

Elodie frowned slightly. "I'm afraid there is no hotel in town at the moment. It burned down last year and has yet to be replaced." Elodie thought for a moment. "The boarding house only serves men, I'm afraid, and the saloon..." She knew no woman who spoke and dressed as finely this would even consider a saloon accommodation. In fact, no women other than the whores who worked there were allowed in. Some considered it bad luck, like the miners who thought a woman entering a mine was bad luck. The miners were a superstitious lot.

"I'm afraid we don't get many women travelers up here." Elodie concluded.

"What am I to do?" cried Hannah to no one in particular. She sank down on the valises where her son had dropped them at the beginning of the conversation with Elodie and stared at the street.

Elodie and the woman's son exchanged glances, then Elodie offered to let the pair stay at her home. She explained her son was away at school and that she had room in her own bed for Hannah.

"You would do that?" asked Hannah, gazing up at Elodie in surprise. "Help a stranger like that?"

"I'm alone myself. I suppose that makes me think kindly to other women in a similar situation."

Hannah stood up, introduced herself and gushed with gratitude at Elodie's hospitality.

"Is there a barbershop hereabouts?" asked the tall, dark-haired boy of Elodie after she and his mother discussed the arrangements for their stay at her house.

"Why would you be needing a barber, son?" asked his mother impatiently.

"I want to look my best when I meet him."

"Oh, good grief," snapped Hannah. "He's only your father."

Elodie was seriously confused now. This woman had introduced herself as Mrs. Hannah Chance—could it be that she was related to the man who owned the saloon? "Excuse me, but wouldn't you rather be staying with your...husband?"

"No, I would not," said Hannah sharply. "I have come to this horrible, remote place to conclude a business matter with my husband and wish to have no other contact with him whatsoever, thank you very much."

Elodie was taken aback by this outburst. When Hannah saw the effect of her words on her new hostess, she immediately sought to make amends. "Forgive me, please. You cannot know of all the grief I have suffered on account of my husband and just the mention of his name is enough to set my nerves on edge. It is a very long story with which I shall not bore you. I am indebted to you for your kindness."

Elodie made a gesture to indicate this was of no consequence, but was actually intrigued by the woman's remarks. The boy agreed to follow Elodie and her children home to deposit their luggage and she promised to direct him to the barbershop. Hannah, meanwhile, went off in search of her husband.

She found the Lucky Chance Saloon with no difficulty, took several deep breaths for courage, then entered the establishment. Brandy was standing behind the bar as usual, wiping out shot glasses. When he didn't immediately look up, she called in a direct voice with an arch smile she couldn't hide: "Brandon Aloyious Chance...your past has just caught up with you."

Brandon's head jerked up, as did everyone else's in the saloon. Women never entered a saloon from the street. Some saloons had ladies' rooms, but they always had secluded side entrances separate from the mens'. When Brandon saw who it was, he sat down the glass he was cleaning, frowned and placed his hands on his hips. "How the hell did you find me?"

"It's lovely to see you, too, Brandon." She walked toward the bar, deliberately oblivious to the staring eyes of all the patrons of the Lucky Chance.

Conor was one of the patrons. He wondered who this mysterious woman was and what her connection could be to Brandy. He smiled at the "Aloyious." She was an attractive woman with dark gold hair styled in the current fashion. She wore fashionable clothes as well, though they were not suited to a climate as harsh as this. From the table where he was sitting, Conor could hear only snatches of their conversation.

When Hannah reached the bar, Brandon repeated his question more softly, "How the hell did you find me?"

"Your mother told me."

Brandon snickered. "Since when have you been on speaking terms with my mother?"

"Since your father died. Or did you even know?"

"Yeah, my brother passed through here last summer on his way to California. He gave me the news." Brandon started to wipe glasses again.

Hannah glanced around the place, surveying it with a look of distaste. "Your mother feared you had sunk quite low. I see now her fears were justified."

Brandy frowned at this jibe. "So you've told me how you found me. Now tell me why."

"We have a business matter to conclude. We need a place to talk in private."

Brandon ushered Hannah into his back room. When they emerged a quarter of an hour later, neither looked pleased. Hannah sailed past Conor on her way out, allowing him to catch the scent of her perfume. Brandy resumed his position at the bar.

Conor could not contain his curiosity. He casually strode over to the bar and ordered a beer. When Brandy made no explanation of the woman's appearance in the bar, he was forced to bring up the matter himself. "A friend of yours?"

Brandon looked up sourly. "A friend? No. My wife."

Conor was stunned. "You never said you were married, Brandy."

"You don't tend to talk about the things you're bent on forgetting."

"When did all this happen?"

"When I was nineteen and stupid."

"Oh." Conor didn't know what to say next. Fortunately, Brandon was seldom at a loss for words and decided to open up.

He began with a disgusted sigh. "She wants a divorce. Got some fool that wants to marry her, so she's gotta put an end to it with me first. I told her it'd be cheaper and easier to just commit bigamy like them Mormons do. Hell, I'd never tell. But no...she's gotta do it all legal and proper." He shook his head.

"A divorce..." Conor mused. He'd never personally known anyone who'd gotten a divorce. He knew Brandon was right in saying they were difficult and costly to obtain.

"She's got a lawyer back home in Texas who wrote to a lawyer in Denver whose supposed to have it all set up. We gotta go talk to some judge there on Friday. I guess I'll oblige her. She says if I don't she's gonna sue me for not supporting her and the boy all these years."

"You have a son?" The revelations just continued.

"Yeah...I do." Brandon was smiling now. "She says she brought him. Kinda lookin' forward to seein' him. I always wondered how he turned out."

"How old is he?" Conor expected Brandon to say nine or ten.

"Let me see now." Brandon looked up to the ceiling, trying to figure. "He was born in '58 and this be '80...how old would that make him?"

"Twenty-two, if he's had his birthday."

"Born in...May." Brandon had a distant look in his eye. Just at that moment, a young man walked up to the bar.

Looking questioningly at both Conor and Brandon, he asked for "Mr. Chance?"

"At your service," said Brandon.

"I'm Josh." He nervously extended his hand. Brandon's mouth dropped open in surprise. He shook his son's hand limply, then covered his mouth with his hand, tears springing to his eyes. Brandon mumbled about needing something from the back room and dashed out.

The boy turned to Conor in confusion.

"I think he's just a little overcome by this...reunion," Conor explained.

"I didn't even know I had a father until last Christmas. My mother had told me he'd been killed in the war. I always wondered why we never had any contact with his parents, seeing as how they lived just over on the next ranch, but I guess there was a lot of bad blood between the families." The boy looked pensive as he solemnly pronounced, "Their marriage was not a successful one."

Conor nodded appreciatively. He sometimes wondered if, twenty years hence, he would have said this about his own marriage. He had loved Allison and was wretched when she died, but their marriage had not been without its problems.

Conor had been obsessed with her from the first day, from the first hour. But after their marriage, their relationship underwent a subtle change from their courting days. Allison was only docile and deferential in public. In private, she was argumentative and selfish, at least to Conor's way of thinking. The difficulties they had experienced on their wedding night set the tone for all future congress between them. Allison did not care for the physical side of marriage and she made that abundantly clear every time Conor got amorous. It was a wonder they conceived a child at all.

The hardest thing to endure was not being able to talk about this problem with anyone. His father was out of the question. His brothers were too much older and treated him already as the little brother who couldn't get anything right. His best friend, Applebee, was still a bachelor at the time and Conor was afraid he would laugh at his marital woes.

At times, Conor even wondered if Allison loved him. An idle remark he once overheard her make to her mother had almost suggested she had married him for his family's money. She wouldn't have been the first to have tried. After her death, he had felt guilty about suspecting her of these ulterior motives. He had even wondered if her dislike of physical intimacy had stemmed from her fear of childbirth—

if perhaps she had known of the danger it posed to her health.

If only she had told him about her heart problems. Abstaining to protect her health would have been far preferable to constantly feeling personally rejected. His mind suddenly left these thoughts to focus on a memory of kissing Elodie's soft mouth and how she had slowly rubbed her face against his in the darkness. Conor blinked, returning to reality.

Brandon returned from the back room all smiles and carrying a bottle of his best whiskey. He kept a private store in the back for special customers and special occasions. He opened the bottle and offered a glass to both Conor and his son. Conor had been favored with Brandy's private stock only three times previously—Christmas, New Year's, and Brandy's birthday in January when they had all been snowed in.

The three men toasted round after round to the father and son reunion. They drank until Elodie's little son, Donal, came wandering into the saloon to fetch Josh home for supper. The little boy came up to Josh and pulled on his coattail.

"Our mamas are mad," said Donal. "You're late."

"Uh-oh," said Josh, wobbly from the whiskey.

"Uh-oh," teased Conor, a bit worse for drink himself. "Brandy, you're sending the boy home to his mother drunk."

"Shame on me," laughed Brandy, pretending to be quite precious. The three men roared with drunken laughter, while little Donal stood by wondering what was so funny.

Donal then recognized Conor and said "Remember me?"

"Uh...why, of course...your name is?"

"Donal—Donal Kelly."

"Donal, of course. How are you?"

"Joe said you were going to be our new pa, but I guess he was wrong."

Brandy raised his eyebrows at this. He leaned over the bar to ask Donal exactly why brother Joe had thought Conor was to be their new father.

"He stayed the night with—"

Conor interrupted. "You're late for supper, remember?"

"Come on, kid," said Josh, good-naturedly, to little Donal. "Tomorrow, then?" he said to his father and the pair left.

Brandy was bursting with drunken mischief. "So...we stayed the night with the pretty little widow, did we?"

"There was a blizzard..." Conor knew in an instant he should never even have begun to explain. Explaining only made him look more guilty.

"You dog, you...and her out to here," teased Brandon, making the shape of a pregnant belly with his hands.

"There's nothing worse than an intoxicated barkeeper," Conor announced with sudden disdain. He was still so sensitive about what had happened that night he was unable to play the good sport about it.

He abruptly turned to leave.

"Told ya she put out more than laundry," Brandon called after him, laughing.

GRANNY ATWATER put Elodie's children to bed so that she could sit in the parlor and converse with her guest. Josh, who was a very helpful boy, volunteered to read to the children once they were in bed. The Kellys had no story books, so Josh said he would read from the newspaper he had picked up in Denver three days before. Elodie asked that he "not read them anything that would upset their slumbers." Josh laughed and said he couldn't guarantee that. Then he called, "*Bon soir, mesdames*," to his mother and his hostess.

Elodie looked to Hannah for an explanation of what he had said.

"It's French. It means 'good night'."

"Your son is quite educated, speaking two languages."

Hannah made an offhand gesture. "His baby nurse was from Haiti by way of New Orleans. She spoke almost no English when Papa bought her."

Elodie's eyes widened at this mention of a slave. She knew people who lived in the Southern United States had owned slaves before the Civil War, but she had never actually met anyone who had. At seventeen, she had come to America as a new bride just after the war ended.

"Josh spoke French before he spoke English because of dear Fleur." Hannah's face and tone of voice made it clear she did not hold Fleur 'dear' at all. How she hated the memory of almond-eyed Fleur. Fleur, with smooth skin the color of coffee with cream in it, who spoke so rarely her voice always sounded new and unfamiliar, whose small face was not pretty, like Hannah's, but exotic and mysterious, as though she were keeping a secret.

Hannah settled into the sofa with her coffee and Elodie sat in her rocker nursing her baby, Corinne, now five months old. Elodie relished having a female friend to talk to. Granny Atwater was so difficult to carry on a conversation with owing to her hearing problem.

"I feel like I should tell you the truth of why I'm here. It's just that I'm afraid you'll think the less of me."

"Speak whatever you feel. I'm the last to sit in judgement on anyone. That is a fact."

Hannah seemed to want to talk to someone. Keeping secrets was a burden to her nature. "I have come to Colorado to divorce my husband."

"I see," said Elodie, trying to sound as nonjudgmental as possible, although the mere word 'divorce' was barely uttered in polite society, not that Leap Year had a polite society.

Hannah shook her head sadly. "This is just killing my poor parents, they are so ashamed. But there is a man, a good man, who loves me and wishes me to be his wife and I want to marry him. Is this really so unforgivable?"

Elodie shook her head and then shifted the baby to nurse at the other breast.

"Brandon and I were happy once. But that was so long ago. We knew so little of life then." Hannah stirred her coffee and smiled as she reminisced. "It was romantic really—like *Romeo and Juliet*— we were the offspring of feuding landowners."

Elodie had received very little in the way of formal education and had never read Shakespeare, so the reference to *Romeo and Juliet* was lost on her. Still, she listened with interest, entertained by her new friend.

"Our fathers were ranchers of adjoining land and fought about everything—boundary lines, water rights, whose cattle strayed on to whose property. But the real cause of it all was Brandon's mother. She was an extraordinarily beautiful woman. I saw her at Christmas last—at sixty, she still can turn heads. She was the acknowledged belle of the county and my father courted her before she met Brandon's father. That was the beginning of the trouble. Do you really want to hear this?"

"Don't stop now," Elodie smiled.

"When Brandon was eighteen, he had a terrible falling out with his father—I think it was over gambling debts, I don't remember. Anyway, my father thought it would be a fine joke to give Brandon a job, just to spite his old enemy." Hannah shook her head. "He would rue that decision for all time."

"Ouch!" Elodie cried suddenly.

"What is it, Mrs. Kelly?"

Elodie smiled in embarrassment. "The little animal bit me." She felt the child's gums with her finger. "Just as I thought—a tooth on the way." She said to the child, "Shame on you. Treat your mother with more respect."

Both women laughed and Hannah said, "My Amy used to do the same thing."

"You have a daughter as well, then?"

Hannah immediately dropped her gaze. "We did have a daughter. The Lord needed her more than we did, I guess." The mention of Amy's name cast a shadow over Hannah. Her thoughts turned back to the day they buried her. It had been a pretty fall day. The leaves were gone from the trees and the flat prairie graveyard was grey and brown, but the day had been warm and sun washed. The big surprise was the arrival of Brandon's family. The whole of the Chance family had shown up, all nine of them. Hannah wondered how they had learned of Amy's death since Brandon had not had contact with them since the time of their marriage and a good deal before that. The minister—he must have told them. They didn't say anything. Just stood solemnly on the opposite side of the grave from Hannah's family. She noticed Brandon looking into his mother's impassive face before the minister asked them to bow their heads. The Chances left after the service, again without a word.

"They could have at least said something," Hannah's mother had fumed on the ride home. "It was their granddaughter, too." The remainder of the day, the house was filled with neighbors and relatives and friends. The commotion helped Hannah keep her mind off the tragedy, but later when she and Brandon were alone in their bedroom— the room that had been her room before Brandon came to share her life, the room with her parents' room on one side and her son's nursery on the other—she broke down.

Curled up in the corner of the room on the floor, she sobbed, she cried, she became nearly hysterical. She was beside herself, not with grief, but with guilt. Brandon sat on the bed, still wearing his funeral clothes. He smoked a little cigar as he sipped whiskey from a bottle he had helped himself to in his father-in-law's study. With a tired expression, he watched her fall apart.

"Hannah, honey, at some point you're just gonna have to dry up."

"Don't you understand? We did this. We're the reason Amy died. We killed her—*we* did."

"The cholera killed her. Just like its killed half this valley. It's called an epidemic and we're damned lucky Josh didn't take it as well."

Hannah shook her head emphatically. "It was us. What we did. God took Amy to punish us."

"It don't work like that, Hannah." Brandon was getting drunker and more annoyed with Hannah and her carrying on.

"She died for *our* sins, Brandy. Because of that awful thing we did."

"Oh, hell, what has that got to do with Amy? You're crazy."

"You know it's true," Hannah hissed as she rose to her feet. "I was carryin' Amy the night it happened. That voodoo witch put a curse on her."

"Leave Fleur out of this. What we did, we did because we wanted to. That's what's really botherin' you—not that you did it, but that you wanted to do it—"

Hannah snapped. She rushed over to him screaming, "How can you talk to me that way? We buried our daughter today!"

In the nursery next door, Fleur covered Josh's mouth to keep his cries from being heard. He woke up frightened by the shouting and crying coming through the wall.

In the room on the other side of Brandon and Hannah, her parents also were sitting up in bed listening to the commotion next door. All the listeners heard the loud slap of a hand against a face and the crack when a head hit a wall and a body sunk to the floor. The bedroom door slammed and heavy footsteps dashed down the stairs and out the front door.

Then there was silence, but for the soft sound of weeping.

When Hannah came to the breakfast table the next morning, her father struggled to keep his composure. Her left eye was blackened and there was a large red swelling on her cheek.

"Where is he?" her father demanded.

"He left last night and didn't come back," she said.

Her father excused himself and went out to have a chat with the ranch foreman.

When Brandon came home that afternoon still dressed in his mourning clothes, the foreman and two of the ranch hands were waiting for him. The hands came up behind him, each grabbing an arm. Then the foreman went to work, as he had been told. "I don't want to see him up and walking for a week," Hannah's father had instructed.

Hannah sat at her bedroom window and quietly watched the beating. Fleur sat in the nursery window and impassively observed from there. Hannah's parents looked on from the big veranda. When it was over, when the foreman stopped his punching, the two ranch hands dropped Brandon in a heap. He collapsed to his knees, vomited, then fell face forward into the dusty ground. Everyone else returned to their business as though nothing had happened.

"I'M SO SORRY," Elodie said, seeing that Hannah was looking depressed at the mention of her dead child. She thought to get her talking on another subject. She liked the sound of Hannah's voice, though she thought she had a funny manner of speaking. Elodie had not heard many Texas drawls before. "You said your father rued the day...?"

"He surely did," Hannah said, smiling sadly. "I guess we weren't really like Romeo and Juliet. After all, they killed themselves, and Brandy and I tried to kill each other."

Elodie chuckled, thinking this a figure of speech.

"No," said Hannah. "We really tried to kill each other. I stabbed him with a letter opener and he pushed me through the dining room window."

ELODIE KELLY was the last person Conor had expected to show up at the door to his room over the saloon. Her cheeks were red with the cold. The mountain was in the grip of a fierce spring storm that promised to dump even more snow than they had received all winter. Her brow was furrowed with alarm.

"They're lost...we must try to find them," she said.

Against his better judgment, he allowed her to enter his room. It was inappropriate to invite a woman into one's lodgings at all—not that the present landlord would mind—but this impropriety was preferable to speaking to her in the hall where anyone might see. She did not remove her woolen cape, which was covered with melting snow, so she probably would not stay long.

"Who is lost?"

Elodie finally caught her breath. "Mr. and Mrs. Chance. They left yesterday to go to Denver. Their son is in bed with a fever and couldn't make the journey—he's at my house."

"Why do you think they're lost?"

Elodie swallowed to compose herself. "Mr. Ranney of the livery stable. He came to tell the son about the two horses the Chances had hired yesterday. Well, it seems two rough types turned up at his livery this morning wanting to sell the very same animals. He recognized them immediately. He asks them where they got the horses and they say they found them in the wilderness."

Conor folded his hands across his chest and leaned against the door. The story did not look good, he had to admit. He had been cross with Brandon for teasing him, but he was genuinely concerned for him.

He considered Brandy his best friend except for Applebee.

"Does the sheriff know about this?" Leap Year did not have its own law enforcement, but the sheriff in Columbine served the whole area.

"They've sent word, but he hasn't arrived. The storm was so bad last night that travel is slow going."

"I wonder what could have become of them. I suppose they could have perished in yesterday's heavy weather and the two characters came upon their horses in the manner they claim."

"Those men stole those horses from the Chances. I can feel it in my bones, Mr. McAllister. I just pray they didn't kill them in the bargain."

"What do you propose I do about the situation?"

"We should go searching for them. If they're alive, every moment that they're out there the danger grows. I've promised young Josh. He asked me to come here."

"You said 'we.' Surely you are not intending to go yourself?"

"I am. I've made all the arrangements. Granny Atwater is going to mind the children and care for Josh until he is well enough to go out. My neighbor is going to care for little Corinne—that's my baby."

"This is out of the question."

"I'm going whether you do or not. There's no more discussion on that. Besides, I'm worried about Hannah. She isn't safe alone with that man."

Conor thought this an odd remark. "That man is her husband."

"Aye, and he tried to murder her the last time he saw her. Even if she's safe from the thieves and the storm, she's not safe from him."

"Oh, this is silly..."

"Mr. McAllister, I know what it is to be married to a brutal man." She spoke these words simply without passion, just a statement of fact. Had she been histrionic, she would not have made half the impression on Conor.

"How soon can you be ready?" he asked, thinking he was probably making a terrible decision.

"I'm ready now. I've already hired two horses and a sleigh. I've packed food for two nights. How soon can you be ready?"

Conor's head was spinning. "I'll just need a few minutes, I guess." As Elodie left his room, he called after her: "Be honest...did you ask me to accompany you because I was the only one ignorant enough to go out in a storm like this?"

She did not answer, but smiled in a mischievous way that

answered "yes."

ON THE PRIOR afternoon, after the two men had stolen their horses, money, watch and jewelry at gunpoint, Brandon and Hannah had walked for four hours in the snow. The robbery had occurred at just past midday and the light was now fading from the overcast sky. Brandon was grateful the robbers had left them unharmed—he sized up the pair as just hungry vagabonds down on their luck—but he now feared for their safety from the elements. Hannah's clothing was not suited to the weather, not even close. Her outfit was suited to a chilly day on the Texas prairie, not a Rocky Mountain spring blizzard. He cursed himself for not dressing more warmly. He had worn his best clothes. He felt this was necessary in order to appear in a court of law and talk to a judge.

"I'm gonna build a snow cave. We'll have to tough out the night in that." He found a large drift and began to scoop it out with his gloved hands.

"Brandon?" said Hannah in a low voice. Brandon stopped his task to look up. Her face was filled with both confusion and concern. "I...can't feel my feet."

Brandon had feared this development. Frostbite. Certainly a common, though dangerous fact of life in the mountains. "You'll be all right," he lied, not wanting to scare her. The last thing he wanted to deal with was Hannah falling apart in one of her nervous fits.

Hannah sat down in the snow, exhausted and shivering. She watched her husband work and it never occurred to her to offer to help. He had been laboring about half an hour, when she felt compelled to ask: "What is it you're building, again?"

"Shelter, woman. See those clouds down the canyon? They're bringing in another storm for tonight. There's about half a chance we'll last til morning."

"What's wrong with that cabin over there?"

Brandon stopped and whirled around to where his wife was sitting. "Cabin?"

"Yonder...there." She pointed. "Isn't that a chimney of some sort?"

Brandon squinted his eyes in the fading light. It did look like a chimney sticking out of the snow drifts about a quarter of a mile away. "Why the hell didn't you say something before this?"

"I assumed you saw it, too. No need to get surly."

"Well, come on, for God's sake." He was ready to start running, but the depth of the snow made that impossible. Hannah just sat there.

"I can't walk. My feet are frozen. You'll have to carry me."

"Like hell I will."

"Like hell you won't." Hannah had never sworn before and found the experience almost exciting.

After further wrangling and much cursing on the part of Brandon, he agreed to pick her up and half-carry, half-drag her the short distance to the cabin.

It was a tiny one-room affair almost entirely buried by snow. If it had any recent occupants, they weren't alive inside. Brandon dug out the door and kicked it open. Inside were a few sticks of furniture and a stone fireplace that took up almost all the back wall of the cabin. The walls were rough-hewn logs and the chinking was nearly all intact. Brandon guessed this cabin belonged to a prospector who worked the placer mines in the gulch in the summer. Placer mining came to a halt during the snow season.

"If this chimney draws, I'm ready to say our miserable lives are saved." He broke up a rickety chair to use as firewood. Some newspaper was stuffed in the frame of the cabin's one window and he used that to get the fire going. Both he and Hannah held their breath as he lit the paper. Smoke rose up the chimney. Both sighed with relief.

While waiting for the fire to grow, Brandon turned his attention to his wife's frost bitten feet. "Get your shoes and stockings off," he ordered.

"I will not." Hannah was indignant, but she wasn't sure why.

Brandy was meanwhile removing his coat, taking off his vest, dropping his suspenders and yanking out his front shirttails. "You will if you want to keep them toes."

"What?"

"Frostbite, Hannah. If your toes freeze up they cut 'em off."

Brandon's manner was so matter-of-fact, she knew he must be serious, even though she had never heard of anything called frostbite before. How could there be anything really wrong when she felt no pain? In fact, she felt nothing at all from the ankles down. She removed her shoes and wet stockings as she was told.

Brandon moved on his knees over to where Hannah was sitting. Hannah was apprehensive. She didn't trust him and couldn't figure out why he seemed to be removing his clothing. Kneeling in front of her, he said to "Hand 'em over," meaning her feet.

"What have you got in mind?" Her brow was furrowed suspiciously.

"We're gonna do what the Indians do."

"And what might that be?" She giggled with curiosity this time, convinced her long estranged husband was flirting with her.

He took an ankle in each hand and jerked her toward him with such force, she slid onto her back, the back of her head bumping the dirt floor of the cabin in the process. Brandon noticed several of her toes were white, just as he had feared. He drew a deep breath, bracing himself for the shock, then plunged her feet under his shirt and against the naked skin of his abdomen. He let out a gasp of pain to feel her feet like two blocks of ice on his warm belly.

Hannah didn't feel anything, but—far from appreciating his sacrifice on her behalf—still assumed he was attempting to seduce her. "I bet this is all an elaborate plot to look up my skirt," she teased, still as much a coquette as she had been at seventeen when they met.

Brandon shook his head with disdain. "Like I ain't seen everything you got a thousand times or more."

Hannah chuckled and shook her head at this remark, so typical of Brandon. Then she sighed theatrically. "If only we had something to eat and someone to cook it."

Brandon rolled his eyes at his spoiled wife's view of their plight.

The fire was beginning to take away the deadly chill of the room. Hannah studied Brandon's face and, for a moment, saw the boy she'd fallen in love with all those years ago. "It's been awhile since I've laid on my back and looked up at you, Brandy."

"Not long enough," said Brandon, unkindly.

Hannah sighed. There was no spark left. She had been mistaken. Still, she longed to get something off her conscience.

"Bran, I never got the chance to say something. It's bothered me all these years. I never got the chance to say...I'm sorry."

Brandon's face softened. Having serious, honest discussions was something he and Hannah had never been good at. "Why should you apologize? I'm the one to do it. I caused all the problem."

"It wasn't just you. I feel truly grieved over what I did."

"Damn it, it was me in the wrong."

Hannah smiled sadly, shaking her head. "Listen to us. Now, we're arguing over who's sorrier."

Brandon started to smile. "We're a sorry pair and that's the God's own truth." He suddenly felt almost amicable to this woman—whom he'd spent the better part of two decades trying to forget. He pulled Hannah into his lap. She wrapped her arms around his neck and lay her head on his shoulder. The thoughts of both drifted back to the violent night that had ended their marriage.

THE EVENING had begun innocuously enough with the wedding of the young minister. The congregation threw them a grand reception. All the families in the valley attended, including both Hannah's and Brandon's, though they kept a discreet distance. Brandon got drunk and loud and disagreeable, picking a fight with one of his brothers, then his father. Hannah and her father angrily told him to go home. He complied without an argument and backed away from them with smile so malicious, it frightened Hannah.

Hannah stole away from the reception, and rode home as fast as the horse she borrowed would carry her. She stomped up the porch steps in a rage and ran directly to where she knew she would find her inebriated young husband—in the arms of Fleur.

Hannah threw open the nursery door. "I knew it!"

"*Mon dieu*," whispered the half-dressed Fleur.

Brandon stood up with a defiant expression and put his hands on his hips. He mentally congratulated himself on his impeccable timing. What he did not anticipate was Hannah rushing back down the stairs to her father's study. He called after her, then followed.

He found her frantically pulling out desk drawers. Oh, God, she's looking for a gun. "Calm down, honey, calm down, now."

Hannah's eyes fell on the silver letter opener that gleamed in the moonlight that fell across the desk. She grabbed it and charged at her husband. She aimed for his heart, but missed, catching him in the shoulder.

Brandon yelped at the unexpected pain, not quite able to grasp that she had stabbed him. She lunged a second time, but he caught her hand, mid-thrust. They struggled and lurched out into the dining room. Hannah's strength in her murderous fury amazed Brandon. He made one last effort to fling her off and back she went—through the air...through the dining room window.

Brandon watched in horror as Hannah disappeared in an explosion of shattering glass. He ran to the window and looked down. She lay on the ground outside flat on her back, as still as death.

Upstairs, Fleur hastily packed her few belongings in a blanket. Little Josh, awakened by all the commotion, watched her in confusion. "Where are you going, Mama Fleur?"

"Away...away far, *mon petit*. Shhh."

"Don't go, don't go. *S'il vous plait*, Mama Fleur. I'll be good, I promise." His lip trembled with the approach of tears.

Fleur paused for a moment and took the little boy in her arms. "*Je t'aime, mon chere, mon petit garcon.* But I must go. This place no good for Mama Fleur no more. Everybody gonna blame me."

"*Mais, je tu fils,*" Josh insisted.

"No," Fleur said sharply. "You have a mama and a papa. You tell them to love you now."

Fleur slipped out the back door and ran into the darkness of the vast prairie.

Little Josh ran after her until his three-year-old legs would carry him no farther. "Mama Fleur, don't leave me," he pleaded as he ran. "Please don't leave me."

No one heard him but the starry night sky.

"YOU WERE the lucky one, Bran. You don't know what it was like after you left," said Hannah, still leaning her head on his shoulder. "Can you imagine going to church on Sunday and finding yourself the subject of the sermon?"

Brandon chuckled, trying to picture this. He relished how this must have galled his pompous father-in-law.

Hannah didn't appreciate his snickering. She was absorbed, as usual, in self-pity. "Did you really run away with Fleur?"

"Hell, no. Where'd you get that idea?"

"She left the same night you did."

Brandon shrugged. "I thought I'd killed you. When I found out I didn't, I was too ashamed to come back. Figured your pa would see me dead, if he got the chance."

"He claimed he would often enough," Hannah giggled.

"Wonder what ever happened to old Fleur?"

"I hope she's burnin' in Hell by now," Hannah spat out.

"Now, Hannah, you know that night wasn't her fault."

Hannah bit her lower lip in a pout. She would much prefer to view the breakdown of her marriage as entirely Fleur's doing than take any of the responsiblity herself. She knew Brandon referred, not to the night they tried so hard to kill each other, but to a night much earlier in their marriage, a night they strayed so far off course, they never quite made it back.

Hannah shut her eyes in an effort to block the memories of that night from surging back. Memories of Fleur and her cursed voodoo ritual. The innocence of the evening, a proposed game to determine the gender of the baby Hannah carried, evaporated quickly after Brandon killed the rooster and Fleur began drawing strange signs on Hannah's pregnant belly with the rooster's blood.

At what point had the evening turned sexual? Who began it? Who kissed whom first? Hannah drew a quick breath to cleanse these thoughts from her mind. She quickly changed the subject.

"So how'd you come to end up here, Bran?"

"Got gold fever. The papers said there was gold in Colorado, just south of Denver. The papers lied, but I liked the mountains and I stayed. You'd like the weather here Hannah."

"I don't think so," she interrupted. "Didn't this lovely weather almost kill us?"

"But the summers, Hannah. The summers are so cool and nice. Butter don't melt here in August, I swear to the world."

"Cool in the summertime? That I can't imagine. Guess I'll have to take your word for it, since I'll be long gone by then."

"Couple years ago, there were real gold strikes up here along the Tenmile. I had to come up and see for myself. First night in Leap Year, I won the deed to the saloon in a poker game—been a proprietor ever since. How's that for luck?"

"Oh, Brandon," Hannah said with a tired tone of voice. "I thought we were finally having a nice conversation and now you're trying to get up my skirts?"

"Who said I was trying that?" he insisted, all innocence.

"Who do you suppose has their hand on my knee, then?"

Brandon grinned wickedly. "Force of habit." He removed his hand. "You look good after all this time, Hannah, I gotta admit it."

Hannah, ever vane, preened under this flattery. She felt slightly sinful, flirting with her soon-to-be former husband—she was unofficially engaged to another man, after all.

"Oh, Bran," she laughed. Then she sighed plaintively. "Here we are alone in the whole world and maybe this is our last night on earth."

Brandon raised a cautious eyebrow. "Are you sayin' what I think you're sayin', Hannah?"

She smiled seductively and wrapped her arms more tightly around his neck. "I'm saying—if you don't want to get kissed this minute, you'd better duck."

Brandon laughed and didn't duck and thought for a moment of the seventeen-year-old girl he'd found on a swing at the church social all those years ago.

CONOR DID not know how to drive a sleigh. Fortunately, Elodie was more than adept. The heavy snows of the previous night had left twenty new inches on the ground with drifts of more than ten feet in places.

"With last night's snow, there will be no tracks to follow," Conor pointed out, more to make conversation than to make a point. The sun was starting to break through the clouds in the mid-afternoon. He was worried about how late a start they had gotten. He did not relish spending a night out in sub-freezing temperatures, however well equipped Elodie claimed they were. He thought the whole adventure would prove fruitless, though he didn't have any better plans for the day and, as Brandy was his friend, he would like to have the feeling he had done all he could to help him, though, in his own mind he was starting to accept the possibility Brandon and his foolish wife must have certainly perished.

"The trails through here are narrow," reasoned Elodie, who had given the matter a great deal of thought. "If they didn't become lost and start to wander, we should come upon them."

"A big 'if,' Mrs. Kelly."

"I've told you before, you may call me 'Elodie'."

"And I've told you before, I do not wish such familiarity, Mrs. Kelly."

"You've been as familiar as any man could be, sir." She was looking straight ahead, but stole glances when she could.

Conor groaned. "Do you ever foresee a time when I shall be allowed to forget that shameful night?"

"No," she replied, turning her face to him with a flirtatious half-smile.

"I give up," said Conor, helplessly. "I don't know what you want from me. I have tried to be a gentleman about what happened, but you won't let me." Conor shook his head in exasperation. "Surely...surely you do not expect me to marry you."

Elodie only laughed. To change the subject, she said, "That's a nice sweater you're wearing. Did someone make it for you?"

"Uh...my mother," lied Conor. "She sent it to me for Christmas." He hated lying, but he couldn't admit that a prostitute had knitted the sweater for him. He felt guilty dragging his mother into it. She didn't know how to knit, but if she did, she would surely have produced a sweater of higher quality than Angel's, which contained many dropped stitches and had one sleeve longer than the other. Still, the sweater was extremely warm, so Conor wore it often.

Elodie could hardly keep a straight face. Her innocence in asking about the sweater had been entirely feigned. She knew exactly who had made the sweater—Leap Year was too small for secrets—and had asked him about it to see if he would tell the truth.

They rode along in silence for a while, looking for any sign of their friends. At about four in the afternoon, they encountered a mail wagon on its way up to Leap Year.

Elodie drew the sleigh alongside the wagon and Conor asked the driver if he had seen anyone on foot between Columbine and the road northeast to Denver.

"On foot today? After the storm that came howling in last night?" laughed the driver. "Who'd be fool enough to be out—'cept you folks and me?"

Conor thanked the driver. The two wagons had traveled less than a quarter of a mile when the driver called back to them.

"It'll be dark soon. If you and the Missus are worried about a place to pass the night, I saw a cabin back about an hour or so with a fire going. Reckon they'd put you up maybe?"

The driver bid them farewell a second time and Elodie and Conor continued their odyssey. Elodie smiled with mischief at the old man's assumption that they were man and wife. Conor frowned at first, then couldn't keep from chuckling himself.

"Maybe the folks in the cabin have seen them," Elodie offered after a long silence.

"Perhaps." Conor wanted to ask Elodie where she had gotten the money to hire a sleigh and a pair of horses from the livery. Such hires were expensive. He rationed himself on how often he borrowed a single horse. Where did a poor miner's widow get such money? The specter of prostitution still lingered in his mind, though he didn't want to believe this. There was something about this woman he genuinely liked, though it was hard for him to admit it. He might actually have considered courting her, had they not gotten off to such a bizarre and ignoble start.

"I've never heard the name Elodie before. It's very pretty."

Elodie wrinkled her nose. "I've never really liked it. I was named after my least favorite aunt, you see."

"I have you beat. I was named after a box of breakfast food."

"What?" Elodie giggled.

"My mother grew up eating 'Conor's Cracked Wheat' for breakfast every day and she grew fond of the name. I was ten years old before she confessed where she got the name. By then it was too late to change it. Everyone thought it was funny except me. Of course, by now, even I think it's funny."

To the tune of "Jimmy Crack Corn," Elodie began to

mischievously sing, "*Conor crack wheat and I don't care, Conor crack wheat and I don't care—*"

"Elodie melody," Conor shot back.

They laughed at their own foolishness and glanced at each other and then both shyly looked forward again. In a more somber mood, Elodie said, "May I ask you a personal question, Conor?"

"Why not?" answered Conor, with an edge to his voice and a wry half-smile.

Elodie ignored his sarcasm, because she found him funny in an odd way. She liked him because he always seemed to be doing more thinking than talking—a welcome change from the boastful, blustering men who inhabited Leap Year, her late husband among them. And best of all, he seemed capable of laughing at himself. "How did you lose your wife?"

Conor hated talking about Allison. His family and friends knew better than to bring up the subject. Time had passed, though, and this diverting new environment had drawn him away from his obsessive grief. "She died giving birth to our daughter."

"I'm sorry. I was afraid that was it. No wonder—" She stopped short.

"No wonder, what?"

"I'm sorry. If I had only known...I might not of—" She glanced at him guiltily, then pretended to be absorbed in driving the team, though the journey had so far gone easier than she had anticipated.

Conor silently accepted her apology and decided to change the subject. Enough had at last been said about their fateful night together and a truce of sorts had been reached. "How is Joe getting along? He stayed at school, I take it?"

"Oh, fine, quite fine," Elodie enthused, brightening. "When I see him, he complains a lot, but I think everything is really all right."

She chattered on about his school and the family he was staying with. Conor studied Elodie's profile as she spoke. She was really very pretty, even though most of her face was swaddled in a woolen scarf. Her cheeks and nose were rosy from the cold and her blue eyes were bright. Riding along on their rescue mission, Conor found himself enjoyably entertained. He considered the possibility of perhaps becoming friends with this woman, who could be charming when she chose to be.

Just when he had guiltily concluded that he was having too much fun for such a grave adventure as searching for friends who may at this moment be in mortal danger, the cabin the mail carrier had described came into view. The fading early evening light made it difficult to see, but smoke was rising from the chimney.

As they approached, they could see that the cabin was almost entirely buried in snow. Drifts came up to within ten inches of the top of the door and nearly to the top of the one window as well. Elodie and Conor sat in their wagon and pondered the situation.

"If I could climb to the top of that drift, I could rap on the window," Elodie offered.

"Let me hold on to you while you do it," said Conor, not having any better idea.

Elodie scrambled up the drift with ease and began reaching for the window pane. Conor was following up the drift and just as Elodie touched the window the combined weight of the snow and Elodie and Conor caused the window to collapse, sending both crashing through the window with a resounding thud.

Conor landed on top of Elodie and as soon as the pair sat up, they confronted the startled pair of cabin occupants.

"Well, I'll be damned," breathed Brandon Chance in surprise.

"Oh, my," said his wife.

"Hannah!" cried Elodie, stunned both by their unexpected entry into the cabin and by finding the object of their search in good health.

"Brandy!" said Conor, flush with their success. He had never rescued anyone before.

After several minutes of excited congratulations and recountings of adventures, it began to dawn on Elodie and Conor that they had discovered the objects of their rescue to be on somewhat more than civil terms with each other, in fact on much more intimate terms than one might expect from a divorcing couple. Brandon and Hannah were not fully clothed. To be precise, Elodie and Conor had found them in bed wearing as little in the way of clothing as the chilliness of the room would allow.

"Did you bring any food?" Brandon eagerly demanded of his rescuers. He and his wife had not eaten in nearly thirty-six hours.

"Surely, we did," Elodie said, glancing at the broken window and the snow slide coming through it and wondering how to get back out to the wagon.

"Elodie, could you help me?" Hannah said in a loud whisper. She had gathered up her clothing and carried it to the far corner of the little cabin. Elodie rushed over and held a blanket aloft to shield her friend as she dressed.

Conor discreetly turned his back to the women and spoke to

Brandon, as he sat on the bed, pulling on his trousers and buttoning his shirt. "You don't waste a minute, do you?"

Brandon grinned back. "Life is short."

Conor whispered, "I thought you hated her."

"Let's just say I found a few parts I still fancied." Brandon was ever the one for the risque remark.

Conor chuckled and shook his head. He couldn't wait to tease Elodie about her fears that Hannah's life was in danger from her husband. He then climbed back out the broken window to retrieve the food from the wagon and secure the horses. All had concluded that they would spend the night at the cabin and begin the journey home at first light.

After their "supper" of hominy cakes and coffee made from melted snow, the question of sleeping arrangements presented itself.

"I think we should let the ladies have the bed," Conor said to Brandon.

At this suggestion, Brandon and his wife exchanged such pathetic, disappointed glances, that Elodie spoke up. "I don't care to have the bed, though I thank you kindly for the offer. I'm so cold I want to sit up by the fire."

"Oh, Elodie, are you sure?" asked Hannah, with obvious insincerity.

Brandon shrugged with a helpless smile and goodnights were exchanged.

The reunited couple lay abed whispering and giggling like a pair of newlyweds, Elodie and Conor sat uncomfortably on the floor near the fire in silence.

Elodie was doubly uncomfortable in that she had now gone more than eight hours without nursing her baby. She felt as though her breasts would explode from the pressure, but there was nothing she could do to relieve it.

Her face, in the firelight, showed her discomfort to such an extent that Conor was moved to ask if she was unwell.

She smiled apologetically, not knowing how to delicately explain. She patted her bosom and said simply: "I'm missing my baby."

Conor, being ignorant of the mechanics of breast feeding, assumed she was gesturing to her heart and that she was expressing homesickness. "We'll be home soon. Are you warm enough?"

"I'm a little chilled," she admitted, hoping this might elicit an offer to sit closer. It did. Conor moved over next to Elodie. He put his arm around her shoulder and allowed her to rest her head upon his chest. He got virtually no sleep and neither did she, but they did not speak again until morning. They just sat there listening to the crackling of the fire and the wind whistling in around the makeshift barrier over the broken window. At some point in the night, Conor leaned his cheek against the top of Elodie's head. Her hair still smelled like the wind before a rainstorm.

THE FOLLOWING morning bloomed sunny and surprisingly warm as Conor and Elodie returned to Leap Year with their friends. They found young Josh to be fully recovered from his fever and overjoyed to see his parents alive again. Brandy insisted on the entire party adjourning to the Belle of Colorado Cafe to celebrate with a huge noontime meal. All thought this a capital idea, save Elodie who begged off, saying she must attend to her children. This disappointed everyone since it was Elodie who had occasioned the entire rescue effort, but she would not be dissuaded. Finally, she asked only that they save her a piece of cherry pie—this being the restaurant's specialty though the pie had to be made from tinned cherries.

The celebration lasted late into the evening. Before the meal ended, the Chances announced that they were reconciled—at least for the moment. This fact emerged gradually and seemed to have been arrived at by stages with neither party actually aware of it until the final decision was made. Conor was responsible for initiating the discussion when he asked, as delicately as possible—if the couple knew when they would be resuming their ill-fated journey to Denver.

Hannah looked uncomfortably at her husband, who frowned back at her. "Well...soon I expect. I must return home to Texas before spring's end."

"To marry Mr. Haworthy," added Josh, making a disgruntled face. It was obvious his mother's intended was not his favorite person.

"Just who is this Haworthy fella, anyway?" asked Brandon, nursing a glass of whiskey.

"He's a librarian," said Hannah primly.

Brandon hooted. "You—marrryin' a librarian? You—who could never spell 'cat'?"

Hannah ruffled at this jibe. "He's a very fine person."

"Just what kind of 'fine person' courts another man's wife, I'd like know?"

Conor felt out of place witnessing a family squabble of this intimacy. He glanced across the table at Josh who was studying his sparring parents with great interest.

Hannah was reluctant to answer her husband's question, but finally did since she felt he deserved the awful truth. "I told him you were long dead."

"You need to divorce a dead man, do you?"

Hannah shifted in her seat and with a low tone directed solely at Brandon, explained: "Your family knew you were still alive and I was afraid they'd make trouble if I married again."

"Bigamy's an ugly word, ain't it?" said Brandon to Conor, in a sly tone to ridicule his wife.

Conor wisely remained silent.

"Hannah...just tell me one thing. Do you love him?"

Hannah looked embarrassed by this question. "He's the finest man I've ever met."

"Do you love him?"

"He's kind and generous and educated."

"Do...you...love...him?"

Hannah drew herself up in a haughty manner that she was a master at. "I'm very fond of him."

"*Fond*? Hannah, I'm fond of lotsa things. I'm fond of good whiskey and a fine round of poker and a fast ride on a horse on a cold, clear morning when the sun's so bright it hurts your eyes to look at it. I asked...*do you love him?*"

Hannah's face screwed up and she looked as though she were going to cry. Conor wished Brandon would stop being so hard on his wife. They had just been through such an ordeal, after all. He said nothing, however, knowing it was not his place to offer an opinion.

Hannah stared down into her lap at her hands as she wrung them together. In a tiny, strangled voice, she admitted, "No...not like I loved you. There—are you satisfied?"

"I knew it!" Brandon crowed. "I knew it!" He was delighted by this admission and his cynicism fell away like a curtain. His son laughed at his sudden change of demeanor. Even Conor smiled.

"Oh, Brandy," whispered Hannah, who had tears in her eyes now.

"Hannah Chance," Brandon began in a grand tone. "I can't ask you to be my wife because you already are. But I can ask you to start *bein'* my wife again. What do you say?"

"Oh, you fool," said Hannah, crying openly and daubing her cheeks with a hanky. "Oh, all right. I'll try if you will."

The entire restaurant, who had been eavesdropping on this marital confrontation, burst into spontaneous applause. Brandon enjoyed the attention, but his wife was mortified and hid her face behind her handkerchief.

When the commotion died down, Josh inquired of his mother what she planned to tell Mr. Haworthy.

Hannah smiled ruefully. "I guess I'll just have to tell him I found out my husband was alive after all. Not much he can say to that."

Brandon rolled his eyes. "Tellin' the truth for the first time in her life. Watch out, Hannah, if might get to be habit formin'."

After several more rounds were drunk to the happy couple, dessert was served—cherry pie. Josh volunteered to take Elodie her piece.

Brandon objected, saying he wanted his whole family together tonight to get reacquainted. He asked Conor to do the honors, buying a whole pie for Elodie and her brood. As Conor was leaving, Brandon caught his eye and gave him a lewd wink. Conor knew exactly why Brandon had designated him to call on Mrs. Kelly. He playfully frowned at his friend's silent suggestion and headed out into the snowy night.

By the time he had walked to Elodie's cabin, it was nearly ten o'clock and only a single light was visible—probably the fire in the parlor. He feared the whole house had gone to bed, but as he approached he saw a figure emerge from the back of the house to gather more firewood.

"Elodie?"

"Who's there?" she answered in a voice that sounded both startled and frightened. She raised a log defensively as a weapon.

"It's me—Conor. I've brought your cherry pie."

She let out a relieved sigh and dropped the logs she had just picked up. "You nearly scared the life out of me."

The moon was bright enough that night he could now see her face. She was smiling.

He rushed over—as fast as the deep, heavy March snow would permit—and handed her the pie. Then he gathered up her firewood and carried it into the kitchen for her.

"You must let me make you some coffee to go with our pie," she said in a soft voice. She was speaking quietly so as not to awaken the rest of the household. She did not remove her woolen shawl and then Conor realized she was in her night gown. She went to the pump and drew water for the coffee.

"I've had more than my fill of pie, I'm afraid, but I would be grateful for the coffee."

They sat together at the table as Elodie ate a small piece of the pie and they drank their coffee. For once, Conor was the talkative one, sharing the events of the celebration dinner. Elodie was delighted by the news that Hannah would be staying in Leap Year. She had longed for a new female friend.

With the pie eaten and the coffee finished, the evening was drawing to a close, yet neither Conor nor Elodie seemed anxious to end it. Elodie stared down at her empty coffee cup and said slowly, "It's time for bed." Then she glanced sideways to catch Conor's reaction.

Conor drew in his breath with a sense of here-we-go-again. His heart started pounding, but he managed an even voice to respond. "I suppose you're right."

They smiled awkwardly at each other and, without discussing it further, Elodie took his hand in hers and they adjourned to her bedroom.

Chapter Eleven

"EVAN, DO you think there are drug dealers holed up in these mountains?" We were at a game of Siamese Twins, which was when we always had our best talks.

"Who told you there were drug dealers up here?"

"Celeste, that waitress at the Tenmile Cafe."

Evan rolled his eyes. "She was probably talking about me."

"What?" I was shocked and yet not totally surprised.

Evan grinned. "Let's just say I used to take the Dormouse's advice too often...I already told you that."

I gave him a puzzled look, completely lost by this cryptic remark.

When he saw my questioning glance, he drew apart and sat up in bed. "I did it! I finally did it! I stumped you at Lyric Trivia!" He laughed with delight.

I sighed with mock annoyance, still waiting for an explanation.

"The Dormouse said to feed your head. Grace Slick? 'White Rabbit?'" He was triumphant.

"Before my time." I tried to be nonchalant in defeat. I still wanted to know about this drug dealing remark. "Evan are you serious or not?"

Evan gestured that this was not a major thing. "I used to do a little transport work to make ends meet, that's all. There's a line that runs through these mountains to serve all the big ski resorts. My outlaw days came to a real swift close when the guy I used to work for over in Avalanche Creek took three bullets in the back of the skull from some unexpected out-of-town company." He shook his head slowly. "Scared the shit outta me. I don't think I ate or slept for three weeks after that."

"This is all in the past?" I was worried—for either Evan or myself, I'm not sure which.

"Yes, ma'am. I walk the straight and narrow with a vengeance these days. Not that I don't miss it sometimes. I mean, some of the best moments of my life have been pharmaceutically enhanced ones."

"For example?"

"The day Reilly was born. I was stoned out of my head. It was the most—"

"You fainted."

Evan grinned. "I'm never going to live that down." He drew me closer. "That summer, we were living on a commune in Canada and we used to sleep on the roof of this big old farmhouse—unless it rained. We used to lay with our sleeping bags zipped together—Reilly in between us—and count the stars or watch the sun come up."

I pictured this in my mind and suddenly wanted to *be* Sandy— laying on that roof with Evan and watching that sun rise—holding that baby. These baby-cravings were coming on me with greater and greater frequency. It was scary.

Evan was just starting to get amorous again when the phone rang. It was my mother. I motioned to Evan it was going to take awhile and he left to go downstairs to get something to eat.

"Where have you been?" she practically shouted. "I've been calling this number for three days!"

I'd mostly been at Evan's house, but didn't want to tell her this.

"I don't know," I murmured.

"I've been worried sick about you, dear."

She had been accusing me of worrying her sick for the last twenty-six years. I took a deep breath and told her about my accident. As I knew she would, she had a fit—wanted to jump on the next plane, wanted to haul me back home immediately. I was her baby again. I was purposefully vague on when the accident had actually occurred. I didn't want to hurt her feelings that I had taken so long to tell her, though I was now glad I had waited since she had reacted exactly as I had predicted.

I got her settled down and eventually convinced I was being well looked after by my extremely friendly neighbors. I was vague about who these neighbors were exactly, almost implying they were a married couple. It was too soon for me to go into the New Boyfriend recital and all its attendant cross-examination.

To change the subject, I asked if she had made any progress on finding grandma's genealogy. She said it still had not been located. I asked her if she had ever heard of an ancestor named Conor McAllister.

"McAllister was my grandmother's maiden name. You don't remember Grandma Simpson, she died before you were born, but her maiden name was Beatrice McAllister. She was related to the McAllisters of McAllister Boots."

"We're related to McAllister Boots?" I was surprised. I had worn McAllister boots.

"Only distantly. I don't think they're planning to leave us any stock in their wills. Too bad Grady didn't get any, though."

"So maybe Grady was Grandma Simpson's half-sister. This Conor guy must have married twice, once in Philadelphia and then again in Colorado. That must be how we got a Colorado branch to the family. I wish I knew more."

"I'll call my Aunt Evelyn in the nursing home. She knows a lot of family history. She can't remember what she ate for breakfast, but she's great on anything that happened before to World War II." Before hanging up, her voice turned steely cold. "Darcy, your sister told me you quit your job at the Randall Gallery. I thought you were just taking a vacation."

"I didn't know when I was coming back. I didn't want my boss to hold my job open indefinitely."

"Darcy, when exactly are you planning to come home? You can't just up and leave all your family and friends—"

"What friends? After I married Keith, I stopped having any friends of my own."

"If only you had tried a little harder with Keith—"

"Don't start with me, Mom!" There was silence on the other end of the line, then the sound of crying.

"I just miss you so much, darling."

"I know," I said quietly. "But, Mom, you have to understand. This is important to me. I needed to get away for a while." My mother just sighed and said goodbye. Nothing like news from home to cheer you right up. I had just put down the receiver when Evan reappeared in the bedroom. It was a rainy afternoon, which meant his job had been called off for the remainder of the day. He had not found anything to eat except breakfast cereal and brought a box of that with him.

The sound of my mother's voice still filled my ears when I suddenly saw a vision of Evan through my mother's eyes. It was depressing. I knew she would never see past the ponytail and the earring, the worn-out clothes and the chronic welfare dependance. The fact that he had three children out of wedlock didn't help either, though surely she would give him some credit for taking on the responsibility of raising them. How many men did that nowadays? The one aspect my mother probably couldn't appreciate was that Evan's appearance and lifestyle, by Tenmile Canyon standards, was not only the norm, but a tad on the conservative side, if anything.

"Your mom on the phone?"

I nodded, still lost in the reappraisal of my lover. "I finally told her about my accident. She came unglued."

"All mothers are alike. After my big accident, my mom came out from Chicago and took care of me and the kids for two months. Nothing like slave labor, I always say."

"I told my mom to stay put—that I already was being well looked after." I gave him a little kiss.

Evan added some obscene references to what else was being done to me, taking me in his arms and teasing me out of my depressed, post-mother's phone call funk. He was a genius at putting me in a good mood.

"Hey, some time we're gonna have to explore that hole you fell into. When are you going to feel like walking that far?"

"I don't know. My foot still swells really bad, every time I do very much walking."

"You've got to get better in time for the meteor shower. It's just a little over a week from now." Evan went on to explain that every year he and his kids would hike up to a special location on a nearby mountain and camp out. Annually, in August the Perseid meteor shower would put on a guaranteed show in the night sky. This meteor display was the Old Faithful of meteor showers, appearing with clockwork regularity every August as the earth passed through the tail of a comet called Swift-Tuttle.

"Now...we're going to be entirely clothed for this event, right?"

"Of course," said Evan, looking puzzled. "It'll probably be thirty degrees up where we're going."

"With your family, I'm never too sure which activities are clothing-optional," I teased.

Evan frowned. "Credit me with at least half a brain. Jeez, Darcy."

"It's not really going to be thirty degrees in August, is it?"

"You've still got a lot to learn about living at altitude, kid." Evan had recently taken to calling me 'kid.' I hadn't yet figured out if this was 'kid' as in 'child' or 'kid' as in 'Here's looking at you, kid, á la Humphrey Bogart. I guess I was sensitive about the difference in our ages. I had never been involved with anyone older before. On the other hand, Evan seldom seemed older so I don't know why I had a problem with this.

Evan had to leave to run some errands and he had no sooner left than my sister, Jane, called.

"Mom said you fell off a cliff or something and broke your foot."

"Not quite a cliff. And I'm okay. A walking cast for six weeks, that's all."

"So...who's the new man in your life?"

"What? I didn't say anything to Mom about a man. What's the

deal?"

"She's psychic. She has boyfriend radar, you know that. She thinks you don't want her to come stay with you because you're conducting some hot and heavy love affair."

Maybe she *was* psychic. "So she called you up to get you to do her dirty work for her?"

Jane sighed. "You know Mom as well as I do. So, come on, what's the skinny? I'll have to tell her something."

"Tell her...okay, tell her I'm in love with a semi-employed carpenter with a ponytail, an earring, and three illegitimate kids."

Jane burst out laughing. "Okay...now tell me what's really going on."

I was having fun with this. "That *is* what's going on, Janey, dear."

"Okay...play hard to get." Jane was annoyed with me, but this was a semi-regular occurrence. "I knew this living-alone-for-the-summer thing would last about five minutes."

"What do you mean by that?" Now I was getting a little annoyed.

"Some people can live alone and some can't. You're the latter. You were born to be half of a couple and that's the way it is."

I let out an audible sigh to show my disagreement with her assessment of me, but refused to let her bait me into a full-blown argument. We steered the conversation into more neutral waters and I received a lengthy recitation of her three-year-old daughter Brittany's latest accomplishments.

She tossed in one more little tidbit before hanging up. "I saw Trev the other day. I was out to lunch with Jacy and he came over to our table. He asked if I'd heard from you."

Trev Randall was my former boss. He owned the art gallery I managed. I went to work for him straight from college, the summer before I married Keith. He was a gifted sculptor who created bizarrely distorted nudes of men and women. His art was so disturbing it never really found an audience, but fortunately he had an adoring and wealthy grandmother who had set him up with his own gallery. "See—being nice to old ladies pays off," he had teased me when I received the news of Grady's legacy. His best talent, however, lay with shrewdly judging the art of others and his gallery started breaking even in merely a year.

"He wanted your new phone number, but I told him I didn't think you had a phone. He said the idea of you without a Rolodex in front of you, much less a phone—was too tragic to imagine."

"Ha-ha," I groaned. The truth was, I didn't want to talk to anyone from back home. I knew it would only make me homesick. Plus, Trev was too knowledgeable about my breakup with Keith. I wanted to leave the past in the past. Leap Year was my chance to do that. Leap Year was my gift, my chance to start over without all that unpleasant baggage to drag around.

Trev had been as doubtful as Janey about my plans for the summer. He had refused to accept my resignation from the gallery. "Let's call it a leave of absence, a sabbatical. You'll come back in the fall, you'll be refreshed, you'll have the color back in those cheeks."

At that point I had stuck two fingers down my throat and pretended to gag myself so he started laughing, "Okay, okay—I'm a little over the top, but I'm sincere. I'll be your safety net. You can always come home to Old Trev."

"Old Trev" was actually only thirty-two, but he had always hovered over me, especially during the divorce period, lending me his shoulder to cry on throughout. He had been more supportive than my own family during that miserable time. Maybe I was overly sensitive, but I always felt my mother and even my sister blamed me for the breakup. They considered Keith the catch of a lifetime and I would certainly never do better.

I somehow bring out the mother hen in people. They seem to take one look at me and assume I can't handle even the smallest problem. I had already sensed this in Evan and even his kids. "I'm never coming back, Trev. Never." I hadn't really meant this, but I thought it sounded good.

"You sound like that nutty soldier in *Apocalypse Now*. The one they sent on the mission to kill Kurtz before Martin Sheen. He wrote that crazy note back to his wife saying, 'Sell the house, sell the children, I'm never coming home, never!'" Trev was a film buff in addition to all his other pursuits.

Jane continued, "I always thought you and Trev might get together after you split with you-know-who."

"Janey, Trev is gay."

"No! You're kidding—but he's so cute."

"And he has a very cute boyfriend." I was being too hard on Jane. Trev was not the flamboyant type and his boyfriend, Dan, even less so. Dan was still so far in the closet it was almost painful to witness. He was a young lawyer with a large downtown firm. Trev said he lived in abject fear of someone from the office finding out.

Whenever Dan stopped by the gallery, he would pretend he was on business as Trev's lawyer, which was actually how they met. "Uh-oh, another business lunch," Trev would joke when he saw Dan walking in the gallery at lunch time.

"I wish my lunches with Keith were tax deductible," I used to tease. Of course, Keith and I didn't really have any lunches together, tax deductible or otherwise. He was always in class or at the library or so he said....

To be ornery, I used to flirt with Trev in front of Dan. To be really wicked, I would sometimes flirt with Dan, making him extremely uncomfortable. Trev couldn't confess that he had told me about the two of them because he had been sworn to secrecy. "You were a very naughty girl," Trev would chide me after one of these escapades.

Trev was never fond of Keith. He even had warned me not to marry him after just one meeting, which I thought was presumptuous. I ignored his warning—the wedding being 72-hours away—but he turned out to be as shrewd a judge of character as he was of art. Over the next three years, I gave him so many opportunities to say "I told you so" he should have been canonized for not taking them.

Hanging up from my sister's call left me feeling depressed and homesick, just like I feared it would. A rainy afternoon with no television and no more Evan until dinner—he had invited me to his house, sevenish.

"SO WHAT'S your latest theory on the Hidden Vein, Sherlock?" Evan asked as he handed me another wet plate. He was washing and I was drying after dinner. The Allender kitchen had a dishwasher, but it had broken six months earlier. Both Evan and Reilly had taken a shot at fixing it without success. They could not afford a new one just now because they were "maxed out" on all their plastic.

The dinner had gone nicely. Evan had grilled Orange Roughy over coals on the deck. He was easing back into flesh consumption. Reilly had been absent, which was the norm recently. The twins were more subdued than usual and both wore sunglasses throughout the meal. Evan didn't ask for an explanation and they didn't offer one. After dinner they scurried out to soak in the hot tub while Evan and I cleaned up.

"I found out a few new things—Grady's parents' names were definitely Conor McAllister and Elodie Kelly. I even found their wedding announcement in the newspaper. She had *five* kids. He sure was brave."

"How many is too many?" asked Evan with an edge to his voice.

I realized I had maybe offended him. "Four," I answered, teasingly.

"Good answer."

"Have you ever worn McAllister Boots?"

"Nope. Too rich for my blood."

"Well, Grady was related to that family."

"So the Widow Kelly found herself a nice, rich husband. With all those kids to support, I don't blame her."

I had to put in my two cents worth. "Conor probably wanted someone to cook his meals and wash his clothes—not to mention somebody to warm up his bed on cold, mountain nights."

"Amen to that. Sounds like a match made in heaven to me."

I began to sarcastically sing: "I'll use you and you'll use me. Oh, how happy we will be."

"Uh-oh. Here comes Battle of the Sexes—Round 8,946." He handed me another plate and waxed philosophical. "Sometimes I think all the women of the world are trying to get even with me, personally, for ten thousand years of male oppression."

"But you deserve it," I offered with feigned innocence. "I think Conor's head was probably turned by the first pretty face he saw. He was out here, homesick, lonely—probably wasn't thinking clearly. Why is it that the only thing men seem to care about is a pretty face? How can they be so superficial? I mean, looks are important to me too—"

"Well, thank you," said Evan with playful sarcasm.

"But they're not the whole game," I continued. "I look at the big picture—personality, compassion, intellect, character, sensitivity."

"I never knew I had so much going for me."

"Be serious—just for half a minute."

"Okay...let me lay it out for you." Evan stopped washing and dried his hands, then folded them across his chest as though ready to deliver a lecture. "Men and women are different—"

"Wow—news flash."

"Stay with me here. Men have to get it up."

"That's it?"

"Yep. The species has to keep reproducing and if it takes a pretty face or good lookin' legs or—" he leaned over inches from my face, "—great tits to get the job done, then that's what it takes."

I must have looked as blank as I felt, so he went on to add: "Educated discussions of art or existentialism may be all well and good, but they *don't get ya hot.*"

"Oh, Evan," I complained in irritation. "You sound like Vanessa, my old college roommate."

"Hey, I didn't make the rules. I didn't design the universe. What's the deal on Vanessa?"

I told him about the notorious Vanessa, dorm roommate of my freshman and sophomore years. Vanessa was two years older than me. We started both freshmen, but she had taken off two years between high school and college to "find herself." In the process, she'd found a number of men. On rare nights when Vanessa didn't have a date, we would sit up talking, drinking cheap wine and eating awful things like nearly raw brownies until we were sick. The much more worldly Vanessa would explain the mysteries of life for me. I was completely in awe of her. One of her discourses:

"Men say women are difficult to understand, but that's because men, by comparison, are so simple. The only thing you need to know about men, Darcy darling, is that their every thought, word, or action is controlled by a single organ of their body," expounded Vanessa one night about three a.m. when we were supposed to be studying for midterms.

"Their brain?" I offered in the absolute state of my freshman innocence.

Vanessa groaned at my ignorance. "I was thinking of something much further south."

"Oh." I pondered this for a moment. "Wait a minute...I think you're selling the male gender a little short. I mean, men have produced great poetry and art—"

"Because they want to get laid."

"They've made great scientific discoveries—"

"Because they want to get laid."

"Built huge multinational corporations—"

"Because they want to get laid."

"Fought wars, led battalions into combat—"

"Because they want to get laid *a lot*."

All the while I was telling the Vanessa story, Evan was clowning around, trying to look down the tank top I was wearing. Reilly had been perfectly honest in describing his father as a "breast man," when we had first driven down to the Tenmile Cafe all those weeks ago. Evan couldn't seem to keep his hands off me. He was worse than a sixteen-year-old boy when it came to copping feels. What I found objectionable in all this was the fact that he often did it when his kids were around. We would be sitting in the living room watching television on the couch. The twins would be sprawled on the floor in front of us. Evan would put his arm around me and I knew a grope was on the way at any time. If one of the girls happened to get up or look our way, he would remove his hand chastely to my shoulder. Still, it was annoying.

"Evan...can I ask you a personal question?"

"No, of course not. Whatever gave you that idea?"

"I'm serious."

"God damn right, we're serious tonight. Just why is it you think you need to ask permission at this stage of the game?" Evan turned back to the sink and resumed washing the dishes.

"Game" was probably the right word for us, but I tried not to take it seriously. Whenever Evan adopted his current tone of voice, it made me feel the ten years' difference in our ages—like he was trying to remind me of my place or something. "Evan, why didn't you ever get married?"

Still facing the sink, Evan decided to stop joking around. "I don't know. I came close once, real close."

I moved over behind him and put my arms around his waist and rested my head against his back, waiting for a further explanation.

"It was Beth, the twins' mom. Believe it or not, the twins weren't an accident. We had decided to have a kid together—unlike Reilly who was the definitive backseat baby."

The top of my head came only to the top of his shoulder, but looking up, I could see the side of his face. He was staring out the window over the sink and smiling with nostalgia. He always took on a wistful sadness when talking about Beth.

"The week the twins were born—man, I was on a high no drug could produce. I called my mom and told her we were getting married. She said—" he mimicked his mother's voice, "'Well, it's about time, you big jerk.'"

"Your mother called you a 'jerk'?"

"Yeah, well, she said it with a lot of affection."

"So what happened?"

Evan sighed. "Beth came home from the hospital and...I don't know...reality kicked us in the head real hard. The twins were just so much work and Reilly was giving us hell...it was never the same again."

"Where is Reilly, by the way?"

Evan turned instantly surly. "Where do you think?"

"Marlena?"

"Bingo! The little lady wins a prize." Evan was wiping up the counter top, frowning. "He's practically moved in with her. I said, 'Great, let *her* put you through college' and he said, 'She's already offered to.'"

"How nice," I offered innocently.

Evan exploded. "Nice? *Nice*? Darcy, my son is prostituting himself to get a college education."

"Has it occurred to you they might actually love each other?"

"In the immortal words of Tina Turner—What's love got to do with it?"

"I think you're jealous of him."

"Why is it that the only people who know how to raise kids are the ones that don't have any?"

"Back off, Evan. I'm only trying to help—"

"Maybe I don't need any help."

"Oh, so I have to listen to you bitch about all your problems, but I'm not allowed to offer an opinion?"

"Maybe I don't need the opinions of some spoiled, preppie twenty-six-year-old."

In a grand gesture, I threw the dish towel on the floor. "I don't know what you need, but I'm starting not to care." I headed for the door.

"Darcy...Darcy, wait." Evan rushed between me and the door, blocking my exit. "Shit, I'm sorry. It's not you I'm mad at. Christ, you're about the only thing good in my life right now. If I lost you—I might as well hang it up."

I was still furious. I stood there with my arms crossed over my chest. In a voice I tried to keep from sounding angry, I asked, "Is that really how you see me?"

Evan grinned apologetically. "Sort of. Doesn't mean I don't love you."

I still felt like pouting. At least he had said he loved me. It was only the second time. I was never sure if the first really counted. "I love you" said in the context of "God, this feels so good," seemed suspect.

"Here, hold on—I got something to show you. Something I've been working on." He pulled me away from the door and toward his bedroom. All over his bed were spread topographical maps. "I've been planning our trip. You know, meteor night."

I sighed, unimpressed. "I've told you, Evan, I can't hike with this cast. It's out of the question. You and the kids will have to go without me."

"I've been looking for a jeep road. Something we can four-wheel to. We can use your jeep, can't we? My transmission is so iffy I'm afraid to get beyond the reach of a tow truck."

"Well..." I was apprehensive. I was pretty sure that taking the jeep off road was in violation of my rental agreement. I was growing fond of the jeep. I was even considering buying it. I had never owned a car all my own before. In high school, I shared a car with my sister. I didn't own a car during college. Then Keith and I shared a car during our marriage, which he got in the divorce settlement.

"This is going to be a special year for the Perseid shower. Old Swift-Tuttle only comes by every one hundred and thirty years. It was last seen in 1862. Then it was back last winter, leaving its trail of ice and dust. Now the earth is going to pass through the debris and the show is going to be better than the Fourth of July," Evan enthused.

"A hundred and thirty years? I thought you told me the meteor shower came *every* August twelfth?"

"It does. The earth passes through the trail every August 12. The comet passes by—oh, hell, I'm no astronomer—just trust me. This year is special."

I couldn't turn him down. It would be almost unscientific, or so he would have me believe. "Sure, okay."

He leaned close. "Forgive me?" He was doing his irresistible little boy face. I sighed, ever the lap dog.

THE FOLLOWING day, I got a chance to hear another side of the Evan-Reilly feud: Marlena's version. I stopped by the Tenmile Cafe for an early lunch of scrambled eggs and toast and mocha latte—I'd begun to develop a taste for the stuff. I was sitting at the counter when Marlena made a point of coming over, pretending to clean the counter next to where I sat even though it was not dirty.

"How's life up in Leap Year treating you?" she asked with a smile on her face, but not looking at me.

"No complaints." I tried to sound as casual as she did. This was difficult, given the fact that every time I saw her now, I kept trying to imagine her and Reilly together.

"You seem to be getting around good on your cast. How's it feeling?"

"No pain. I'm almost used to this darn thing. Do you suppose I'll miss it when it comes off?"

"My ex-husband broke his leg in a car accident and wore a cast to his hip for three months. When they cut it off of him, he took one look at his leg and fainted dead away. He'd never fainted in his whole life. The doctor said everybody reacts differently. Some get dizzy, some feel sick to their stomachs, some don't notice a thing."

I smiled and shrugged and continued to eat.

She busied herself at the counter again and then said, without looking up, "How's Evan?"

"Oh, fine," I replied cautiously.

She sighed and put down her rag. "I'm just sick about this distance between Evan and Reilly."

I tried to smile sympathetically. I knew in an instant I was being used as a go-between. I didn't mind. I wanted peace in the Allender family as much as Marlena. Still, being a pawn in a game with emotions running so high was risky. I was still the newcomer.

"I know it's all my fault, but what could I do? Lord, I love those boys. I feel like I've raised 'em both."

I nodded, then shrugged, trying to vaguely convey my empathy along with some ambivalence.

"Well...anyway," Marlena murmured and drifted away.

A large elderly man sat down next to me at the counter. It was Jim Knobe. I recognized him by his cowboy hat and neck brace. Apparently the talented Greta had not cured his neck pain.

"Howdy, young lady. Remember me?"

I told him I did. We had been introduced by Evan that first morning he had taken me to the Tenmile for mocha latte. He asked about my leg and I gave him my standard story. It rolled off my tongue with ease, I had recited it so often.

"You want to know something about your family and mine?" he asked with a twinkle in his eye after the conclusion of the formal accident discourse.

I nodded with interest.

"My daddy was once engaged to your aunt, old Miss McAllister."

"Really? When was this?"

"It was in the early part of this century. Before he met my mother, of course, and that was just before the Great War. He must have been engaged to her around 1915, maybe. She was a pretty thing back then. I've seen a photograph of them, taken at their engagement party."

"Why didn't they get married?"

"It's a mystery. My pa never did figure out why she broke it off. They were engaged for more'n a year, then her mother died. She just came to my father one day and said she couldn't marry him and gave him his ring back. She was like a different person, he said. He thought she must've found someone else, but she didn't."

"She never married, I thought."

"Nope, she didn't. My poor old father had quite the broken heart for a while. Left the state, went to California. He met my mother there and got married. Then he came back here. Even got to be friends with your aunt, eventually."

"That's kind of sad, somehow."

Old Jim had a mischievous look. "Bet I can tell you something else about your aunt you don't know. She was a bootlegger during Prohibition."

"No!" I giggled with delight. An outlaw in the family?

"I swear to the world it's true. She and her two brothers, Don and Joe. I can remember them from my childhood. The three of them were all living up there by themselves. Used to operate a still that supplied three counties. Of course the brothers eventually went to jail for it."

"Why didn't my aunt get in trouble?"

"They say the sheriff was sweet on her and wouldn't believe she could be so lawless."

"So my dear old maiden aunt was a bootlegger."

Jim leaned in close with a bashful grin. "She may have been a dear, but she wasn't any 'maiden'."

"*No*," I challenged, teasingly. "Nuh-uh."

"Yes, Ma'am. That sheriff. They were a hot item. I was just a sprout at the time, but I can remember all the gossip. I used to go up to Leap Year and run errands for her and her brothers, do odd jobs after school and the like. Sheriff's car spent a lot of time parked up there."

"How do you know they were lovers?"

"I saw 'em kissing on more than one occasion. And then the sheriff's wife sued him for divorce, named your aunt as the reason."

"Wow, I had no idea." I thought back on how little I really ever knew about Grady. When we corresponded, she was always more interested to know about me than tell about herself. She wanted to hear about my science fair projects and my prom dresses. With the egotism of adolescence, I was only too happy to talk about myself. Only now did I appreciate my lost opportunity—that she was the one with the interesting story to tell.

"Whatever happened with the sheriff?"

"He lost the next election. Had to move away. People back then weren't too forgiving, you know." Jim sighed. "Your aunt was a looker, a real heartbreaker. But she was an independent one, always went her own way."

"Do you, by any chance, know what happened to the rest of her family? I think she had some sisters as well."

"She told me her sisters married and lived elsewhere, but they stayed in touch. One sister moved to Denver. The other married the son of the local saloon keeper and moved to Texas, where he had inherited a big ranch. You know the Lucky Chance?"

The Lucky Chance was a bar and pool hall in Columbine. I had been there once with Evan when a band he had wanted to hear was playing there. It was a dark, smoky dive. I didn't really like it, though they did have good hamburgers. The dirtiest looking places always do.

"Well, that place is named for a saloon that once existed up in Leap Year. It was the first saloon in town and the rowdiest, according to the tales you might read in the old newspapers. It burned down sometime around the turn of the century."

Jim finished his beer and said he had to leave. I thanked him for all the information on my ancestors.

Celeste, ever braless, came over to give me my check. She leaned in close, signaling the need for a confidential chat.

"It's none of my business..." she began. "But you seem like such a nice person."

Oh, brother...where was this leading? I gave her look that said 'please continue.'

"That Evan Allender is just no good. I know he comes on real charming and all, but you've got to watch out "

"Watch out?" I now remembered the coolness Celeste had shown to Evan that first day he and Reilly had taken me to the Tenmile.

"A few years back he was dating my best friend and—" She broke off, her attention drawn to something in the parking lot. I turned to look. A large black man was emerging from a very small Porsche convertible.

"That's my honey," said Celeste, with obvious pride.

I decided to play the know-it-all. "Didn't he used to play for the Broncos?"

"You follow football?" she asked with surprise, pleased that her boyfriend was famous.

I shrugged modestly, hoping my knowledge wouldn't be put to the test.

Then Celeste sighed wistfully. "He wants to marry me, but I don't know. It would kill my parents. They're like total racists."

"I'm sorry." I felt like Dear Abby today. Then Celeste remembered what she wanted to communicate to me about Evan.

She whispered tersely. "My friend was going with that Evan and he got her pregnant, then he just turned his back on her and said something jerky like, 'This is your problem. Deal with it'!"

Mike entered the cafe and our conversation went no further. I wanted to defend Evan, tell his side of the story, how this girl had lied to him. Then I realized I had no idea whether we were talking about the same girl.

METEOR NIGHT arrived at last. Evan and I and the girls stuffed ourselves into my jeep and drove off for my first night of sleeping outdoors in the mountains. The girls and I had to hold most of the camping equipment on our laps since the cargo space in the little jeep was nearly nonexistent.

Evan had picked out a scenic spot on National Forest land that was accessible by four-wheel drive vehicles. He thought the view would be good for sky watching. We drove down Tenmile Canyon, past the SKY Chutes, and over Follow the Sun pass. We missed the unmarked turn off the first time and had to double back.

We slowly crept up the rocky path, Evan trying to ease over the worst bumps, saying he was afraid every jar would hurt my foot. We finally found a camping spot with a good vantage point for meteor viewing. Evan built a campfire from dead branches the girls gathered. We all sat around it roasting hot dogs and later marshmallows as the summer sky slowly darkened. Just as the sun disappeared beyond the western wall of mountains, it cast an eerie golden-yellow glow against the head wall on the opposite side of the canyon. We watched it creep up the granite slope until the last rays turned the small bits of summer snow orange-pink, then faded. The air picked up a sudden chill and we all pulled on our jackets and sweat pants.

We all talked and talked, everyone in high spirits, until Winter mentioned that this was the first year Reilly hadn't joined them on this annual family outing. Evan's mood darkened as he stared into the fire.

"Reilly's growing up, girls. He's not gonna be around that much any more, probably."

The girls seemed downcast by this. I thought it an appropriate time to do my duty as Marlena's go-between. "I was at the Tenmile the other day. Marlena asked about you."

"How sweet," muttered Evan through gritted teeth.

"I think she's upset to have come between you and Reilly."

Evan only frowned.

"I also ran into Jim Knobe."

"How's old Jim?" Evan looked up, brightening.

"He's still wearing his neck brace." I threw this in as a dig against my 'rival' Greta. "He told me Grady was a bootlegger during

Prohibition."

Evan laughed. In an Old Western accent he said, "These here hills is full o' outlaws. Right, girls?"

"Right!" yelled the twins in unison, flattered by this distinction.

By ten, the sky was fully dark and Evan doused the campfire. Evan and I had a double sleeping bag that zipped together and we snuggled down into. The girls placed their bags about ten yards away. We could hear them talking, but couldn't hear what they were saying.

The girls started giggling about something, then started pretending to sneeze. Loud ah-ah-ah-choo's were heard. The girls were taunting us, apparently expecting us to make love.

"Pipe down, over there," yelled their father, with good-natured irritation. Then the first big meteor zipped across the sky. Everyone heaved a collective "ooh" then an "aaahh" at the next and the next.

"This is the best year ever," whispered Evan, after watching a meteor go by so large it had its own tail and made a sizzling sound.

"I'm so lucky to be here," I whispered back.

"We all are," said Evan, philosophically. "I could make a lot more money somewhere else. I know I could. I'm good at what I do, damn it. But every morning I wake up and look out my window and I'm ready to pay the Mountain Tax all over again."

"The mountain tax?" I was afraid there was some new assessment I hadn't heard about yet. I already had enough tax troubles.

Evan chuckled at the obvious apprehension in my voice. "You have to take a vow of poverty to live up here, unless you're a trust fund baby or you find gold or silver like old Reynolds did a century ago."

"The owner of the Northern Star?"

"Yep. He made millions—only to end up dying broke. The Silver Panic of 1893 wiped out all the silver kings and all their towns with them."

"Like Leap Year?"

"Yeah. Some stayed on. Like Grady. Living up here...something happens to you. It's like a drug you can't get enough of...a high so incredible you never want to come down."

"A *Rocky Mountain High*?" I asked to needle him for being so corny.

"Hey, Big John knew what he was talking about. That song was real popular when I was in junior high school. I was living in Chicago and I made my mother buy me a plaid flannel shirt and my first pair of waffle stompers."

I didn't know what waffle stompers were, but didn't want to

admit my ignorance.

"How'd you get so good at Lyric Trivia, anyway?" Evan asked.

"Remember Vanessa?"

"The cynical college roommate?"

"She used to play a radio 24 hours a day. For two years of my life, I heard a radio play, day and night, waking and sleeping. I probably absorbed a lot of it in my sleep."

The magical night wore on and the twins grew silent, probably asleep. The meteor show got better and better, but at some point it became old hat. Even miracles get boring with constant repetition. The lyrics to *Rocky Mountain High* were still on my mind, the part about coming home to a place you'd never been before. Big John *did* know what he was talking about.

Evan and I cuddled closer for love and warmth and I thought about Evan's love for this place and all the sacrifices he endured to stay up here. Grady must have felt the same. I wanted to love something that much.

Evan pointed up into the starry night sky. "Second to the right and straight on 'til morning."

"More Lyric Trivia?"

"Peter Pan. Those were his directions to Neverland."

I stifled a chuckle at the irony of Evan quoting Peter Pan. I nodded off with my head on his chest, thinking I've never been happier, I'll never leave this man, I'll never leave this place, I'll never come down, never come down...*never come down.*

Chapter Twelve

I hope not to shock you, Darcy, but I'm sorry to say my parents' life together began in sin...

CONOR WAS awakened by a soft knocking at Elodie's bedroom door and the sound of an infant crying. Cold white sunlight already filled the room. Conor vaguely remembered bringing Elodie her cherry pie the night before, but it now seemed like a million years ago.

"Come in," Elodie said in a voice still filled with slumber. She slowly stirred herself. She gave Conor a sleepy smile. Her curly hair was in wild disarray, but Conor thought that only made her more attractive.

The door opened and thirteen-year-old Mary Rose carried the baby in, saying in a timid voice, "Corinne wants her breakfast."

"Bring her here," sighed Elodie.

The girl regarded Conor with wary eyes as she carried the baby around to Elodie's side of the bed. She handed the child to her mother, still staring at Conor.

"You remember Mr. McAllister, Rose," said Elodie in a sharp voice. "Say 'good morning,' girl."

"Good morning, sir," said Rose gravely in a voice barely above a whisper.

Conor nodded his reply, feeling very awkward once again to be seen by Elodie's children in her bed. The girl made a quick exit, shutting the door behind her. There were sounds of others beginning to stir in the house.

Elodie calmly unbuttoned the front of her night dress and put the baby to her breast. Conor discreetly looked away.

"I don't mind if you look," smiled Elodie. "You saw it all last night, now didn't you?"

"I suppose I did," said Conor shyly. He looked on with interest, now that she had given him 'permission.' He was curious. He had never seen a woman nurse a baby before. Elodie relaxed back into the pillows she had propped behind her. She watched him watching her. He reached over and pulled the night dress off her other shoulder, exposing the other breast. Drips of pale milk appeared at her nipple. He caught one of the drips on his finger tip.

"Going to taste it?" she challenged, amused by his curiosity.

Conor blushed and dried his finger on the quilt. Elodie shifted the baby to her other breast.

In a playful mood, Conor whispered to baby Corinne. "Hurry up, little one, I want your mother back all to myself."

Elodie smiled broadly at this, pleased by Conor's attentions. When the baby finished and had fallen back to sleep, Elodie placed her in a pulled-out drawer of her chest among her linens and set it on the floor next to the bed as a makeshift cradle.

She looked back at Conor in her bed and, with a strange, almost defiant expression, let the nightdress drop to the floor.

"You're beautiful," he whispered.

Then she looked down at her body and said, somewhat sadly, "I wish you could have seen me before all the children."

Conor looked her up and down as though taking inventory. Small and dark-haired, she was not his type. The tall, willowy, blond Allison had been his type. And it was true—all the pregnancies had taken their toll. Her belly was marked and misshapen from this. On the other hand, he loved her swollen, milky breasts.

"You're beautiful," he repeated, knowing now he was falling in love with her whether he planned to or not. Warily, still defiant, Elodie climbed back into bed. Knowing he had been aroused by her nursing, she offered him her breast. He took it eagerly, but when hot milk shot into the back of his mouth, he jerked away in horror.

"I...I...I'm sorry," he stuttered. "I don't know why I did that. Forgive me." He rolled over onto his side away from her, ashamed to face her.

Elodie tugged at his shoulder, trying to get him back. "But I wanted you to. It's all right."

"No, it's not," said Conor firmly. "What I did was wrong, perverse, depraved...I'm sorry. It won't happen again."

"Conor, Conor darling. Forgive me for speaking ill of the dead, but I think that wife of yours put some strange notions into your head of what's proper and what's not between two people who love each other."

Conor reluctantly rolled back to face her. He looked up at her, still miserable.

As if to illustrate her point, she put her hand on his crotch and began to caress and stroke him. Allison had certainly never done that.

Other women had—most recently, Angel, but not Allison, not on a single day of their marriage. Then Elodie did something no woman had ever done: she put her mouth where her hand had been.

"Oh, my God, Elodie, stop it!" Conor cried in alarm. But soon it felt so good he didn't want her to stop it and in a few moments more he begged her to stop because he couldn't hold back any longer, but she didn't stop and he ejaculated into her mouth. He covered his face with his hands, slightly horrified at what they had just done. When he looked up at her again, she was wiping her mouth on the bed sheet and grinning down at him mischievously.

He smiled weakly. "Where on earth did you learn about that?" He barely knew about the practice himself. It had been whispered of by the boys at school and one night years later, when Conor was walking home late, he had passed an alley. There he had seen a man leaning back against the wall and a woman kneeling before him. Conor had hurried on, both aroused and disgusted by what he had seen.

"One of my laundry customers was a lady who worked at the saloon where you live. You probably know her better than me," she teased.

He chuckled. "No, I swear to you, I don't."

"Anyway, I guess she thought I had too many children because once she drew me aside and said she had some advice for me lest I ever get married again. A way, she said, of pleasing my husband mightily but with no risk of more children. Oh, and she also said if you swallow it, it will cure the consumption."

"Perhaps I should tell my brother Ned. His wife is consumptive." They both burst out in laughter. Then, more soberly, Conor added, "You understand, what we just did is forbidden by law in most states."

"Well," said Elodie, provocatively arching one eyebrow, "I guess we're both outlaws."

Laughing still more, Conor took her in his arms. Then they heard sounds of others stirring in the house. "I shouldn't have stayed so long already. I was planning to leave before your family awakened."

"It's all right," she said. She kissed his brow, quite certain he was the handsomest man she had ever seen, and undeniably the most well-groomed.

"It's not all right. You know that." He held her closer and sighed. "*I have more care to stay than will to go.*"

Elodie smiled, contentedly.

"That's from 'Romeo and Juliet.'" He didn't want Elodie to think he was taking credit inappropriately.

Elodie was puzzled. This was the second reference to this couple in a week. Who were these people, anyway?

Conor read Elodie's confused expression. "Shakespeare," he explained. "It's a play about a pair of doomed lovers."

"Oh, a play." Now she understood, or at least thought she did.

"Are you familiar with Shakespeare?"

Elodie shook her head, regretful at her lack of formal education. Book learning had not been a high priority for girls where she came from.

"Shakespeare was an English poet and playwright. He lived a long time ago." Conor began to recite the only sonnet he could remember:

"Shall I compare thee to a summer's day?
Thou art more lovely and more temperate.
Rough winds do shake the darling buds of May,
And summer's lease hath all too short a date.
Sometime too hot the eye of heaven shines—

—something, something, something." Conor's memory was failing him. He could only come up with the last two lines:

"So long as men can breathe or eyes can see,
So long lives this, and this gives life to thee."

"Very pretty," said Elodie, thinking she had heard the whole poem and not getting much out of it.

"He was making his mistress immortal by writing this poem about her," Conor explained. "I've tried to do the same with my drawings."

"Pictures of...your wife?" ventured Elodie, cautiously.

"No, you, of course."

"Of me?" Elodie preened at this. "May I see them?"

Conor frowned and admitted, "I didn't save them." He would have been embarrassed to show her the nudes, anyway.

Elodie turned immediately downcast, jutting out her full bottom lip. "I'll make new ones, better ones—now that I have you to pose in the life." He kissed her and wanted to make love to her again, but there was growing commotion from her children in the kitchen. "I suppose I'd better be going."

"Don't go...please don't."

Conor sat up. "But I have to—"

"No, you don't," Elodie pleaded. "I could make you happy. I know I could."

"You already have," Conor chuckled, raising his eyebrows. He got out of bed and began to dress.

"More than *that*," she said.

Conor didn't honestly know what more there was at this point. He certainly wasn't in a position to support a family of five. He didn't even contribute to the welfare of his own daughter. He immediately suspected Elodie of trying to trap him into marriage.

As though she were reading his mind—which he almost suspected her of having the ability to do—she spoke to this very point.

"You don't have to marry me. I can live without that honor. It's you I want, just you. I make no demands of you—just that you love me and live with me."

"You're suggesting that we live together, openly, without marriage?" He was shocked by this proposal.

"Yes."

"Well...I don't...I don't know," he stammered.

"Are you worried about your reputation?" she asked, stifling a giggle.

"I'm more worried about yours," he replied earnestly.

"I don't have one, so stop worrying."

She was so matter-of-fact on the point, it was he who was forced to laugh. "You're a frighteningly determined woman, Elodie Kelly."

"It's the altitude," she said, with a wicked grin.

ELODIE GOT her wish. Within a week, Conor informed Brandon Chance that he no longer needed the room above the saloon. This announcement pleased Brandon who wanted the room for his son, Josh, because it was heated. He gave Conor quite a time about his new choice of lodgings. Conor endured the kidding with grace, having braced for it.

Within a month, Conor was writing letters home to his parents and his mother-in-law to advise them he would not be returning home in the late spring as originally planned. His career in journalism kept him in the West, he wrote, and, in truth, his column for Applebee's paper was more popular than ever. His account of the rescue of the Chances—discreetly edited, of course—was to become a great success.

He told them he would return to Philadelphia sometime in the summer, but he did not return in the summer or the fall or the winter. Living with Elodie and her family proved as natural and effortless as breathing. The children accepted him, not as a father figure, but as a friend. At first, the noisy chaos of the house overwhelmed him, but soon he grew to relish it. Growing up essentially as an only child, he had never known what it meant to live in a house filled with children.

He was especially close to Joe. They had formed an intense bond, spending a summer fishing in Tenmile Creek. Conor wished his own father had not been so elderly when he was born. He would have liked to have spent such a summer as father and son with him. Of course, even Conor's older half-brothers did not get this kind of attention. Their father had been too preoccupied with building a successful business. To take an entire afternoon off to do something as worthless as fishing would have been unthinkable to Ben McAllister, even when he was Conor's present age and the sons of his first marriage were schoolboys.

Little Donal and Kitty adored Conor. They knew they could count on him to bring them sweets, when their mother was not looking. Only Rose was shy of him. But even she warmed up when he presented her with a charcoal portrait of herself on her birthday. Life with Conor in the house was so different from the one they remembered with their real father. Now there were no more drunken rages, no boxed ears, no screaming arguments late into the night punctuated by the crash of broken china, no more running errands for a mother hiding a bruised face from the neighbors.

Living 'in sin' with Elodie had not proved as socially uncomfortable as he had feared. Such an arrangement would have been impossible back home, but Leap Year often reminded him of a foreign country in which he was daily becoming acquainted with the local customs. Perhaps Elodie was correct in her assertion that people really did live by a different set of rules up here. Closer to heaven, she had once said. If this were the case he had no desire to venture down ever again.

Their lack of formal vows played a noticeable role occasionally. One such incident occurred the week Conor spent writing a profile of Northern Star Mine owner Reynolds. Mrs. Reynolds arranged a dinner party in honor of the event. She made a point of inviting only Conor, though the fact that he lived with Elodie was well known. Elodie didn't make a fuss and Conor innocently thought only men had been invited. When he arrived, however, he realized that all the Northern Star investors, plus the head foreman, had been invited along with their wives.

When Conor returned home, he was seething at the slight he felt had been directed at Elodie. He slammed the door of the cabin as he entered, causing Corinne to wail in Elodie's lap as she sat before the fire waiting up for him.

"Was the food that bad?" she laughed, as she tried to quiet the baby, hoping not to awaken the remainder of the sleeping household.

"The food was adequate, the company was not."

"Whatever is the matter?" His angry mood surprised her, so seldom had he fits of temper.

He slumped into the sofa next to her and stared at the fire. "Hypocritical son of a bitch. I'm sorry, forgive me for using language like that. It's just that—"

"What did Mr. Reynolds do to you that was so unforgivable?" She found his pouting face amusing and irresistibly little boylike.

Conor sighed bitterly. "It wasn't what he did to me." He was slowly calming down and now wishing he hadn't begun the explanation. He didn't want Elodie's feelings hurt, but now knew no way to avoid telling her the source of his irritation. "All the other men's wives were invited to the dinner party."

"I'm not your wife, Conor," Elodie reminded him quietly. The baby was asleep again against her chest.

"They're hypocrites, all of them. I hate them."

"It doesn't matter," Elodie lied. "I don't care, really I don't." Another lie.

"Just wait until old Reynolds sees what I write about him. Perhaps I should share with the reading public just how often the morally superior owner of the Northern Star visits the cribs behind the Lucky Chance!"

"Oh, hush, now. You'll do no such thing. Mr. Reynolds is the most powerful man in this town. You'll do nothing to annoy him, no matter what the provocation. We may be sinners, but we're not fools— am I right?"

Conor put his arm around her. "I suppose you're right. I'll sleep on it at least." As they prepared for bed, a disturbing thought came to him. Could it have been possible that Elodie had once been old Reynolds' mistress? That would explain the existence of Corinne as well as how Elodie seemed to have so much more money than a laundry business would suggest. She was a beautiful woman and possibly desperate for funds after her husband's death. Had Reynolds exploited this, seducing her with his wealth?

Oddly, this thought made him ponder the relationship of his own parents. Had his seventeen-year-old mother also been dazzled by the wealth of an older man? Conor hated himself for thinking along these lines. He was casting both Elodie and his mother as little better than common prostitutes, trading their youth and beauty for financial security. While falling asleep that night, he tried to put this disturbing speculation out of his mind.

As the months wore on though, his nagging sense of guilt about the immorality of their living arrangements began to increase and never more so than the afternoon he came upon little Donal sitting by the roadside, perched on a large boulder, crying his heart out. After considerable coaxing, Donal shared the source of his misery. It seemed two older boys at school had tormented him with the news that his mother was going to spend eternity burning in Hell.

"Why would they say that?" asked Conor, upset for Donal's sake but remembering the politics of the playground well enough to know little boys seldom needed reasons to inflict cruelty upon one another.

"They said she was a 'forn-i-crator'."

Conor bit his lip to avoid smiling at Donal's mispronunciation, but at the same time felt shamed that his living arrangements with Elodie were causing her children to be taunted or ridiculed.

"Donal, have you ever known your mother to be anything but kind and good?"

"No." Donal sniffed loudly and wiped his wet and swollen face on his sleeve.

Conor handed him a handkerchief to blow his nose on. "And good and kind people don't go to Hell, do they?"

"No."

"So, obviously, these boys are wrong, aren't they?"

Donal looked up at Conor uncertainly, then looked down again and nodded slowly.

Conor couldn't tell if he had convinced the boy or not. He then mentioned that the mercantile had just received a new shipment of licorice. Donal perked up immediately at the mention of his favorite treat and the two of them headed off for the store with Donal now happy and Conor now miserable.

That night after the children were in bed, he informed Elodie that he had been taking unconscionable advantage of her feelings for him over the last few months, that they were setting a bad moral example for the children, and that he could no longer bear to subject them all to the shame caused by their lack of convention. For these reasons, he felt he must move out.

The words had no sooner left his lips than Elodie threw herself at his feet, wrapped her arms around his legs and set up such a wailing, he feared the children would hear and come down. She begged him to reconsider and implored him to tell her what she had done that had so displeased him.

"Nothing, nothing," Conor assured her, completely stunned by the melodrama of her outburst. "I...I just didn't want you to suffer anymore on my account."

"I'd suffer any torment to be near you," she sobbed, still carrying on. "I'd bear any shame, I'd walk through fire if I had to, I'd—"

"All right, all right." He pulled her to her feet. "I didn't mean to upset you. Of course, I'll stay." He hugged her to his chest and thought about how neither of them had mentioned the other obvious solution to end their dishonor: marriage.

Conor knew he should marry her, but every time he thought about it he felt as though he were standing on the brink of a frightening precipice. The prospect of taking on the legal responsibility for her and all her children was simply too daunting. Still the debate in his mind continued on an almost daily basis.

Just before Christmas, he finally reached a decision. The decision had been influenced by many things, not the least of which the fact that Elodie, who had weaned her baby in the fall, was now getting sick in the mornings. Conor knew what that meant.

But there was more to it than wishing to spare Elodie's already questionable reputation further stain. In her, Conor was beginning to feel he had at last found his soulmate, the true partner of his heart. With all the previous women in his life, he had experienced either love or passion—never both at once. He wondered if it were some failing on his part or if this were simply how the world worked. There had been that friend of his mother's who had relieved him of his virginity at nineteen and that girl at the company picnic—both examples of sexual fireworks without any love attached. At the other end of the spectrum was Allison, of course. He had loved her desperately, but connubial bliss had eluded them to such an extent it almost amounted to a cruel joke. Kathleen, too, was nearer Allison's end of this spectrum, though he knew their affair might have taken a different turn had they met later in life, that is, when at least *he* been more mature. But now he had Elodie. He loved her with his heart and his body. Was she his reward for all those years of failed or marred relationships? He was not going to let her slip away.

"I suppose we had better think about getting married," he said to her one morning in bed as she was chewing on dry toast in an effort to control the nausea.

"Why?" she asked, through a mouthful of toast.

"Well...isn't there a child on the way?"

She nodded, still chewing.

"Then I expect we'd better get married. I mean, neither of us need any more illegitimate children, right?"

She swallowed. "Don't tell me you—the noble and impossibly correct Mr. Conor McAllister of Philadelphia, Pennsylvania—has fathered a child out of wedlock?"

He chuckled at her teasing. "I'm afraid so. I mean, I suppose so."

"You suppose? You don't know?" She took another bite of toast, this time out of hunger. The sick feeling had passed.

Conor shrugged. "I never knew how it turned out. Her father was one of my father's employees, the head tanner, in fact, and—"

"Employees?" Elodie interrupted. "You told me your father was a cobbler."

Conor smiled in embarrassment. "*You* said he was a cobbler, El. I told you he made boots. He owns a bootworks."

"And he employs people?"

"About eighty," said Conor.

Elodie's eyes widened, reevaluating the man who shared her bed. "I had no idea."

Conor gestured to indicate this matter was of little consequence. He had been pursued too much in his earlier youth for his family's wealth. It had been refreshing to be with someone who had no knowledge of it.

"Tell me about this girl," said Elodie, sensing that Conor didn't want to talk about his family.

Conor sighed, shaking his head. "It was not a pleasant thing."

"Now that I won't believe," teased Elodie.

Conor laughed. He liked the light way Elodie could joke about sex. "I meant the aftermath, of course. We met at a company picnic. My father gives one every summer for the employees and their families. My mother held a picnic basket auction to benefit a children's charity she works on.

"I bid on a basket and got to eat with the girl who brought it. She was lively and kind of pretty. She was...forward. I know that's no excuse for me, only an explanation. What I'm trying to say is it's not as though I talked her into doing anything."

"No one's calling you a cruel seducer, my darling," laughed Elodie.

"The girl's father certainly did," said Conor bitterly. "He practically implied I'd forced myself on her." In fact, quite the opposite had been true. The laughing, flirtatious girl had informed Conor before the picnic meal was eaten that she thought they should find a more secluded location to share the afternoon. Conor was foolishly only too happy to oblige her. His last thought as they left the party was, "And to think I hadn't wanted to attend this damned picnic."

"A couple of months after the picnic the girl and her father showed up in my father's office, demanding that I marry her. I mean, it was so absurd. My father called me to his office and drew me aside and asked if there were any truth to this. I admitted I'd had her—just the once, of course. Then he asked if she had been a virgin. I told him I didn't think so—I was hardly an expert on such matters, but I was pretty certain. I remembered him sighing with relief. He patted me on the shoulder and said not to worry, that he'd handle it. I couldn't believe he was taking my side for once. Not that he was happy about the situation. But for just that moment, it was as if he was treating me—I don't know—like we were friends."

"Well, he was your father, Conor. How was he supposed to treat you? Like a stranger?"

Conor chuckled. "More or less. We were never close." Conor went on with his story. It felt good to finally tell it to someone, now that all the crisis was long in the past. He had never talked about this to anyone outside his immediate family, except Applebee, who had advised him to run away and join the Navy. "My father returned to his desk and went into action. He was a lion when it came to negotiation. Good old Dad—how he loved a challenge. He told them that marriage was out of the question, that they had no proof I was the father. He even implied that it was an outright extortion attempt. The girl started crying at that point. I felt really awful. I wanted to comfort her somehow. She had this bruise on her face. I think her father must have hit her."

Elodie frowned furiously at this part of the story. "The old monster."

"I made some move toward her, but my father gave me such a look. He made it clear we were going to stand our ground. But this man was not stupid. He said if I would not own up to it, they would bring a lawsuit."

"A court could make you get married?"

"No, but they could make me support the girl and her baby. They had us on this. Even if they didn't win the suit, the scandal would have been terrible. You see, my family was prominent enough that a lawsuit like that would have made the papers. My father would not let my mother suffer through something so...sordid. They argued back and forth a long while and finally reached an agreement on a sum. I remember how during the negotiations, the girl and I just looked at each other miserably. When it was over, my father and her father stood up and shook hands, like it was all just an ordinary business deal. The man even continued to work for us."

"All quite civil, thank you very much."

"Exactly. She was sent to live with a relative in Baltimore. That was part of the agreement. I never knew how it all came out. Whether she had the baby, whether it was a boy or a girl, whether it was even mine or not. I guess I'll never know."

Conor thought about that meeting, about how, after the man and his daughter had left his father's office he had hoped to slip out as well. He had almost made it to the door, almost gotten his hand on the knob, when his father barked his name. He spun around.

"Do you understand how fortunate you are that this man values his employment with us, Conor?" Ben was scribbling notes to himself at his desk and did not bother to look up at his son as he spoke.

Conor didn't follow his father's line of thought and said nothing.

"If he didn't," Ben continued, "he and a couple of his friends would be beating you senseless in an alley somewhere."

Conor shifted uncomfortably. Even at twenty-five, he understood that men did not appreciate having spoiled, young rich boys defiling their daughters. The girl's words at the picnic—*You're trapped*—had come back to him just then in a brand new and unnerving context.

Ben sighed and sat back in his great leather chair. He pushed his spectacles up over his forehead and gazed out the window as though there were something to look at other than another brick wall. "Glad I never had any daughters," he murmured. Then he turned his attention back to his son. "I don't want this to happen again. Is that clear?"

"Yes, sir."

"You're too old for this kind of nonsense. When I was your age, I was already married with two children."

"I don't have anything against marriage, Father. I just haven't found the right woman."

"All those girls you go out with—I find it hard to believe one of them couldn't fill the bill."

"But I want it to be perfect—"

"Nothing in life is perfect, Conor. Marriage is a gamble. *Life* is a gamble. We can't control the outcome, we can only hope for the best."

"But, it's just that—"

"I'm awfully busy, Conor," interrupted Ben, beginning to scribble again. "Another time perhaps."

"THE POOR THING," Elodie mused about the unfortunate tanner's daughter. "I mean, even if she were a fast one, I still pity her."

"I guess I do, too." Conor was soft-hearted. He had never had any real feelings for this girl, but had felt bad about how he'd behaved, sorry that he'd caused her grief—even if he were just a pawn in a clumsy extortion scheme. To him, the bruise on the girl's face had spoken more about the situation than any words that had been exchanged.

Then another thought occurred to him. Perhaps Elodie's compassion for this girl sprung from her own experience. He took a deep breath and finally asked a question that had bothered him since the day he had met her. "El...I swore I'd never ask you this, but...I can't help but wonder."

As usual, she seemed to read his mind. "You want to know about Corinne."

He nodded, unable to face her directly.

Elodie suddenly looked tormented. She turned her face toward the window as though looking out of it, oblivious to the fact it was curtained at the moment.

"Elodie..." Conor said softly. "Were you...attacked?"

"Yes," she replied quickly. "Yes, by...a stranger. I never saw him again."

Conor was instantly furious at this stranger who had harmed his soon-to-be wife. "I wish I could kill him," he muttered.

"Oh, hush...it's long passed." She put her arms around him and hugged him. "Let's talk about *our* baby." She smiled brightly, forcing him back into a good mood.

Conor grinned and pulled up her nightgown. He studied her abdomen and noticed the slight swelling just below her navel. He gently placed his hand there. "Is this it?"

"Yes," she answered, suddenly shy.

"Do you ever feel it kicking?"

"Not yet, of course. That doesn't happen until quickening."

"Which is when?"

She laughed at his ignorance. "In a couple of months, I guess. It's always near the middle. The bulge will be much bigger by then. You know, for a man who's been married before, you don't seem to know much about this process."

Conor playfully groaned. "Oh, El—would you believe I never even saw her naked?"

"No."

"I hate to admit it, but it's perfectly true." For the first time ever, he began to find the absurdity of it funny. In fact, his entire, miserable marriage to Allison suddenly seemed hilarious to him.

"Oh, Conor, stop teasing me. The pair of you had a child together, for God's sake..."

"I said I never *saw* her. I didn't say I never *touched* her!" They were both laughing now. Elodie shook her head, still not completely believing this, but also contemptuously thinking what an over-bred, hothouse flower Conor's dead wife must have been. But in the same instant, she worried that perhaps Conor liked demure women. She, in her eagerness to do anything to please him, must have seemed a complete wanton by comparison. She quickly pulled her nightgown skirt back down to modestly cover her limbs, but Conor's thoughts were far away.

He was remembering how his last argument with Allison had been prompted by the innocent desire to feel their baby kick. He had come home from her father's law office early that day. He was reading law there. Her father had promised him a position in the firm if he could pass the Bar. But Conor was finding the study of law excruciatingly boring. He had accepted the offer only because it gave him an excuse to leave the bootworks. He had left the office library in the middle of the afternoon on the pretense of a headache, though he really just couldn't stand another hour of reading the lofty pronouncements of long-dead judges in the moldy smelling casebooks.

He sat in the windowseat of their bedroom enjoying a cup of coffee laced with a shot of whiskey. Allison was sitting before her mirror, pinning and unpinning her hair, trying to design a new style. Suddenly, she sucked her breath in and held her hand against the side of her belly.

"What's the matter?" asked Conor, walking over to where she sat. She was very near her time. The doctor had told them the baby could arrive any day now.

"Oh, nothing. Just the kicking again. This child never gives me a moment's peace, day or night."

"Let me feel the kicking."

"No." She slapped his hand away.

"*Allison*, it's my baby, too." He sat down next to her on the vanity bench and frowned at her reflection in the mirror.

"Must I forever cater to your lecherous whims?" she snapped.

"My 'lecherous whims' as you call them happen to be the normal desires of a loving husband. I wish you had some context within which to comprehend this."

"Normal desires? I would call them base and demeaning. You despise me because I refuse to allow you to drag me down to your level."

Though Conor had never struck a woman in his life, the urge to slap his wife's petulant face almost overpowered him. But he thought men who hit women were cowardly and disgraceful, so he used words to hurt her instead. "I think sometimes you are quite seriously insane. They put people as confused as you are in asylums for their own safety."

This opened the expected floodgate of tears. Between sobs, Allison muttered, "If I had known what a vile, insensitive, perverse man you were, I would never had consented to become your wife!"

"And I wish to heaven every day you had not!"

Allison wailed even louder at this and Conor left the room, but not before nearly knocking down his mother-in-law who had apparently been eavesdropping on the other side their door. Conor rushed out of the house and did not return...until it was too late.

ELODIE'S VOICE pulled Conor back into the present.

"I think we should build a larger house," she was saying.

"Oh, El...I agree we need more room, but I don't have that kind of money."

"But I do."

This brought up the second troubling mystery concerning the woman whose life and house he had shared for the preceding nine months. She never seemed to be short of funds. Conor still had no idea where the money came from and Elodie was adept at dodging his tactful inquiries. He wasn't in a position to complain about the situation. He could not begin to support her large family on what he made writing for Applebee's paper. He had a small income from a trust left him by his grandfather McAllister. That saw to his personal needs, not much more. He knew he should feel grateful to finally have found a woman who was not trying to marry him for his family's wealth, but the source of Elodie's funds remained a disturbing puzzlement. Despite her claim to be a rape victim—which really hadn't come out very convincingly, Conor still caught himself wondering about Mr. Reynolds.

They were married on New Year's Day by the Methodist preacher. Just before the ceremony, Elodie asked Conor once again if he were happy about the baby they were expecting. Rather than giving her the usual 'yes, of course,' he thought about his answer for a moment.

"This is what I think about children," he whispered. "I think that every time a child is born, the world starts over again. And maybe I could use a second chance."

Elodie's children, Granny Atwater, and Brandon and Hannah Chance were the only witnesses. Hannah was huge with child, due any day. Elodie was convinced Hannah and Brandy's baby had been conceived in the snowbound cabin the night before she and Conor had rescued them. She was certain this was a sign from heaven above that the reunion was meant to be. Hannah agreed, but her husband would only roll his eyes at this fanciful speculation. According to him, conceiving babies was "as common as dirt" and there "wasn't nothin' mystical about it." As the owner of a brothel, he had certainly ample opportunity to witness the miracle of life in its basest manifestations. Indeed, the alleyway behind his saloon, and the fourteen other saloons which now lined the main avenue of Leap Year, had come to be known as "Stillborn Street" for all the dead infants found in the trash heaps.

Leap Year had experienced a spectacular growth spurt since Conor had first arrived. The town now boasted, not only fifteen saloons, but eight restaurants, four hotels, still only three churches, and—to Elodie's delight—a school.

The Chances had prospered despite the new competition. They had just completed construction of a grand new home. Conor was fairly certain this new house had inspired Elodie's request for one. Conor had promised her a house would be built as soon as the snow melted in the spring. Conor was tired of the dark pine cabin, with its rough-hewn walls. He longed for a fine frame house with the elaborate trim of his parents' home in the East.

The Chances toasted the newly married couple with a party at their new house. Brandy, after several rounds, announced he was taking full credit for bringing the couple together. He claimed it was his suggestion that Conor bring Elodie her cherry pie the night after the famous rescue that led to this moment. Elodie blushingly acknowledged this was true, while Conor felt Brandon's remarks inappropriate in the presence of Elodie's children.

Throughout dinner, Hannah observed the new bride with a critical eye. Finally, she leaned close and asked her friend in whispered tones if a baby had prompted the sudden nuptials. Elodie's brilliant smile was her only reply. With a self-satisfied smirk, Hannah turned to her husband and whispered, "I was right."

Tragedy cut short the newlyweds' bliss the following week when Elodie suffered a miscarriage. She woke up one morning with strong cramping pains and her nightdress covered with blood. By noon, it was all over.

Conor was terribly upset. He feared for Elodie's health. All the old anxiety of Allison's death came back in a rush, making him nervous and depressed. Granny Atwater's response to his anguish was a shrug and a "These things happen."

Elodie, who should have been receiving comfort over her loss, instead found herself offering it to her new husband. Over and over, she insisted her health would return, that they would try for another baby in the spring. She was afraid he would lose interest in her if she could not provide him with a child. On a purely practical level she feared he would go back on his promise to build a new house.

ANOTHER, MUCH older problem reasserted itself the week after Elodie was back on her feet. She was alone in the house, but for a sleeping Corinne. Granny Atwater had taken Donal and Kitty to the market and the two older children were at school.

He entered the kitchen door without knocking. His sudden appearance gave her a start. She eyed the distance between herself and the carving knife on the pantry wall.

"Good day to you, Elodie, dear."

His very appearance sickened her.

"What are you doing here?" she whispered fiercely.

"That's no way to talk to me, girl. Haven't seen you in more'n a year. Isn't that so?" He fingered his beard.

"Haven't missed you, either." She slowly edged toward the kitchen, as he sat himself down at her table. She noticed his limp was worse. Perhaps the cold weather had worsened it or perhaps his health was on the decline.

"Married again, I've heard." His tone was evilly taunting.

"Aye, and it's no business of yours."

"I think it might be my business. I think it might be very much my business. I'll grant you he's a pretty fellow. You always liked 'em good looking, now didn't you?"

Elodie let out an angry sigh. "What exactly have you come for?"

"To see you, of course. And conduct a little business."

"I'll be needing more money than usual. I want a new house."

"A house! You're dreaming, girl, if you think I'll be giving you that much."

"You will and you'll like it," Elodie snapped, in a voice as cold and hard as granite.

"Simmer down. How much are we talking about?"

"Two thousand, maybe three."

His eyes widened, then narrowed. "For that you'll be giving me a little sugar, now, won't you?"

"Give me the money and get out. You'll never lay a hand on me again. I have a husband now. He'll protect me from the likes of you." Elodie held her anger at bay and tried a new tactic. She smiled coolly. "Maybe he'd like to come in on the game."

The man jumped up with a murderous mein. "You tell him and it'll be the last thing you'll ever do."

Elodie held up her hand to warn him to keep his distance. Her other hand, behind her back, was securely on the carving knife now. "I was just joking. You know I'd never tell."

Noises were heard from the road. The man glanced out the front parlor window nervously. It was Granny Atwater returning from the market with the two little ones.

"Quickly," Elodie whispered. "The money—hurry up!"

"All right, all right." He tossed a grimy handkerchief on the table filled with gold coins. It landed with a *ka-chunk* and two of the coins spilled out.

"Get out, quickly," she commanded as she snatched up the little bundle.

Chapter Thirteen

WELL, IT HAPPENED—reality finally reeled me in. Hardly a month into the affair of the century, it was over. Over, dead still, no going back. Stopped like an electric clock in a momentary power outage and flashing 12:00 ever since. So much for summer romance.

The day after Meteor Night, I received an unusual phone call.

"Is Evan there?"

"No, sorry."

"He gave me this number."

"I can give him a message."

"You his old lady?"

"Uh, yeah." I took an instant dislike to this man's tone, but I didn't know why.

"Look, tell him Frank called and I'm gettin' fuckin' tired of waitin' for him to make up his mind. I gotta know if he's in by tomorrow—*no later*. You got that?"

"What are you talking about?"

"He'll know. Just tell him." *Click.*

I put down the receiver in slow motion. I felt a fifty-pound weight in the pit of my stomach. I wasn't the worldliest woman around, but I had watched enough TV to realize I had just probably conversed with a drug dealer.

I was stunned to think Evan had lied to me when he told me all his outlaw activities were in the past. I had generously excused this as a youthful indiscretion. What a naive fool I'd been. The lying bastard.

A rage mixed with hurt, disappointment, fear—a kaleidoscope of negative emotions—brewed inside me. For hours, I just sat in Grady's bay window, staring at the floor.

In the early evening my mother called. The ringing jarred me out of my hypnotic trance of anger. She was in a rare cheerful mood, talkative enough for both of us. I wanted to rail against the villainous treachery of men, but couldn't. She would not have sympathized. Her reaction would have run along the lines of "lie down with dogs, get up with fleas," or some other equally unsavory aphorism.

"I talked to Aunt Evelyn in the nursing home. She remembered a few things about her mother's family. Grandma Simpson never really knew her father. He left Philadelphia when she was only two and she was raised by her mother's parents. He came out to Colorado and ended up marrying an Irish woman with a lot of children."

"Elodie Kelly. She had five kids," I interjected. I was irritable and disappointed that I wasn't learning anything new.

"Anyway, after this marriage, plans were under way to send Beatrice out to Colorado to live with her father. She was about four or five at the time and Evelyn said Beatrice remembered this event. The year was 1882."

"What happened?"

"He never came back to pick her up. He just disappeared. They never found out what happened to him. His family even hired private detectives to look for him, but no luck. His new wife said he just never came home one day."

"God, how weird."

"The other thing she remembered was that this Irish woman—the step mother, I guess—sent Bea a huge check as a wedding present. They had kept in touch a little bit over the years, but they never met. This huge wedding gift—it was like $5,000, which was an enormous sum of money back then—came way out of left field."

Before hanging up, my mother asked in a quiet, non-argumentative tone for once, "Darling, when are you coming home?"

I mumbled forlornly, "Soon, I guess. As soon as I sell..." My voice trailed off. As irrational as it seemed, I no longer wanted to sell Leap Year. The old town was like a stray puppy that had followed me home. I'd grown to love it and didn't want to give it up, even if its owner could be found.

"Soon," I repeated.

I resumed my meditations in the bay window. I should have been more interested than I was in this new information on Conor. I had been eagerly awaiting more family news about Grady and her parents, but just now I was too overwhelmed by my own problems to care about anything else. Darkness slowly filled the room and then, just after nine, Evan arrived bearing Chinese food in a brown grocery sack.

He dropped the food off in the kitchen, calling to me. "Darcy, you home? You won't believe it—I got to play midwife. Scarlett had her puppies, six of 'em. Darcy? Why are all the lights off?"

He entered the living room and saw me sitting in the bay. The smile drained from his face. "What's wrong? You look like somebody died."

"I have a phone message for you," I said in a low voice.

"Huh?" He stood warily in the arched entryway to Grady's parlor.

"Frank called."

Even in the low light, I could see the color drain out of his face.

"Oh, shit," he whispered.

"Evan, you told me that was all in the past and I believed you."

He moaned as he swung around and slammed his fist into the door frame. He turned back to face me, cradling his painful hand against his chest. He slumped into the nearest chair and stared at the floor between us. "I didn't want you to know."

"And that would make it okay? Is that your point?"

"Look, it's no big deal—"

"The hell it isn't," I exploded.

"I needed to pick up some extra money, okay? Since Greta split, I've had trouble making ends meet. That's all. Kids are expensive, Darcy. A couple of drops a month for Frank and I don't even need to build houses."

"And you were just not going to tell me—"

"Why would I tell you? So you could go ballistic? So you could treat me like a criminal?"

"Excuse me—*Hel-lo*. You *are* a criminal!"

"By some people's definition —"

"By *everyone's* definition. We're talking major felonies here."

He made a face to indicate he thought I was being—what? Provincial? Nit-picking?

"Evan, I thought I knew you..."

"You do know me. I'm still me." He shrugged.

"But drugs are—drugs are—" I sputtered in my frustration.

With a sad smile, he said, "You don't need to lecture me on the evils of drug abuse. Christ, that's why Beth and I broke up." He raised his eyes to the ceiling as though looking back in time. "I never realized she had such a problem until it was too late. I mean, sure, there were drugs around, but it was all strictly recreational, you know? I was gone a lot. I was playing in that band I told you about. We were going out on gigs nearly every weekend during ski season. Beth was stuck at home with the twins and Reilly. One day I came home and found her giving a blow job to a friend of mine in exchange for drugs. That was the end of the Beth and Evan Show."

He sat silently reflecting for a while, then continued. "Since then, I've blamed myself. God knows, I was no angel myself during that time. My opportunities to get laid were endless when I was out on the road with the band. Sometimes I played the faithful husband and sometimes I didn't." He shrugged with a resolute sigh. "I just couldn't live with a coke whore, though, you know?"

After another long silence, I simply said, "I don't want to talk anymore. Just go."

After he left, I threw out the Chinese food. I had no appetite. The very smell of it sickened me. I went to bed that night feeling more alone, more betrayed than I had the night Keith had announced he wanted a divorce.

AS IF MY life needed a further blow, I had a checkup on my foot the following day and was about to leave when the accounting clerk waylaid me at the door.

"Ms. Close, we didn't know where to send this. Do you have a post office box yet? Cause we don't get home delivery, you know." She handed me a fat envelope.

"I guess I didn't realize. My aunt has a mailbox right next to her door." I had sort of wondered why I hadn't received any mail. I knew that the car rental bills were being charged to my mother's credit card, but I hadn't gotten anything from the utilities yet.

The girl chuckled. "Old Miss McAllister was the only person in the county that got her mail delivered. Mr. Peterson at the post office used to worry about her so he'd drive up to Leap Year once a week to give her mail and see how she was doing. Everybody used to kid her about getting special treatment from the U.S. Postal Service and she would always laugh and say, 'I deserve it'!"

I smiled and thanked the girl and opened the envelope as I walked out to the parking lot. I casually scanned the blurry computer printout listing all the charges in connection with my foot. When I found the bottom line, the figure hit me like an electric shock: $1,486.12.

Nearly fifteen hundred dollars! How could one broken foot cost so much? That was more than half my entire net worth at the moment. I drove home in a daze wondering how I was going to pay the bill. I couldn't ask my mother for any more money. She had already lectured me on the dangers of not carrying health insurance. I had been living without it since the divorce.

As I made my way up Leap Year Road, a telephone company truck was driving down. I wondered what brought them up here. I hadn't reported any service problem. The road was so narrow, I pulled off as far as I dared to allow them to pass. When they got closer, I could see it was my two pals, Barry and Steve. I waved at them, but they didn't even turn their heads as they buzzed on by, spraying my jeep with gravel as they passed.

Well, that's nice, I grumbled to myself as I turned back onto the road.

The day was made complete when I walked up my rickety front porch stairs only to have the spongiest step give way under my only remaining good foot. My ankle got scraped, but no other damage was done except to the broken step. I sat down on the porch and cried—cried over my problems, cried over losing Evan, cried because I now hated Evan, cried because I owed so much money, cried over the broken step. At least I knew of one carpenter I would *not* be calling to repair it.

The next morning, I looked through the county's slim phone book and began calling carpenters. One was able to come out—or 'up,' as they always termed it—late that afternoon. I moped about the house all morning, yearning for a television set, then decided to drive down into Columbine for lunch. That would kill a couple of hours while waiting for the repairman to arrive.

I stopped at the post office to get a box rented.

"You're lucky you came in today, young lady," said the elderly Mr. Peterson. "I have some mail for you in General Delivery. I was about to send it back."

"Lucky? These both look like bills," I weakly joked, getting an awful sinking sensation in my stomach. One was from the electric co-op. The other from the telephone company.

While eating, Marlena came over and asked how Evan was.

"Evan and I are no longer together." I tried to say this as simply and unemotionally as possible. I also knew that in announcing this fact in the Tenmile Cafe, I had effectively communicated it to the entire world. This made it official somehow and that gave me a sense of satisfaction. I had been trying to focus on all the reasons I was better off without Evan. He was too old for me. And he didn't shave often enough which made my face raw from his kisses. And we didn't really like the same music and I was tired of always pretending to have the same tastes as the man I was with. I did that the entire time I was with Keith and if I ever have to listen to another Elvis Costello song I will become seriously ill. Besides, when was the last time a man pretended to like the music I liked just to please me? Did I ever get taken to any R.E.M. or Sting concerts? No-o-o-o.

"Sorry to hear that, honey," said Marlena to the Evan news.

"Oh," I shrugged carelessly, "These things happen."

"I thought Evan had really found someone in you. That you'd be good for him. That Greta—that was a disaster waiting to happen."

"What was Greta like, anyway?"

"Oh, she was pretty. No doubt about that. Tall, skinny, high cheek bones, very blond. Really striking. She even did some modeling when she was young. That's what brought her to America in the first place. She was just a teenager at the time."

"When was this?"

"Long time ago. The Seventies. She's a couple of years older than Evan, I think. She was a has-been in the modeling world by the time she was twenty-two. She went back to school, learned this acupuncture thing—which I always thought was right up there with voodoo—and she came up here to the mountains because she liked to ski."

"Well, how nice for her," I murmured sourly, half to myself.

"I never cared for her much. Kind of aloof, a real cold fish. Evan's kids didn't get on with her either."

"I know." I smiled slightly, thinking back to how Reilly and the girls had virtually plotted to get us together. I had almost felt as though it were a Nineties remake of "The Parent Trap."

"Honey, are you sure you're okay?" Marlena asked with real concern. "You look like you're about to cry."

I was touched that a woman I had known only a few weeks could be so caring. Then again, it wasn't as if Marlena and I didn't have something in common—namely, being ex-Evan girlfriends. I guess there was some kind of sorority in that alone—a growing and huge sorority, come to think of it.

"I've got money problems," I sighed.

"Don't we all?" Marlena laughed, trying to cheer me up.

"Mine are pretty bad. I don't know how much longer I can stay here. And I was just starting to get really attached to Leap Year—Evan or no Evan."

"It's probably no comfort to you, but you're not alone. Most people who come up here can't make ends meet. Some last a year, some last a month, but most end up going back where they came from. I wish it were different. If you could tough it out till ski season, you could get on with the ski resort at Avalanche Creek."

"Isn't that awfully far away?"

"About forty miles, but the resort runs a free shuttle bus into Columbine—that's how many locals work there."

I shrugged and Marlena drifted on down the counter to talk to another friend.

Before I left, Celeste came my way and leaned over the counter with a big smile.

"I heard you broke up with Evan," she whispered in a low voice. "Good for you. You're too fine a person for him. I could tell that right off. You can trust my advice on some things, truly. And besides, he's not the only fish in the sea. During ski season, you should see how the county fills up with men. They all come to work at Avalanche Creek. Of course, they're not exactly what I would rate as marriage material."

"They want to have fun-fun-fun until their daddy takes their T-Bird away?"

"In this case, their Rossi's," she laughed. "Still, they're cute and it beats sitting home alone nights."

I ARRIVED back in Leap Year just ahead of the carpenter. He followed me up the winding switch backs, tailgating the entire route. I guess I was driving too slow for him although I had thought I was able to make the journey in fine time these days and had been proud of that fact until now.

He was young, early twenties, and his name was Nick. He brought his dog with him, a big Irish Setter called Horse. All the construction workers seemed to do this I had noticed. Evan said he took Rhett with him to job sites, but I thought this was some unique quirk of his until I began seeing big dogs around every house under construction in the county.

Nick asked if it was okay to let Horse run around the yard and I said 'sure.' He got his tools and a piece of lumber out of his truck. I had measured the broken step for him and given him the directions over the phone because he wasn't too keen on making two trips up the mountain if he could help it.

He was a cheerful type, with sun lightened brown hair that fell in ringlets around his face, giving it a cherub quality. His upturned nose and sharp chin completed the cherub picture.

"You know you have a carpenter living just down the way from you?" he asked as he pried up the broken board with a crow bar.

"Yes," I replied curtly.

"You know Evan?"

"Yes."

"So, like, he was busy?"

"Yes, he was busy." This guy was awfully nosy, but I guess it did seem strange I wouldn't have my only neighbor fix something like this.

Nick chuckled and shook his head. "That Evan—what a head

case."

"Why do you say that?"

"Ah, I don't know. I like the guy, he's a friend. We've worked a lot of jobs together. I don't know. You'd just think, if a guy had a woman in love with him that was...like a goddess, a Scandinavian goddess...he'd have sense enough not to go out on her."

I told the carpenter I had to go make a phone call. I didn't care to hear any more about Evan. I stood over the sink at my kitchen window, contemplating the Evan break up. I felt now more justified than ever. A clear picture was emerging of him as having a recurring fidelity problem in addition to his lack of ethics. Was that the real reason Greta left him? Had she gotten fed up with his running around and eventually left to find someone else?

I paid Nick what I considered an exorbitant sum for the step—the mountain tax no doubt—and watched him drive off. Yes, the infamous bumper sticker was in evidence: THERE ARE NO RULES ABOVE 10,000 FEET. This arrogant, outlaw slogan now left a bitter taste in my mouth. This place could use a few rules, in my opinion.

As Nick's truck disappeared down the first switchback, I saw a telephone repair truck approaching. I wondered what could be wrong since this was the second time I had seen them in two days. They did not drive into Leap Year, but veered off on the path toward the old mine instead. I vaguely hoped they would stop by for coffee, but they didn't return.

I tuned the radio to one of the two stations that I could almost receive without static and settled in for another night alone. I didn't need Evan. I didn't need anyone. I could be just like Grady. I thought about her letter and how her parents had met up here and lived happily ever after, I guess. I thought I would be like them, but now it seemed I was destined to be like Grady. I could be happy with that life. It would just take some adjustment.

I could live happily ever after in Leap Year, if I could only quit hearing all those noises. I hugged the pages of Grady's letter to my chest, feeling sentimental and wishing I had known her better. I even wished—in purely a fantasy sense—that I could have known her parents. I wanted to feel the presence of their ghosts in the house, but instead fell asleep thinking about the weird mountain people.

Chapter Fourteen

The loss of their child was not the last tragedy my parents would face, but, sadly, the first of many...

ON THE FIRST day of May, Conor received both good news and bad news. The good news was that Elodie had told him before breakfast that she was nearly certain she was with child again. This filled Conor with both happiness and apprehension. He feared as always for Elodie's health. He was beginning to think he was cursed in matters of procreation. Elodie did not share his fears and assured him over and over that this time would be different. She promised him she would make an effort to take it easy and rest more, though she knew such measures had little to do with the outcome of her pregnancies. She had worked ceaselessly though her first five and delivered healthy infants and had actually had more ease during the last with its unhappy result. Still, she was willing to do or say anything that would calm Conor's anxiety. Keeping him happy was important to her.

Conor's bad news came in a letter from back home. His brother Ned had lost his wife to consumption. In his letter, Ned announced his intention to take a leave of absence from the bootworks and travel for the summer. He would be paying a visit to Conor about mid-June.

Conor was sitting at the dining table reading this letter as Elodie prepared the noon meal. With the older children at school, the younger children playing in the yard and Granny Atwater entertaining baby Corinne in the upstairs bedroom, Elodie and Conor were relatively alone. As she approached the table to spread the tablecloth, she noticed his worried expression.

"Bad news?" she asked with concern.

"Oh, uhm...one of my brothers. He has lost his wife."

"I'm sorry to hear that," she mewed with perfunctory compassion. She was pleased it was not something worse, something that might call Conor back to the East. She worried periodically that he might get the urge to see his daughter and, once back in the comfort and luxury of his family, he might never return. She felt a nagging, ignoble jealousy concerning his little daughter. The daughter represented Conor's old life, the life he had left so far behind in Philadelphia. This child was a kind of rival, not so much for Conor's affections, but for his allegiance to this new life he had made in this high place. "Was this the consumptive one?"

"Yes. I never passed on your medical advice." Conor and Elodie exchanged embarrassed smiles. Then Conor continued hesitantly, "There's something else."

Elodie stopped her work momentarily and awaited his explanation.

"Uh...my brother is embarking on a long journey. He wants a distraction, I think, to get over his loss. He's going to go traveling across the country, all the way to California. He says he won't stop until he sees the Pacific Ocean."

Elodie's eyes widened. "Oh, quite a trip. And will he stop here for a visit on his way?"

"Uh...yes. He says he wants to stop here around the middle of June. He'll wire his exact plans when the time is nearer."

Elodie furrowed her pretty brow. Her complexion had bloomed again with her new pregnancy. Her breasts were fuller, her eyes brighter. Conor had never seen her looking more beautiful. "Our new house won't be ready until at least July. Oh, but no matter. We'll find the room for him somehow. Don't worry."

Conor did not share his wife's optimism, but his difficulty had nothing to do with the new house not being completed in time for his brother's visit. It was time to confess something. "It's just that...I've never, you see, told my family...that I've—we've...married."

When Conor saw the look on Elodie's face upon the utterance of these words, he wished he had died before he had said them. "I kept meaning to write," he mumbled, knowing there was not much he could say to improve the situation.

"Four months," Elodie said with a look of devastation. Her arms dropped limply to her sides. "Four months to the day, we've been wed. I wondered why I never received any letter from your family. I didn't ask, maybe I was afraid to ask. Afraid of the truth."

"Truth?"

"That you're ashamed of me. Ashamed to claim me as your wife. Not good enough for the high and mighty McAllister clan."

"It's not that," Conor began miserably, but the awful truth was, Elodie was right. He had been ashamed to tell his family about her. He knew only too well what their reaction would be. Elodie was an Irish immigrant and a Catholic, though she didn't practice her faith as far as

Conor could notice. She was poorly educated and really not much different than the servants in his mother's kitchen. They would not have been pleased by the fact she was a miner's widow with five children and the last illegitimate, no less. They would never have understood that society was different on the frontier. Social and cultural norms and distinctions faded here, gave way to the shared hardships and the daily gamble that was life up in these unforgiving mountains.

"I'll write them today," Conor promised, with sudden resolve. He realized it might be fun to annoy his father in this way, especially when he was so far from feeling any immediate effects of his father's considerable appetite for disapproval.

"I'll write my mother and my father," Conor continued with enthusiasm. "I always send them separate letters, I have no idea if they compare them. Then I'll write Ned, of course, and tell him we look forward to his visit. And then I'll write my in-laws. After all, Bea should know she has a stepmother and...that she'll have a new brother or sister by Christmas."

Elodie smiled faintly, only slightly mollified. Conor knew he needed to do more.

"And there's one more thing," he added.

Elodie waited with a questioning glance.

"I'll need a photograph to send them."

"A photograph? Of me?"

"Of course. I want them all to know just how pretty you are." Conor was getting almost shameless in his flattery at this point, but Elodie, for once, let her vanity rule her stubborn cynicism.

"A photograph...of me," she repeated, thrilled by the idea. "I've never had my likeness taken at all."

"We shall go into Columbine today and you shall sit for that man who takes the photographs." The photographer in Columbine was actually the undertaker. He made a good living photographing live subjects as well as recently deceased ones.

Conor knew he had redeemed himself with the suggestion of the photograph. He now remembered how fascinated Elodie had been with his photographs of Beatrice. His father-in-law was an avid amateur photographer and regularly sent him photos of little Bea. There had been Bea's third birthday, Bea's Christmas, Bea with her new puppy, Bea on her favorite pony. Conor had quite a collection and Elodie had gotten excited every time one had arrived.

They hired a buggy and drove down into town, getting stuck in the mud only once. Conor ruined his best clothes extricating the wheel.

The task was made especially difficult by the fact Elodie refused to get out of the buggy while he worked on it. She did not care to soil her finest frock in the sloppy road. Conor was annoyed at her attitude, but said nothing since he was still trying to make amends for the failure to advise his family of his nuptials.

Conor had planned on a portrait of them both, but the ruin of his suit made that impossible, so he had Elodie sit alone for the picture. A single sitter was less expensive anyway. The undertaker led them into a back room he used as his studio. The room had large windows that bathed the room in light from the south. Conor did not care for the smell of death that he thought pervaded the place, but he dutifully accompanied his wife who was apparently too excited to notice.

Elodie looked beautiful sitting before the photographer's fabric backdrop. She had spent a great deal of time dressing her hair and it now showed to good advantage. Conor didn't care for the hat she'd chosen, but even that did not detract from her considerable good looks this day. Still, he convinced her to sit for one pose without it. The faintest of smiles held to her lips during the long seconds of the exposure. The light caught her dimpled chin just so.

After the session, the pair took tea in a small cafe in Columbine before heading back up the mountain to Leap Year. Elodie chattered happily all the way home, confirming in Conor's mind that he had now been forgiven. He even wondered as they drove if they dared to make love that night. He worried that this might disturb her pregnancy somehow and yet they had made love—and rather vigorously—only two nights before with no harm done. Of course, Conor hadn't *known* about the baby two nights ago. He was in a quandary. He wanted to make love to her so very much.

Thoughts of love vanished when they arrived back at their cabin. They had just dropped off the buggy at the livery and were walking home when they saw a man running from their cabin. He was a filthy, dirty fellow with long matted hair and beard. He must have seen them coming and was now dashing away as fast as his limping gait would carry him.

Conor ran up to the house and grabbed a stick of firewood for a means of defense. He owned no weapon other than a hunting knife, which was now in the top drawer of Elodie's dresser. He chased after the intruder, but lost sight of him in the dense pine forest behind the cabin. He returned to see after Elodie who was now in tears with fright.

"Where are the children?" he shouted as he reentered the yard.

"I don't know," Elodie replied, her voice shaking with emotion.

"The house is empty."

"We'll check with the neighbors to see if they're there," said Conor, trying to calm his wife, afraid now this shock might harm her in her delicate state. He put his arm around her as they walked in the spring's late evening sunlight to the Clarkson's cabin next door, a distance of about two hundred yards. There they were relieved to find Granny Atwater and all the children sharing supper with the family. They had given up on Conor and Elodie getting home in time and had accepted the Clarkson's dinner invitation.

The next morning, Conor proceeded directly to his friend Brandon's saloon to ask his advice on purchasing a revolver. Conor and Elodie had gotten little sleep the previous night, holding each other, feeling tense and fearful but unable to admit their fears. Conor had tried to convince himself this was an isolated occurrence. That it was probably a miner down on his luck, driven by hunger to steal something—most likely food—from a house. But it was no use. They both feared the intruder's return as they shared a breakfast looking worn and tired, still jumpy from the evening before.

Brandon was full of advice on the subject of guns. He owned several, a rifle for hunting, and two revolvers, one of which he kept under the bar for protection when matters got out of hand. He had never actually shot anyone, but had threatened many a drunken miner who had gotten into an argument over a saloon girl or become convinced someone was cheating at cards.

The other revolver was kept at home for Hannah's protection, although Brandy and Conor joked about the wisdom of allowing Hannah access to a deadly weapon considering their marital history, which Brandon had shared with Conor on one late and somewhat inebriated evening the previous winter.

Brandon offered to sell Conor the gun he kept at the saloon. He had his eye on a fancier piece he had recently seen at the gunsmith's in Columbine. He even offered to show Conor how to shoot it. Conor had never owned a handgun before. He had never owned any gun, in fact. He had borrowed Brandy's hunting rifle when taking young Joe hunting the pervious summer. Before that, his only experience with firearms was a few quail hunting trips with his brothers.

In the middle of the afternoon, when business at the saloon slowed down, Brandon left his son Josh in charge and took Conor to a vacant lot where they could target practice on empty bottles. Josh was pleased to be left to cover for his father. He had just returned from a seven-month visit home to Texas to his grandparents' ranch. He truly liked Texas better than the mountains of Colorado, but he missed his mother and wanted to see his new baby brother, Samuel, so he had returned.

Conor enjoyed the target practice. Brandon did too. He had a huge store of empty whiskey and beer bottles which he saved up for just this purpose. By supper time, the two men had grown tired of their pursuit and Conor agreed to buy Brandon's pistol. He took it home and showed it to Elodie who shivered at the sight of it. She feared it falling into the hands of one of the children. Just the summer before, a four-year-old boy had been accidentally shot by his six-year-old brother who had been playing with their father's gun.

"We'll hide it in a location only you and I can reach," Conor assured his wife. He suggested on top of the china closet and Elodie reluctantly agreed. They debated whether or not to advise Joe of the gun's existence. At thirteen—nearly fourteen, he was considered old enough to operate a gun. Conor felt he should be told. He thought Joe could help protect his mother and siblings, but Elodie resisted, still feeling Joe was her 'baby.' Conor agreed to postpone the decision for a while, personally believing Elodie would get used to the idea of the gun after a while.

Soon letters begin arriving from Philadelphia with reaction to the news of Conor's remarriage. His mother expressed bewilderment at this unexpected news, but in the most delicate terms. She tried to be kind but questioned Conor's choice of mate. Her letter began: *My dearest son, what could you have been thinking, to make a decision of such magnitude so far from the counsel of your loving family?*

But now I have a new loving family, he thought to himself defensively after reading this. He received a similar, but less personal letter from his mother-in-law relating Beatrice's confusion over the news in the letter he had written to be read to her.

Conor was surprised by the mildness generally of the reproaches he received concerning his marriage. The only really negative remarks came in a rather insulting letter from Allison's father who suggested that he had tarnished Allison's memory with this sudden and uncouth marriage. Conor was not bothered overmuch by this abrasive assessment. He was no longer as sensitive as he once was concerning his late wife and he knew his father-in-law had never liked him very much.

He felt much lighter of a burden, now that he had told them about Elodie. He was rotten at keeping secrets. They gnawed at him and made him miserable.

Ned arrived by the morning mail wagon on a bright and unusually warm day of June. Only traces of snow remained in Leap Year and the roads were still quite muddy. The air was fresh and the summer wildflowers were beginning to bloom.

"This is quite a place," said Ned as Conor helped him down from the wagon. Conor thought Ned looked awfully tired, even haggard. He had arrived by train in Denver the morning before and immediately wired Conor. He said he must rest overnight there before proceeding to Leap Year, which Conor thought was odd. Perhaps travel did not agreed with him. Then there was the stress of losing his wife only three months ago. Conor had not seen his brother in nearly two years, but he seemed to have aged ten in that time to judge from his appearance and demeanor.

"Look at you," Ned laughed, patting Conor's bushy beard. "You look like a man of the mountains." He grabbed a handful of hair at the back of Conor's neck and playfully gave it a jerk. Conor hadn't gotten his hair cut since he moved to Colorado and it now hung in a curly mass well past his collar.

The thin air caused Ned to pause often to catch his breath as they walked to the cabin. Elodie had wanted to come into town to meet him, but she was unable to leave the noon meal she was preparing and had fussed over since dawn. Conor called to her as they entered the cabin which was filled with the delicious aroma of elk stew and freshly baked bread. When Elodie emerged from the kitchen to see they had arrived she yelped in alarm and dashed off to the bedroom without even saying hello. Conor knew her vanity was at work again. She didn't want to meet his brother in her stained apron with her face dripping from the steam of the kitchen and her hair sticking to her face in ringlets.

"Not afraid of me, I hope," said Ned to Conor as Elodie disappeared.

"I guess she just wants to make herself presentable," Conor said to explain his new wife's odd behavior. Corinne was standing next to the sofa, she still held on occasionally for added stability though she had been walking for several months. She began to wail with all the commotion. Conor instinctively picked her up and began comforting her.

Ned pointed to Corinne and asked tentatively, "Yours?"

"Oh, no," laughed Conor. "But I am the stepfather to five now."

"Five. My, my, my, and one back home."

"And another on the way," Conor added in a low voice, but beaming. He didn't want Elodie to know he had told Ned she was with child. Conor felt certain Ned already knew. He had written it in his letter to little Beatrice and he knew the way his mother-in-law gossiped.

Ned was tempted to tell him he may well have two more in Baltimore, but thought better of it. He found it amazing that when he added up all of Conor's children, both natural and stepchildren, he had more than anyone in the family. This, from the little brother whom no one thought would ever settle down. On the other hand, they had never mistaken him for being celibate. The McAllisters had at first been stunned and mystified by Conor's wedding announcement, but when Allison's mother told them his new wife was pregnant, they issued a collective, "Oh, so that explains it." Andrew had even remarked to Ned, "He's too far from home for Dad to buy his way out of this one."

"Conor never could keep his trousers fastened," brother Bob had sourly commented after a family dinner at their father's house. It had been a farewell dinner of sorts to mark the beginning of Ned's big journey. The wives had retired to the parlor for their coffee and the men—patriarch Ben and all four McAllister brothers, the first set—sat with their after-dinner brandy at the table as the two servants cleared. The brothers and their father were careful not to make disparaging remarks about Conor having married an Irish immigrant, since both servants were recent arrivals from Ireland. They had mixed feelings about this anyway. After all, Ben's father had originated in County Kerry, but he had come over so long ago—before the turn of the century—that they felt little in common with the influx of potato famine refugees. They didn't even have a common religion with their forebears. Ben's father, upon arriving in America, had changed his Catholic faith as quickly and effortlessly as one might change a suit of clothes and the McAllisters were henceforth Protestants and would remain so for all future generations.

Ned leaned closer to Bob and whispered, "He's made up for a slow start, that's for sure."

Bob threw back his head with a laugh. At this, their father roused himself from a near doze to ask, "What's that, now?"

"Nothing, Dad," Ned answered quickly.

"No, nothing," Bob chimed in, then exchanged glances with Ned that said, So the old man was not asleep after all. Ben was getting on in years, there was no doubt of it, and the collective opinion of his sons was that perhaps he was starting to slip a little. They were all now men of their middle years and frankly anxious to be taking over the family business from its majority shareholder.

The source of Bob and Ned's jest was an incident long past. On Conor's eighteenth birthday, they had decided their special gift to him would be to arrange for the loss of his virginity. After an evening on the town of dining and drinking, they took him to an expensive brothel. They didn't tell him in advance where they were going because they wanted to surprise him and they didn't tell anyone else in the family because no one else would have approved.

Conor was still rather an innocent in the world and did not at first comprehend what kind of establishment it was, but when he was introduced to a woman named "Guisella" who said she would be happy to entertain him this evening, he began to get the picture. When she took him by the hand and led him upstairs to a gaudily over-furnished bedroom, the picture became clearer still. Before he entered the room, he cast a nervous glance over his shoulder and caught sight of his two brothers standing together at the bottom of the staircase. They had broad smiles on their faces and Bob was giving Conor a thumbs-up sign. It was all so ludicrous and vaguely dreamlike.

Though the October night was chilly, the bedroom was suffocatingly hot. Conor undid his collar pin.

"Now, now, let me help you wit dat," said Guisella, in heavily accented English. She began unbuttoning his vest. She was in her late thirties or early forties and wore a great deal of cosmetics on her face.

Conor still was not completely convinced this woman was a prostitute. What if his assumption were wrong? It could prove very embarrassing. He decided to put matters out in the open. "Did my brothers...pay you...for this?"

"Now don't you vorry about dat," said Guisella, misunderstanding his concern. "Dat's all been taken care of."

Conor broke into a cold sweat. He didn't like the way this woman smelled and she was as old as his mother. He didn't like her touching him and he particularly didn't like her touching him *there*, which she was doing just then and discovering what he already knew: that he was too intimidated by the situation to perform.

"Relax, relax," coaxed Guisella, but everything she did to try to arouse him only put him off still further. Finally, she gave up, begging him not to tell his brothers "nothing happened" or else they might demand their money back. Conor agreed to say nothing. At least he had seen what a grown woman looked like naked. The evening had not been a complete waste.

On the carriage ride home, Bob and Ned eagerly demanded to know the details of Conor's evening with Guisella.

"So how did it go, baby brother?" asked Ned, with a wicked twinkle in his eye.

"Oh, fine," answered Conor without any enthusiasm.

The two older brothers exchanged worried glances. "She was all right, wasn't she?" asked Bob.

"She was fine." Conor was terrible at telling lies. He stared at the floor of the carriage, dejectedly.

It was obvious to the brothers by now what had happened, or not happened. Ned sighed. "It's all right, Conie-boy. Tonight just wasn't your night."

Conor, in addition to feeling completed humiliated, now felt guilty that he had wasted his brothers' money and disappointed them as well. "I really wanted to. It was just that...I don't know...I just...." He let out a sigh of exasperation.

"Don't let it worry you. It happens to us all now and then," Ned assured him.

"It doesn't happen to me," asserted Bob.

Ned gave Bob an irritated sidelong glance that said, *You're not helping.* "I told you Guisella was a poor choice. She's too old for him. We should have gone with Tess."

"No one's better than Guisella," insisted Bob.

"Boys Conor's age don't need the kind of sophistication Guisella has to offer."

The brothers argued the rest of the ride home over the differing merits of the various girls employed by the house and it became clear to Conor that they were not strangers there. Conor was surprised by this. They were both married men and he did not understand why married men would seek out the services of a prostitute when they shared a bed with their wives every night. But Conor was just eighteen and had a lot to learn about the world. He would even have to wait more than a year to finally lose his virginity.

Bob and Ned never told anyone about their disastrous birthday gift to Conor, but for years joked about it between themselves. They were especially amused by the fact Conor later blossomed into such a ladies' man. Neither had thought of the Guisella incident since the death of Allison which had plunged Conor into a seemingly interminable state of melancholy. But now the specter of him remarried and possibly a shotgun wedding at that, indicated to them he was his old self again.

"You mean this has happened before?" Will, the youngest and least worldly of the brothers, asked innocently as another round of brandy was poured.

Ned filled him in on the regrettable incident involving the head tanner's daughter.

"*Our* head tanner's daughter?" Will questioned in surprise.

"Yes," sighed Ned. "He's the older fellow, the one who's been with us for ages."

"I know who you mean," said Will, a bit defensively. "He's the one with the gold tooth."

"Which I no doubt paid for," grumbled Ben, still convinced Conor had been the unwitting victim of an extortion plot. "He and that girl of his took us for a pretty penny."

"I wonder whatever happened to her," mused Andrew, the oldest.

"She had twins," announced Will to everyone's amazement. The entire assembly snapped to attention.

"How do you know this?" demanded Ben.

"She brought them to the company picnic last week," replied Will, pleased to be one up on the rest of the family for a change. "I served the whole family punch and I remarked on how alike the two little boys were—couldn't tell them apart if my life depended on it. Fine-looking little fellows, about five or six years old, I should reckon. Lord...I had no idea. The father said his daughter was home for a visit, that she lived in Baltimore. I assumed that was why her husband didn't accompany her to the picnic."

"Five or six. That would be about the right age," said Ben, half to himself. "But we still never had any proof it was Conor."

"Did they look like him?" asked Bob with interest.

Will shrugged. "I'm no judge of these things." He furrowed his brow and frowned at the tablecloth in an effort to remember what the little boys looked like. "They did have big blue eyes, with those lids."

"We all have lids," laughed Ned.

"Conor's are larger than most," stated Will with authority. "I would have to say that these boys had eyes very like his, for whatever that's worth. Imagine that...our baby brother has fathered twin sons and he doesn't even know it."

"Can't fathom why the boy should have so much success with women," remarked Ben to no one in particular. "He always acted so shy around them."

"Ah, but women love that, Dad," said Andrew.

Ben frowned, not really accepting this.

"And, let's face it. He's just plain good looking. Only one in this family who can make that claim," said Bob, not altogether happy with the fact. With almost a malicious delight, he added, "Say, Dad, did you and Lilly ever know about Conor and that little seamstress?"

Ned cringed. Bob would never have known about the seamstress had not Ned told him and now he wished he hadn't.

"Seamstress?" grumbled Ben.

"Let it go, Bob. It's ancient history now," said Ned. But Bob would not let it go and he proceeded to regale the group with more of Conor's errant exploits. Ned sighed through this. Conor had been remarkably discreet concerning the little redhead. Ned would never have found out about it had not Lilly loaned her entire household staff to Ned and Irene for their daughter Jennie's wedding. The girl had sewn Jennie's wedding dress and done an extraordinary job, though she had annoyed both Jennie and Irene with her saucy, direct way of speaking. She didn't seem to understand her place, but she was so talented with a needle they were obliged to put up with her outspokenness. On the day after the wedding, Irene told Ned she needed to discuss some unpleasant news with him. He was worried the news concerned Jennie, but she said it was servants' gossip about his half-brother. It seemed Lilly's cook told Irene's cook who told Irene's personal maid who dutifully reported to her mistress that Conor and the irritating little seamstress had been involved an affair of several *years* duration, that everyone in his father's household knew about it except his father and stepmother, and what was he, Ned, going to do about it?

"What can I do about it?" Ned had shrugged.

"You should inform your father, or at the very least have a talk with your brother and tell him what a terrible error he's making."

"This is just gossip," Ned had insisted. "We have no way of knowing it's true or not." So he did nothing and was bent on forgetting the matter. Conor was a grown man and he could take care of himself. Besides, Ned wondered what Conor could possibly see in such a vexing young woman. On the other hand, Conor had an offbeat outlook when it came to many things and he was just rebellious enough to take up with someone as unacceptable as the little redhead.

Ned hadn't thought about the situation in months when one evening he and Bob were dining out, entertaining some potential clients. He glanced across the room and who should be dining there also but Conor and his friend Applebee with the seamstress in question seated between them. They were laughing and talking and having quite a wonderful time from all appearances. Bob saw them too and asked Ned who Conor's new girl was. They had both witnessed the girl feed Conor a bite of food from her own fork. Conor, laughing, had then gently brushed a tendril of the girl's curly hair back from her face and had whispered something in her ear that made her laugh. Both were gestures of such casual intimacy that the two men knew immediately that the girl was with Conor and not his friend. Bob had wanted to go over to their table and say hello, but Ned told him not to, saying he'd explain later. On the way home, after parting from their dinner guests, Ned shared all he had learned from Irene's gossiping servants. Bob thought they should tell their father what Conor was up to.

Ned discouraged this. "Lots of men keep mistresses."

"McAllister men don't," Bob insisted, self-righteously.

"We both know one who did."

Bob frowned. "But that was long ago...and anyway Dad ended up marrying her."

Bob and Ned then shared a laugh, saying "like father, like son," and resolved to say nothing to Ben. Conor was having enough trouble getting along with his father at the moment and they did not want to make things worse, impending scandal or not.

When Bob concluded his seamstress story, which he had embellished quite a lot, everyone was amused except Ben. Ben just shook his head at his youngest son's misdeeds.

"You know, Ned, you'll be seeing Conor in a couple of weeks," said Will. "Maybe you should tell him about the twins."

"Absolutely not," commanded their father with a finality that ended the discussion.

ELODIE RETURNED with a fresh outfit and smoothed coiffure. Conor introduced the new Mrs. McAllister with great ceremony. Ned kissed her hand in a flourish of gallantry and Elodie blushed and curtsied. She put Corinne in her baby chair and led the gentlemen to the dining table and began to serve. She had arranged for Granny Atwater and the two youngest children to dine elsewhere this noon. "Always trying to get rid of me," Granny had grumbled, but was really joking. She knew Elodie wanted the opportunity to converse with Ned without the distractions of a huge family present.

Throughout the meal, Elodie described in detail the new house they were building. It was in the framing stage at the moment. Conor spoke with enthusiasm of his new business enterprise. He had decided, with quite a bit of prodding from his wife, to start a newspaper in Leap Year. He had been doing a lot of research into the venture, getting a wealth of advice from Applebee, of course. Applebee was nervous that the time Conor spent on his own newspaper would interfere with his column writing. Still, he was happy for his friend. His life had seemed to have at last found some course of direction.

After the meal was completed, Conor offered to take Ned over to view the new house under construction. Ned had expressed much interest in seeing it, though he insisted on taking a nap first. Conor also noticed him swallowing some medicine from a small bottle he kept in his vest pocket.

"Are you all right, Ned?" Conor asked when Elodie was out of earshot.

"Nothing, nothing at all. Damned headaches. Probably the altitude. Don't mention it to—" he jerked his head toward the kitchen where Elodie was humming as she cleaned the dishes.

Ned took a long nap, not waking up until after six. Conor took him on the promised walk to the new house while Elodie fed the children their evening meal. On the way to the construction site, they stopped into the Lucky Chance for a drink. Conor introduced his brother to Brandon, who declared their drinks to be on the house in honor of Ned's visit. Conor was pleased and surprised by this gesture. Brandy seldom gave away his merchandise.

Conor bought an extra bottle of whiskey and took it with them to the new house. The two-story house was completely framed and some of the walls on the first story were already in place. Ned was appropriately impressed with the dwelling and generous with his compliments. The evening was wearing on and the two men sat on the unfinished side of the first floor with their legs dangling over the foundation. They sipped their whiskey, passing the bottle back and forth.

"Ned, I've been waiting for a quiet moment to tell you how sorry I was to hear about Irene."

"Thank you, Conor." Ned looked pensive. "She was so terribly ill for so long...when the end finally came it was like a blessed relief of sorts."

"And how are your children?"

"Oh, fine, fine...busy with their own lives." Then Ned brightened. "On the night before I left, Jennie told me she was going to make me a grandfather again. She said it was my going away present."

"Congratulations." Conor raised the liquor bottle in a kind of toast and took a swig. Ned did likewise.

"I want to thank you for all your good advice about schools to Eddie," said Ned. Eddie was Ned's youngest son and was to start college in the fall. "You're the expert—the only college graduate in the family."

"I think Will would have finished college had the War not intervened, don't you?"

"Ah, well, the War changed everything, now didn't it. Of course, you're probably too young to remember."

"Oh, no, I remember everything. I was twelve when the War began. The boys at school and I were obsessed with it. We knew every general's name, followed every battle, even memorized casualty totals. Then, of course, there were the inevitable telegrams calling boys home because they'd lost fathers or older brothers. Our family was so lucky."

"Amen," said Ned. "But remember, two of the four of us never saw any fighting." Ned and Andrew had "office" posts during the war and never risked any injury greater than a paper cut.

"Still, I was proud of you." Then Conor confessed, "I used to be so ashamed that my father was too old to fight. A lot of the other boys' fathers were nearer your age than his."

Ned chuckled and patted Conor on the knee. Conor had never felt closer to any of his half-brothers than he felt at this moment to Ned. Maybe the oppressive presence of his father had blocked this kind of fraternal intimacy from ever taking root. Now, so far from home, so high up on this mountain, everything was different. It was almost as if he were seeing Ned truly for the first time. Conor no longer felt like an only child.

As they watched the orange rays of the setting sun slowly make their way up the eastern canyon wall, Ned broached a sensitive topic.

"Tell me to mind my own business if you must, little brother, but just how is it that you can afford to build this fine house and start a new business *and* support a growing family. I mean, I know as well as you how far that trust fund Grandfather left us will go and surely your friend Applebee can't be paying you anything close to what it would take...do you know what I'm saying?"

Conor smiled toward the canyon wall, wondering how to answer his brother's well-meaning inquiry. He decided to tell the truth, maybe not the whole truth, but some portion of it. "My wife has money," he said simply.

Ned raised his eyebrows at this. "Pretty *and* rich. You know how to pick 'em. So Conor has married an heiress. Wait until the family hears about this. You were much too coy in your letters home. I have to tell you they all think that...well, that is, they assume that your lady...umm, being in a family way...that perhaps that prompted the marriage, shall we say."

Conor frowned in embarrassment. Although what his brother suggested had been literally true, he did not want his family thinking this about his wife. Once again he told a portion of the truth. "Well, they're quite wrong to think that. Elodie and I were married on New Year's Day."

"But that was nearly six months ago. Why did you keep it a secret?"

"I knew how the family would react to the news. I knew Father would have a fit when he found out I married an Irish immigrant and a Roman Catholic, at that."

"He did," Ned grinned.

"But that's really so ridiculous," Conor fumed. "Our family was originally from Ireland. And we were originally Catholic. I know the whole story about Grandfather coming here. Why does Dad have to pretend we came over on the Mayflower or something?"

Ned sighed. "Try to understand him, Conie. He was the son of an immigrant. He made a grand success and he wanted to fit into this new crowd he was with, but he never got over feeling like the son of an immigrant."

Conor shook his head, not agreeing with this assessment. "Dad took over a thriving business from Grandfather. His was not some rags-to-riches story."

"I don't know. Humor him, then. He's getting old. How much time does he—or any of us—have left?" Then Ned nudged Conor in the ribs. "You should have told him she was an heiress. That would have pleased his vanity."

Conor smiled bitterly and took another swig of the whiskey. The sun was gone now and the evening chill was rising. He chose not to correct Ned's assumption that Elodie was an heiress. In truth, he still had no idea where her money came from. He had privately begun to think Brandy's story about her late husband stealing gold from the Northern Star was true. That was the only plausible explanation he could come up with. He did notice that once he started living with her, she had ceased to take in laundry. Had the laundry business been only a ruse so people wouldn't question how she was able to feed her large family? Was his moving in her new ruse? So that now her neighbors just assumed he was supporting her, when in fact the opposite was closer to the truth? Conor had made a slightly unethical decision to stop asking Elodie questions he didn't want answers to.

The brothers sat quietly for awhile watching the canyon darken. Seeing someone from home had made Conor suddenly nostalgic for his old life. He had taken so much for granted there. A rush of homesickness swept over him, a longing to see his mother again, and Applebee, and...his daughter. He felt guilty that his own daughter, the only remnant he had left on earth of his love for Allison, was a stranger to him. He was closer to Elodie's children and he knew that was wrong somehow. And yet were not his in-laws eminently better qualified as parents than he was? Maybe he would be a better father to this new child on the way. Maybe this child would be his second chance just as he had predicted to Elodie on their wedding day.

"I suppose we had best return," said Ned, breaking the graceful silence of the June night. "Your charming wife will be wondering what's become of us."

"A little while longer maybe...it's just so pleasant."

Ned nodded in agreement and the two finished the last of the liquor. It was serving to take the chill off now.

"Do you remember Guisella?" Conor asked, after another long silence.

Ned burst into a great, loud laugh. "Lord, whatever made you think of that?"

Conor laughed too. "I have no idea. It just popped into my head. The sight of you and Bob standing together at the bottom of that staircase looking up at me—I must have looked such a fool."

"You didn't look foolish at all—just terrified." They both laughed again, then Ned sobered a bit. "We honestly thought we were doing you a favor. Can you ever forgive us?"

"There's nothing to forgive. I knew you both meant well. I just wasn't quite...ready...for Guisella."

They both collapsed into laughter again. "You'd be shocked to know who finally accomplished the task," said Conor when he had recovered enough to speak again. He instantly wished he hadn't mentioned this. It must have been the whiskey talking. He was usually a gentleman when it came to these matters.

"Well, little brother, are you going to tell me or not?" Ned was grinning, waiting for Conor's story. He fully expected Conor to name the little red-haired seamstress.

Conor sighed guiltily. "I really shouldn't—"

"Oh, come on."

"Oh, well...what does it matter now? She and her husband moved to London years ago."

Ned's jaw dropped open. "Not Lydia Bryson? The banker's wife?"

Conor shrugged and smiled. As ignoble as he knew it was, he was filled with male pride to have impressed his brother in this way.

"Lydia Bryson, lovely Lydia," murmured Ned, just as shocked as Conor had predicted. "Good Lord, you did aim high. When did this happen?"

"About a year after my unsuccessful night with Guisella. I'd known it was coming. She'd been flirting with me and teasing me for ages."

"Lydia Bryson, I can't believe it. Everyone wanted Lydia. Everyone lusted after Lydia. And our little Conor got her."

Conor was amused that Ned still called him 'our little Conor', even though he stood a full foot taller than his older brother. And actually, it was she who got me, if we want to be precise about it, Conor thought. Lydia Bryson was his mother's best friend. She, too, was the much younger second wife of a wealthy, successful man. Ben McAllister was forever courting Lydia's banker husband for new loans so the couple dined often at Conor's parents' house. Lydia first caught his attention because she did not talk down to him like most of his parents' friends, but rather treated him like an equal. At age nineteen, this flattered him a great deal.

Lydia was lovely, just as Ned had remembered. When Conor met her she was in her mid-thirties, but she seemed much younger. Her every word and gesture was calculated to garner male attention and she usually succeeded. Having a shapely figure and lustrous raven hair didn't hurt either. She had large, striking dark eyes, a pale complexion and a mouth perpetually fixed in a provocative half-smile. Her elderly husband bored her and ignored her by turns and she felt this gave her the excuse to discreetly pursue all sorts of adventures, Conor being one of many.

"She invited Father and Mother and me to their place in the country one autumn weekend for some hunting with her stupid husband. I knew something was going to happen when she put me in a bedroom on the opposite end of the house from everyone one else...and it did," Conor concluded lightly. His first two experiences with sex may have been awful, even traumatic, but his third was sublime. When it came to pleasing a man in bed, Lydia Bryson had few peers and Conor came away from their first night together feeling like he had *invented* the act of love.

"Imagine that—under the nose of her old husband and your parents as well. The pair of you was downright brazen. Did the affair go on long?"

"Not very long, really. I got obsessed with the idea her husband would find out and might hire someone to kill me!"

Ned slapped his knee at this and they both shared another laugh.

"Ned, can I ask you something serious?" Conor asked after the mirth died down. Ned shrugged amiably and Conor continued. "Did you hate my mother?"

"Oh, Conie, how could anyone hate a charming and lovely woman like your mother?"

Conor was silent, so Ned knew he was not going to be able to get away with a superficial response. "All right...the whole truth is...I didn't like the pain she caused my mother. Not that she ever meant to hurt anyone. She's much too sweet and it's really not her we blamed."

"So it was true," murmured Conor, finally receiving the confirmation of years of vague remarks and innuendoes. But Ned was too kind to tell Conor the actual events of that time. The sons of Ben McAllister's first wife had revolted at the news of their father's remarriage. For years, they had actively despised Conor's beautiful young mother, considering her a shameless gold digger who had made their father a laughingstock among his friends and business associates. But Lilly McAllister was not nearly that sinister or complex and gradually they came to realize this. At some indeterminate moment, they had all become a family again.

"Oh, forget it now. Your mother and father have made each other very happy all these years. Father's indiscretions as a husband surely have a statute of limitations at some point."

Conor smiled faintly and was compelled to finally ask another question that had bothered him since childhood.

"Is that why none of you seemed to like me?" he asked, referring to the first set of McAllister brothers.

Ned laughed at this question. "Wherever did you get that idea?" When Conor's look told him he did not accept this answer either, Ned once again was forced to be candid. He sighed. "Maybe there was a touch of jealousy at play. Father spoiled you so."

Conor was forced to laugh. "If Father spoiled me, I never noticed it!"

Ned chuckled. "Children take everything they have for granted, Conie. Believe me, you were spoiled compared to the rest of us. Of course, Father was a great deal better off by the time you came along. Do you think we got imported nursery maids and private tutors and every plaything ever created when we were young?"

Conor had never stopped to consider this. It had never occurred to him that his father had not always been wealthy.

Ned continued. "There was nothing you ever wanted for when you were little, you know. And then you grew up and the good news just continued. The girls were all mad about you. You practically had to hire a bodyguard to keep them at bay."

Conor smiled in embarrassment at this. His brother was exaggerating, but not too much.

"It was as though you led a charmed life. As though nothing bad could ever happen to you."

Conor snorted at this. His mood instantly reversed.

Ned backtracked. "Well...the matter of Allison, I know...a terrible tragedy. Forgive me for that last remark."

"Ned, could I tell you something I've never told anyone and would you promise not to repeat it?"

"Of course, of course."

"Nothing was ever right between Allison and me. I don't know why. I loved her to distraction before we were married, but after..."

Ned was surprised to hear this admission from Conor. Allison and his little brother had always seemed like the ideal couple, both so good looking and smartly dressed and well-bred. The first set of McAllisters had even invented a derisive nickname for the pair because they seemed too perfect: Prince Charming and Lady Faire, they called them behind their backs, or The Charmings, for short. "Are we dining with the Charmings tonight?" they would ask of their wives. Their wives would roll their eyes and cluck their tongues at their husbands' foolishness.

"Problems in...uh...the bedroom?" asked Ned discreetly.

"Well, yes, but more than that. That was just a symbol of everything that was wrong between us. And...and I did something awful...something I've never been able to forgive myself for." Conor hesitated, unsure of whether to confess this or not. He had carried it inside for so long, but now he finally wanted to share it with someone and he was feeling so close to Ned at that moment. "The night Allison died...I was with someone else."

"Oh, good lord," murmured Ned, sympathetically.

"You see, we'd had this terrible fight—Allison and me—and I'd stormed out of the house...and...I ran into someone on the Square...someone I used to know."

"Lydia?"

"Oh, heavens, no. Someone else. Someone I used to care about a lot. She was headed for the train station. She had been in town visiting her sister-in-law who'd just had a baby—anyway, I insisted on buying her dinner and...we ended up spending the night together, taking a hotel room as man and wife. I know that's terrible of me." Conor shrugged miserably. Conor had never repented of his indiscretions before his marriage. He had always thought them to be just that—indiscretions, surely in the realm of forgivable sins. But adultery was a different matter entirely in his mind. "It was just so good to be with someone who—I don't know—we just *liked* each other so much. We laughed and laughed and talked about old times," Conor paused, he was getting the familiar lump in his throat and he wanted to avoid this.

'Like' was the essential term. He and Kathleen had so truly, deeply *liked* each other. Conor would not have felt half so guilty about that night, had he not enjoyed it so much. They had even gotten the physical part right for once. In the six years they had been apart, both had grown more experienced and sophisticated. And not the least of the night's pleasures for Conor had been a vengeful sense of getting even with Allison for the irritating nightmare their marriage had turned out to be.

"Would this young woman by any chance have had red hair?"

Conor looked at Ned, surprised. "You knew Kathleen?"

"She made my Jennie's wedding dress."

"Oh, yes, I remember that." Then Conor cocked his head skeptically. "And everyone knew about her and me?"

"Not everyone."

Conor rolled his eyes and sighed, then continued his story. "Well, I put her on the train at six a.m. and walked home and when I arrived, the doctor was just leaving. He saw me as he was getting into his carriage—he was in a hurry to attend to another call—and he said, very sarcastically, 'Glad you could make it.' I guessed at that moment that Allison must have delivered, but when I rushed in, I saw Allison's mother with her head down on the dining room table, sobbing, and Allison's father sitting in the parlor staring at the floor. I knew immediately, without being told, what had happened. I'd deserted Allison on the one night on earth she'd really needed me."

"I'm sorry."

"I haven't even told you the worst part," Conor suddenly blurted out.

Ned raised his eyebrows, wondering how the story could get any worse.

"I actually considered leaving Allison that night. Seriously imagined it. I even invited Kathleen to run away with me."

"What was her reply?"

Conor smiled sadly. "She was always the practical one. She said 'no,' thank God. She didn't want to leave her husband. He was a decent fellow. He needed her. They ran a tailor shop together. And she had a little girl. She was afraid she'd never see her again." Then Conor's face twisted in unhappiness. "How could I have done something so terrible to a wife who was giving birth to our child at that moment...and losing her life in the bargain? I'm the lowest being on earth."

"You're a *human* being, Conor. And we're frightful prone to error. But we can atone for those errors...and be forgiven. You're so hard on yourself."

Ned patted Conor's shoulder affectionately, now understanding many things about his brother for the first time. Conor's seemingly inconsolable grief after Allison's death was placed in better perspective now. Ned could see it as the kind of grief born of guilt, to a large measure. He'd seen a similar grief in his own father after his mother died—the guilt of having lost someone you knew you hadn't loved enough.

Conor's obsessive melancholy was beginning to make Ned uncomfortable, so he sought to abruptly change the subject. "You seem very happy in your present marriage, little brother."

Conor smiled now readily. "I've never been happier."

NED'S VISIT lasted three more days and was enjoyed by all. Conor took him through the Northern Star mine and the surrounding towns. Conor still worried that Ned seemed so tired and took medication so frequently, but Ned kept minimizing his discomfort. On the day he was to leave, Ned bought presents for all Elodie's children and a beautiful scarf for Elodie. He kissed her cheek and told her she was the best thing ever to happen to his little brother. She blushed and thanked him and bid him a safe journey.

"I'm going to tell Father what a gem you've found with that new wife of yours," said Ned, looking down at Conor from the little window of the stage that would return him to Denver. "Just as soon as I return home."

But Ned did not return home. He made his way to California, just as he'd planned and also as he'd planned, he died there. Conor received a letter from Ned, posted posthumously, ten months later. Ned had a cancerous tumor growing in his brain, the cause of his terrible headaches. Only he and his doctor in Philadelphia knew this. Ned had made the decision to die alone because he didn't want to put his children through the suffering of another long illness so close on the heels of his wife's death.

He wrote a loving letter to Conor, reminiscing about his visit to Leap Year and how much pleasure he had derived from the bond they had formed as brothers. He described at length the beauty of the Pacific Ocean and the lovely mild weather of the southern California coast. But by the time his letter reached Leap Year, Conor was too consumed by the tragedy that had engulfed his own life to be touched by anyone else's.

Chapter Fifteen

BRRRRING! went the tiny saw blade that was cutting off my cast. The thing made such a loud and horrifying noise for an instrument so small. The young nurse's aide doing the honors saw the apprehensive look on my face before she began.

"I'm not gonna cut ya," she laughed and, to illustrate her point she touched her own finger to the whirring blade. It stopped instantly. "These things are safe. Pretty safe. I've only cut off two or three feet."

"Ha-ha" I said sarcastically to her lame attempt at humor.

She cut up one side and down the other and off it came in two pieces. "Wanna keep it as a souvenir?"

"No," I murmured. I had originally planned to do just that, but now that it was off I noticed it carried a distinct and terrible odor of decay. I wrinkled my nose in disgust.

"It's just from the dead skin—the smell, I mean. It'll wash right off." She began to rigorously rub alcohol over my foot. "Look how long the hair is," she giggled.

"God," I murmured, observing this also. The hair on my leg was nearly an inch long, as long as the hair on a man's leg.

"Women are always so surprised to see how long it can grow," the smart-mouthed aide continued happily as she worked away.

I was also shocked to see how skinny and wasted my leg looked from the knee down. Even my foot had shrunk. I had never even thought about a foot having muscles before. Mrs. Reno breezed in to take me to the X-ray room. She said not to worry. The musculature would return in about a month or so and I would be as good as new.

When I stepped down, I was surprised at the pain I felt. The foot hadn't hurt for weeks while in its cast. Mrs. Reno assured me this was normal. After the X-rays, I was taken back to the little examining room where I sat and waited a long time for them to send my X-rays over the phone lines to the orthopedic doctor in the next county. High technology was certainly a boon to rural, doctor-deprived areas like this one. Meanwhile, I got dressed, putting on a pair of jeans for the first time in two months. I had worn shorts the whole time I was in the cast to avoid having to slit the leg of any of my slacks and jeans. September was just a few days away and I had been getting pretty cold in the shorts. There had even been snow flurries in the air the day before, though the radio said the snow level was still at 11,000 feet.

Mrs. Reno returned with the good news that the doctor was satisfied with the X-rays. I no longer needed a cast, but was to wear strong, supportive shoes constantly for the next several weeks to aid my foot as it slowly regained its strength. I thanked Mrs. Reno for all her kind assistance and slipped out the clinic door holding my breath that the accounting clerk would not dun me for payment.

I DROVE home to Leap Year and found, to my horror, a sheriff's car parked in front of my house. The officer was peeking in the front bay window when he heard me drive up.

A hot flush of panic seized me. It's a drug bust! He's somehow heard about Evan's return to a life of crime and now he has a search warrant to go through my house since Evan spent so much time there.

"Can I help you?" I called, hoping my voice didn't sound too quaver-y. I hopped out of the jeep as quickly as my tender foot would let me.

The young sheriff's deputy walked out to meet me in the yard with a somewhat sheepish grin, apparently embarrassed to be caught window peeking. He was very blond with a thin blond mustache. He also had a persistent sniffle.

This reminded me of a story Evan once told me involving a couple of young sheriff's officers. He had taken Greta to a bar down valley one night. They were halfway home when Greta discovered she had left her purse behind. They drove back to the bar and Evan knocked on the door since it was now past closing time.

The owner of the bar, who knew Evan from his days with his band, opened the door but did not look too happy to see him. Evan told him why he was there and the man reluctantly let him in.

When Evan entered the dimly lit place he immediately discovered the reason for the owner's discomfiture—seated at the bar was the undersheriff and one of his deputies, with a mirror between them, doing lines of coke. Evan pretended to take no notice, quickly located Greta's purse, but before leaving made eye contact with both law men. "I figure that was my arrest insurance for the next several years," Evan had laughed. "That's why I drive so fast on the county roads." Knowing what I knew now, I wondered if his policy of arrest insurance had run out.

"You live here, ma'am?" the deputy asked me.

"Yes."

He smiled in a friendly manner, but nevertheless announced, "The county assessor's office is after you—if you happen to be Darcy Close, the record owner of the property. I came out to post this notice 'cause the county didn't have an address for you."

He handed me a paper—a foreclosure notice. The notice advised me I owed $2743 in overdue property taxes plus penalties and interest. The property would be auctioned by the sheriff at the next sale date, if the amount was not paid in full. I knew this was coming, but I hadn't expected it so soon. At first, I was so relieved his visit did not involve Evan, it took me a moment to let this new bad news soak in.

"But this isn't fair," I complained, sitting down on my porch steps to reread the fine-printed legalese. "I need more time. Just a little more time is all. I've been laid up for the past several weeks with a broken foot and...and—"

The young deputy sat down next to me. "I bet if you told them that, they might cut you a little more slack. They're pretty reasonable," he offered.

"But I still don't know where I'm going to get the money," I moaned.

"Oh, well, yeah. I can't help you there. You know what they say about death and taxes. And look at it this way—taxes are better."

Then he introduced himself, shook my hand, and walked back to his car. I thought maybe he had been flirting just a little. But with everyone so friendly here, it was hard to tell. I called a question to him before he shifted into gear.

"Do you think I'm safe living alone up here?" Since my breakup with Evan, I had acutely begun to focus on the isolation of Leap Year. My imagination constantly played games with me. I was even irrationally beginning to fear the telephone repair guys, but the mountain men/drug dealers were the main antagonists in my lurid fantasies.

"Safe from what?" he asked.

"I don't know—outlaws?"

He grinned. "You mean like Wyatt Earp?"

"He was a lawman."

"Oh, yeah, right." He chuckled in embarrassment. "Let's see...outlaws. Uh...no, fresh out of outlaws, I guess." He shrugged. "It's pretty quiet around here. The only folks I arrest are drunk drivers and speeders. I got a pretty easy job when it comes right down to it. Don't tell the voters or they'll try and cut our budget."

Either Evan's associates weren't known to him or he was inclined to look the other way. I felt vaguely reassured as I waved to him, then I sat on the porch and stared dejectedly at the dusty street for a long time.

The county assessor had made my decision for me about Leap Year—I would have no choice but to sell it and sell it quickly. Otherwise, I would lose everything outright. I had to smile at the irony of how anxious I had been to sell Leap Year before I saw it. Now that I had no choice, I longed desperately to hold on to it.

I spent the next week inviting every real estate agent in the book to come up to Leap Year and evaluate it for a quick sale. The answer from each was, "hopeless." Leap Year was too remote, the road too difficult, the location too far from the established resorts to have any real commercial value for development. Besides, any interested buyer with half a brain would simply wait for the sheriff's sale and buy the place for the price of the back taxes.

But one agent, a businesslike woman in her late forties who drove a Range Rover—so she must have been pretty successful—made an interesting remark just before leaving.

"I always thought this place had potential as a cross-country ski resort. You know, a cute Victorian Bed & Breakfast, cut a few trails back in through those woods and over the old mine. Maybe in summer, give mine tours—if you could get the Bureau to certify the mine as safe. Getting people up here might be a challenge. Perhaps a shuttle service, something like that. Play on the historical aspect, restore parts of the town as a living history museum."

My head started spinning as this woman, with the unlikely name of Melody Ring—Ring was her married name, her parents weren't really that cruel—reeled off her ideas for the future of Leap Year. I insisted she come in for coffee and she told me she had once proposed this to Grady, only to be ordered off the property at gun point.

We shared a laugh at what a feisty old darling Grady had been, though I think Melody was just feigning affection for Grady to flatter me. I didn't blame her. If someone stuck a shot gun in my face and ordered me off their property, I wouldn't care much for them either.

"It would take a hell of a lot of money to do this up right," she said. "You'd need some investors or some major financing...or find the Hidden Vein." She laughed.

"Amen, to that."

Melody, who was now getting re-excited by her own idea, even expressed an interest in becoming one of my investors, should I decide to pursue it. She had just sold a million-dollar house over in Columbine

Hideaway and was looking for investment opportunities.

"It's the house owned by that football star—you know, the black guy. He's moving to Chicago. Got a manager's job with the team there. I think he was bored with retiring so young."

I knew she was referring to Mike, the former Broncos lineman. He was the only "black guy" in the county, so he was easy to identify. I wondered what this meant for Celeste, his girlfriend. Small towns— here I was worrying over the love life of a woman who poured my coffee.

Melody went on to speculate that the money she had to invest would probably be only a third of what I would need to get started, but if I could secure financing for the rest, I could count her on board. She gave me the name of a local banker and listed out the type of information I would need to present to him.

The moment Melody left, I threw myself into the new Leap Year project. Finally, I had a way to resurrect Grady's town after all. I worked feverishly for the next several days, hammering out a business proposal. Melody even let me use the word processor and laser printer at her real estate office so that my business plan would have as professional an appearance as possible.

The day of my meeting with the banker, I sat at the counter of the Tenmile, nervously rehearsing in my head what I would say to him. I was on my third cup of coffee, which was only serving to increase my jitters, when a tall, elegant woman in her early sixties or so, strode in and sat down at the counter three stools down from me. She was expensively dressed, wearing a leather jacket that was not at all sporty-looking, so I knew she was not from around here.

Her blond-turned-to-gray hair was stylishly coifed and she was smoking one of those long, thin 'ladies' cigarettes. She looked familiar, but I couldn't place her.

Marlena came out from the kitchen and automatically began to fill the woman's coffee cup.

The older woman smiled at Marlena and when Marlena looked up from the coffee and their eyes met, the woman said in a husky voice that could only be achieved with decades of chain smoking, "Hello, Marlena. Are you keeping an eye on that son of mine?"

Marlena smiled in recognition. She drawled back, "Why, Mrs. Allender, you know that's more than a one-woman job."

"All too true, I'm afraid," agreed the woman with a world weary sigh. "I managed to produce a doctor, a banker, a vet...and an Evan. It must have been something I ate during pregnancy."

Marlena and the woman who could only be Evan's mother shared a laugh. For some reason, this remark struck me as hilarious and I had to laugh, too. I tried to squelch it, but it came out my nose. The two women turned to look at me. Embarrassed by my eavesdropping, I pretended to be reading the newspaper in front of me so they would hopefully think it the source of my amusement. They didn't buy it.

"Darcy," called Marlena. "I want to introduce you to someone."

I took a deep breath and tried to smile pleasantly.

Marlena had a slightly mischievous look on her face. "Darcy Close, I want you to meet Virginia Allender, Evan's mother. She lives in Chicago."

"Nice to meet you," I said uncertainly. Mrs. Allender smiled faintly and nodded an acknowledgment.

"Darcy is your son's neighbor," continued Marlena, a regular chatter box today. "She owns the whole town of Leap Year."

"The ghost town?" asked Mrs. Allender, her interest piqued. "You know my son?"

In the Biblical sense, I thought sourly, but answered, "We're friends. You have a couple of darling granddaughters."

A real smile crossed her face at this remark. "They are sweet, aren't they? I'm here to buy them some school clothes. Evan doesn't manage those tasks very well."

My nerves were getting to me, so I excused myself to the ladies room to splash cold water on my face. When I returned to the counter, Marlena was gone and Mrs. Allender was on her second cigarette and her second cup of coffee. If this was her lunch, no wonder she was so thin.

"Darcy—may I call you Darcy?"

"Sure, Mrs. Allender."

"Call me Ginger," she said. She had Evan's strawberry blond coloring and freckles. "Marlena told me you and my son were...more than friends."

Damn that gossiping Marlena. I shrugged noncommittally. "We dated."

Ginger smiled sardonically. "Evan doesn't date. He moves in."

She got that right. She knew her own son pretty well. I was getting affronted at the personal tract this conversation was taking until she added, "Marlena was sorry to see the two of you break up. She said for once my son had chosen a sensible woman, someone who was good for him."

I was flattered that Marlena had said this about me. Since I had broken up with Evan, she had stopped treating me like a dumb pilgrim. I didn't know how to respond so I just stared down at the counter. Ginger apparently knew she was making me uncomfortable so she changed the subject.

"What can it be like to live all alone in a ghost town?"

I launched into a description of my plans for the future development of Leap Year. I was actually practicing my spiel for the banker, but Mrs. Allender—Ginger—actually seemed quite interested. Marlena came back over and started listening, too. Evan's mother asked several intelligent questions, then said, "If you get your financing from the bank, I might be interested in investing as well."

"Really?" I was completely dumbfounded.

"If your development is a success, it will make my son's property a great deal more valuable. It'll be a way for me to help him without actually helping him, if you get my meaning. He's so damned stubborn. Just like his father. Can't help him, can't tell him a thing."

I took Mrs. Allender's phone number and address in Chicago and walked out of the Tenmile barely touching the ground. I walked over to the First National Bank of Columbine feeling almost giddy. It can't be this easy, I thought, it can't be this easy.

It wasn't. I made what I considered a brilliant appeal for financing to a Mr. Perkins, but when I concluded, he sat back in his big leather chair and smiled his banker's smile—the smile that says: Thanks for stopping by.

"Ms. Close, you're obviously very enthusiastic about this project and I appreciate the hard work you've done on this proposal, but..."

The fatal "but." I knew it was coming when I saw the smile.

"I feel that you've seriously underestimated your start-up capital. You'd be amazed what even the most modest development costs these days. And there's the matter of your lack of experience in development. You say you've managed a small art gallery, but I'm afraid that's not the type of experience that will translate to this type of endeavor.

"One of your investors is a real estate broker—Melody, I know her, charming woman—but selling real estate is not the same as developing a resort—however small—from scratch. I'm afraid we at the First cannot at this time...blah, blah, blah...."

At some point his words ran together and I stopped listening. He concluded by suggesting I continue to seek private investors since I had already had some luck in that regard.

I walked out feeling both angry and dejected. Sexist pig. I was convinced he had turned me down because I was a woman. If Evan had walked into the bank with the same identical set of facts, I would bet he would have walked away with the hundred and fifty-grand I was seeking. Well, maybe Evan with a haircut and a tie.

I bought a sackful of junk food and a six pack of beer and decided to spend the evening getting fat and feeling sorry for myself. Before I could settle in, the phone rang.

"I got tired of waiting for you to call me," said Trev's voice in a petulant tone.

"I've been meaning to call you, really I have," I lied.

"Yeah, right, that's what they all say. So how's life in the wild, wild west?"

"Not as wild as it used to be, Trev."

"No outlaws roaming the streets?"

I was about to make a joke about rampant substance abuse being the only local crime problem when a paranoid chill gripped me. What if my phone were bugged? My association with Evan tainted all my perceptions now.

"No, Trev, no outlaws."

"Another myth shattered," sighed Trev with mock disappointment. "More importantly, how are you doing?"

"How are *you* doing?" I shot back defensively.

"Come on, Darcy, let's face it. You were an emotional basket case when you left. And your mother's worried sick about you. When I called her to get your phone number, she unloaded on me for nearly half an hour."

"I'm sorry about that. She was really upset about me coming out here. I think it's tied up with Dad leaving and all that. But I'm doing fine, really. I've made a lot of friends and—oh, hell, who am I kidding? I'm not fine at all. Everything's going wrong." I choked up.

"Darcy, what is it?"

"Oh, everything. Money problems, mostly. Isn't that boring?"

"How much do you need? I could float you a loan."

"No, Trev, I couldn't do that."

"Name the sum. What are friends for? Two hundred—three hundred?"

I sighed. "It's more in the neighborhood of three thousand."

"Oh." There was a long silence, then Trev continued. "I guess that's a pricier neighborhood than I had in mind. Damn, I wish I could hit up my grandmother for a loan but she's in Europe doing the grand tour with one of my cousins. She tries to devote a year to each of her grandkids. I've already had my year—you know, the gallery."

"That's all right—I told you I wouldn't feel good about borrowing money from a friend."

"Employer," he corrected.

I covered the mouthpiece of the receiver so he wouldn't hear me sniffle. It looked like Trev was going to be right. I didn't seem to be able to avoid my fate of returning home, moving back in with my mom, resuming my old job, as though Leap Year had never happened. I felt like I was letting Grady down in such a big way. Grady was so real a presence to me sometimes. And her parents as well, particularly Conor. I identified with him more and more.

"What about your mother—couldn't she help you out?"

"She's in bad shape financially from Dad leaving and besides, she hates this whole Colorado thing anyway. She'd be thrilled to see me have to come home."

Trev began to chuckle. "Looks like Miss Scarlett is going to have to marry Frank Kennedy to pay the taxes on Tara."

I groaned. "Okay, I'll bite—what are you suggesting?"

"Hitting your asshole ex-husband up for a loan. Dan knows him professionally. Says the firm he's with pays their associates a king's ransom compared to most firms. And anyway, he owes you. There's got to be some guilt you can exploit there, surely."

"You're evil, Trev. You're truly, deliciously evil."

"If only I could learn to use my powers for good," Trev sighed playfully.

"Ask Keith for money, hmmmm, I don't know."

"You'd better hurry, though. Dan told me he heard that Keith's getting married again. The new wife might be the jealous type."

This news hit me like a small nuclear blast. As if I wasn't emotionally at ground zero already. Keith, who said our divorce was necessitated by the fact he "hadn't been ready to settle down," was now getting hitched again less than a year after the end of our marriage.

"Darcy? You still there?"

"Yes."

"Hey, I'm sorry to have spilled the beans on old Keith. You know I'd rather spill some boiling oil on him instead. Your mother said there was someone new in your life."

"Uh, no, that's history."

When he started pitying me, I cut him off. "It's all right. It was my decision to end it."

"Oh, I get it."

"Get what?"

"You got dumped by Keith so now you took your turn and dumped somebody else. It's probably all part of the healing process."

"That's not it at all. I had a very good reason for ending the relationship."

"Which you don't want to talk about—"

"Which I don't want to talk about. Correct."

"Have you noticed that you never want to talk about anything that's going wrong? You just want to hold it all in. It's like some kind of macho thing—like to admit you've been hurt would be to admit some kind of weakness."

"That's not true, Trev."

"Think about it."

I knew he was right about my tending to bottle things up—I'll admit that much—but he was way off base if he thought I dumped Evan because Keith dumped me. I mean, I'm pretty sure. Then again, maybe he had a point. Nah. Well, maybe. No, no way. Oh, well, what did it matter anyway? If I moved back home, I would never see Evan again.

"It's too bad I'm not still married to Keith. At least then I could kill him for the insurance money."

"And you say I'm the evil one." Trev chuckled, then, before hanging up, added, "I just thought of one more source of revenue for you. Does your dearly departed aunt have any antique furniture? You might want to have it evaluated by a dealer."

This was a good idea. I thanked Trev for it and we said goodbye—at least I said goodbye and he said, "See you soon."

I STARTED calling antique dealers first thing the next morning. There were three in the county and one was interested enough to make the drive up to Leap Year. He sounded very elderly and said he had known Grady all his life. He seemed excited about seeing the house and said he knew a lot about the history of Leap Year. He asked if he could come over right away, but I put him off until after lunch. That would give me enough time to drive down into Columbine and buy some cookies or something to offer him when he arrived. One thing I had learned about small town living was that business people were never just business people, they were your neighbors as well and expected to be treated as such. The interviewing of all the real estate agents had driven this point home. All just expected to be invited for coffee and a little snack of some sort. I felt bad in retrospect that I hadn't offered Nick, the carpenter who fixed my step, something to eat.

He was probably trashing my name around now as an inhospitable Easterner. Of course, if I were leaving soon, I guess I wouldn't have to worry about my reputation.

The antique dealer, Mr. Sanders, arrived only forty-five minutes later than the time we had agreed upon—another fact of life here: no one is ever on time. One o'clock on Tuesday means "sometime on Tuesday afternoon, unless I'm running late and it ends up being Wednesday morning instead."

Mr. Sanders was a weasly-faced little man with long, stringy gray hair and a baby-sounding voice not unlike the late Truman Capote. I gave him a tour of the house and he showed an interest in the desk and the bedroom dresser. He said they dated from the late nineteenth century. He made me an offer of two-fifty each. I knew nothing of antiques and had no idea if he was being generous or if he was—to quote one of Evan's more infamous maxims—telling me to bend over.

A quick five hundred sounded great to me and I accepted. He said he would come back on Sunday afternoon to pick them up because he would need his grandson to help him. I invited him into the kitchen for coffee and the brownies I had baked in a rare fit of domesticity—from a box mix, of course. He gave me a lecture on how bad caffeine was for my health, so we ended up drinking milk with our snack like a couple of kids. It took me awhile to get him off the subject of old furniture in general, but I eventually got him talking about Grady.

"A remarkable woman. A college graduate—did you know that?"

"No, I didn't. That must have been unusual back then."

"Oh, yes, especially for this area. She told me she got her picture in the local paper—the first woman in Columbine to graduate from college. She lived with a married sister in Denver and taught high school for ten years, then came back to Leap Year during the war—the First World War—because her mother was in failing health. Stayed on to keep house for her two older brothers, half-brothers, really. I first met her during the Great Depression. I was about nine or ten. My friend Jim and I—"

"Jim Knobe?"

"Yes, do you know Jim? That old geezer, he used to get me into so much trouble. Anyway," Mr. Sanders puckered his wizened face into a naughty smile and whispered, "We used to help Miss McAllister and her brothers in their 'home-based' business."

"Bootlegging!" We both laughed.

"You *have* been talking to Jim, haven't you?" Mr. Sanders shook his head. "My mother—God rest her soul—would have killed me, if she'd known what Jim and I were up to."

"Did my aunt ever say anything about the Hidden Vein?"

"Well, she devoted most of her life to looking for it—or so they say. She was always rather closemouthed about it, secretive. But she was fond of me. She used to sit with me on that old porch swing and talk and talk. We talked about the Hidden Vein on a few occasions. You know, I do remember her saying one thing kind of interesting. When her mother was dying of influenza during that great epidemic of 1918, in her delirium, she kept repeating the words, 'The Earth will have to open up again.' Miss McAllister said she couldn't tell if her mother were talking about her fabled gold or her own grave."

Chapter Sixteen

My parents' new house was completed on the Fourth of July in the year 1881. This would be the house I was born in and would live in all my life. I assume you, dear Darcy, may be sitting in this house as you read these pages...

THEY CELEBRATED with fireworks. Conor finally owned a house of his own and he decided to throw a huge party to celebrate. He ordered fireworks from a company in Boston that his father always used. The McAllister Independence Day parties had been legendary in Philadelphia, a town known to celebrate the day even more than most.

Conor knew his party wouldn't be as lavish or as elegant as the ones his family threw, but it would be festive enough by the mining camp standards of Leap Year. Conor didn't want to see Elodie over work herself, what with the move and all, so he hired the Belle of Colorado Cafe to cater the party—over her objections. Elodie was in the fifth month of her pregnancy and insisted to Conor "if I were going to lose it, I would have lost it by now." Granny Atwater, with her decades of midwifery experience, agreed. Still, Conor insisted his wife take it easy.

The day of the party, she looked beautiful. She had made a new dress for the occasion, adjusting the waistline to conceal her pregnancy. Conor and Granny were the only ones in town who knew she was expecting again. After losing the last baby, she was almost afraid, in a superstitious way, to share the news. She hadn't even told her best friend, Hannah. But Hannah had come over to the cabin early that morning to help Elodie move the last of her dishes and household items to the new house. She had remained to help Elodie get dressed and, seeing her without her stays, recognized the unmistakable bulge at her waist.

"I had been hoping you were just getting fat," Hannah teased. "If you got horribly fat, you see, then everyone would acknowledge me as the prettiest woman in town."

Elodie laughed and tossed a pillow at her friend, who was sitting on her bed, not really helping much.

"Maybe I'd even get the nerve to throw myself at that handsome husband of yours," Hannah continued in the same vein.

Elodie didn't find this funny at all. She had a jealous streak where Conor was concerned, though with the ratio of men to women being what it was in Leap Year, it was Conor who should have been the one to worry.

There was a knock at the bedroom door and the sound of a baby crying. Elodie pulled her new dress over her head and opened the door a crack. It was Betty, Hannah's fourteen-year-old maid with little Samuel in her arms.

"What now?" snapped Hannah.

"He won't take the bottle of milk," Betty announced glumly over Samuel's screaming.

"How long did you try?" asked Hannah with visible irritation.

"A long time."

With an angry sigh, Hannah motioned for Betty to bring the baby to the bed where she half-reclined. She unbuttoned her blouse and put the squirming child to her breast. Elodie asked Betty to fasten her dress while Hannah nursed.

"Oh, no!" shouted Hannah in a sudden rage. Elodie and Betty looked over to see Hannah despairing at the wet spot she now had on her blouse. Her left breast had leaked some milk while she was nursing on the right. Elodie shook her head at her friend's distress. She didn't quite understand Hannah's feelings for her baby. She had looked forward to Samuel's birth, but after it occurred, she seemed to lose interest in him. She took care of him as little as possible, delegating every task she could to young Betty. She was now trying to get him weaned—six months earlier than Elodie thought prudent. Elodie always nursed her babies a full year and sometimes longer. Of course, she had rushed her own Corinne a bit last fall, so anxious was she to try to get pregnant by Conor. She had assumed a pregnancy would prompt a marriage proposal from him and she had been right.

Betty took the baby back and left. "Stupid girl," Hannah whispered when she was gone. Betty had been recruited by Brandon to work in the saloon, but Hannah had intervened. She had insisted Betty was too young to be a prostitute and, besides, she needed a baby nurse and a maid as well. Hannah worked Betty so hard and was so short tempered with her that there may have been times when Betty wondered if Hannah had really done her a favor "rescuing" her from a life of sin.

Hannah was not completely comfortable in her role as a saloon keeper's wife. She was particularly embarrassed by the brothel portion of the business, but she enjoyed the money and was willing to spend it, nonetheless.

Now dressed for the party, Elodie stacked up the last of the china. It was sitting out on the floor of the dining room because the china closet and the table had already been moved to the new house.

"Isn't this my husband's pistol?" asked Hannah as knelt to pick up an armload of dishes.

"It used to be," said Elodie. "Conor bought it from him after we had that intruder. We used to keep it over the china closet. Here, hand it to me. I'll put it in the pocket of my apron until we get over there."

The new house was like nothing else in Leap Year. No dark pine cabin was this, but a fine and modern frame dwelling with bay windows and a shingled mansard roof. "Why does the roof come down over the house?" Brandon had asked during the construction. Conor knew his tastes were more educated than the general populace of Leap Year, but Mr. Reynolds admired the house. Reynolds had even agreed to help finance the newspaper Conor wanted to start. The quiet Reynolds was secretly something of a publicity hound and loved reading about himself in the newspaper.

Mr. and Mrs. Reynolds arrived at the party late. "They're making their grand entrance," Conor whispered to Elodie. Conor was still perturbed at Reynolds and his wife for failing to invite Elodie to their dinner party, but he wanted Reynold's money, so he fixed a smile on his face and went to greet his guests.

Reynolds had to practically drag his wife to the event. "I can't be civil to that Irish hussy of his," Mrs. Reynolds told her husband. What she meant to say was Irish whore, but she was too ladylike.

"Oh, Ida, simmer down. I don't like the woman either. She was damned impertinent to me when her husband died. But I like the McAllister boy, so humor me. We don't have to stay long."

The day was lovely and clear and cool, like a high mountain summer day always is. In deference to either Conor's house warming or the celebration of Independence, even the usual afternoon thunderstorms stayed away, making it as perfect an afternoon and evening as one could wish for. Elodie did not think the food was as good as she could have made herself, but Conor warned her he did not want to discuss the matter anymore.

At dusk, everyone gathered in a clearing about a hundred yards below the new house. Conor had instructed Joe and two of his friends in how to set off the fireworks. As soon as he had them ready to begin, he thanked everyone for coming and joined Elodie and the rest of the children on their picnic blanket.

The canyon walls faded to blackness and the show began. From the first burst, the assembled crowd "oohed" and "aahed." Many in the group had never seen fireworks before. Conor turned to Elodie with a satisfied smile only to discover her glancing nervously back up at the house instead of enjoying the bright bursts of color in the sky.

"I have to check on something," she said, rising from the blanket.

"Not now, you'll miss—"

"I'll be right back," she whispered, and hurried off.

Conor wondered what the problem could be. All the children were accounted for. Corinne crawled into his lap and he continued to enjoy the show. Five minutes passed and Elodie did not return. Then ten minutes. Conor was concerned. Perhaps Elodie was ill and didn't want to alarm him. He decided he must investigate and sat Corinne down between Donal and Kitty.

The house was completely dark when Conor reached it, but he heard noises coming from the kitchen. It sounded like scuffling of some sort, then there was a muffled cry and Elodie's voice saying something like "Stop it!" and "No!"

Conor raced to the kitchen and upon arriving could see nothing in the darkness. In the next second, the room was illuminated by the explosion of another glittering firework and in the green tinged light he saw the form of a man on his kitchen floor and his wife struggling under him. The man was attempting to pull up Elodie's voluminous skirts and she was kicking him and pummeling his head with her fists.

In a rage he had never felt before he dove on the man and ripped him off his wife in a single motion, flinging him against the dining room table. Elodie scooted away backwards, still on the floor.

Conor grabbed the man by the throat and began smashing him in the face with his fist. Conor hadn't hit anyone since his school days, defending Applebee and his smart remarks, but he had not forgotten how to throw a punch. A red rocket exploded in the sky outside and bathed the room in a red glow. Conor looked down at the man, whose nose was bleeding profusely now, but did not recognize him.

He slugged the man again, hoping he would lose consciousness, but instead the man kneed him in the groin, dropping Conor to his knees. Then he kicked Conor viciously in the jaw. The man tried to get past the still doubled over Conor, but Conor caught hold of his legs, tripping him and causing him to whack his head against the bricks beneath the wood stove as he hit the floor.

The man collapsed in a heap, let out a strange, sighing groan, and did not move again. Conor crawled on his hands and knees to where the man lay to examine the situation. A white fireburst filled the sky and the whiteness lit up the room again.

"Elodie," Conor managed to whisper, though his jaw was either broken or dislocated and the pain was so excruciating he could hardly stand to move it.

"Yes, yes, my darling," came her voice through the dark kitchen.

Conor tried to say, "Are you all right?"

Elodie rushed to his side. "I'm fine, I'm fine, but how are you?"

"He'sh dead," Conor slurred, then spit out some blood and two of his teeth.

"God bless you, my darling." Elodie was crying now, on her knees, holding Conor's face against her bosom.

"Some icesh," Conor requested.

"Ice? Yes, yes, of course." Elodie got up and hurried to the ice box and pulled out several small chucks of ice. She wrapped them in a dish rag, and returned to Conor's side. She pulled him half into her lap and held him in her arms while he applied the ice to his swelling jaw.

"We'll need to call the sheriff," Conor mumbled into Elodie's bosom.

"No, no, hush now."

"It'll will be all right. The man was attacking you. I was defending you. I won't be in any trouble. Don't worry. Now you must go fetch the sheriff and tell him what has happened."

Elodie stiffened. "No, we cannot go to the sheriff. Let us just bury this man and be done with it. What does it matter, anyway? He got what was coming to him, didn't he?"

Conor sat up and faced his wife. The ice was numbing the awful pain in his jaw and he was able to speak more easily. "I know this is unpleasant for you. I know women don't like to have it known that they have been...attacked in this way, but we must tell what happened. We have no choice. A man is dead."

"No, we cannot let anyone see him," Elodie whispered tersely. Her face was lit by a red burst outside and Conor saw in it, not modesty or shame, but fear and determination. He then realized he didn't know the full story.

"Why?" he demanded, suddenly fearful himself, but of what he did not know.

"Don't ask, please don't ask," she begged, her face twisted up in tears now. She grabbed a fold of her long skirt and wiped her cheek.

"I've killed a man, Elodie. We can't pretend that never happened." Conor was still struggling to comprehend what had just transpired. He had taken another human being's life. Someone, this terrible stranger, was no longer alive on this earth because of him. Conor's heart began to pound and his breath came in short bursts. But he had done it for the purest motives in the world. This ruffian was trying to rape his wife, his pregnant wife. No one would criticize what he had done. In fact, he would be a hero. Why didn't Elodie understand this?

"Conor, we must hide this man's body so that no one will ever find it."

"Elodie, that's ridiculous. Someone will come looking for him, someone will miss him."

"No," she said firmly. "No one will miss him. You see...to the world, he's already dead."

"You're not talking sense, Elodie."

Elodie hung her head and began to speak in an eerie, low tone, devoid of emotion, of any human quality. "This man lying here...is Kyle Kelly. My husband."

"Oh, my God," Conor gasped.

"The sheriff would recognize him, you see."

Conor was dizzy with pain and now horror. He struggled to grasp what she had just told him. The moon, which had been hiding behind a thin layer of clouds now appeared and shown brightly through the windows, bright enough to cast shadows in the silent kitchen. In the faint, gray light, Conor saw Elodie was staring blankly at the floor. She continued in the same flat voice. "Kyle was deep in the Number Five shaft the day it collapsed. But he was in deeper than the collapse itself. He said it started with an explosion, but then there was a great shaking of the earth itself. He turned and looked and saw at the end of the shaft a stream of light. He said it was like heaven shining down to him. He followed the light and climbed straight out of the mine. He ended up on the high ridge above the Northern Star."

"He survived...?"

"He was bad hurt. A boulder had fallen on his leg and the great sound had made him nearly deaf, but he had survived."

"But why did he pretend to be dead?"

Elodie was silent a long while. The fireworks show was nearly over and the crowd was clapping and cheering. "What everyone said about my husband was true. He found a rich vein of ore no one knew about. Now that this secret opening was to be had to the Number Five and now that everyone was thinking he was dead...."

"He could steal with impunity," Conor concluded. "Elodie, what was your role in all this? Why did you marry me, for God's sake, when your husband was yet alive?"

"I hated him. He made my life a living torment."

"He supported you rather well," Conor remarked with a sudden savagery.

"Aye, he paid me for my silence. I was the only link to the world he had. I threatened many times early on to go to the authorities, but..."

"In time you got used to having all that money—and you didn't want to give it up."

Elodie lashed back. "It's so easy for you to sneer at me. You, with your rich father and your easy life. You don't know what it's like to have nothing, to wonder if you'll watch your own children starve to death. I love you Conor, but who are you to judge me? Did you ever want for anything in your life? Ever?"

Conor was silenced by this reproach. He didn't know what it was to be poor, to worry about the future, to wonder where your next meal was coming from, to have a brood of young children depending on you for their very lives.

"Why didn't he just disappear? Why did he stay around here and risk getting caught?"

"Because he's the devil." Then Elodie sighed. "He wouldn't give me up and he missed the children sometimes." Then Elodie began to sob and whine, "He wouldn't leave me alone. I never knew when he might show up and when he did...he would insist...that I be a wife to him."

Conor knew Elodie was saying that her first husband forced her to have intercourse with him.

"I used to beg him not to. I know it was his right, but I didn't ...I was afraid I would have another child and everyone on earth thinking him a dead man...and in time that's just what happened." She started sobbing even harder.

"Corinne."

"Yes, Corinne. She's his child, of course. But I couldn't tell anyone. And him—he laughed at my suffering and the shame I had to endure. He said, 'Enjoy the money, you're nothing but a whore now anyway,' From that moment on I wanted him dead." Elodie raised her head. "But then I thought better of it. I thought, I'll take his filthy, criminal money and I will enjoy it. I'll become a criminal, too. I'll make a good life for my children and I'll find a way to protect myself from him in the bargain. God must have approved of my decision because he sent me you."

"Elodie, we—"

"Arrrgh."

Conor and Elodie both jumped in horror at the sound of the dead man *groaning*.

"Oh, my God, El—he's still alive!"

Elodie and Conor sat, staring, transfixed by the sight of Kyle Kelly turning his head slightly and moving his lips. Then Elodie got up and walked directly over to where her kitchen apron hung on the back of the door. She pulled it off its hook and quickly returned to the two men. She knelt down beside Kyle.

"Elodie, what are you doing?"

Elodie didn't answer, but pulled the pistol from her apron pocket. She calmly wrapped a corner of the apron around her hand—she had heard that people who fire guns get powder burns—and then cocked the pistol.

The metal of the pistol caught the moonlight and Conor saw it. "My God, El, don't do it!"

But in an instant Elodie had wrapped the remainder of the apron around Kyle's head and in time with the last big explosion of the fireworks show, she discharged the pistol against Kyle's temple.

Conor's mind screamed, *This can't be happening*. He sputtered helplessly, "Elodie...Elodie...you've just killed a man."

She turned to him with a face hardened into cold resolve.

"You can't kill a dead man," she said.

MUCH LATER, in bed, in the dark, Conor began to cry. The fact that the woman he loved, that he had chosen to live with, to marry, to be his life's partner, to be the mother of his children, was capable of killing someone—her own husband, no less—and showing no remorse for it overwhelmed him.

He had not cried when Allison died. He had not cried since childhood. Not since the age of twelve, those first few homesick nights at boarding school. Then he had buried his face in his pillow to hide the fact. He couldn't let the other boys in the dormitory catch him crying. They might have called him a baby or a girl. Men were not supposed to cry. That fact had been drilled into him early on by his father who would whip him for crying and whip him still more if he cried over the whipping. Thus he was well trained to be dry-eyed at Allison's funeral.

They told him he behaved rather oddly at her grave site. His memories of this were hazy. He recalled standing there between his parents and Allison's parents listening to the minister drone on and on. At some point, he stopped listening to the minister and just wandered off. He walked away from the grave site and all the attending family and friends and just kept going. Lilly tried to go after him, but Ben grabbed her elbow. One person in the family making a fool of themselves was enough.

Conor walked all the way downtown, a distance of four miles from the church where Allison was buried. He wandered until he found an open saloon—not easy at ten o'clock in the morning. When he did, he walked up to the bar and ordered a whiskey.

"How's life treatin' ya, pal?" asked the friendly barkeeper.

"Never better," replied Conor, with just a touch of sarcasm. He downed the whiskey and requested another.

Conor's manner was odd enough, that the barkeep asked for payment up front. Conor felt in all his pockets—trousers, waistcoat, overcoat, vest. He had no money with him.

The bartender looked annoyed and began drumming his fingers on the bar to indicate his impatience.

Conor sighed. Then he pulled his gold wedding band off his finger with some difficulty and offered it to the man for payment.

The astonished barkeeper picked up the ring and examined it. "This real gold?"

"It doesn't get any realer." Conor knew "realer" wasn't exactly a word, but he was in the mood to imitate the way the barkeeper spoke.

"You're sure you want to give me this?"

Conor shrugged. "I don't have any money."

"If this is real gold, you can have the whole bottle." And he handed Conor just that.

Conor had worked his way through half the bottle, when he decided he had better sit down. He surveyed the room. It was empty, but for a taxi dancer who was yawning and stretching in the far corner of the room. Then his gaze fell on an ornate upright piano. He made his way unsteadily toward it and sat down.

He opened the cover and began to play. He hadn't played in more than ten years, but somehow his fingers still found the keys to an elaborate composition of "Greensleeves," which was his mother's favorite. He used to always play it for her on her birthday when he was a boy.

The taxi dancer came over and leaned on the piano. When Conor reached the end of the piece, she said, "You sure can play pretty."

"Eight years of lessons," said Conor. Four at home and four more at boarding school. For a moment, Conor recalled how kind the music tutor he'd had at home had been to him, always treating him with candy whenever he played a piece flawlessly. The music tutor at school had been quite a different story. He would stand over his pupils with a ruler and rap their knuckles every time they missed a key. One day when Conor was fifteen years old, he decided to rebel. Every time the elderly teacher would whack him, he would deliberately play worse. In ten minutes time, his knuckles were bleeding all over the keys of the piano. The teacher became enraged when he realized the keys would have to be cleaned and struck Conor across the side of the head with the ruler, laying open a scalp wound which bled profusely, staining the broad white collar of Conor's school uniform. That day marked the end of Conor's musical education.

Conor was staring at his knuckles when the barkeeper joined them at the piano. He took a more critical look at Conor now.

"Those mourning clothes you're wearing?" he asked.

Conor gazed up at the man and replied casually, "I buried my wife this morning."

The man frowned and sighed, unable to take advantage of a young man grieving over the death of his wife. He pulled the ring from his pocket and tossed it on the piano keys. "Do yourself a favor, pal. Go home and sleep it off."

Conor fingered the ring, flipping it back and forth between his thumb and forefinger. He looked up at the taxi dancer. She wasn't very pretty and she was missing a couple of teeth, but she seemed fairly clean. He offered her the ring. "Would you like to spend an hour or two with me?"

She grinned and snatched the gold band. She bit it. Satisfied it was real, she answered, "For this, you can stay all day." She took him to her room, but Conor had a lot of trouble. He kept losing his erection. He couldn't seem to concentrate and all the whiskey didn't help either. Finally, he gave up and asked the girl to simply hold him.

"Don't make no difference to me," she replied happily, thinking this the easiest money she had made in a long time. "But...I still get to keep the ring, right?"

"Yes," he mumbled into the curve of her neck. He wondered how he would explain the loss of his wedding band, should anyone ask. It would probably show up in a pawn shop in a day or two. If he could find which one, perhaps he could purchase it back. The woman held him in her arms and patted him in a comforting manner.

Comfort...that's what he wanted and that's what he got. Easily worth the loss of the ring.

CONOR AND Elodie hid the body of her first husband in the china closet for disposal of some sort in the morning. Conor still wanted to go to the sheriff and confess everything, but Elodie talked him out of it. It wasn't really the talking that convinced him to see it Elodie's way, but rather the moment in the middle of the night when their baby kicked for the first time. Elodie gasped when she felt it. It was always exciting to feel that for the first time with each of her pregnancies. She grabbed Conor's hand and pressed it to the spot.

"Is that...?"

"Yes," she whispered. "That's our son. Remember our wedding day and you said that the world starts over every time a child is born? We have to think of him now. We have to do this for him."

He no longer wished for a second chance or another chance, but only to make the world go away somehow. It was this overwhelming sense of hopelessness, a frightening feeling of not wanting to live anymore that made him start to cry.

Chapter Seventeen

THE EARTH will have to open up again. *The Earth will have to open up again.*

Oh, God, it couldn't be, could it? Had that strange crack in the Earth I had fallen into been the key? The magic entrance? Had I stumbled *literally* into the Hidden Vein? I was thrilled, almost giddy. The eerie luck of it. What if there were still gold down there? I could save Leap Year after all. It was as though Grady had reached out to me from the grave—or urn, as it were. Wait until I tell Evan!

Evan. For an instant, I had forgotten that Evan was no longer a part of my life. But who could I ask to help me get back down into the crevice or cave or whatever it was? I wasn't going back down, not for all the gold in the world. I needed someone who could rock climb. Evan. I had no choice.

I debated how to resume contact without giving the wrong message. I opted for in person. If the twins were around, it would limit what could be said of a personal nature. It was getting late, nearly supper time, but I drove down to Evan's house anyway.

I knocked. I could hear the stereo on inside, but none of the usual chaos and chatter. Evan answered the door and looked surprised and apprehensive to see me.

"Hey, Darce. What's shakin'?"

"Evan, I need to ask a favor."

"Sure, babe, anything—a kidney transplant? A cup of sugar? Someone to father your children? Just name it."

"I'm serious, Evan. This is really, really important. I need someone to climb down into the hole I fell into. I just figured out something that about made my head explode."

Evan crossed his arms over his chest and leaned against the door frame as he listened to me summarize my grand theory. I was calling it the Earthquake Theory. After Mr. Sanders, the antique dealer left, I spent all afternoon on the telephone to the county geologist.

"The county has its own geologist?" Evan asked, incredulous. Then he shook his head and rolled his eyes. "My tax dollars at work."

"He's only part-time. I had to track him down at his dad's auto parts shop in Brownleaf. Anyway, back to the Vein—" I had started calling it "the Vein," for short. "I asked him about seismic activity in this area. He called me back after checking with some computer records and confirmed it. Seismic activity was recorded in 1878—that big one that caused the Northern Star to have a cave-in—then again in 1896 and 1990.

"Okay, so this is my theory: The first quake caused the crack to open up, the second made it close, or something, then the third reopened it."

"I don't remember any earth tremors in 1990. I guess I was still living down in Columbine then. Oh, well, go on."

"The geologist said my theory was a longshot, but possible, it was *possible*."

I then related the story of Grady's mother's delirious ramblings and how the telephone repairmen had heard my cries for help *through* the old mine shafts. At the end, I was breathless and probably looked more than a little ridiculous.

"I agree, we've got to take a look down there now. No question." Then Evan sort of cringed. "I'll have to ask Reilly for help."

"You need two people?"

"Yeah, one's got to belay the other, sort of. It's the only safe way to do it."

I didn't understand climbers' jargon, but I didn't bother to ask. Just then a little gray puppy came running to the door. Evan scooped him up before he could escape. He cuddled the pup in the crook of his arm and began to stroke him like a cat.

I smiled at the cute little thing and was now heartened by Evan's apparent interest in the project.

"Will you ask Reilly? Please?"

Evan frowned and sighed. "Oh, hell, I guess I've been looking for an excuse." Then he looked down at my feet. "Hey, you got your cast off. Nice boots."

I looked past him into the house and casually asked where the twins were.

"My mom took 'em to Denver for a big shopping trip. They're gonna visit Beth for a few days. I gotta go down and pick them up on Saturday." Then Evan started grinning. "You made quite an impression on Big Mama Allender."

I had to suppress a smile. It was funny to hear of such an elegant woman as Ginger Allender referred to as 'Big Mama.'

"She gave me the third degree over why we broke up. Said I

must've been an idiot to let go of you. She didn't chill out until I convinced her that *you* dumped *me*."

"Did you tell her why?"

"Hell, no, there are some things you just don't tell your mother, right?"

"There are a lot of things you don't tell people, Evan." I started to head for my jeep.

Evan shrugged. "I can't believe you're so upset about something that doesn't even concern you."

I spun around angrily. "The fact that you lied to me concerns me. The fact that you would even *consider* criminal activity, much less be blasé about it, concerns me. Some of us play by the rules, altitude or not!"

"Mighty high talk from a lawyer's wife—"

"Oh, shut up! You don't know what you're talking about anyway. But since you brought Keith into this—yes, I am tired of being involved with men I can't trust, so maybe I'm not ready for *Keith, the Sequel*."

"I'm not Keith, damn it."

No, you're worse, I thought as I looked off down the canyon. Keith was easy to hate.

Evan put his hands on his hips and stared at the ground. "Darcy, we had something good started. We both know that. You could decide to give me another chance, you know. Like maybe I've been going through some pretty heavy changes here this summer, too. Like some shit's gone down that stopped me cold, made me think. Like maybe I'm getting too old for the revolving bedroom door. Like maybe I owe it to the kids to—I don't know—settle down."

"And get married?"

"Well, maybe not quite *that* far down." He grinned his old self-deprecating grin that said I was supposed to take this as a joke.

I sighed and shook my head. Staying mad took more effort than I was willing to invest at the moment. "It doesn't matter, Evan. We're just too far apart here. And I'm probably not going to be staying around much longer anyway."

"Unless we find the Hidden Vein."

"It's going to take at least that. I'm broke. The county is going to auction Leap Year right out from under me for back taxes if I don't get my hands on three grand quick."

"I could loan you some money."

"I thought you were so broke."

"I'm gonna be flush pretty soon."

I groaned. Don't tempt me. Don't, don't tempt me. Was Evan the Devil in disguise? "I can't, Evan."

"Oh, come on. You don't want to lose Leap Year. You don't want to leave here. You've started to love this place as much as I do."

Like a drug you can't get enough of? Thinking about drugs made me angry all over again.

"I don't want your fucking drug money!"

"Wooo—the Princess of Philadelphia uses the F-word. Okay, okay, I get the message."

I wanted to slug him, but forced myself to cool down. I had to focus on why I had come here. "Look, are you going to climb down into that hole or not?"

"Let's see...gotta go to Denver on Saturday—would Sunday work? If Reilly's available?"

"Yeah."

I drove home with my emotions bouncing back and forth between elation that I would soon find the fabled Hidden Vein and confused and conflicted over the exchange with Evan. What did he think—that he could just snap his fingers and I'd come running back? Did he think he could lure me back with his ill-gotten gains? If I had learned anything from my debacle with Keith, it was to be more careful with my heart.

As I undressed for bed, I glanced out of the bedroom window and thought I saw a light in the distance. I turned out the lamp in the bedroom and sat down by the window to take a second look. I saw it again. It seemed to be car lights up near the road to the ridge, it wasn't really a road at all, but more of a path. Who could be up there so late at night? Too late for hikers. Campers? The mountain people? I made sure all the doors and windows were locked or fastened shut. I tossed and turned half the night thinking I heard noises and dreaming weird dreams about the mountain people.

EVAN PICKED me up early on Sunday morning. We squeezed into the cab of his truck with Reilly in the middle, just like that first morning when the two of them, who I took for brothers, drove me down to the Tenmile Cafe for mocha latte. Summer and Winter were visiting Marlena and riding her horses.

The father and son seemed conciliatory, if not exactly warm to each other. I did as little talking as possible and so did they. All of us, if not particularly happy to be with each other, at least were excited about our mission. I think the Allenders were expecting to split any treasure we found. I hadn't offered anything, but I would probably feel obligated to do something in this regard.

We drove as far as Evan's truck would manage up the ridge, then walked the rest of the way. My foot was still painful, but gaining strength. It was a warm day and the jeans I wore were hot, but I didn't want anyone, especially Evan and Reilly, to see my still-shriveled leg. Vanity, vanity....

I found the crevice without too much difficulty and Evan and Reilly discussed how to tackle it. They decided Reilly should be the one to go down in because he was the smaller of the two. They both donned climbing harnesses and began anchoring the climber's ropes to allow Evan to belay Reilly. As Reilly disappeared into the hole, I could see the worry on Evan's face. It reminded me that Evan came with the same emotional equipment common to all parents, no matter how offbeat or unconventional their parenting style happened to be.

"Hey, Darcy, I see some of your blood," Reilly called up cheerfully on the little walkie-talkie he had taken with him. He must have passed the place where I had hit my forehead. The cut had bled profusely. Now I had only a pale pink mark above my eyebrow.

Evan chuckled at his son's remark and smiled over at me. Was he remembering the night he had taken me home with all those injuries?

"Okay,,,I'm here," came Reilly's voice again.

"What do you see?" I asked eagerly, sharing the walkie-talkie with Evan.

"Give me a minute. I don't have much range with this headlight. "Some of it looks like a mine for sure, but some of it doesn't."

"This sounds good," I said to Evan. "It could mean the shaft Kyle Kelly was working in was just below us." If only I could have gotten that book at the library that had the schematics of the old shafts.

Evan shrugged. "Cool." I could tell he was more interested in Reilly's welfare than in my theories. To the walkie-talkie he said, "Any gold down there, Sidewinder?"

"Not yet," answered Reilly.

"Why do you call him 'Sidewinder'?"

"I don't know," said Evan, sounding a little testy. "Why not?"

Reilly's voice came back on. "There's something here. I can see that there's been a lot of digging."

"Does he know what to look for? Maybe we should get someone who has experience, Evan."

"He knows what he's doing. He's been in mines before. He's seen what a vein of gold or silver looks like. He was raised in mining country, remember?"

"I see something—it's part of a vein. It looks good."

Evan and I looked at each other and simultaneously shrieked.

"I'll take a sample," said Reilly. We then heard chipping sounds.

"Oh, God, Evan," I whispered. I was starting to shake, I was getting so excited. "Oh, God, oh, God, oh, God."

Evan grinned at my enthusiasm. "Calm down."

"I'm gonna follow this down in farther," said Reilly. The radio crackled and hummed.

"Not too much farther, Reill."

Before Reilly could answer, we heard a piercing scream over the static of the radio. Evan's face contorted with fear for his son's safety. "Reilly! What happened?"

The next sound on the receiver was one of embarrassed laughter coming from Reilly. "I'm sorry. I sorta freaked. I just found a body down here!"

I gasped and looked at Evan and he looked at me, both of us wide-eyed. I asked Reilly to describe it.

"It's a skeleton. A real skeleton of a person. I guess it's a man, from the clothes. Looks real old, like a long time ago. He's like laying on some kind of rug or something. There's a big hole in the base of his skull."

"Reilly, is there any sort of identification on the body?"

"I found a pocket watch. I'll bring it up. I got some ore samples. I wanna get out of here, okay?"

"Sure, let's go," said Evan.

"Belay?"

"On belay," replied Evan to his son's strange inquiry, and began taking up the slack in the rope as Reilly started climbing back to the surface. I at first assumed that Evan was going to somehow pull Reilly out, but I could see that he was exerting no effort on the climbing rope, just taking up slack. I asked him about this and he explained that his only job was to brake the rope that ran through the little belaying device which would catch Reilly if he should start to fall. He tossed around terms like "locking carabiner" and "A.T.C." which went over my head.

Reilly made his way back to us on the ridge without any difficulty. In one hand he held out the handful of glittering particles he had chipped from the rock wall. With the other hand, he placed the watch in my sweaty palm. It was dusty and corroded a bit, but you could still see the elaborately engraved patterns on each side. I couldn't get it open, so Evan loaned me his pocket knife and I pried it. Inside the watch face had blackened with decay, but the inside cover still held the photograph of a woman. She had dark hair and a heart-shaped face. She was pretty though her eyes seemed troubled or too serious. Her pointed chin had a dimple in it.

"Who could this be?" I whispered.

"Maybe it's Grady's mother," said Evan, coming over after helping Reilly bundle up the climbing gear.

I nodded. Judging from the hairstyle, he could be right. But whose body was hidden down in that shaft along with the Hidden Vein?

"There's definitely a vein down there, but it's been mined big time."

All of a sudden I was crying.

"Hey, Darcy, what's the deal?" said Evan. "We found it. They've been looking for it for a century and you're the one who found it. You're gonna be rich—maybe. And even if there's not much left, at least you got a neat pocket watch out of the deal. And we had fun today, didn't we, Sidewinder?"

Reilly didn't answer quickly enough and I saw Evan elbow him. "Uh, yeah. Yeah, right, we did."

"I don't know, I don't know. I just have a really bad feeling all of a sudden. Grady said that damned gold was cursed and she was right—at least one person got himself killed over it. I just wonder who it was."

Evan chuckled. "Obviously somebody who knew too much."

I was silent on the trip home. I couldn't stop wondering who the skeleton was. I thought about what Mr. Sanders had related from Grady—the gold or the grave. The crack in the Earth had yielded both.

"Darcy, it's none of my business," said Reilly as I got out of the truck, "but shouldn't you be sorta more excited than this? I mean, you've been looking for this the whole summer."

"I'm happy, really, I am." I tried to smile. Evan and Reilly exchanged glances, obviously puzzled by my confusing reaction to it all. They left to drive down to the community college to give the ore samples to a friend who could analyze them. I stayed behind to wait for Mr. Sanders to come pick up the furniture.

I went to work, emptying the drawers and removing them. I had trouble with the top drawer. It would only come out halfway. I yanked and yanked and finally it gave way, knocking me backwards onto the floor with the stubborn drawer landing in my lap. From my vantage point on the floor, I looked into the cavity where the drawer had been and saw them: a couple of crushed up papers, that had obviously fallen behind the draw when it was stuffed too full.

As though in a dream, I reached in and retrieved them. They had Grady's shaky, faded handwriting on them. Maybe this was the answer, at last.

I quickly got up and called Mr. Sanders, asking him to come for the furniture another day. He informed me rather curtly that if this was an attempt to get him to raise his price, I could forget it. I assured him it wasn't, that I just needed longer to clean out the drawers. He said he would try to come up the following evening if his grandson was available.

I curled up in the porch swing to read what I had found. Grady related the terrible "crime" she had alluded to on the first page of her letter. It seemed her mother had married Conor McAllister, my great-great grandfather, knowing full well that her first husband, Kyle Kelly, was still alive. I knew without being told by Grady how he had escaped the mine collapse. He had obviously climbed out of the hole just as Reilly and I had.

Grady said her parents were deeply in love and everything would have been perfect but for this little surplus husband problem. So they killed him. Grady said her mother actually pulled the trigger, but Conor conspired to keep the secret—and the gold, of course.

Chapter Eighteen

My parents' crime would soon come to poison every aspect of their lives together. They tried to pretend as though nothing had happened, but their terrible secret weighed upon them in a thousand ways...

CONOR MCALLISTER was never the same after the night of Kyle Kelly's murder. Superficially, life went on as before. Elodie cared for the children and the new house. Granny Atwater continued to live with the family and help out as best she could, though she was becoming increasingly frail. Conor went on writing for Applebee's newspaper, though much less frequently than before. He took less interest in his plans to start a newspaper in Leap Year, though he sold articles to the Columbine paper on a regular basis.

He stopped corresponding with his family in Philadelphia. They became concerned about him, fearing him ill, but Applebee reassured them that the articles kept coming, often with a brief note or salutation. His mother and mother-in-law were left confused by this and were tempted to blame his new wife. Both felt vaguely threatened by this unknown woman who had taken over Conor's life, causing him to turn his back on his prior family in favor of his new one. The fact that Ned had written after his visit to Leap Year that the new Mrs. McAllister was a charming, attractive, and possibly wealthy woman did little to endear her to the remainder of Conor's family.

He was drinking more than he should and his demeanor was perpetually downcast, even morose. The children were puzzled by this change in him. They had previously enjoyed such a fond relationship with their stepfather. He had been far kinder to them than their own father had. But now he was silent at the table and often cross and short with them.

"What's wrong with Uncle Conor?" they would ask Elodie out of Conor's hearing. They had taken to calling him "Uncle," though little Corinne, now two, called him "Papa" since she had never known another father.

"He has a lot on his mind," was always Elodie's perfunctory

response. But she worried. She didn't like his drinking. She knew she should be grateful he did not become loud and violent when inebriated like her first husband. She had often ended up with a black eye or a split lip after one of Kyle's binges. Conor had never raised a hand to her in all the time they had lived together.

But loudness and even violence she understood and knew how to cope with. The silent place Conor retreated to when he was drinking frightened her more than any of Kyle Kelly's drunken rages. She couldn't reach him there and she never knew for sure if he would return.

And then there was the matter of their marriage—the physical part. From that terrible night forward, it was completely absent. Throughout the remainder of the summer and into the fall, Elodie's pregnancy progressed uneventfully and her waistline grew and grew. Elodie knew some men didn't like this and avoided their wives during this time, but Conor shunned her utterly. They slept together every night, but never exchanged a kiss, a touch, a caress—nothing. An invisible but impenetrable wall existed between them in their narrow bed. Conor seemed even to avoid looking at her whenever he could help it.

She felt she was being punished by his coldness. Of course, she deserved punishment—after all she had committed the greatest crime one could commit—but she thought somehow she could make him see why she had done it, why it needed to be done, why she had no choice, why it was better for them and why one had to put the needs of one's children before all else, even one's mortal soul. She wanted to tell him all this but she could not because he would not speak to her. The only words they exchanged were the day-to-day necessities, civil and courteous. What shall we have for supper? Will you bring in some more firewood, dear? Will you mind the little ones while I finish preparing the meal? I'm going out for a while, but will return before luncheon. Is there something you need from the market?

During the fall of 1881, only the crisis with Mary Rose drew them together as man and wife. Rose was fifteen and had begun to work occasionally for Hannah Chance, helping Betty, Rose's current best friend, with chores around the house and with baby Samuel. It was no secret that Rose's motivation for working in the Chances' house was to be close to Josh Chance, who apparently returned her affection.

One evening, Rose asked that Josh be allowed to dine with them. Rose had been putting off this invitation for some time, owing to the fact her mother and stepfather's relationship seemed so distant and strained. She had waited weeks for the situation to right itself and had finally given up and invited Josh anyway.

The young couple were quiet during the meal, but Josh was dressed so formally Elodie and Conor were forced to exchange smiles and Elodie whispered, "Is it a wedding or a wake?"

After supper, Josh asked if he might have a word with Conor. Mary Rose made herself scarce, taking the little ones upstairs. Conor asked Elodie to return from the kitchen, since he had a fairly good idea what was coming. He was not Rose's father and he felt any decisions should be made by Elodie.

Just as expected, Josh was asking for Rose's hand in marriage. He had blurted out his request before any of them had reached the parlor to sit down. Conor glanced back at Elodie for guidance. She was standing behind him, still wiping her wet hands on her apron. She was frowning, so Conor knew what answer to give.

"I'm afraid that's out of the question, son," said Conor, feeling as though he were being called upon to act much older than his just-turned thirty-three years. He felt silly calling Josh "son" since the boy was only about ten years younger than he was.

Josh looked crestfallen and ill-at-ease, he didn't know what to say next. Conor pitied the boy. It was only a few years earlier that he had endured the agony of calling upon Allison's father with the same request. He had received a positive response, but not before being cross-examined on his ability to support a wife and family. At least Josh would be spared that indignity.

"Rose is only fifteen," Conor went on to explain, "and marriage before the age of..." Conor turned back to Elodie and mouthed the question, Sixteen? Elodie nodded. "...sixteen, at the very least, is unthinkable. Besides, it is the wish of her mother and myself that Rose finish school before marrying."

Conor once again glanced back at Elodie. She smiled approvingly. Elodie was adamant that Rose and all the children finish the eighth grade. Rose's education had been so haphazard, it would take a long time for her to complete this level, even with Conor's tutoring. He had been helping Joe and Rose with their schoolwork since nearly the day he had moved in with Elodie, a year and a half before.

Josh went home disappointed and Elodie went upstairs to give the news to Rose.

"How did she take it?" asked Conor, when Elodie returned downstairs to the parlor.

"How do you think?" said Elodie with a tired sigh, as she slumped into a chair near the fire. "She thinks she's in love."

"We're going to have to forbid her from seeing Josh anymore," announced Conor matter-of-factly. "I had no idea matters had gotten this serious."

"Why on earth?"

"He's too old for her."

"It's just puppy love. It's harmless," Elodie protested.

"Josh is a young man of—what, twenty-one, twenty-two? Trust me, Elodie. There's nothing harmless about it. Boys Josh's age will do or say anything, *anything*, to get...what they want."

Elodie shrugged and picked up her darning. "Josh is a nice boy."

"Nice boys, bad boys. It doesn't make any difference. From seventeen to twenty-five, their bodies do their thinking for them and their brains go into temporary hibernation. Trust me on this."

"Surely we are not talking about Mr. Conor McAllister at twenty-two," Elodie teased. She then realized this was the first real conversation they had embarked on since...that night. In her thoughts, she always just called it *that night*.

Conor put down his paper and looked directly at his wife. "When I was Josh's age, I was keeping a mistress."

Elodie put down her darning, in astonishment. She had assumed that the girl he had gotten into trouble at the company picnic had been his only indiscretion ever—until meeting her. He always had seemed so straitlaced and shy, it was difficult for her to accept that he had such a past. "And just how did you support a mistress? You told me you were in school until the age of twenty-four."

"I had help from my parents," Conor joked.

Elodie raised her eyebrows in disbelief. She could never tell when Conor was kidding. "Your parents?"

Conor couldn't keep the tease going any longer. "They didn't know anything about it. She worked for my mother. She lived in our house."

"How convenient," said Elodie, primly, with intentional sarcasm.

"Actually, it was. She used to sneak into my bedroom after midnight and leave before dawn." Conor suddenly grinned. "My mother was forever asking me why I looked so tired at breakfast!"

Conor and Elodie both began to laugh, but when their eyes met, the merriment drained away and the conversation died. Conor returned his attention to his newspaper and Elodie began to darn again. In a while, she said, "It's getting late."

As she slowly, awkwardly rose from her chair, Conor asked, "Are you feeling all right?"

"Oh, fine. Just tired, that's all. Only a few more weeks, I should think." Then, with a smile, she placed her hand on the side of her large belly. "He must have heard me talking about him. He's kicking me again. Want to feel it?"

"No."

Elodie sighed, disappointed. "Will you be coming to bed now?"

"You go on up. I'm going to read for awhile longer."

"Suit yourself."

THE CRISIS began the following morning with little Kitty banging on their bedroom door.

"Darling, whatever are you shouting about?" demanded Elodie as she rubbed her face to wake herself. Conor sat up as well, blinking and trying to focus.

"She's run off, Mama. She's gone and she's taken all her clothes and hair ribbons and *my* comb and brush. She even took Uncle Conor's picture of her off our wall!" Rose and Kitty shared a bedroom. Elodie pulled Kitty into her lap.

"Rose has run off? But when?" she asked.

"I don't know," wailed Kitty. "I just woke up and she was gone!"

"I came to bed at eleven," offered Conor in an effort to be helpful.

"That awful boy has stolen her!" cried Elodie.

"He was a nice, harmless boy last night, according to you," Conor remarked.

Elodie glared at Conor over Kitty's head. Conor suggested they get dressed and go over to the Chances' house to see what they knew of the situation.

They arrived on the Chances' doorstep at eight-thirty. Betty came to the door and informed them that Mr. and Mrs. Chance were still asleep.

"Well, wake them up," snapped Conor.

Betty hesitated uncertainly for a moment, as though trying to decide whether to brave Conor's displeasure or Hannah and Brandon Chance's. Then she dashed off, up the stairs, leaving Conor and Elodie standing in the entry hall.

Elodie thought Conor was overly sharp with the dull-witted girl, but she was too upset about Rose to remark on this. She assumed Conor's often condescending attitude toward servants was born of his having been surrounded by them all his life. She wondered sometimes how he had ever adapted to life at her house, where everyone was expected to fend for his or her self.

"A new carpet," murmured Elodie, noticing a fine new Turkish carpet in the entry hall. She and Conor had not dined with the Chances in a very long time. Conor had lost interest in social engagements and anyway had always complained that Hannah's constant chatter got on his nerves.

In five minutes, Brandon came down the stairs, buttoning his shirt and pulling up his suspenders. His wife, in her dressing gown with her hair still in a long braid hanging over her shoulder, peered down from the second floor bannister. Anyone who knew the Chances knew they seldom rose before eleven.

"What might you need, Mac?" asked Brandon, through a stifled yawn.

"Your son. Is he here?"

"Suppose so," said Brandon. He then hollered down the hall for Josh. Josh slept in a room off the kitchen on the first floor. He had a room on the second floor, but refused to sleep there because it was next to the nursery and he didn't like being constantly awakened by his infant brother's crying.

When no answer was forthcoming, Brandon mumbled, "Oh, hell," and ambled back to the boy's room. He returned with a puzzled look. "Not there."

"I knew it!" cried Elodie, beside herself. Conor put his arm around her, still able to at least pity her, if not love her.

"Knew what?" asked Hannah, in alarm, as she hurried down the stairs now, holding her dressing gown closed with both hands.

"He's run off with my Rose!"

"She's underage," announced Conor. "We could have him charged with statutory rape."

"Oh!" squealed Hannah.

"Now, hold on, hold on," said Brandon, always the practical one.

"Would Betty know about it?" Elodie asked, with sudden inspiration.

Betty was immediately brought back into the entry hall.

"I don't know anything," she mumbled, clearly intimidated by the situation. She nervously twisted the pocket of her apron and stared at the carpet.

"That's a lie, now tell us right now," said Brandon, pinching the girl's chin.

Betty winced from the pinch and looked like she was going to cry. "I promised I wouldn't," she whispered, miserably.

"You'll tell us right now or I'll knock those freckles off your face!" Hannah shouted, raising her hand to strike Betty.

"They run off to get wed," Betty squeaked, twisting the pocket of her apron more furiously than ever. "They been planning it for ever so long. Said they'd go to Texas and live with Josh's grandparents if things didn't work out here."

"We've got to go after them," announced Conor. He and Brandon began to debate this matter when the boy from the telegraph office appeared in the open doorway.

"Oh, you're both here," the boy said, clearly pleased that he would be making one stop, not two. He handed both women telegraphs and departed after Conor tipped him.

Conor looked at them both and announced they confirmed Betty's version of events. The eloping couple had departed Leap Year after midnight, found a justice of the peace in Denver and were married just before dawn. They were about to board a train that would eventually take them to Texas when they sent the wire.

"Well, it seems we're related, folks," remarked Brandon to no one's amusement.

Conor and Elodie walked home in silence. Conor was concerned that all the fretting over Rose would be detrimental to Elodie's condition, but he didn't know what he could do about it. When they reached the front porch of their house, Elodie sat down in the porch swing and began to cry.

Conor sat next to her and put his arm around her. He offered her his handkerchief. "It'll be all right. Josh seems like a nice young man. Didn't inherit any traits from his parents, that I can see." Conor meant this as a joke, but Elodie was not in the mood for levity.

"I'll never see her again," she sobbed.

"Don't say that." But Conor thought she was probably right. "We could invite them to come back, at some point."

"We could?" asked Elodie, hopefully.

"I don't care." Conor's voice sounded tired, even bored.

He didn't care about anything anymore, that was the problem, as Elodie saw it. At least he was sitting here with her, talking to her. She decided to seize the moment.

"The child, our son...he'll be here soon," she began hesitantly.

Conor said nothing, but wondered where she was going with this. He had begun lately to dread, rather than anticipate Elodie's confinement. He had morbidly decided she would die in childbirth like Allison had and he would be left alone with all her children to care for.

He knew he was only legally obligated to support his own child since he had never adopted Kyle Kelly's children, but he was too soft-hearted to see them sent to an orphanage or worse. And he had grown to care about them.

"You...still want him, don't you?"

"Of course," said Conor with little enthusiasm.

"I want you to be *happy* about it," Elodie insisted.

"Well, I guess you can't get everything you want, Elodie."

"How dare you! How dare you! A woman risks her life in childbirth—does that mean nothing to you? You, who've already lost one wife?"

Her angry words stung him. He apologized. He was about to rise from the porch swing when Elodie grabbed his jacket sleeve. "There's something else. It's about money. We're running out."

"I've been wondering how long it would take before you got around to that subject." Conor lounged back in the swing and gazed into the cold blue sky of late October. He smiled bitterly. "I guess if we're murderers, we may as well be thieves."

"You'll do it, then?"

Conor didn't answer immediately. He thought about his own hypocrisy. About how he had been content to live on the money as long as he didn't know where it came from. The proverbial fool's paradise, he reasoned cynically. For the first time in his life, he had been independent of his family's money. It had felt so good to be free. And yet had he not traded one sort of dependence for another?

"You'll do it, then?" she repeated.

The last week of November, Elodie was awakened just before dawn by the familiar pains. They always began in the small of her back. She lay on her side without a sound, trying to think of how she might get Conor out of the house for the next several hours. She had to get rid of him because he worried too much. Christmas was a month off. She composed a shopping list of presents she would insist must be bought today and that they must come from Columbine. They would need to be sending the presents to the folks back East soon anyway. And she wanted to send a special gift to Ned in California. They hadn't heard from him in some time, but Elodie had such fond memories of him from his June visit.

The pains increased with astonishing frequency and Elodie was forced to awaken Conor. She convinced him to undertake the shopping mission, but with a great deal of difficulty. Before leaving he kept calling up the stairs to ask why she wasn't taking breakfast with them.

By that time, the pains had increased such that she could barely get through a sentence.

Conor returned from his shopping trip much earlier than expected. He had found everything Elodie had requested in Leap Year, thus saving himself the trip to Columbine. It was nearly time for lunch and he was hungry. He was just coming up the porch steps when Hannah Chance appeared in the door.

"Well, if it isn't Papa," she said with a broad smile.

Conor frowned at her, puzzled by her remark. He noticed what appeared to be blood on her apron. Then it hit him—the baby. He dashed up the remaining steps and almost shoved Hannah aside. Dropping his parcels in the front hall, he ran upstairs and burst into their bedroom, breathless.

Elodie smiled faintly. "A son," she whispered in a voice hoarse from screaming. "A fine, healthy son, just like I promised." Nestled at her side was a little bundle with a tiny, sleeping, red face.

Conor stared down in amazement. She wasn't dead. The infant survived as well. It seemed impossible to him.

"Be happy," she implored wearily. "Please be happy. Would you like to hold him?"

"No," he said, taking a step back lest she force the child on him. Infants made him nervous. He hadn't held Beatrice until she was seven or eight weeks old and even then he hadn't enjoyed it. He had lost some of his fear of babies when he began to live with Elodie and she would unceremoniously shove Corinne into his arms whenever she needed a free hand to cook dinner or attend to other chores. Still, a newborn was another creature entirely.

"Elodie, if you don't mind, I was thinking perhaps we would name him Edward after my brother Ned."

"Edward McAllister. A perfect choice." She smiled up at him weakly.

He gently sat on the bed at her side and picked up her free hand. He pressed the palm of her hand to his lips.

CONOR AND Brandon were the only mourners at the grave site of Hannah and little Samuel. The Methodist minister had spoken a few words and then hurried off to attend still another funeral. It seemed he did little else in the three weeks since the small pox epidemic had swept down the Tenmile Canyon like a warm, wild Chinook. He idly thought how it was lucky it was already April and the ground had started to thaw, otherwise they would have had trouble burying all the victims.

The dreadful disease ravaged the mining communities where the men worked in such close quarters.

Conor had forbidden Elodie to attend the funeral or even visit her friend during her illness, so fearful was he that she might catch it and spread it to the children. Quarantine signs were appearing on doors all over town.

"Seems like I got her back just to lose her," Brandon remarked.

"I'm...sorry," Conor mumbled, unable to think of anything else to say. When he had lost Allison, all the well-meaning words that had been offered had seemed so pointless. There did not seem to be anything worthwhile to say on such an occasion.

"There's a part of me wishes she'd never come back at all."

"Oh, Brandy, you know you don't mean that."

"Hell, I was never cut out to be a husband anyway. Who was I kiddin'?"

The two men stood silently watching the hired man fill in the grave, one muddy shovelful at a time. Wet April snow began to fall.

"Maybe it was for the best," Brandon mused after a while. "Hannah would've hated to live with scars on her face. She was always vain of her looks."

"She was a beautiful woman."

"True. But vain. A vainer woman never drew a breath. Never really got a chance to know little Sam. Hell, I never really got to know either one of my boys."

"The other one's going to make you a grandfather in a few months," Conor said.

"The hell you say—"

"Elodie got a letter from Rose last week. We assumed you got a similar letter. We would have come over, but Hannah and the baby were so ill." Conor had received another letter just that morning that did not convey such happy news. The letter had been written by his brother Ned and posted posthumously by a lawyer handling Ned's affairs. Conor now faced the unpleasant task of going home to inform Elodie their infant son's namesake was dead.

"Can I ask you a favor, Mac?"

"Anything."

"Would you write Josh a letter and...you know, tell him about his ma and all?"

"I'd be happy to. Is there anything you'd particularly like me to say?"

Brandy shrugged and ran his hand through his hair. "Say she

didn't suffer much and...her last words were—I don't know—about him, that she loved him or something."

"Can you remember her exact words?"

"Oh, damnation, her last words were crazy crap about how she didn't like the color of the curtains in our bedroom. She was out of her head."

"I'll come up with something nice." He patted his friend's shoulder and said he would return home and start on the letter immediately after supper.

While he wrote the letter, his head began to pound terribly. He planned to do some editing on his first draft of the Reynolds biography, but the fierce throbbing forced him to put his head down on the dining room table. He decided to turn in early.

By midnight, the chills began. He awoke Elodie begging her to put more blankets on the bed. He could not stop shivering. She felt his forehead, just like she did when the children were ill.

"Oh, dear Mother of God," she whispered in fear. "You're burning up with fever."

Conor was delirious for two days. On the third day the fever broke long enough for him to sit up in bed and watch the small red spots appear on his face, reflected in the hand mirror Elodie kept on her armoire.

She brought some soup in to him, sat it on the chest next to the bed and snatched the mirror from his hand.

"I always got so much attention from the way I looked," he said cynically. "I guess I won't have to worry about that anymore." It was ironic that someone from an upbringing as privileged as Conor's had never been inoculated against the smallpox, but his mother was more afraid of the inoculation than she was of the disease. This was because one of her sisters had died in early childhood from a tainted dose of the vaccine.

"Don't take on so. Not everyone with the pox is scarred for life. I got it at the age of three and I survived. Look at me."

"You never told me you survived the small pox." There was a great deal she had not bothered to reveal. She never liked to speak of her past. The only thing Conor knew about his wife was that she had been born in County Cork, the seventh of nine children. Her mother had died when she was eight and the family had been miserably poor. The father had tried to keep the family together, but one by one the children were sent off to live with relatives until they were old enough to fend for themselves, which came at a shockingly young age, to

Conor's thinking. At fifteen, Elodie met Kyle Kelly, a handsome young man with dreams of running away to America. When he asked her to marry him, she had accepted without a second thought and had arrived in New York a bride of seventeen, about to give birth to Mary Rose.

The next day, Conor's fever returned and he knew nothing of his surroundings for the following week. In his delirium, strange dreams came to him, some of them frightening, some just disturbing. Sometimes he thought Elodie was Allison. *Adultery is a terrible thing*, Allison would say with narrowed eyes. Sometimes Elodie's children confronted him over the death of their father. *Murderer, murderer!* they would cry. Sometimes Beatrice would say, *Why did you desert me?* And then there was the girl at the company picnic. *You're trapped*, she kept saying, but her teasing smile had been replaced with a malicious, threatening sneer, *You're trapped, you're trapped....*

And most chilling of all, little Edward would appear, not as the five-month-old baby that he was, but as a small child, and he would look at Conor with mournful eyes and say: *I will have to die for your sins*.

On the tenth day, Conor sat up in bed and knew he would survive. He felt so good, he called to Elodie to tell her.

Instead of joy at the news, she covered her face with her hands and began to sob. And it was obvious her tears were not those of relief.

"I though you'd be pleased," Conor joked weakly.

She sat on the bed with her back to him. "We have lost him."

"What?" Conor asked in alarm. "One of the children? Did they take it? The baby?"

"He died an hour ago."

"Oh, my god," whispered Conor, overwhelmed by the tragedy, still dizzy from weakness.

"All of them took it. Except Joe and me. I think Donal and Kitty will survive. Granny was the first to go."

"And Corinne? What of Corinne?"

"The day before yesterday," Elodie whispered, then breaking down again. Conor pulled her close. They rocked back and forth as she sobbed. "I don't think my heart can bear this."

Conor caught his breath. He was not certain whether he felt worse about the loss of his own little son or that of two-and-a-half-year-old Corinne. She had come to seem like his own as well. Maybe it was because he had made love to her mother on the night she came into the world or maybe because she stood in place of his own Beatrice, but he had always considered her his daughter.

One of the children began crying for her, so Elodie stood up and dried her eyes. "Joe and I are going to bury them ourselves. They're starting to bury the others in mass graves and I...I could not...stand that...not for my darlings."

"I'll help you," said Conor, trying to rise from the bed.

"You'll do no such thing," Elodie returned, fiercely. "We don't need to lose you as well!" She left, then stuck her head back in the door, still angry. "And just who might Kathleen be?"

During his fever, not all of his dreams had been nightmares.

THEN CAME May, the muddy month, full of raw winds and chill and dirty, leftover snow. Conor was drinking too much. Often he would stop in at the Lucky Chance in the late afternoon and not come home until closing. Some nights, Brandy would help him get home. Other times, he would give one of the more sober miners two bits to do it.

It took him a long time to recover from the small pox. The marks were healing but it was still unclear how many would leave scars in their place.

Elodie was more lost on how to reach him than ever. The awful silence that had followed Kyle Kelly's murder and had abated somewhat after the birth of Edward, was back, redoubled, tripled. Elodie had entertained vague hopes of trying to have another child, but that was a foolish wish. Conor and she were more estranged than ever. He had gotten slightly more affectionate with her in the past winter, though never to the point of actually making love to her. Now even that was gone. Passion had once been the centerpiece of their love and now it was barely a memory, for nearly a year had elapsed since they had come together as man and wife.

He would sometimes seem happy, sometimes very happy for brief spells. Elodie sadly thought back on how last Christmas had gone so well. On Christmas Eve, Conor and the children had sat before the fire on the floor of the parlor singing Christmas carols. Conor had taught them a carol in German, one he had learned from his German grandmother, his mother's mother. He had even agreed to hold month-old Edward in his arms. The infant had cooperated marvelously, falling instantly asleep. Conor had been amazed by this, looking over the heads of the children from his place on the floor to Elodie where she sat on the sofa. He pointed to the sleeping babe tucked in the crook of his arm and mouthed the words: "I can't believe this." He had always told Elodie how he had only to walk near Beatrice when she was small and she would begin to wail. Elodie had smiled back, thinking if only, if only we could be happy again. She then remembered how more joyful still the previous Christmas had been—Conor had just proposed marriage and she thought her life would at last be perfect. It was as though this were the existence she had been waiting to lead all her life and now it was upon her.

But his black moods always returned. And in the weeks following the deaths of the children, it looked as though he would never be happy again. At times, she didn't think she could go on like this, but what could she do? She was his prisoner. If she displeased him, he might tell the authorities what happened last July Fourth. On the other hand, it might be a matter of his word against hers. Their awful secret had made prisoners of them both.

"Do you believe in curses, Elodie?" he asked her one night when he happened to be drinking at home. They were sitting in the parlor before the fire. Elodie had sent the children to bed early because she didn't like them to see their stepfather in that condition.

"Stuff and nonsense," she curtly replied.

"Brandy once said Hannah believed in curses. They lost an infant daughter to the cholera and she was convinced it was because of something they had done."

"Don't be silly," she replied, though feeling edgy. She didn't like his mood. It was even odder than usual.

"But it would make sense of something senseless, wouldn't it?" Conor stared into the fire as one enchanted. "God getting even—and in the cruelest way possible."

Elodie approached him, knelt between his knees and tried to put her arms around his waist. "We could have another child, Conor. Please, let us try."

He shoved her away and she had to catch herself from falling backwards. "We're cursed, Elodie. Nothing good will ever come from our union. And get off the floor—stop degrading yourself!"

With sudden inspiration, Elodie tried a new tact. "Conor, there's something we must do."

"A felony or a misdemeanor?"

"Oh, stop it, please. I've been thinking of your daughter in Philadelphia. She should come to live with us. We should have done it right after we married, but I...I was afraid I'd be too busy with the new baby to be a good mother to her. But we need her now and she needs you."

This proposal took Conor off guard. Elodie had never before expressed an interest in Beatrice. Conor had even sensed her jealousy, though she had tried to hide it. He thought for a moment, then said, "Out of the question. Do you seriously think I would remove her from a life of comfort and safety to expose her to the dangers of living up here? Haven't we lost enough already? Do we need more fodder for the epidemics and the cold and the wild beasts and the savages?"

"She needs her father," Elodie recited in a calm, measured voice.

"No."

"She's being raised by her grandparents. I'm sure they love her and can give all sorts of fine clothes and such, but they're old. Remember how often you told me how lonely you were as a boy? Raised by an elderly father who never had the time or the energy to play with you or even get to know you ?"

A slight change crossed Conor's face and Elodie knew she was beginning to reach him. "Conor, I could be a good mother to little Bea. It would soothe my sore heart to have her here. After all we've been through."

Conor stared into the fire again. "I'll think about it."

Elodie rose and left him alone for the rest of the evening. She glanced in on him periodically and was pleased when she saw him writing a letter. He sealed it and addressed it and laid it on the dining table. She came out of the kitchen and glanced at the letter. She was not good at reading handwriting, but she made out the word, "Philadelphia," and knew she had convinced him. He saw her and asked when she was coming to bed.

"Just now," she answered and hurried to join him on the stairs. He put his arm around her waist as they climbed the stairs together.

"It's a good idea you've had, El," he said as they entered their cold bedroom. Elodie smiled to herself. It was the first time in so long he had called her by his pet name for her.

As she struggled to unhook the back of her bodice, he crossed over to her side of the room, took her by the shoulders, turned her around and began to unhook the dress for her. When the stiff fabric was free of her neck and shoulders, he began to kiss them.

THE NEXT morning, Elodie sang to herself as she cleared the breakfast table, disturbing the silence of the big house. She was alone and she had been alone so rarely in her life, it seemed unnatural. Joe and Donal were at school and Kitty was playing with a neighbor child. Conor had left the house before Elodie had awakened. She wondered where he was, but assumed he had walked into town to post the letter before the arrival of the first mail wagon.

Midmorning, he finally returned.

"You were off early for someone who got so little sleep last night," she teased with bright smile. They had carried on like newlyweds. All the passion they had ever shared had come back in a rush last night. Elodie had fallen asleep in Conor's arms certain that the dark year of their unhappiness was finally over.

Conor did not return her smile. In fact, he looked more morose than ever. Elodie frowned slightly to notice he was tracking mud in on her new carpet—the carpet she had talked Brandon Chance into selling her after Hannah's death. "We've made a terrible error inviting Bea to come here. I posted the letter to my in-laws first thing this morning, then I went for a long walk and watched the sun rise. What could I have been thinking of last night? It would be insane to bring her here. I walked back into town to retrieve the letter, but it was too late. The first mail had already left."

"Conor, my darling, it's not a mistake. Everything will get better, I promise you. Think of last night. It was just like we used to be. I made you happy—you can't say I didn't."

Conor shrugged. "Physical pleasure? What does that signify?" Then he smiled bitterly. "I guess it did mark the first time we ever *legally* consummated our marriage."

Elodie grew nervous. She knew his moods only too well. He was even worse than usual just now and he wasn't even drunk.

"Sit down, my dearest, I'll fix you breakfast or lunch—whatever you want." She nervously twisted her apron between her hands, like a servant at the mercy of the master's whims.

"It's no good, El. And it never will be. Can't you see that? It's hopeless. We're...we're *damned*, but in life as well as death."

"Conor, no—you're wrong. You're just upset about all that's happened. You're still recovering from the pox and you're in grief over our children, but it will get better. I know it. The pain will ease with time."

"Stop trying to deny the obvious, El. Nothing will ever be right again...unless—"

"Unless what?" She had great difficulty keeping herself from shrieking the words.

"You know as well as I do," he stated calmly, though his marred face was still distraught.

She knew exactly what he was talking about, though they had not discussed it since the night of her husband's murder. She knew the guilt was eating away at him. Momentary happiness distracted him—the birth of Edward, for example—but the gnawing guilt always returned.

"We must go to the authorities."

"No!" She did shriek this time. "What would that accomplish? To tell them we've killed a man they think is dead already?"

"Does the fact that we committed a 'perfect' crime—one that we'll never be suspected of—make us any less guilty? Are your morals really that flexible, dear?"

"How can you say that to me? Do you think I haven't suffered? Do you think it's easy to live my life, knowing that the only thing that waits for me at the end of it is the yawning gates of Hell?"

"Oh, Elodie, save the melodrama for someone who enjoys that sort of thing. And anyway—I'll take the blame. I'll tell them it was all my doing. They'll believe it. Second husband finds out first husband is yet alive—gets rid of him. And steals the first husband's gold—another motive still. I'll say you knew nothing about it."

"And what will that accomplish? Sending you to the gallows and the rest of us to live in poverty? Conor, this is madness!"

"The life we've been living is madness and I'm tired of it—that's all. I want to confess. You should understand that—you're a Catholic. Isn't that what Catholics do? Confess their sins?"

"Conor, you're frightening me," she whined. She was trembling with anxiety. She tried to tell herself to remain calm. She could handle this situation if only she were to remain calm. "Conor, even if you don't care about me anymore and what I would suffer, at least think of the children. Do you want little Bea to grow up the daughter of a murderer? And what of my children? You're fond of them, too. Think of Joe. Think of the little ones. They adore you."

"I'm sorry for them, but it doesn't matter. Our crimes are too great and they continue. They continue daily. Some things transcend--"

"NO, THEY don't!" She was truly frightened now—desperate. He was serious this time. She looked about the room, frantically. She was not going to let him ruin her life.

"Calm down, El. You're getting hysterical. We'll talk this out, make plans, but before this day is over...there'll be an end to this. Once and for all." Paradoxically, as she was getting more agitated, he was growing more tranquil. The more he spoke his thoughts aloud, the more comfortable he became with them. His throat was dry. He passed by his wife on his way to the kitchen sink to get a drink of water, touching her gently on the cheek as he went.

"Conor," she began in a small voice. "I'm begging you. Reconsider."

"Do you remember the day we met?" He smiled out the window, between sips of water. "You offered me an apple and warned me it might be from the Tree of Knowledge. I guess I should have taken you at your word. But you were just so beautiful...."

Her voice got louder, more shrill, "Please, please, think of the children, yours and mine, please, for the love of God, *think of the children*!"

Conor's back was to her as he stood at the kitchen sink, finishing his glass of water and setting it down in the basin. "There's nothing more to discuss."

Chapter Nineteen

WITH TEARS in my eyes, I read the last of Grady's letter:

If only she could have told him. If only she had known at that moment, it might have changed everything. She might have been able to reach him, change his mind, keep him from leaving. But she didn't know, wouldn't know for weeks that they had another baby on the way—and that baby was me!

Almost eighty years have passed since my mother told this awful tale. My eyes fill with tears and I must set down my pen and cry for the father I never knew. My mother wore mourning clothes until the day she died, for everyone concluded he took his own life.

She said my father told her on their wedding day that he believed the world started over every time a child was born. She said that was literally true in my case. Her old world had ended and a new one begun. She said I was a comfort to her, but also a torment. I resembled my father, you see, and every time she looked into my face, she saw his again.

I never found the gold my mother claimed existed, though rumors of the Hidden Vein persisted for decades. I don't know whether I hope you find it or not, Darcy. I spent my whole life looking and for what? I realized too late in life that gold doesn't love you back.

I am an old woman now and I have passed up so many opportunities for love because something else was always more important or more sensible. And yet does not our search for love define us? I know you have not asked for my advice and must follow your own path, but don't repeat my mistakes.

I am leaving you one treasure, dear Darcy. A treasure mined, not from the earth, but from the human heart. I hid it in the mattress of my bed. Best Wishes and thank you for your patience with me and my parents' story.

I sat Grady's letter down on the porch swing and I gazed out over the remnants of Leap Year and thought about Conor, my ancestor, wondering how the end had actually come for him. I blinked back tears.

The afternoon sun blazed in its late summer glory, warming all but the shadowy pockets. I slowly rose and walked into the house and up the stairs to the bedroom like a sleepwalker.

I examined the mattress and finally found a slit in the side that had been stitched up. I got my nail scissors and began to cut it open. I gingerly reached in and located a large, flat, lightweight, cardboard box, tied up with aging twine. My hands shook with anticipation as I cut the twine and lifted the lid.

"Oh...my God...I can't believe it," I whispered when I finally beheld Grady's precious gift. Inside the box were drawings, sketches, charcoals, pen-and-inks, dozens of them. All of them signed: "C. McA."

His drawings, Conor's drawings. Grady said he was an artist. They were probably the only thing she ever had to know her father by since he had died long before she was even born. I carefully sorted through the drawings. Oh, Conor, Conor, I whispered as I gently lifted out and studied each one. He couldn't have been more real to me at that moment, had he stood there in the flesh.

Nearly half were of Elodie. I recognized her from the photo in the watch. Some of the portraits were traditional and pretty, some were sensuous, almost erotic. A few of the portraits—were they later ones done after the murder of Kyle?—were dark and strange, disturbing. Were they the product of a sick mind? An incurably depressed one? Poor Conor, born too soon for Prozac. Yet could even modern psychiatry cure a spirit as ravaged by guilt as his?

The pictures of the children were more cheerful. Elodie was pictured holding a baby in several, but I had no way of knowing which baby this was. I knew it wasn't Grady since she hadn't been born yet.

Then there were general sketches of Leap Year and the Northern Star Mine. If I could ever get enough capital to restore the town, these pictures would be an invaluable tool. There was even a couple of pictures of the house, the one I now lived in, when it was at various stages of construction.

I carefully placed the drawings, now brittle with age, back in the box. At least the dry climate had protected them from mold. Even if the Hidden Vein turned out to be worthless, what a souvenir I now had. I debated whether to show them to Trev. If he panned them or said they were amateurish, it would break my heart.

I decided to take a walk up on the ridge and revisit the infamous hole in the earth that had affected the lives of everyone who ever knew of it. At least now I knew whose body was down there. Poor old Kyle Kelly. Evan was right, he had known too much. I headed up the hill, not feeling as unhappy as I had before. I felt privileged that Grady had singled me out to receive both her terrible family secret and her wonderful treasure. I had to be aware of one to appreciate the other.

A strange sight presented itself when I reached my destination. Two men were on their hands and knees leaning over the mysterious hole.

"Hey! This is private property," I yelled when I was close enough.

Both men looked up, startled.

When I saw who it was, I smiled. It was Barry and Steve. My rescuers from the phone company. "Hi, guys. What are you up to?"

They looked stricken. Barry turned to Steve. "Shit. She's seen us now. What the hell are we gonna do?"

"Grab her!"

My mouth dropped open in surprise as the two men rushed towards me and did just that, "What's going on?"

"What are we gonna do, Steve?" Barry demanded again.

"Hell, I don't know!" Barry answered frantically. "She'll turn us in."

I tried to reason with them. "Look, if you think there's gold down there, you're wrong. You're out of luck."

"Like hell we are, lady. We've found the Hidden Vein—or at least you did when you fell down to it. We been watchin' you. We saw you and your boyfriend send that brother of his down there this morning. We saw you get pretty excited, so we know there's something down there."

"The only thing down there is a hundred-year-old murder victim!"

"Maybe you oughta join him," sneered Steve, getting nasty. "We shoulda thrown the old lady down there as well."

"Shut up, Steve!" Barry looked really scared.

"Did you break into her house?" I struggled, but they each held my arms back, pinning my elbows almost together and positioned themselves in such a way that I couldn't kick at them.

"We didn't steal nothin'!"

"What did you do to her?"

"Nothin'! We didn't do nothin' to your aunt," said Barry,

quickly. "It wasn't our fault, anyway. She just tripped and fell in the kitchen. She was yellin' at us to get out of her house."

"You killed my aunt?" I sputtered in shock. Now I was truly afraid.

"Hell, no, we didn't hurt her," said Steve. "We just wanted to talk to her, that's all. It was her that flew off the handle."

"Murderers!"

"What are we gonna do now?" cried Barry again.

"You're gonna let her go," said a new voice.

All three of us, in a tangled unit, whirled around to behold an incredibly dirty stranger, with scruffy, ragged clothing, long, greasy hair and a tangled beard. He had a dirty backpack thrown over one shoulder. He looked like the man I had seen in Marlena's parking lot. Marlena had called him a mountain man and I had remarked how he didn't look anything like Robert Redford.

"You and what army's gonna make us?" Steve returned, snickering.

The man calmly slung the backpack off his shoulder and pulled out the biggest handgun I had ever seen. "Unless you want a skylight in your skull, turn her loose, pal."

They did as they were told, immediately releasing me and putting their hands above their heads.

"Hey, back off, man," said Steve, nervously. "We don't mean any trouble. We could even cut you in—"

"Shut up," said the man to Steve. He jerked his head to indicate I was to come over to him. He said to me in a low voice, "See that rope over there? Tie their hands behind their backs, then tie them together."

I hurried over to the opening of the hole where Steve and Barry had been leaning over before I arrived. I found a rope, a video camera, and a battery lantern. I picked up the rope as the man had told me to do and went over to Steve and Barry, who nervously complied without hesitation.

"Hurry up," the man urged, but not unkindly.

My hands trembled as I worked, causing me to fumble my tying efforts. When I finally completed my assigned task, the mountain man told me to call the police.

"Uh...it's going to take me a while to get back down to my house to make the call," I stammered.

"I got a cellular in my bag," he said.

I rushed over to the backpack and gingerly unzipped the filthy thing. The grimy interior contained not only an expensive cellular telephone, but huge wads of cash. Was he one of the fabled drug dealers everyone claimed hid out up here? I hurriedly dialed "911" and reported my problem. While I made the call, the man forced Steve and Barry to climb into the hole. Tied together, they were too big to fall in, but were securely held pending the arrival of the authorities.

"So long, assholes," the man said cheerfully to my two would-be captors. He walked over to me, picked up his backpack and deposited his gun and phone. He gave me a friendly salute, threw his pack over one shoulder, and began to walk down the other side of the ridge toward the closest line of trees.

"Wait a minute, you can't leave now," I sputtered, feeling every inch the damsel in distress.

"You wait for the cops. People in my line of work aren't too fond of law enforcement."

I tried to fathom his age. He could have been anywhere from twenty to forty, but he was looking more like Robert Redford to me all the time. He kept on walking.

"Thank you," I called after him, helplessly.

"My pleasure. Anything for a friend of Evan's."

"Are you Frank?"

The man stopped, "No, Frank's a business associate of mine. He said Evan was thinking about coming in with us again, but then he backed out at the last minute—said his old lady wouldn't let him. That you?"

"I guess," I murmured, stunned by this revelation.

The man laughed and I thought he mumbled something like, "Pussy-whipped." He started walking again.

"There's not very much gold down there, you know."

He turned back and with an informed grin said, "Yes, I know." He resumed walking, but added over his shoulder, "Been played out since '91."

"Is that 1891 or 1991?" I shouted. He was almost out of sight.

I heard laughter float up as he disappeared into the dense forest beyond treeline. If he answered me, his words were drowned out by the chopping whirl of the sheriff's helicopter as it made its way up the canyon.

Chapter Twenty

THE DAY on the ridge, now more than two years ago, was the turning point—both for me and the future of Leap Year. The sheriff's deputies had no more than handcuffed Steve and Barry and read them their rights—just like on TV—when a young reporter from the mountain bureau of the Denver Post drove up. She had picked up my call for help on a scanner that allowed her to eavesdrop not only on the police calls but on peoples' cellular phone conversations as well.

She was very nice, but looked so young. She said she had graduated from college the previous spring with a masters in journalism. She offered me a ride back down to my house, and I excitedly spilled my guts to her about the story of the Hidden Vein, my great-great grandfather, my aunt—everything.

We had just reached the house when Evan came charging up Leap Year Road. He had seen two sheriff's cars speed by his house. He had flagged down one to ask what was going on and the officer told him they had received a call that some woman had been assaulted up near the old mine.

The reporter and I continued the interview. She loved the drawings and the story of Conor and Elodie and Kyle. I told her my suspicions about Grady's death as well, but she said she'd have to check with her editor before printing anything about that, due to liability fears. It wasn't clear at that time whether charges were going to be filed against Steve and Barry for anything besides their assault on me.

Evan sat patiently through my story, then made the big announcement: The ore samples did indeed look like gold to the guy at the college. We would not have a definitive answer until tomorrow when he could assay them at his lab.

The reporter got really excited by this and said it was going to make a great human interest piece for her paper. When she left, Evan joined me on the porch in the swing. I thanked him for all his help and he apologized for not being the one to have rescued me. I told him what the mountain man looked like and he thought he remembered him from his drug running days.

The mention of Evan's outlaw days cast a momentary pall on the afternoon. We sat in silence for awhile, then I asked the question I had awaited all afternoon to ask.

"Evan, that guy up there. He said you backed out of the deal at the last minute. Is that true?"

"Well, yeah. So?"

I waited for him to say more, but he didn't. I guess he didn't want to admit I was the reason for his change of heart. But why? Maybe his pride wouldn't let him. I wanted to think that was it, at least. But I felt cheated, somehow. I wanted him to make some full blown declaration of love for me, that he had changed his ways for me, given up a life of crime for me. I would have to be satisfied with his decision to stay on the straight and narrow and leave the credit alone.

After another silence, he turned to me.

"Darcy, help me out here. If it were me who just found out I owned a famous lost gold mine, I'd be running around screaming, shouting, dancing—something. You're just sorta sitting there looking like somebody died. What gives?"

"Somebody did die, Evan."

"You mean Kyle Kelly?"

"And probably Conor—Grady's father. They all died because of the damned gold. Plus there's Elodie—her life was no picnic."

"Let's not forget old Elodie. Lady MacBeth of the Rockies. She offs one husband, then drives the other one to suicide—why can't I meet great chicks like that?"

I smiled at his little joke. I stared into the distance as though hoping to see my future. "If we get any kind of real money from the Vein, I want to do something good with it. After I pay my debts and taxes."

Evan snorted at this.

"Some of us take our financial obligations seriously, Evan."

"Okay, okay, don't get mad."

"Anyway...what I'm trying to say is, I'd like to loan Reilly some money so he could go to C.U. instead of the community college."

"Great, then he won't have to fuck Marlena for it."

"Stop it! Marlena loves him."

"I know what Marlena loves. I know Marlena real well, remember?"

"And Reilly loves her," I insisted, like I knew what I was talking about.

Evan sighed and shook her head. "Reilly is eighteen—"

"Reilly is about forty, he just looks eighteen."

"Why do you want to do this for him anyway? It's not like you're related to him or anything."

"If you and I got married someday, I'd be his step-mother." I loved him, whether I wanted to admit it or not, I loved him. He truly made me happy in a thousand ways. I couldn't do a complete one-eighty for him, I couldn't just forget or excuse his moral lapses, but maybe I could bend a little. He dropped his plans for an outlaw career, presumably for my sake, if I could believe the guy on the ridge. And we were above ten thousand feet, after all.

Evan twisted sideways in the swing to stare at me. "Are you proposing?"

I began to laugh. "That sounded like a proposal, didn't it? Well, this is Leap Year, after all."

"Last Tuesday you pretty much said we were through. Now you're proposing? Is this one of those PMS mood swings I've been hearing about on TV?"

I started laughing even harder. "Probably. I don't need an answer right away. I do need to know if you're coming to dinner tonight. I think I'm entitled to some major celebration, somehow."

"I'll have to consult my social secretary, but I'm certain something could be arranged."

I playfully punched him. "And bring the twins. Reilly, too, if he's available."

He hesitated about half a beat. Adding the kids into the equation immediately shifted the focus, defusing the sexual tension. But he said, "Sure."

When Ginger Allender observed that her son doesn't date, he moves in, she wasn't kidding. Evan and the girls came to dinner that night and essentially never left. I felt like I was truly heeding Grady's advice—listening to my heart for once instead of just my head. After all, marrying Keith had been the sensible thing to do and look how that had ended up. Hard to do worse.

"I always wanted to live in this house," Evan remarked casually about three days later.

"Oh, really?"

"A fantastically remodeled bathroom—obviously the work of a master craftsman."

THE YOUNG Post reporter wrote a long story about Leap Year and her editor loved it. The Post sent a photographer to illustrate it and a one-and-a-half page feature ran in the following Sunday's edition. They included a big photo of me posing next to the mysterious hole on the ridge. The story was titled, "The Woman Who Owns a Ghost Town," and the nickname stuck. Henceforth, I would become Darcy Close-the-woman-who-owns-a-ghost-town. It was like having one of those descriptive Indian names.

The morning after the photo story, there was a knock at the door. It was a reporter for CNN with a camera crew. The broadcast networks showed up the next day using crews from their Denver affiliate stations and from that day on, the world was at Leap Year's doorstep.

Suddenly, I found myself in the center of a cult phenomenon. Everyone was clamoring for more information about the history of Leap Year, my ancestors, the Hidden Vein—I had to immediately hire a security firm to keep fortune hunters and curiosity seekers off the property. The banker who had stiffed me for a loan the month before was now more than happy to save this "important local landmark" from a tax sale.

Several major publishing houses made offers to me for a book on the story of Leap Year. The rights were eventually auctioned and the final figure was astounding, thanks to news media having bestowed upon Grady's town its fifteen minutes of fame. The book was rushed into print the following spring, to capitalize on the Leap Year mania before it died. I spent the whole, snowy winter working with the Post reporter—she agreed to ghost-write it for a nice cut. One of Conor's moodiest charcoal drawings of Elodie graced the cover and it was titled "The Hidden Vein."

When "The Hidden Vein" began to climb the bestseller list, all hell broke loose. Book tours, talk show appearances, threatened lawsuits...it was a heady and exhausting time.

The McAllister Boot people were particularly difficult to deal with. They tried to sue for rights to Conor's drawings which, owing to the success of the Leap Year story were going to be published in a coffee table-style book in the fall. Since I was a direct descendant of one of Conor's daughters and the sole legatee of the other, my lawyers told them to "go fish". Their suit was dismissed on a summary judgment motion—whatever that was—and they decided to change their tactics. In an effort to "make nice" with me, they invited me to visit their factory in Philadelphia. What the hell—it was a great photo op. I was becoming quite the publicity whore.

I toured the place, viewed all the portraits on the wall of their founding family—Andrew, the immigrant cobbler who started the company, his son Ben—Conor's father—the capitalist supreme, then Conor's four half-brothers. The people at the factory took measurements and made me a nice pair of riding boots. I didn't have the heart to tell them no one would be caught dead wearing English riding boots in the Rocky Mountains, but I accepted the present graciously.

The grandson of a Ned McAllister—one of Conor's half-brothers—took me to lunch. He was the only member of the McAllister family still involved with the business. He was a dapper, charming man of about seventy-five with snow white hair and ruddy cheeks. He brought with him what I had been longing to see and hoped still existed—the McAllister family album.

He carefully opened the album to a marked page. "Well, here he is," Richard McAllister announced with flourish.

I gazed down in wonder at the photograph. The faded ink of the caption read: "Conor and Allison, Wedding Day, October 15, 1876." A handsome young couple stared solemnly at the camera lens. My foolish thought was: Conor—at last, we meet. I've heard so much about you.

"Conor and Allison—they were my great-great grandparents."

Conor was very good looking. And I was surprised how much Grady, from early photos of her I had found, resembled him. They shared the same heavy-lidded blue eyes. Finally seeing his picture gave me a lump in my throat. I felt so much like I knew him. And yet, some part of him still lived on in me, some remnant of his genes still persisted through four generations and eleven decades.

"Oh, my, I'm afraid I'm getting all choked up," I said helplessly.

"This was the only adult picture we could find of him," said Richard. "There is a baby picture, however. It's pretty funny." Richard opened a little box that held a daguerreotype of a two-year-old Conor on his mother's lap. His mother was a very pretty young girl, who looked barely out of her teens. Little Conor looked like a girl, with long, curly hair and a lacy baby dress.

The waiter brought us our coffee and dessert. Richard chatted at length about his family and the history of his company. He had never known his grandfather, Ned McAllister. He was long dead before Richard was born. In fact, the only member of Conor's family who was still alive during Richard's lifetime was his great-uncle William, the youngest of Conor's older siblings, but he died when Richard was just a child. Then Richard looked suddenly embarrassed and blurted out an apology about the lawsuit. He assured me it wasn't his idea and wished the whole matter had never gotten started. I accepted his apology and told him I didn't hold a grudge—which was only partly true.

We were nearly finished with our lunch when Richard looked over to see an elderly woman approaching our table, moving along slowly, followed by an attentive maitre d' who was carrying a parcel for her.

"That must be her now," said Richard. "I've a surprise for you, Miss Close."

"Hello, hello, you must be Richard McAllister," said the little woman of about eighty in a surprisingly deep voice. The maitre d' helped her into her chair as Richard rose to introduce us.

"Miss Close, may I present Mrs. Nancy Banks, the granddaughter of Thaddeus Applebee. He was the publisher of the *Tuesday Gazette,* the paper Conor McAllister wrote for as a correspondent."

"Sit, sit," ordered Mrs. Banks, as though Richard were a pet dog. She extended a shaky hand to me and I shook it delicately. "Nice to meet you, honey. Loved that book of yours. Caused me a trip to the attic, though. You see, I inherited first editions of all my grandfather's newspapers—twenty-eight years worth. That's a lot of old paper, believe me. I thought of throwing them all away about a thousand times. Glad I didn't now."

She opened up the large manilla envelop the maitre d' had carried in for her. She pulled out photocopies of all of Conor's articles and slapped them down in front of me.

"Oh, Mrs. Banks, this is wonderful," I gushed. "I can keep these?"

"If you publish them, give me a plug," she said. "I'm not interested in making any money off them. Got plenty of that. And," she looked pointedly at Richard McAllister, "some of us are not so greedy." Richard, obviously embarrassed, refolded his napkin in his lap. "But I'd get a kick out of seeing my name in print, honey."

"I don't know what to say. This is wonderful. Are you sure about letting me publish them? My publisher will go nuts when she finds out we finally found these. In fact, she wants to publish a new, expanded version of my book next fall for the Christmas sales. There's also going to be a calendar—if we could quote—"

"Take them, take them," Mrs. Banks interrupted. "Bet you didn't know that my grandmother was one of this Conor McAllister's old girlfriends."

"No, I didn't." This sounded juicy.

"Long story, won't bore you with it."

"I'm not bored," I almost shouted. I was ready to twist the old lady's arm if I had to.

"Well, here's the *Cliff Notes* version. My grandfather had quite a crush on my grandmother when they were real young, but she had it bad for this Conor fellow. She ended up marrying somebody else, but years later, when the news was out that Conor had disappeared, she contacted my grandfather to find out what happened. She was a widow by then and they started a romance that ended up leading to a thirty-year long marriage. Had five kids. They were quite a pair. Especially my grandmother—what a pistol. They say that's where I got my red hair." Mrs. Banks patted her now-silver locks.

I tried to get her to go into more detail, but she was tiring and wanted to go home. The lunch ended and I thanked Richard and Mrs. Banks for their time.

I hurried home to my mother's apartment to read the articles. I sat up until three in the morning before I finished them all. When I was done, I felt I'd finally met Conor, and I liked him. He had a wry, offbeat sense of humor that came through wonderfully even when he was writing about something serious or mundane. He was insightful and intelligent—more than I expected from a spoiled, handsome rich boy.

Between October of 1879 and May of 1882, Applebee published fifty-seven articles. Some were illustrated, some were not. I counted twenty-seven new sketches in all. These sketches provided still another dimension. While all the drawings Grady had were pretty much focused on family life, these newspaper drawings were descriptive of life in Leap Year generally. The miners, the mines, the smelting process, the rebuilding of the Northern Star Hotel, old Gideon Reynolds, the silver baron of Leap Year, Brandon Chance, the wily saloon owner, his wife Hannah, the spectacular growth of Leap Year during those boom times, and finally, the small pox epidemic. That last article was difficult to read, it was so heartbreaking. Not that Conor indulged himself in the self pitying prose the Victorians were famous for. He was remarkably self-contained. But the horrifying facts spoke for themselves. Apparently he and Elodie had lost a couple of kids in the epidemic and Conor himself had just barely survived.

On a lighter note, Conor's account of his first Christmas in Leap Year was a hilarious gem. He spent it in the saloon with seventy-five other single men and it was outrageous and irreverently funny even by today's standards. I wondered how the oh-so-proper Victorians reacted to it.

The Christmas article the following year was almost as funny. It concerned Conor's attempt to get his friends to believe him when he told them of the then-novel tradition of decorating a Christmas tree. Apparently Conor's mother's family was of German origin and had brought the tradition over with them from the old country. He failed to convince anyone that it would be a good idea to cut down a tree and bring it into one's house and stick candles and ornaments all over it. They all thought this ludicrous.

The most touching article of all was not written by Conor, but by his friend Thaddeus Applebee. In an editorial, he explained to his readers why there would be no more "Letters from the Gold Fields." I was grateful to Mrs. Banks for thinking to include this with the rest. Applebee begins by saying he has lost a friend as well as a valued member of his staff. When Conor failed to arrive in Philadelphia on the date he had specified in his letter, his in-laws contacted Applebee to see if he had heard from him. Applebee sent a telegram to Conor in Leap Year, only to receive a cryptic wire in reply from Elodie Kelly McAllister which read simply: "Conor Missing."

Applebee immediately contacted Ben and Andrew McAllister. Several more wires were sent to Elodie, asking for more explanation, but she failed to answer them. The sheriff in Columbine was contacted by wire as well, but he replied he had no information on Conor other than that he had simply been reported "missing" by his wife. Missing person reports were commonplace in such wild country and not taken too seriously because the person would invariably either return or be found dead. By the end of the week a frustrated Applebee and Andrew decided to hire a private investigator out of Denver to search further.

The investigator's report turned up very little. Conor was last seen alive by a mail carrier on the morning of May 13. He had just posted a letter. Conor's wife and friends were interviewed and all said pretty much the same thing: that Conor had not "been himself" for nearly a year, that he had a known drinking problem, that he was particularly grief-stricken over the recent deaths of his son and stepdaughter, and that he was still recovering himself from the effects of the deadly small pox epidemic which had left him badly disfigured. The investigator's conclusion was "probable suicide."

Applebee, in his editorial, refused to accept this explanation, defending his friend as being a "sober, responsible, and decent man" who would never shirk his responsibilities to his family. Applebee supported this claim with the evidence of Conor's letter to his in-laws, posted the day he disappeared, stating his intention to arrive in Philadelphia at the end of May to pick up his little daughter and return with her to his family in Colorado. He finally states that the riddle of his friend's disappearance may never be solved and that perhaps that was the hardest fact of all to accept.

As a curious side note, Applebee includes a report made to the sheriff by one Virgil Cooper who stated he saw Elodie McAllister, or someone who looked like her, up on the ridge over the Northern Star Mine in the early morning hours of the day after Conor mysteriously vanished. He claimed she was "lugging something that was too heavy for her." It was something rolled up in a carpet. Virgil, who had been sleeping off a night of too much drink in the woods, stated that he rubbed his eyes to clear them and when he looked back at the woman, her bundle had disappeared and she was walking quickly back down the hill. Virgil's report was not taken seriously as it seemed to make no sense. Besides, Virgil was the town drunk and a known liar in the bargain.

I took a deep breath. I realized Virgil's story was ignored because neither he nor the sheriff knew of the existence of the hole up on the ridge. But Elodie knew...and so did I. Something wrapped in a carpet— Reilly had said the skeleton was lying on a rug of some kind.

"Oh, my God," I said loudly enough to wake my sleeping mother in the next room. I dug through my purse and pulled out the pocket watch Reilly had found. I always took it with me when I traveled because I was fond of showing the photo of Elodie to people who had read *The Hidden Vein*. I carefully examined the watch. The name of the jewelers was inscribed in tiny letters on the back, "Burnbaugh and Sons." I pulled out the Philadelphia yellow pages and turned to the listings for jewelers. Sure enough, there was a big display ad: "Burnbaugh and Sons, serving the City of Brotherly Love since 1859."

Conor's watch. Conor's body at the bottom of that hole. And Reilly had said the skeleton had a big hole in the base of the skull. I was no forensics expert, but a bullet wound in that location didn't sound self-inflicted.

She killed him. *She killed him.*

How could Elodie have been so...so—I don't know, incredibly selfish? She loved him. Did she kill her second husband for her children like she did her first? What a monstrous perversion of maternal love.

I had to call Evan. I had to share this with somebody. As I dialed, my mercenary instincts were already drafting a press release. This discovery was certain to get Leap Year back into the news.

"Huh?" came Evan's very sleepy voice on the line.

"It's me. I've got a major news flash—Conor was murdered!"

"What time is it?"

"It's almost two, your time. Isn't this like totally shocking?"

"You woke me up to tell me somebody got murdered a hundred years ago?"

"Well...yeah." I suddenly felt a little foolish.

"So what am I supposed to do—dig up a suspect?"

"Ha-ha." I sighed. I loved Evan, but he did not share my Leap Year-mania to an appropriate degree. "I know who did it—Elodie. The greedy bitch."

"No shit? She offed *two* husbands. Far out." I heard him yawn. "Don't get any ideas."

We both laughed and I was about to hang up when I suddenly blurted out: "Evan...I want to get married."

"Husband-killing puts you in the mood to get married?"

"I'm serious. At least, I think I am."

"Got anybody in mind?" he asked.

"You, of course, asshole."

"Okay."

I sat there in disbelief. "That's it?"

"Wasn't that the answer you wanted?"

"Of course, but..." I exhaled with exasperation. "You've spent your entire adult life avoiding the altar and now you're just like, 'okay'? That's it? I don't have to twist your arm or anything?"

"Let's review the facts: A wealthy and famous woman whose net worth grows as we speak has just asked a former welfare recipient, yours truly, to marry her. Do I look stupid? Duh!"

Thus the Mustang was finally roped. I supposed if he'd gotten all mushy about it, he wouldn't have been Evan and I wouldn't have loved him.

We didn't wait for the wedding to start a family. My biological clock was ticking so loudly, it was keeping me awake at night. It may have been beginner's luck, but the home pregnancy test said, "Bingo," after a single month's effort, so wedding plans shifted into overdrive.

The wedding was held in Leap Year in the newly rebuilt and restored Northern Star Hotel. The hotel was to open that winter as an inn for cross-country skiers, realizing Melody's and my dream at last. The old Victorian hotel was a beautiful and charming setting, but how many brides have to endure a guest list that includes least four of the groom's former bed partners? On the other hand, it was interesting to finally meet all these women I had heard so much about. Beth was aloof and silent throughout and came only to please her daughters, who looked adorable in their matching bridesmaids' outfits. Sandy was off-the-wall and a little obnoxious, especially after she got drunk at the reception. Her cowboy lover was in tow, he was recovering from still another rodeo-related accident. His arm was propped up in an uncomfortable-looking traction device. He got drunk, too, but he was a funny drunk and kept everyone entertained with his rodeo stories.

Greta was just as icy and beautiful as everyone had led me to believe. She had the good taste not to bring her young boyfriend, which would have destroyed Evan's day. She drew me aside at the reception and told me to call her when the baby's due date neared. She told me she could perform acupuncture to ease the pain.

"No need for poisonous drugs," she said in her low, seductive Swedish accent.

I politely thanked her for her offer and promised to consider it, but if she thought I would let one of Evan's old girlfriends stick needles in me, she was dreaming.

Marlena was a dear. She arranged for the catering of the affair. She and Evan were on better terms these days, since Reilly had transferred to CU-Boulder. Reilly was his dad's best man. He insisted on wearing sunglasses throughout the ceremony. His very unusual new girlfriend from school wore sunglasses as well. She refused to speak to anyone, leading many at the wedding to believe she was a foreign exchange student who did not understand English. "She's, like, *above* chit-chat," Reilly defensively explained when anyone asked.

Evan's mother decided to attend when she was assured no press would be there. She brought with her Evan's sister, Joni, and his older brother, Michael, the banker. The other brother, Sam, the cardiologist, could not get away, but sent a fabulous gift: two airline tickets to St. Martens.

I was amused when I met Joni. She looked so much like Evan, she could have been Evan in drag. She was tall and thin and angular and had the same shaggy, unkempt strawberry blond hair. She had a disturbingly dry sense of humor, however. It was hard to know when she was kidding, which was unnerving at times.

Michael was every bit the robo-yuppie Evan had described. Unlike Joni, who came to the wedding dressed as though she had just presided over a calf breech birth—which was literally the case—Michael was impeccably dressed in Armani and kept glancing conspicuously at his Rolex throughout the day.

My mother even had the gall to pull me aside and pointedly ask why I hadn't chosen *that* brother. She was not crazy about Evan. This irked me, of course. Especially in light of the fact that Evan had gone out of his way to make a good impression on her. He had even offered to *cut his hair*. I didn't let him. That would be too great a sacrifice on his part. I requested only a neatly combed back ponytail. Still, I was gratified he had offered in the first place. I guess I had my own lap dog now.

My mother did manage to hit it off with Ginger Allender. Both former Junior Leaguers, they realized quickly they were sisters under the skin. They got into a friendly one-upmanship over who had raised the most money for which charity.

My sister Jane was unable to make it, being too pregnant with her second baby to travel. She promised to come out when my baby arrived, in six months. Jane ended up delivering the morning of the wedding—continuing her longstanding tradition of upstaging me at every turn.

Then there was the surprise guest—every wedding has one. My wandering father decided to interrupt his quest long enough to witness his younger daughter tie the knot for the second time. He had read about me in an English language newspaper in Bordeaux where he was employed as a grape picker. He had called my mother and she told him I was getting married again. Somehow, he had managed to make it all the way up to Leap Year.

His hair was shaggy and he had a beard. He looked more like a vagabond than a former insurance company executive. He hit it off with Evan immediately. They ended up ditching the reception before it was even over and went down into Columbine and got drunk together at the Lucky Chance—the sleazy biker bar that was the namesake to the saloon that had once stood in Leap Year and was now also being restored and rebuilt on its original foundation.

They staggered in sometime after two in the morning. How they ever negotiated Leap Year Road in their condition, I have no idea. Evan spent the rest of the night vomiting and sleeping on the floor of Grady's fancy bathroom. When he finally came to bed he moaned, "Why don't you find Elodie's gun and just put me out of my misery? You'd be doing me a favor."

I went down to the kitchen the next morning to find my father humming and rosy-cheeked, fixing himself some breakfast.

"I hope you're proud of yourself," I fumed. He looked sheepish and poured me some coffee. "Thanks to you I got to spend my wedding night listening to my husband—"

"—drive the porcelain bus?" My father gave me a guilty grin.

Then he shrugged nonchalantly. "I wanted to get to know the boy. We just had a few beers."

"A few beers? Dad, according to the morning paper, Coors stock went up five points last night because of you two."

Dad threw back his head in a loud laugh. I was too angry to enjoy my own joke, so he tried to get serious, a little. "Wedding nights aren't what they used to be, anyway. It's not like you hadn't already done the deed, you know." He leaned close to me as he buttered me a piece of toast. "You're mother gave me the news—the blessed event alert. I'm having grandchildren right and left, it seems."

He sat back in his chair, looking suddenly wistful. "You young people today don't save anything for the wedding night. It's sad in a way. Now your mother and I—*that* was a wedding night."

"I don't want to hear about it, Dad."

"It was wonderful," he continued, dreamily.

"I don't care to hear about it, *thank you*."

"Both of us virgins," he said, his impish, bad boy grin returning. He leaned forward to confide in me. "She's still got the hots for me, even after all these years."

I rolled my eyes. "What are you saying here?" I tried not to smile, but couldn't help myself. His good mood was catching. He had changed so much in the last two years, it was hard for me to grasp. The old insurance exec dad would never have even considered boasting to me about his sex life.

"I'm saying I didn't sleep on the couch last night."

I made an irritated face. "At least somebody got laid on my wedding night."

"Oh, Kitten, don't be mad at your old man. I promise, I'll leave you're new husband alone today. Say...was that tall blond with the Swedish accent really his former roommate?"

"What's your point?" I exploded, him having just gouged a raw nerve. "That you can't believe he left Miss Sweden for Plain Old Me?"

"My, my, but we're touchy. I didn't think that at all. I mean, you're the one who's rich and famous now. Right?"

My parents did not ultimately end up reconciling. My father's bohemian ways were more than my mother could tolerate. She told him to take a hike and he ended up back on my door step. He and Evan have decided they are soulmates, possibly brothers in a past life. It's kind of cute—Dad follows Evan around like a puppy. My mother now has three reasons to be upset with me: 1) I left Philadelphia and her, 2) I married a "hippie," and 3) I'm harboring a criminal—my father. You can't please everybody so at some point, you stop trying.

A GRAND Jury refused to indict Barry and Steve for the murder of Grady. There just wasn't enough evidence. Like Applebee's frustration over Conor's disappearance, I suppose I'll never really know what happened to Grady and what role, if any, those idiots played in her death. My two assailants finally pleaded guilty to assault and attempted kidnapping. They got only about six months in jail. I think their sentences were light because they didn't have any prior criminal histories.

My mysterious rescuer was never heard from again. I wished I could thank him but I suppose my "inability" to give the sheriff a description of him was the kind of payback he was most interested in. ("All I can remember, Officer, is that he was wearing jeans and hiking boots." "Well, Ma'am, that sure narrows it down.") The newspapers dubbed him "The Lone Ranger", which was fitting, I suppose. The sheriff also guessed him to be a drug dealer. He said a "whole tribe" of them live way up there somewhere. "My office has nowhere near the manpower it would take to flush them out of a place that remote. The Feds aren't very interested in getting involved—I guess these guys are too small time. Kind of surprising one would end up playing the hero."

The Leap Year phenomenon just kept growing. My book signings took me all over and I met fascinating people, some who were even distantly related to me—or at least thought they were. I met a woman in Baltimore who claimed she, too, was a direct descendant of Conor McAllister, although she admitted she couldn't prove it. According to her family history—folklore really—her grandfather was one of a pair of twins born to a woman whose father had worked for McAllister Boots. The twins were illegitimate and the father was listed as "unknown" on their birth certificates, but the family rumor handed down was that the twins were fathered by one of the McAllisters. The woman had done a lot of research and had checked out the ages of all the McAllister men at the time the twins were born. Conor was the only one young enough to fit the family story which held that the girl's "seducer," as the Victorians used to say, was as young as she was.

I told the woman I didn't know anything about Conor having any illegitimate twins. She produced a photograph, taken in 1890, of the twins graduating from secondary school. Having just seen Conor's wedding photo, I was immediately struck by the obvious resemblance (or was I reading this in and just wanted to see a resemblance, who knows?). For some reason, I didn't mention this to the woman. I don't know why, maybe I was feeling proprietary about Conor, like I "owned" him and didn't want to share him. I felt strangely threatened by the fact that this woman might have an equal "claim" on him, somehow. Oh, well, Conor's wedding picture would appear in the next printing of "The Hidden Vein" anyway, so she could draw her own conclusions and, hell, write her own book.

At a Dallas book signing, I met a family who was "pretty sure" they were descended from Mary Rose Kelly and Josh Chance. They weren't thrilled to claim Elodie, the murderess, as kin, but they said they enjoyed the book, nonetheless.

Evan was keeping busier than he had been in years supervising the renovation of Historical Leap Year, Inc. He had always dreamed of commandeering a big work crew and now had his wish. Melody was coordinating the project, getting history and anthropology students from various local universities to donate research time into making our renovation as historically accurate as possible. I had in mind something along the lines of Historical Williamsburg, though on a much smaller scale, of course. My funding for the project was hardly in the Rockefeller league.

With the wedding finally accomplished, I was looking forward to devoting some time to what Evan called the "Allender Under Construction". If it turns out to be a boy, I'm going to name it "Conor," of course. I'm praying it won't be a girl, because I feel sort of obligated to name a girl after Grady, whose real name was "Gertrude"—ugh.

I guess I did the right thing marrying Evan. I mean, it's not like he has a great track record for longevity of relationships. I made my mind up that afternoon on the porch to heed Grady's advice and somehow I just knew she would have approved.

He really is exactly what he looks like—an aging flower child. He seems to care very little about material things. Even though we have plenty of money now, he still dresses in the same old ratty clothes and he still drives the same old junky truck. I keep telling him to buy a new one, but he always shrugs and says he will when the transmission finally gives out. No wonder Grady liked him. He even accepts with grace occasionally being called "Mr. Close."

Love can be a cruel and crazy thing. Why did Conor have to have Elodie? After the murder of Kyle Kelly, wasn't it obvious to him she was as poisonous as a Black Widow spider? He could have probably gone home to Philly and had women lining up around the block to be the next Mrs. Conor McAllister. But no, he chose to stay in Leap Year. What hidden vein in the human heart is so vulnerable that once tapped, no wisdom can reach it? Evan had found that vein in me and here I was, marrying the fool when logic screamed at me to run in the opposite direction. What kept us here, Conor and I? The love of a person or of *this place*? Was Evan right when he said that living up here was addictive, like a drug you couldn't get enough of?

These thoughts were filling my brain as Evan and I drove down into Columbine to the clinic for a prenatal visit. I apparently drove too fast to Evan's way of thinking—which must have been really fast since he himself drives down Leap Year Road like a maniac sometimes.

"Don't you think you're hitting those switchbacks a little hard, Darce?"

"Am I?" I asked, all innocence.

"You're driving for two now," he reminded me.

"I thought, 'to brake is to admit defeat.'" I was feeling kind of bratty.

"You can be irritating, you know that? You're rich, but irritating. I liked you better when you were poor and nice."

"No-o-o, you didn't," I sing-songed. Then I hit the accelerator again. I wasn't afraid of these winding mountain roads anymore. I was their master, not the other way around. I was the reigning Miss Kick-Butt Colorado, right?

Evan shook his head and sighed. "I don't mean to whine. It's just that when a car begins to travel in a *sideways* direction on curves, I think it's fate telling you you're either gonna slow down or die within the next ten seconds."

I looked over at him, raising my eyebrows and smiling provocatively as I took yet another turn way too fast. "*Life just keeps happening to you.*"

~ * ~

Printed in the United States
54063LVS00001B/77